From
Mountain
to
Marshland

From Mountain to Marshland

TRISH HOWELL

ISBN: 978-1-7371256-0-0

Cover design and maps by: Trish Howell

Library of Congress Control Number: 2021910222

Printed in the United States of America

DEDICATION

For Pop, who loved a good story, and enjoyed telling one
even more.

ACKNOWLEDGMENTS

Thanks to my family and friends, who given me so much encouragement. A special thanks to Kandy and Sandy, who have read this, and given me both support and feedback, and to Betty, who encouraged me, and helped with publishing information.

MAP – THREBANT

TRISH HOWELL

MAP – BRIDLAND

MORIMOND

BRIDLAND

MAP – MORIMOND

MAP – ELSTOW AND AMADEE

WILLIAM'S LINEAGE

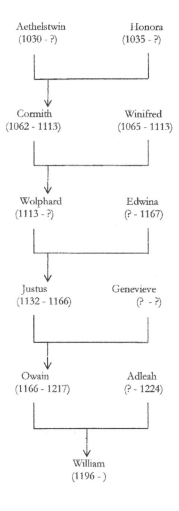

Aethelstwin
(1030 - ?)

Honora
(1035 - ?)

Cormith
(1062 - 1113)

Winifred
(1065 - 1113)

Wolphard
(1113 - ?)

Edwina
(? - 1167)

Justus
(1132 - 1166)

Genevieve
(? - ?)

Owain
(1166 - 1217)

Adleah
(? - 1224)

William
(1196 -)

CLAIRE'S LINEAGE

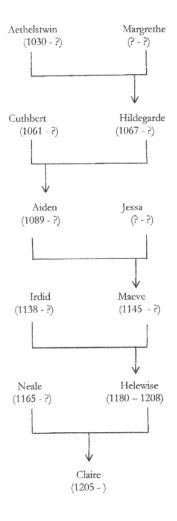

Aethelstwin
(1030 - ?)

Margrethe
(? - ?)

Cuthbert
(1061 - ?)

Hildegarde
(1067 - ?)

Aiden
(1089 - ?)

Jessa
(? - ?)

Irdid
(1138 - ?)

Maeve
(1145 - ?)

Neale
(1165 - ?)

Helewise
(1180 – 1208)

Claire
(1205 -)

BREONA AND CEONALD'S LINEAGE

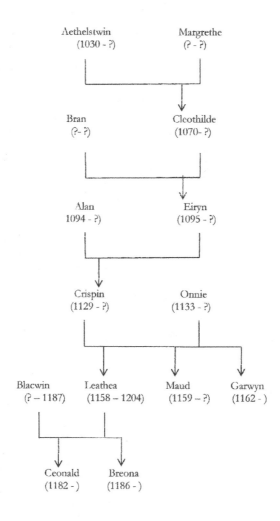

CHAPTER ONE

Dark clouds hung low over the forest and blackened the swift flowing Oberon. Small streams twisted through the hickory, the ash, the elm, and the oak, adding their burdens to the great river, still swollen with snow melt escaping to the sea. Shadowing the river, a narrow road wound through the trees, disappeared at each shallow tributary, and reappeared on the opposite bank, neither able to alter the other's course.

Heat more like August than June enveloped the forest, the air humid and close. The residents of the Brightwood had disappeared, retreating into their burrows and dens and an ominous silence blanketed the forest. A horse-drawn wagon crept along the road, and the sound of the horse's hoof beats and the rhythmic creak of the wagon wheels, echoed and hung in the air. No living thing seemed to mark its passage, with the exception of the occasional low-hanging branches that grasped and clawed at the wagon, protesting the disturbance.

If the merchant had once advertised his wares, the symbols had long ago weathered to the same, monotonous gray as the wagon. Signs of recent repair were hidden by days of dust from the road, but the sleek horse testified to the prosperity of its owner. The silence, or the weather, or the combination of both, made the horse nervous; its back twitched and quivered as if plagued by horseflies, although none could be seen.

Reaching the third ford of the day, the driver, as he had at previous crossings, brought the wagon to a stop and climbed stiffly down. He pulled a felt cap from his head and wiped his brow, leaving dark streaks in the furrows and creases of his worn face. He knocked the worn cap against his leg, sending up a cloud of dust, which, like his previous efforts, only succeeded in redistributing the dirt. With this new assault on its senses, the horse's head jerked back, nostrils flaring.

"Hey now, there's no need for that." Herbert kept his gruff voice low and studied the forest, but the shrubs and trees lining the road kept their secrets. "It's just a storm brewing that's got you on edge," he said. Still, the day had a strange smell and the horse had been steady enough until now.

Herbert looked uneasily at the sky, then scratched the horse's neck slowly. "You'll be safe undercover afore dark," he said, "and none the worse for a few drops of rain." By all the saints, steady horse or no, he'd be glad enough to be on horseback again. He'd eaten so much of the road in the past week, he'd be able to take up farming if he could but swallow the plow. Aye, a few more hours and they'd all be safe at Windrush, weather be damned. He looked back at the wagon. Its occupants were quiet.

He leaned forward. "You've done a fine job up to now," he said, "and your part in this is almost done. I can tell you, you've never hauled a more precious cargo."

Who would ever dream the High King's Queen and their four children rode concealed from view? For that matter, who would believe him playing both nursemaid and lady's maid? Well, if the story was ever told, there'd be no man dare twit him about it, or come next tourney they'd feel the prick of his lance fast enough.

The horse calmed and he gave it an encouraging pat. Ahead, the stream was shallow, the soft mud on both banks smooth and unbroken. Good, no one had crossed here recently. "Not that it should matter," he said to the emptiness; they rode away from danger, not toward it. By now the High

King's armies would well have reached their assembly point and if his luck held, Herbert would join them before the foul Cedric drew near. "By heaven's grace," he said, "I'll bloody my sword yet." His hand went to his side, then fell away. He was traveling merchant one final day.

The close association with his passengers seemed to have loosened his tongue after years of one-syllable sentences. They would reach Windrush just in time, another couple of weeks and he'd out-talk the women folk. Herbert grinned. Even so, he'd never best the little one. He'd always known women talked a lot, but he hadn't realized they started out all voice, and wound down, as they grew older. Given what young Mistress Elspeth was like at three, she would not give anyone any peace until she was fifty. Strange Her Grace was so easy on the ear.

"Enough," he said. "I'm either chattering like a magpie or off wool gathering. Herbert, you're a changed man and not for the better."

He led the horse forward to the stream bank. "I'll give you time to drink your fill," he said, "then we'll give our passengers a chance to stretch their legs."

The horse stood fixed, ears cocked, eyes intent on the road ahead. Behind them, the dust raised by their passage had dissipated, and the road ahead was as deserted. Herbert knelt and put his ear to the ground. Hoofbeats resonated deep in the earth. Not the leisurely pace of a Bishop's mare, or the clip-clop of a fat friar's donkey, but riders, and more than one, coming at a goodly pace.

"I'd give a fair piece if you could tell me who they'd be," he said. The horse flicked one ear.

Just their bad luck, and only a few hours left to the journey. A merchant's smock hardly made him one; he'd fool no one who knew him and worse yet, start tongues to waggling. Who did he know who wasn't already with the High King? Who rode to a purpose on the High King's road? Herbert shook his head; the coming storm afflicted more than the horse. Then he shrugged. It was a young rabbit that knew only one way back to the warren.

"Prepare to meet an enemy and live to greet a friend," he said, and hurried to the caravan.

At the rear, he untied the ropes fastening the canvas covering and pushed the flaps aside. The hot smell of last night's wood-smoke still clinging to his passengers rushed out. In the closed confines of the wagon, dust churned up by their journey still hung in the half-light. Bolts of silk and velvet and fine linen were stacked hindmost in the wagon, while spools of ribbon and gold and silver thread filled one of the chests. Too fine to be purchased by all but the wealthiest, they nevertheless added realism to myth of he being a merchant, and had the further advantage of disguising the family's wardrobe, to be fashioned after reaching Windrush.

Claire, wife to William, Queen of Bridland and High Queen of Threbant, leaned against the side of the wagon, blinking in the changed light. Her three boys slept sprawled out around her, while young Elspeth napped in her mother's lap.

"Are we there?" Claire leaned forward, massaging the small of her back. The boys stretched and yawned, Elspeth sat up, rubbing her eyes.

"No, Your Grace," Herbert said. "It seems we will soon have company. I did think it preferable that you and the children do come out of the wagon and I meet up with them alone." Even in the gloom, he did not miss the arched eyebrows.

Claire's bones knew every rut; her elbows and back burned where the coarse fabric had rubbed, as the wagon swayed and lurched. Every muscle ached. Earlier she would have been glad for the break, but now she wanted only to stay, for the wagon to continue, for this interminable trip to be done. "Let's go on. We've met with people before."

He shook his head, no. "Just to be on the safe side. No sense tempting Providence."

Cautious, always cautious. It was hard to believe he was a knight of the realm. "I've been sitting in the back of this wagon for days, precisely so no one would see me, and now that someone is coming, you want me to get out? Exactly how, pray tell, will my standing by the side of the road satisfy the need for secrecy my lord husband does so desire and you have so strictly enforced?"

Herbert sighed. He lacked the honeyed tongue and had missed it more than once these past days. As for Her Grace standing by the road, that's the last thing he wanted. She had an over-sharp tongue at the moment and besides, she wasn't wearing her wimple. Not that he blamed her for either. She looked hot and tired and he was more than willing to ignore the temper, but as for her costume, he could make no such allowance. A highborn woman might scorn the head covering, but no ordinary, self-respecting, God-fearing woman would be seen without it, even in the heat. She would wear it in public, Queen or no.

He tried again. "It'll be cooler under the trees. There's a nice stream and you can have a bit of a break.". He could tell she wavered. "Humor an old man who's only trying to do his job. It'll be the last stop before our journey's end."

She flung one heavy braid over her shoulder and leaned back, but said nothing when Richard jumped down from the wagon followed closely by his brothers.

Richard disappeared. "I don't see anyone," he said. "How do you know somebody's coming?"

"The horse told me, and I'll explain how later." Herbert sighed. "This isn't a farmer going to market, Your Grace. This is different."

Edward tugged at Herbert's sleeve. "You're not supposed to call her that."

"Not when we're pretending," James said.

Poor man, the three boys had badgered him the whole way. With neither a wife nor child of his own, Herbert had often been more patient than she had been. Whatever else could be said, Herbert of Amesly was not to blame for her misery. "Go on then, Elspeth," she said. "We'll accommodate Sir Herbert, and do as he wishes." Hitching her skirt up, Elspeth scooted across the floor and held out her arms. Claire followed, climbing stiffly down.

Herbert retrieved her cloak and the once-white wimple, and held them out. "Might start raining."

Claire shook out her skirts. Herbert was overly fastidious given the emptiness of the forest. Surely off the road and out of sight, she could wear as little or as much of her costume as she pleased.

He waited.

"The boys can carry them," she said finally.

"Do you see that big oak up ahead?" he said, handing the cloak to Edward and the wimple to James.

The wild, unshaped trees were a kaleidoscope of green. In the well-tended orchards of Ambridge, where the trees stood in orderly rows, she knew the apple from the plum, the oak from the willow and both from the elm. Now, she could not tell one from the other. "I'm not sure," she said.

"You see where the road curves?"

She nodded.

"The oak is the biggest tree on the right, the one hanging furthest over the road." He looked at the boys. "You know the one I'm talking about, don't you?"

Three heads bobbed.

"I'm going to drive on as far as that tree, so if whoever's coming decides to stop, we won't have to worry about James here talking too much and calling attention to the whole lot of you."

James flushed, but he smiled, and the other two boys laughed. James never said anything Edward could say for him.

"How will we know when they've gone?" Claire said.

"I'll come back for you when they're safe out of sight."

Although still faint, the hoofbeats were now audible. Herbert pushed aside a branch, clearing a passageway. "Go on, lads."

They darted through the opening.

"Stay close to the stream, Your Grace."

"I have no intention of becoming lost," she said, taking Elspeth by the hand and giving Herbert a quick smile to soften the unintended sharpness of her words.

The trees formed a thick canopy, and away from the road, the foliage thinned. Small trees crowded where an older one had fallen, winnowed by disease, or storm, or age. Behind them, the bough still quivered, but both Herbert and the road had disappeared. "That looks as good a place as any," she said, pointing. "We can spread out my cloak and have a nice place to sit." Although tired of sitting, it was too much of an effort to stand.

"I'll do it," Edward said.

Richard made a grab for it. "I'm the oldest."

"No fighting." Next time, if there ever were one, neither threat nor promise would induce her to leave their nursery maid behind.

After several attempts and a few furtive tugs, the cloak was spread out. Claire sank down. She hated the first few minutes after they stopped, when the ground beneath her rocked with the same regularity as the wagon. Instead of becoming accustomed to it, she seemed to grow sicker every day.

"We could have a race," Edward said.

"Too many trees, besides, Herbert wants us to be quiet. Let's go see if there're any fish." Richard glanced at his mother.

"Stay out of sight of the road." They were good boys, but full of energy, and she was not used to their full-time care. Closing her eyes, Claire leaned back against the tree. She must remember to send for Richard's tutor; he could come up with the nursery maid. The other two might as well start their lessons, it was nearly time anyway and would keep them occupied.

Elspeth!

But there was naught to fear. The child was with her brothers. The four were lying on their stomachs, hanging over the banks of the stream, engrossed in the water world. They'd be filthy, but the servants at Windrush would see to them; better they were occupied.

The lapping stream blocked the sounds of the forest. Or

7

perhaps, masked their absence. Claire did not notice the void or consider the difference. She stretched out, enjoying the luxury. Herbert was right, it was cooler and she was glad for the rest. He had taken excellent care of them; she must remember to mention it to William. And send word about the tutor. Herbert could take a letter back. She would have him stay at Windrush until she'd written it.

Was that a cry?

Claire opened her eyes, surprised to find they had closed. The children were still by the stream, but Richard lay with his head turned toward the road. He touched Elspeth on the arm, and put one finger to his lips. It was not her imagination. Edward and James had taken their cue from Richard, and all four children lay rigid.

Hoofbeats. A trot or a canter maybe. The pounding grew louder. Her heart echoed the beat.

The horses splashed across the stream. A man spoke, random syllables swallowed by the forest. A second laughed, a deep laugh that penetrated where words could not. Elspeth buried her face in the dirt and covered her ears. Slowly the hoofed tattoo faded. Claire cleared her throat and found fear had a taste. Her racing heart slowed, she remembered to breathe. Without a word the children crept back.

The afternoon resumed its normal course but the chill laugh had cast its pall, and she waited impatiently for Herbert's return. Try as she might, Claire could hear no sign of him. They waited.

When she could bear it no longer, she whispered to Richard. "Go look and see what's taking Herbert so long, but don't go out onto the road."

He was gone only a moment and returned, face pale. "I can't see him. It's kind of far to see but I think the horse is gone."

She stared. He was only ten; he must be mistaken. "He must be there," she said. "We'll surprise him and save him the trip back."

"Where did he go?" James whispered, when they reached

the road. Except for the wagon, the road was empty, the forest still.

"He must just be on the other side of the wagon, where we can't see him," Claire said, forcing a smile. "Come along, we'll find him."

They crossed the stream, stepping from one flat, broad rock to another, and on each bank left faint footprints, which along with the impression of wagon wheels and the pock-marking of horse's hooves, recorded the day's activities. High overhead, the trees rustled and swayed. The same barrier of thick shrubs lined the road, but the trees now hung lower, crowding closer. No foot race was proposed, no contest to see who could spot the most squirrels. All eyes focused on the road. Every few steps, Claire stole a look behind her, but the road and the forest remained void of life.

With a loud caw, a large crow swooped down from its hidden perch, and landed on the top of the caravan, then strutted back and forth, head bobbing, as it looked down on the road ahead. The children moved closer to their mother.

A few feet from the wagon, Richard pulled at her arm. "What's that?"

A dark shape lay just beyond the wagon.

"Stay here." When Claire reached the wagon, the crow flapped its wings and lumbered away.

"Wait for me!"

Richard followed, a dozen steps behind, quickly closing the distance, while the other three waited as they'd been told. Claire was angry, but relieved for the company, and felt at once a little braver for having the need to appear so.

The abandoned wagon tongue rested on the ground. Beside it, the dark form lay in a still darker pool. One arm was unnaturally bent, the other lay across his chest, and Herbert clutched a hole in his tunic, as if by pulling the fabric together, he could himself become whole. Blood escaped through his fingers, seeped down his side and dyed the earth. His eyes were closed, his breathing hoarse and irregular.

She crouched beside him. "Herbert?" she whispered.

When there was no answer, she reached over and gently touched his face.

He moaned. His eyes flickered open, vacant, empty.

"My Lord," she said. He blinked, seemed more aware of their presence. Perhaps she only wished it so.

"What should we do?" To her mind, her calm voice concealed well her fear.

Still silence.

She wanted very much not to look at him, to look beyond, at the road or the trees, to wake from the nightmare. Her eyes, though, were inexorably drawn back. They had planned for every contingency save this. Her whole life had been prescribed by custom and nothing new arose but what someone was there to direct her. Was there a protocol for being left alone with four small children and a man who might be dying? The wind whispered but did not answer.

She took a deep breath. "What should I do?" Did Richard sense her panic?

"Go," Herbert said in a low voice. From one corner of his mouth, a trickle of blood slid out, ran in a ragged path down the side of his cheek and onto his neck. He lifted his good hand a few inches above his chest and waved it about weakly, but if he meant to point to the north, or to the south, she could not tell.

"The boy," he whispered.

"He's right here." She motioned to Richard.

"The boy." The words now barely inaudible. With a trembling hand, he tried to motion.

Claire took his hand in hers, held it for a moment, and laid it gently back on his chest.

"We'll go," she said. "We'll get help." Her voice broke. Tears flowed unnoticed. We'll get help. A fine promise but it was a sorry distance to Windrush. Even if they reached the castle, would he live long enough to see help return? And yet if there was help closer, she did not know where. She may as well toss a feather to the wind to decide their direction.

Richard touched her arm lightly, then knelt on one knee

next to Herbert. "We will not forget you, Sir Herbert of Amesly," he said, "and I will have the bard, Ceonald, write a song so that all men know of your bravery."

The boy had this day grown much older.

Herbert looked at the boy and tried to speak. With a groan, he raised his good hand to Richard's chest and patted it once. His hand fell back and he stared once more into the void, his breathing even more shallow and ragged.

Claire leaned forward and made the sign of the cross on his forehead. "Go with God," she whispered.

With one hand on Richard's shoulder, she struggled to her feet and stood, her hands held out stiffly.

"Mother."

She did not move. Could not.

"Mother."

The boy looked so pale.

"He said we should go away."

She walked to the side of the road. The labored breathing followed. Claire stripped leaves from one of the bushes, and when her hands were as clean as she could get them, let the leaves fall, littering the road with crimson-stained green. She turned and nodded.

"Where will we go?" Richard said.

"I don't know."

CHAPTER TWO

Overhead, the oak leaves rustled and a few floated down, one landing on Herbert's chest. He groaned and attempted to lift one palsied hand. If anything, he had grown paler. A branch cracked. Another. Claire jumped back, pulling Richard along with her. She cried out, as two browned legs dropped and flailed about, trying to gain a purchase that did not exist.

"There's naught to fear," their owner said in a thin voice. A barelegged boy in a brown tunic dropped down and scrambled to his feet. "I'm sorry I scared you." he said. "I was thinking out the best way to tell you I was there, and then all of a sudden like I wasn't."

Claire's eye's filled with tears, and overcome for the moment, she covered her face with her hands, heart pounding.

"You're a bad boy." Richard said. He put up his fists and scowled.

"Ow!"

Edward? James? The wagon blocked her view.

Elspeth shrieked.

Claire ran, Richard and the uninvited boy close behind. The wagon had grown longer. An eternity passed with each step. She could hardly breathe. Had the riders returned?

12

The children were alone. Edward held Elspeth at arm's length, clutching the back of her dress. "She bit me," he said.

James stood in front of Elspeth, blocking her escape.

"Let go," Elspeth said between sobs.

"Edward."

"You said for us to stay here." He released his hold. At that inopportune moment, Elspeth jerked away, and fell. Her crying grew in pitch and intensity.

"Are you hurt?" Claire bent over the child, but her eyes were drawn to the horizon. Who else might hear?

"No," Elspeth said, continuing to cry.

"Get up then," Claire said. "We have no time for this." Be quiet or they'll hear us, she wanted to scream. But then it wouldn't have been the child's crying that alerted them, but her own despair. Her voice had been sharp, curt, as if belonging to someone else. Was this really happening?

"You should come away afore they come back."

Claire started. She had forgotten the stranger. Elspeth's eyes grew large. She stopped crying and her thumb crept into her mouth. Like their sister, the boys stared.

"Are you real, or . . . or . . .". Richard stood, hands clenched.

"Richard." But the boy did seem half wood-nymph. The boy glanced at the children, then looked back to her.

"My name is Jeremy," he said, bowing.

"Do you live here?" Edward said.

"I—"

"How come you were in the tree?" Richard said.

Jeremy opened his mouth to answer.

"What tree?" Edward said, moving a few steps closer.

"Where's Sir Herbert?" James said.

"Enough," Claire said, stopping the inquisition. Whoever he was, he was right, they needed to go. Pray, he could help them.

"I promised him I'd help," Jeremy said, nodding toward the wagon. He leaned toward Claire and whispered, "He won't stop bleeding. I tried . . ." He looked down at his hands. "He said I should help, but he wouldn't answer when I said who . . ." He straightened and looked at Claire. "Then I heard something, so then I climbed back up in the tree, and then you came."

Seemingly older than Richard, Jeremy stood a full head taller, but had a slighter build, and his wiry body hung from straight shoulders. He did not have the look of a beggar-boy; his tunic was neatly patched and his hair looked no worse than her own boys, who had started out the day decently enough.

"We need to get help," she said. "What's closest?"

"Lamberton," Jeremy said, "My father's gone to Allyntown, but my mother is to home. It's that way." He pointed north.

Relieved, she nodded. Past the wagon, past Herbert, but in the right direction. Away from Ambridge and away from the riders.

"You can come home with me," Jeremy said. "My mother will know what to do." He looked at Elspeth, who pulled her thumb out of her mouth, and thrust the offending hand behind her back. "We can walk the first part of the way in the woods," he said. "It might be better."

"You won't get lost?" Claire said, worrying, but relieved all the same. The children might hear Herbert's breathing but would not see his tortured face or the darkening circle beneath him. This Jeremy had his wits about him, to look to Elspeth and see the need.

"I know the way. I come here most all the time, when my mother doesn't need me."

A curious thing to do, but what did she know about the life of a peasant boy? The boy had a steady look about him, his face open with the eagerness of the young. "We'll rely on you then, Jeremy," she said. She hesitated. Should she send the boy and stay with Herbert? What if he couldn't get someone to help? What if the men came back? But would they?

The crow returned, sending a branch overhead swaying, and peered down at them in silence. That and the shadows beginning to creep out from beneath the shrubs along the side of the road, decided her. She could not help Herbert and she couldn't risk the men's return. She went quickly to the wagon. Trampled and torn lengths of cloth covered anything that might have been left, including the basket she wanted. Hopefully it wouldn't be needed. She nodded to Jeremy, and as she turned away, caught a glimpse of some nuts between folds of fabric.

"Edward," she said, "climb in and get anything you can find to eat, and give it to me. It's a game to see how fast you can find things, so best hurry." Neither of the other two boys would be so quick. Richard would have done it, but without much enthusiasm, and James would have been too easily distracted. She had hardly finished speaking when Edward swung himself into the back and handed out his first find, the basket she had missed earlier. It was empty but he quickly found some of the dried apples, the nuts and a few pieces of broken oat cakes.

"I'm done," he said, grinning and thrusting his chest out. "Did I win?"

"You did, indeed," she said. "Scramble out and let's be off." Jeremy had been watching anxiously, and now nodded. There wasn't much in the basket, but hopefully it would satisfy the children if they didn't reach Lamberton until after nightfall.

Once again, they abandoned the road, and Jeremy set a brisk pace. Claire concentrated on each step; a tree root threatened to trip her, a dead branch caught her skirt. She was compelled to look behind her every few yards, to see if they were followed, to remember they must get help and then to hurry on. Even after they passed by the wagon, and knowing they would make better time on the road, Claire could not force herself to propose their return. It was Richard who broke the silence.

"How come they hurt him?" he said.

"I don't know," Claire said. "I suppose they think they can get away with their thievery, since their lords are with the King." He had spoken quietly, as she did. The road seemed far away, but the forest seemed to be listening. Thievery . . . Much had been gone through and some things ruined, but had anything been actually stolen? What did it mean if they hadn't been? The nightmare did not end.

"My mother said they were bad men." Jeremy kept his voice low as well.

She grew cold. "Do you know them?"

"Not exactly. There was three of them. Two came to Lamberton yesterday. The other one I never saw before, but maybe he came after I left this morning, or maybe I just didn't see him."

Didn't see the one and how many others? She felt nauseous. "When we get to Lamberton," Claire said, "is there someplace we can wait out of sight, while you get your mother? It might be better to speak to her privately."

He hesitated. "Well, there's the church," he said.

"Wouldn't the priest be there?" Claire said.

He gave a soft grunt. "I doubt it."

Still, might someone come to the church if the priest was wanted? "We wouldn't want to bother anyone," she said.

"I have a better idea," Jeremy said, flashing a quick smile. "Come on, I'll show you." Veering right, he headed deeper into the forest, and quickened his pace.

Having chosen him, they had no option now but to follow. He had a steady look, Claire repeated to herself. She should never have allowed Herbert to go on without them. Still what choice did she have and what difference would it have made? He wore death's mantle bravely, she would tell Ceonald, if that was Herbert's fate. Let the bard work that into his song. What would Ceonald say of his High Queen's role? Until now, she had never felt the sting of his caustic tongue. Still, what else could she have done?

Although the forest seemed the same, Claire could tell by the ache in her legs that the land had begun to slope upward. She carried the basket and her arms hurt as well, although it was meagerly filled. Her own boys trudged along in silence, while Jeremy trotted ahead with Elspeth on his back.

When they reached a small clearing, Jeremy stopped. "Wait here," he said, "I know it's safe, but let me make sure."

This clearing seemed no different to Claire than any other, except that on the other side of the clearing, a steep hillside blocked their path. She blinked back tears. She did not have the energy to climb it. Jeremy slid Elspeth off his back and darted across. When he reached a thicket of shrubs and vines hugging the hillside, he stopped and tugged at one of the branches. A large opening appeared and he disappeared from view. In a moment, his head popped out.

"Come on," he said. "I'll show you the Hermitage of St. Declan of the Forest. You'll be safe enough here, I warrant."

She stooped slightly as she entered. The little bit of light that shone through the door, revealed log walls, which had weathered to deep silver. The floor was rough stone. In the middle of the room was a cold hearth; the smoke vent above them had presumably been choked shut long ago. An oak bucket and a wooden ladle rested on the hearth. Behind her to the right, a tall cupboard filled the corner. A bench and small table completed the furnishings. Although unseen, the sound of a bubbling brook filled the room.

"Who lives here?" she said.

"It's a place for a hermit," Jeremy said. "But there hasn't been one in ever so long. For years and years and years my mother says."

The floor was swept and it smelled as if it was aired regularly. "It looks lived in," Claire said.

"My mother keeps it clean. Sometimes I help, but nobody else ever comes here. It's a holy place you know, so needs to be kept. There should be a blanket in the cupboard, if the mice haven't ruined it. Can you hear the water?"

She nodded.

"A whole creek comes right out of the hill. That's how come this is a holy place and St. Declan came here. My mother says he can make you well if you get sick. You can stay here, and I'll go get her."

The room was small, the walls thick. "It seems safe enough," Claire said.

"It's a holy place," Jeremy said, nodding.

Richard stiffened.

Claire shook her head slightly. The boy did not intend the insolence. By his tone, she was sure he meant his response as reassurance, and did not mean to imply her concern for the hermitage's safety unwarranted. "Tell your mother to see our wounded companion gets help first," she said.

Jeremy nodded.

"Say nothing to anyone but your mother, Jeremy," she said. "And ask her to keep this private until we have spoken. Do you understand?

Jeremy looked perplexed. "If we don't tell anyone, how can we get help for him?"

"I suppose you must have more than your mother's help," Claire said, "but keep our presence here secret from all but her."

"I swear," Jeremy said.

"Can you find the way back even in the dark?"

"Sure," he said, straightening his shoulders. "It's easy. You just need to follow the creek. Lamberton is on this side of it and there's nothing but forest on the other."

CHAPTER THREE

When the door to the hermitage closed behind him, Jeremy ran toward home, leaving a trail of swinging branches that created the illusion of a breeze in the stillness. He vaulted over the logs in his path, swerving only when he reached the old oak man, as he had called the fallen giant for as long as he could remember. The shadows in the forest lengthened, but for the first time, Jeremy was not afraid of being alone in the Brightwood after dark. His mother always said St. Declan protected those who carried on his work, and today he knew he had the saint's blessings. He could even have jumped over the oak man, Jeremy thought, but it might be cheating to try on a day when he had the clear advantage.

At the edge of the forest, he turned away from the creek. The Bywater field was fallow this year, so Jeremy could cut across the clover-choked furrows without incurring wrath. On the other side of the field, the village smithy loomed large and dark against the deepening purple of twilight. When he reached it, Jeremy slowed to a walk. There was no point in the whole world knowing his business, and besides, he was out of breath. He walked past the cobbler's house. Benjamin's dog, Boyo, curled around the corner and barked. Jeremy whistled softly. The dog fell silent, but stayed in the shadows instead of rushing out to greet him. Even Boyo could tell he had changed.

Next to the cobbler's, the baker's dovecote wore its nightly silence. Jeremy walked quietly by; there was one dove in the cote that when startled, was worse than a rooster for calling out an alarm. He trotted past the widow Edith's cottage. She was sure to be abed and even if she wasn't, didn't hear all that well. He and Benjamin had proof of that! From there he ran to the back of the church, crossed to the south side to avoid the churchyard and stopped.

In front of the church, the road to Ambridge widened. Across the road, white-gray smoke from the inn's chimney climbed lazily against the dark sky. Light streamed from the windows. His mother had either decided to leave Jeremy's chores for his return or had been too busy to fasten the shutters. Other than that, the inn looked the same as it did every evening. The same, and like Jeremy, different. He wondered if his mother would be able to tell.

Ever since there was going to be a war, when he had the time, Jeremy had climbed the big oak on the road to Ambridge and pretended he wasn't an innkeeper's son. Now, the man pretending to be a merchant lay bleeding under the self-same tree. Under the tree where Jeremy had closed his eyes when the scar-faced man pulled his knife. When Jeremy had finally opened his eyes, the man he hadn't helped, looked up at him and his mouth opened, but the only sound was a rasping groan. The scar-faced man had kicked him then. Laughed, when the bone snapped, while the other two unhitched the horse like they had all the time in the world, which they did.

"Protect her," the man who wasn't a traveling merchant had whispered, after Jeremy climbed down from the tree where he had watched the lords and their knights and their squires and their pages ride to war. The boy had called the man, Sir Herbert, and if he was a knight, the boy's mother must surely be a lady. Like the miller's wife in Allyntown, who was ever so rich, the lady wore a sleeveless tunic over her dress instead of an apron like his mother wore. And two thick braids hung to her waist. Jeremy had never seen anyone else's mother with her head uncovered, not once in all the village of Lamberton. He had bowed with his very best bow, learned from one of the pages accompanying a knight passing through Lamberton this past spring.

As for the children, the one who'd been under the tree looked to be the oldest. Next to the lady, he liked this boy the best. Imagine, knowing a real bard and asking him to write a song. The little girl was different, her face was red and her nose needed blowing and she made him glad he didn't have a sister. Alone, neither of the two little boys was worth noticing, and he had to look more than once before he realized it wasn't that they were strange, merely that they looked just the same that made them so different.

Protect her. The wounded man had not sworn Jeremy to his secret, but all the same, Jeremy decided he would only tell the parts he had to. He wouldn't tell anyone about him not being a merchant, even Benjamin, who was his best friend in the whole world.

"Sir Herbert of Amesly," Jeremy whispered. He had sworn a holy oath to a knight of the realm. Of course, he didn't know he was a knight when he swore it, but it still counted. A knight, even wounded, could hardly ride to Lamberton in an ox cart, or swing himself onto a draft horse, and ride clinging to the forelock, as the horse was led slow-footed into the village. A knight must have a proper horse and that meant Father Ambrose.

Jeremy didn't want to tell Father Ambrose how he had closed his eyes and not tried to help. How the crooked arm had begun to swell. Or how he'd held on to the tree and tried not to throw up. He didn't want to tell Father Ambrose how he'd climbed the tree again when he and the crow heard a noise and it flew off. And if he did tell, it would hardly be a secret long, since Father Ambrose's wife would be scurrying door to door at daybreak. He couldn't lie, but he'd leave parts out; it couldn't be helped. His mother was different, he'd tell her all of it and maybe she could help with the priest. He hoped she was alone.

Jeremy darted across the road. In the public room, his mother stood next to a table with a flagon of ale in her hand, ready to replace an empty one lying on its side. Wisps of hair strayed from beneath her wimple and clung to her flushed face. Something was clearly amiss.

At the table, a thin man with greasy hair that hung to his shoulders, bent over the remains of his dinner. "Well, what have we here?" he said, looking up. "A boy who's been up to no good I'll warrant." He stuffed the last of his bread into his mouth. As he stared, he scratched his head, stopping when he found something and giving it a quick squeeze, before flicking it onto the floor.

Jeremy was silent.

"Where've you been, boy?"

"Jeremy," Phoebe said. "Your chores aren't done. See to the animals, then I'll dish up your supper." She set down the tankard and waved him toward the door.

Jeremy wished he'd gotten a better look at the others, but at least the man didn't have a scar. He took a step back.

"Not so fast. He goes when I say so."

With eyes fixed on Jeremy, the man grabbed Phoebe by the arm and pulled her closer. "I said, where've you been, and I'll thank you to speak up when I ask you something and do it directly." He tightened his grip.

Phoebe winced.

The door opened behind him.

"Run, Jeremy!" She jerked. Almost pulled free.

He wanted to. The laugh stopped him. The back of his neck grew cold, but not from the draft of the open door.

"Where've you been, boy?" the greasy-haired man said, unperturbed by whoever had come into the inn and now stood behind Jeremy. A man with a cold laugh and sharp knife.

Jeremy formed the words. No sounds came out.

A rough hand grabbed his neck. "We're waiting." His voice was pleasant, but his fingers dug into Jeremy's neck.

"I've been swimming . . . it was hot so I went swimming,"

Jeremy said. A flicker of a frown crossed his mother's face; she knew he was terrified of the water.

"Swimming?" the greasy-haired man said. "Aren't you afraid you'll get sucked down and eaten by the fishes?"

"I'm not afraid of anything. Or, anyone." Jeremy twisted and pulled away. He could hear nothing but his heart. They must hear the pounding too.

"So how come you're not wet?"

Jeremy was pushed aside. The scar-faced man swaggered past, pulled a second bench up to the table, and knocked both tankards onto the floor. The ale darkened the clean rushes.

"A fresh drink for my friend," the scar-faced man said. "And get me one, along with whatever he's been eating."

The greasy-haired man released Jeremy's mother. But she didn't run and she didn't get the ale. Run, Jeremy screamed silently!

"You, boy. We're waiting." He pulled a knife from his boot and outlined his scar with the tip.

"I was waiting to dry off," Jeremy said. "I fell asleep."

"You're quite the brave boy there, aren't you?" The scar-faced man said snickering. "Going swimming all by yourself and then falling asleep, sweet as you please, all alone in the woods. Now that's a scene I'd like to come across." His eyes narrowed. "T'would be a pity if you took ill from the exposure. If only I'd known, I could've helped you. I like little boys. I could have warmed you up right good. You wouldn't have fallen asleep, I'll wage that." He flipped his knife. The long blade arched upward, fell, and stuck quivering in the table next to him.

"Fetch me my knife, boy."

"Jeremy has chores. Tell him to let me go and I'll get your knife and then your dinner."

"Touch my knife, Mistress, and my knife touches you."

Phoebe nodded, her face pale. Jeremy rushed across the room, pulled out the knife, and drove it as hard as he could into the table, a few inches from its owner's hand. He took two quick steps back and stood, teeth clenched.

The scar-faced man laughed, his eyes hard. "You're a plucky lad and I like that. Maybe we'll take you with us when we go and see what you're really made of."

Both men laughed.

"Of course, you may come to regret you lost your chance with the knife." He wiped it across his tunic and laid it on the table.

"He'll go nowhere with the likes of you." Phoebe said.

"My, my," the greasy-haired man said. "He gets his courage from his mother, does he?" His arm lashed out and he grabbed her by the wimple and pulled hew down until her face met his. "Maybe you'd rather be the one to have some fun."

"Leave her alone," Jeremy said.

The scar-faced man laughed. "Tsk, tsk, such bravery all around. Maybe we'll take you both along. Might add to the entertainment." He began cleaning under one fingernail with his knife while he watched Jeremy.

Outside a dog barked. Jeremy turned. The door remained closed.

"Don't get excited," the greasy-haired man said. "We're expecting company. You can fetch dinner and drink all around, Mistress. We can't leave out our friends." He released his hold. "Could be they'd want to share everything, Seth." He hunched forward, watching his companion, face impassive.

So, the scar-faced man had a name. Seth and Sir Herbert. Jeremy would remember both.

"Well what do you say to that, boy? Should we keep back a little, just for ourselves?" Again, that laugh.

Jeremy looked from one to the other and shrugged. Did they mean his mother was to give the men food without something to drink? Or maybe ale, but no dinner?

Seth jumped up and twisted Jeremy's arm behind his back. "I think we'll keep our treasures to ourselves," he said. "I saw a storehouse in back earlier, and I'll warrant it has a strong lock." His knife slashed up and rested across Jeremy's cheek, the tip close to his eye. "Come along nice like, Mistress

Innkeeper, or else maybe my knife will slip. Of course, maybe the boy would like a little decoration." He laughed and twisted Jeremy's arm tighter.

Jeremy tried not to cry. Sir Herbert hadn't.

"Don't hurt him! We'll do what you say."

"Well now, that's just fine," Seth said. "You'd best keep nice and quiet if you know what's good for you. And if one of you gives us any trouble, the other one gets to pay the piper. Understood?"

They nodded. Jeremy and Phoebe were shoved stumbling from the inn and thrust into the storeroom. The door closed and the key turned in the lock. They were trapped in the darkness.

CHAPTER FOUR

In the hermitage, Claire sat staring into the darkness. She had tried to sleep, lying down next to the Elspeth, but when her eyes closed, she could think only of Herbert, with the ever-widening circle of blood-stained soil beneath him. She willed herself to think only of the rushing water, of the gardens at Ambridge, of the message she should send to William, of any of a thousand subjects that were not Herbert, but she could not vanquish him. Finally, she resolved to stay awake until Jeremy returned, and moved quietly next to the wall where she now sat. One of the little boys cried out in his sleep, but Claire did not wake him, having no means to comfort his nightmare.

They had gone down to the creek after Jeremy left, following the curve of the hill toward the sound of rushing water. Just as Jeremy described, a creek already several feet wide flowed out of the base of the hill. She didn't think to bring the bucket, so the children knelt on the banks, cupped their hands and drank their fill. Claire dipped her fingers in the water, and then immersed her hands, letting the water flow over them. When her fingers ached with cold, she hurried them back to the hermitage. She split the food into two portions, and divided one of the halves between them. They ate just outside the doorway and afterwards, the children lingered half-heartedly outside. When night settled firmly in the clearing, they went in without protest. Claire pulled the door shut and fastened the latch. Or had she? The dark brought its own dangers. Were there wolves in the Brightwood, with their long snouts ready to catch the scent of dried blood?

Claire rubbed her hands on her skirt; they still did not seem clean. She stood and felt her way to the door. Taking a deep breath, she pushed the door, then pulled at the latch. Both held firm. Even if the smell of blood clung to her clothing, the door was stout. Relieved, Claire returned to the spot she had earlier vacated. Her movement did not go unnoticed.

"Is Jeremy here?" Richard whispered.

"No," she said. "I couldn't remember if I fastened the latch."

"Oh."

"My Lady, Mother?" Richard said.

"Yes."

"Is Herbert dead?"

The room took on a sudden stillness. "He was alive when we left him," Claire said. "You know that."

"But that was a long time ago. How long until he could die?"

"I don't know," she said. Was death an eternity compressed into a single breath? A second of anguish stretched out for a lifetime? The knot in her stomach grew tighter.

"Does it hurt?"

"Go to sleep, Richard."

He was silent a few moments. "I should of killed that crow," he said.

"There would be others," Claire said. Others and worse. Pray Herbert recovered sufficiently to hold the inevitable scavengers at bay until help arrived, or that he had died unmolested. She shuddered. Jeremy had seemed to have no fear of the forest. She wondered his mother let him roam at will.

"He was doing his duty, wasn't he?" Richard said.

"Yes," she said. "He seems a good lad."

"What?"

"Jeremy. He seems a good lad."

"No, not Jeremy, Sir Herbert. Sir Herbert was doing his duty."

"Herbert of Amesly was . . .is . . . a knight and true to his oath."

"It's important to do your duty."

"Obedience is the first part of duty, Richard. Go to sleep." Duty. She was sick to death of the word.

"It's your duty," her own father had said, as he lifted her up to the funeral bier to see her mother. Her mother, with one arm folded against her chest, the other holding a waxen doll, gold circles where her eyes used to be. For years, the glowing coins haunted Claire's dreams and watched her from dark hallways. Had the journeyman's price been paid for the baby who had stolen her mother away to lay with her for all eternity? Claire could not remember and did not know if she'd ever known. As if it mattered now.

"They'll get punished, won't they?" Richard said.

"What?"

"Those bad men."

"Yes," Claire said.

"Will my Lord Father do it?"

"He'll send someone who'll represent him in the matter," she said. The High King would feel the blow that struck his knight and would show no mercy. It was he who had refused Herbert his sword.

"A merchant traveling in Bridland has no reason to be armed and none have complained of any danger, save the usual tribulations of their lot," William had said when the journey was discussed.

"How will he find out?" Richard said.

"I'll have a messenger sent when we reach Windrush," she said.

"How'll we get there?"

So, Edward was awake as well, and probably the other two.

"I'll have someone from Lamberton go to Windrush," she said, "and then the Marsh King will send back an escort for us." An army had been sent from Windrush to fight with William, but Claire was sure the Marsh King had not neglected his own care and comfort, and had retained a goodly number of his retainers to that end. Her needs would be made his, and she would see his men were put to good use.

"How'll they know who to catch?" Edward said.

"Jeremy knows," Richard said.

Jeremy. She should have the questioned the boy more closely. Well, time enough for that on the morrow.

"Go to sleep, both of you." But how could they sleep when she could not? No doubt William slept without worry.

They should never have left. Claire had opposed William's plans from the start. When reason failed, she flattered, she pleaded, and she cried. They argued for days and then late one night, just as she was beginning to prepare for bed, William's squire came and bid her come to the small council chamber. Claire finished untying the ribbons wound through her braids and worked the plaits loose, leaving soft curls flowing down her breasts. He had relented, there could be no other reason for the summons, and she had vowed that kind word would meet with gentle response.

The room was half-hidden in darkness, but by the smell of musty parchment, she knew the door to the tall cupboard in the far corner was open. Absorbed in the papers before him, William sat at his table in the middle of the room. The two candles on the table flickered, sending up thin lines of smoke. The chair opposite him was empty. She walked quietly to table and pulled out the chair.

William looked up, but there was no welcome. "Leave it," he said. "This won't take long."

Her face grew warm. She waited.

William bent over his papers. He read slowly, his ink-stained finger underlining each word. Hardened to the rein, trained for the hunt and callused by the sword, his hand was ill at ease with the quill. His finger rested. He paused, tapped the parchment twice, and then sat back in his chair. "We must discuss your journey to Windrush," he said.

"I'm not going."

William stood, leaned forward and gripped the edge of the table. He was a stranger, white-faced, with nostrils pinched.

"We would remind you," he said, "that we are both your husband and your King and as such, you are doubly obligated to obey us. We have no more time for your hysterics and there is no more time for your arguing. Get yourself and your children ready to leave."

He had the gall then to wave her away as if she were a page . . . no, not even that, the knife boy . . . and then he walked to the window, where he stood as if the empty night might reveal its secrets.

Claire didn't see him again for a week. When she did, she tried the role of seductress. "Please let us stay," she whispered, when she was sure he would be unable to say no.

"As husband, I might weaken Claire, but as King, I will not," he said. "You leave at the next new moon."

She gave up. "At least send us with a proper escort," she said. "Surely you can do better than to send your wife and children unattended like simple peasants."

"That is exactly the plan, Claire, and you well know it," he said. "Once you're at Windrush, if there be a need, the Marsh King has only to close up his castle to see you safe, but I cannot spare an army to get you there. And with a large escort, the trip will take twice as long as needed. With a small one, you call attention to yourself without the benefit of adequate protection. You will travel as we've planned, with Herbert of Amesly as escort. Speed and secrecy will see you safe."

William's curt tone, which would have caused his councilors to gauge their words, only intensified her anger. "Well if you can't spare a few men to safeguard your family in their own home, I suppose it's understandable that you can hardly afford to send more than one to take us away from it," she said.

His face reddened. "The plans are final, whether they meet

with your approval or not."

"This is Reginald's war, leave it to him."

"I did not seek this war, but on my honor, it is mine," he said. "Reginald may be King of Norwood, but I am High King and he is my subject as much as the woodsman in Brightwood or the farmer at Mullendown. Reginald is pledged to my aid and I must to his. If I do less than I am charged, I am the one lessened. Besides, it is over-late for this debate. Cedric is determined to make this my battle and his challenge must and will be met."

"Have your battle then, but I still don't see any reason to leave Ambridge."

"You choose not to listen, Claire," William said. He wore the face of suffering husband; she had seen it often enough on others, but never on him. "I've told you time and again," he said, "this place was built after the peace of Longraithe with no thought to its defense. If our enemy prevails at Mullendown, there would be no way to defend Ambridge. I will see my family and my lineage kept safe."

"It seems you start your war defeated."

It was as if she struck him. "See that you and your children are gone come daylight," he said coldly, and turned away.

They obeyed, as in the end she knew they must, and Claire resolved to put a cheerful face to it. No one would say the High Queen did not know her duty. But he was not there as witness. The wagon left early the next morning without another meeting.

In the hermitage, she shifted, but the floor gave no greater comfort with a new position. Her lord husband had commanded her to Windrush and at Windrush she would be. He could have his battle lust and when that fire was consumed, then let him then try to dislodge her.

Claire pulled her cloak closer and waited for Richard's next question, but there was only the sound of the creek. When she woke, the door of the hermitage was open and she was alone. She jumped up and ran outside, blinking in the sunshine.

The children walked toward her. Perched high on

Richard's back, Elspeth wore a crown of white daisies on her snarled curls and clutched a small bouquet. The boys' heads were damp, their tangles flattened. Richard was well scrubbed, but a line on Edward's cheek and a similar one on James, showed where their efforts had ended. Elspeth's face at least was clean. Had she been crying? Never mind, she was happy enough now. When they reached Claire, Elspeth scrambled from Richard's back, and forming a ragged line, the boys bowed and Elspeth curtsied.

"For you, milady," Richard said. He nodded to Elspeth.

"Oh," Elspeth said, and held out the nosegay. "Some flowers for your chair."

"Did you hear that?" Edward said. "For your chair." He nudged James and they collapsed in laughter.

Elspeth looked down, her face turned red and her lower lip began to quiver.

"She was supposed to say, for your good cheer," Richard said.

"Well you said it nicely," Claire said, "and the flowers brighten my morning." But the clearing behind them was empty.

"Jeremy hasn't arrived?" she said.

Richard shook his head.

"Maybe he forgot," James said softly, but his face was still hopeful.

"Maybe he forgot and we're going to stay here forever and ever and get eaten by wolves," Edward said.

Elspeth began to cry in earnest.

"Of course, he hasn't forgotten," Claire said. "Let's put an end to that nonsense." Her head began to ache.

"Maybe his mother wouldn't let him come," Richard said.

"It's early," Claire said. "Like as not they've been busy seeing to Sir Herbert. We must be patient."

They ate what was left and by midmorning, she paced outside the hermitage, the daisies limp and forgotten on the table inside. Whatever the reason, it seemed they had been abandoned. "Come," she said, "it seems we must make our own way." They needed food. They needed safe shelter and they needed what William had not provided. Her letter to him would make sure he knew what they had suffered. Claire wound her braids around her head and covered her hair with the wimple, smoothing in the loose strands. Today she had no argument with her dress.

In the daylight, the creek sparkled with resolute cheerfulness. The water was deeper than she imagined it to be the night before, and under its crystal waters, the creek bed was a jumble of large round rocks. Treacherous footing if they were to attempt to cross. Here and there a tree limb or the decaying remains of a fallen tree lay partially submerged, sending the waters swirling around them. When they came to one that spanned the creek, Claire stopped. "I think we would do better to cross to the other side," she said.

"But Jeremy lives on this side," Richard said.

"We will cross here," she said, ignoring Richard's look. He was a child after all. Jeremy did not come back for a reason. It would be better to survey the village from the other side of the river first. The log was well suited to its purpose and they reached the other side without incident. On this path, they were truly alone. She held out her hand to Elspeth. "The day is half gone," she said. "We must hurry."

CHAPTER FIVE

In front of the church at Lamberton, a makeshift pen had been constructed. Too flimsy to hold even the dullest of livestock, it nevertheless restrained the two hundred or so inhabitants of the village, who had, with the encouragement of lance and sword, been gathered there. Others had joined the strangers Jeremy had seen earlier. No random collection of scoundrels, these new arrivals stood guard, wearing Cedric's emblem on their chest, and chain mail under their tunics.

A black-robed cleric, with his ledger and quill, sat at a table in front of the church and scowled in the sunshine. Near one of the ropes, the village blacksmith sat gray-faced, one arm clenched to his chest. A spare, angular woman stood at his back, her toes wedged beneath him, so he could lean against her without appearing to do so. One foot had begun to grow numb, but Biddy had no thought of moving. Better lose the feeling in her feet, than give them the satisfaction of knowing how hurt he was. The pain must be awful bad or he'd have told her to leave off helping.

A red lump on the baker's head swelled as the morning warmed and he felt it often, wincing with each tentative touch. Father Ambrose had an angry welt across his face and would have at least one black eye, which was more than Biddy would have given him credit for, if you'd asked her the day before. The priest's wife fluttered around him, using her apron to dab at his face. Poor thing, it must be a hard life to hide whenever the Bishop rode through, but she was in her glory now. Father Ambrose flinched with each fresh assault and said nothing, but cast furtive looks at his neighbors, as if to see who might be witness to his bravery. As far as Biddy could tell, only the innkeeper and his family were missing. Giles would still be in Allyntown, but Phoebe and Jeremy's absence worried her. Biddy glanced behind her. The nearest guards were deep in conversation.

"Phoebe and the boy are missing," she whispered.

"Hush wife," the blacksmith said. "If they be hidden, let them stay hid."

"I pray them be so," she said.

The door of the inn opened. The cleric pulled his ledger closer and picked up his quill, while the soldiers straightened and fell silent. Clad in the same tunic and mail, the cause of their transformation stepped into the square. A round helmet sat low on his forehead; its thin nose-guard separated one piercing eye from the other and pointed down to his scarred chin. He sauntered to the table and put his hand on the monk's shoulder. The monk, whose arrival the prior evening had forestalled Seth from returning to the storeroom, flushed and sat very still. Seth smiled, enjoying the man's discomfort. He deserved as much, for all he was a plague to have around. Not all men of god cared who you diddled with but this one had a narrow view. Cedric may well have laughed it off depending on his mood, but Seth dared not risk it until their principal work here was done. Still, the monk would be busy well into the night compiling his report and would pay no mind to any of them. Patience would have its reward and their foresight in hiding the innkeeper's wife and her boy would give them an even freer hand. Seth stepped to the end of the table and surveyed the square.

"Begin," he said.

Biddy's back grew cold. Two soldiers walked to end of the

village and stopped at the last cottage.

"What's happening?" the blacksmith said.

"I don't know," she said. "They're down by Tom Carpenter's."

One soldier went into the cottage while the other went around to the back. A pig squealed. Her neighbors shifted nervously, and Biddy glanced toward the table. The scar-faced man stood smiling, one hand stroking the hilt of his sword. She looked away quickly. The soldiers reappeared, spoke for a moment and then one trotted back to the square. There he consulted with the cleric, who nodded, dipped his quill into ink and began to write.

"It is my duty to tell you," the scar-faced man said, "that this village is now part of the kingdom of Oroskree and Cedric is your rightful king and sovereign. I'm sure you'll want to give your new King a tribute of welcome and we are here to suggest a small sum. A tax as it were, to repay him for his trouble in annexing this village."

A soldier near Biddy snickered.

"We owe Cedric no taxes," a voice said.

It sounded like Father Ambrose, but Biddy had been looking at the scar-faced man, and couldn't be sure. To her surprise, the scar-faced man nodded agreeably.

"We'll let each man decide for himself," he said. "Who belongs to that cottage?"

He held up a finger. "One," he said loudly.

Then another. "Two."

And a stub. "Three."

He laughed and then whistled shrilly. Near the cottage, the soldier bent down and picked up a stick. He shielded it for a moment with his body, then stepped back and tossed it onto the roof. A few wisps of smoke drifted up and small tongues of flame began to lick the thatch. As the fire caught hold, a collective moan went through the crowd. A second torch was lit and thrown through the door. The soldier walked to the neighboring cottage.

From the other end of the village, a voice called out. "Who

lives here?"

"Who, indeed?" the scar-faced man said.

The cobbler, stooped from years at his bench, pulled off his cap and twisted it nervously. "It's mine," he said.

"Family?"

The cobbler pointed.

The scar-faced man motioned them forward. A soldier lifted the rope so they could pass beneath it. As the cobbler straightened on the other side, he stumbled, then regained his balance. No one laughed.

"You can pay for yourself and Tom Carpenter as well," the scar-faced man said.

"He knew all along," Biddy said.

"Aye, and what else does he know?" the blacksmith said.

"Now cobbler, your tax—"

"William is our King."

The square was deadly quiet. The blacksmith twisted, straining to see, then grimaced. "Who said it, wife?" he whispered.

"Benjamin."

"Likely they won't do much to a young lad."

Biddy nodded.

The scar-faced man rolled his eyes and put his hand to his chest. "I am wounded," he said, "to think my words carry so little weight, that even the slightest boy can mock me."

"What's he doing," the blacksmith said.

"Play acting-"

"Silence!" A few drops of foamy spittle slid down into his scar. "Are you hard of hearing, boy? Didn't I just tell you that Cedric is your King?"

Benjamin looked down at the ground.

"I don't hear your answer!"

Benjamin's mouth opened, but nothing came out.

The scar-faced man's sword flashed in the sunshine. "As you don't hear," he said, "you don't need the ear."

Benjamin touched the side of his head, then held out his hand out, covered in blood. He turned white, slumped, and fell. His mother screamed. Two soldiers rushed forward. One sword tip pressed against the cobbler's chest and the other wavered between Benjamin's mother and his younger brother. The scar-faced man kicked the boy's thigh.

Benjamin groaned.

"He'll probably live and you'll pay a bonus if he does. Now, I have a few questions before we get to the subject of your taxes, and I do hope you'll pay better attention."

The cobbler nodded, ashen-faced. Biddy crossed herself. More than one mother pulled her child closer. Still no Phoebe or Jeremy. The inn was quiet, and alone in the village, had no smoke rising from the chimney.

Behind the stout door of the storeroom, Jeremy perched on an upturned ale barrel and Phoebe sat in the corner with a sack of meal at her back. Since it was June, the storeroom was more empty than full, but a few sacks of dried beans were stacked next to the meal and round cakes of cheese sat on a high shelf. Two loops of summer sausage hung from the ceiling, separating a fat ham and the last of the onions, braided and hung from hooks the previous fall.

"Who was that?" Jeremy said. He hoped it wasn't his lady. No, she was safe.

"I don't know," Phoebe said. "What do you think they want?"

Jeremy did not answer. His mother asked the question now only from habit and he had given up speculating. "The lady will wonder where I am." Like his mother, Jeremy was compelled to repeat himself. "Do you think it's night all over again?" he said.

"Closer to midday, I think."

"Do you think they forgot about us?" Something smelled different but he couldn't make out what it was.

"Maybe."

"Maybe nobody will ever come."

"Someone's bound to. Your father'll be back from Allyntown soon."

"Today?"

On the other side of the door, a key scraped in the lock. The door swung open. The greasy-haired man stood outside. "I'm letting you go," he said. "I wouldn't be so generous, but the truth is, there's no time now, the army is already here."

"King William's army is here?" Phoebe said.

He snickered. "An army, I said. Wrong King. Cedric is your King now."

"But King William has gone to Mullendown to fight Cedric," Phoebe said.

"Very accommodating, I'm sure," he said. "I guess King Cedric decided on another place and forgot to tell him. You should know, Mistress, that in another time or place, I'd not set you free, but I don't hold with some of Seth's ideas and Seth's a man to be reckoned with. He gets what he wants most times, and them that crosses him don't live long or find they wish they'd died. As I see it, I can't very well free your boy without freeing you and not have him find out about it. So, listen well, both of you. If he does find out, all three of us'll wish he hadn't. And when he's done with you, I'll make you pay for my misery as well."

"I won't say anything," Jeremy said.

"You have our promise," Phoebe said. Seth. She won't forget that name.

"Get you gone before I think better on it," the greasy-haired man said, "and stay out of sight."

At the back of the inn, a large garden showed early promise. Supporting the summer's bean crop, poles extended in long orderly rows leading away from the inn.

"Use the beans for cover," Phoebe whispered, grateful the crop had come on early.

Jeremy nodded.

She gave him a gentle push, then followed, bending low as she ran. By the time she reached the last pole, Jeremy was halfway across the next pasture. She waited until he disappeared into the trees, before she followed. He was waiting just beyond the first tree.

Something burned at the far end of the village and the

greasy-haired man had disappeared. "We look to be safe for the moment," Phoebe said.

"I don't think anybody saw us," Jeremy said. "I watched real close and didn't see anything."

"That was smart." She put her hands on his shoulders, then ruffled his hair. "We must go our separate ways now, son, as we have planned. I pray God keep you safe."

"Don't worry," Jeremy said. "I'll see you real soon, you'll see. God speed, mother."

She hugged him. "And you, my boy."

"We'll wait till you bring help," he said and started running. When Jeremy's side hurt so bad that he couldn't stand it, he slowed and settled into a steady pace. Three times he stopped, whirled around, and watched the forest. No one followed. At the hermitage, he sprinted across the empty clearing. Inside, the blanket rested in a tangled heap on the floor and a few wilted daisies lay on the table. He ran outside.

"Lady! It's me, Jeremy."

He ran to the brook, but the soft moss told no tales. He felt like crying. They were supposed to be there. They were supposed to be where St. Declan could take care of them. Jeremy raced back to the hermitage. Inside, heart pounding, he held up the blanket. No sign of blood. He folded it and put it back in its place, then picked up the daisies. He would save his lady's flowers until he fulfilled his pledge.

They had to be someplace! Unless they had gotten to Lamberton before he left, he would have passed them. Maybe they'd gone back to the wagon. He could easily run there and back before his mother could get to the hermitage with help. Let them be at the wagon. No, better if he found them before they reached it. There were wolves in the Brightwood. He ran. After a long, long time, the back of the wagon appeared ahead through the bushes.

He burst on to the road. "Lady!"

Three soldiers on horseback stared back.

Cedric's men! Jeremy turned and ran.

"Hold there boy!" one of the men said.

They followed, horses snorting as they crashed through the undergrowth. Jeremy veered left. A horse blocked his path. The crashing behind him grew louder. He dodged in the other direction. No matter which way he turned, he was trapped. Jeremy turned and ran back to the road. He had forgotten there were three.

The soldier jumped down and grabbed Jeremy. "I've got him, Hugh!"

Jeremy squirmed, but could not get loose.

"Why did you run, boy?"

Jeremy struggled harder.

"Stop I tell you! I'm not going to let you go."

Jeremy twisted. The soldier's grip began to loosen, then tightened before he could escape.

"We aren't going to hurt you," the soldier said. "We only want to ask you some questions."

Jeremy kicked him, then tried again to pull away.

"Damnation!" The soldier did not slacken his grip.

"Do you need some help there, Stuart?"

The other two were back. The one who asked the question dismounted.

"Only if you're offering, Hugh," Stuart said. "It's of no mind to me, but I wouldn't want to leave you out of the fun all together."

Jeremy kicked as hard as he could.

"Ow!"

"Well, I know you never had the advantage of having had little brothers," Hugh said. "Let me show you how it's done. Just a demonstration mind, I'm sure you don't need my help." He grabbed Jeremy at the waist and hung him under one arm like a squealing pig on its way to market. Jeremy continued to kick, but could only land a few soft blows. Hugh carried him a few feet and then dropped him.

"Now, I don't want to hurt you," Hugh said, "but if you give me a bruise, I'll give one back, understand?"

Jeremy sat in the dirt and glared.

"Tell us about the lady," the soldier on horseback said.

Jeremy pressed his lips together.

"There are ways to make you talk, you know," the soldier said.

Jeremy pulled his legs up, wrapped his arms around them, and tucked his head down. He was not going to betray his oath.

"We'll give you one more chance," Stuart said. "We heard you say 'lady'. Tell us about her and you can be on your way."

"This is serious business," Hugh said. "Answer the question in the name of the King or suffer the consequence."

Jeremy hoped he would be half as brave as Sir Herbert. What hurt worse, bones breaking or the knife? His legs began to shake and he hugged them tighter.

"We've got no time for this," the soldier on horseback said. "You can tell us what we want to know here, or you can go with us. You'll not so easily refuse the questions then, I can tell you."

Would the one called Seth be there? Jeremy swallowed hard and shrugged.

"Percival," Hugh said, "best take the boy with you and tell them what's happened. We'll go on."

"You have a choice, boy," Percival said, "and it's your last one today. You can ride behind if you act decent, or be tied on like baggage. It's all the same to me, take your pick."

There was no escape. "I'll ride," Jeremy said.

"So, you do talk," Hugh said. "Are you sure you won't make this easy and answer our questions?"

Jeremy looked down. He would be as brave as long as he could.

Jeremy's wrists were bound with leather, then Hugh swung him onto the horse, handing the rope to Percival, who tied it around his waist.

Jeremy twisted around. The road on the other side of the wagon was empty.

"We buried him just before you got here," Hugh said, grimly.

Jeremy bit his lip and blinked a few times.

"Do you know where the woman who was traveling with him is?" Hugh said.

Jeremy shook his head.

"But you did see her?"

Jeremy lowered his head, he'd said enough.

"You can tell us later then." Percival spurred his horse.

CHAPTER SIX

As Jeremy ran toward the hermitage, Phoebe hurried north. She avoided the road, sure the scar-faced man would somehow know her plan and follow. When she had walked far enough to think the chance of discovery unlikely, she moved onto the road, anxious to speed her journey. By mid-afternoon, the trees grew sparser and bright clearings appeared. At first blackberries and thin saplings both claimed the light, but soon the hopeful oaks gave way to the vine. Where a last oak stood lonely sentinel, the road twisted, said farewell to the forest and disappeared into the great marsh that spread out south and east of the Windrush, giving the castle its name. Phoebe looked reluctantly at the oak and took a deep breath before continuing.

In the marsh, rushes moaned in the constant wind, a thousand whispering voices in an undulating sea of green. Even though you could hardly go a few feet from the road without flushing a bird, the Marsh King had little fear of poachers. Few men went willingly into the marsh and far fewer returned. Whether the constant murmuring was the muted cry of men held under the marsh's spell or the sighing of their souls, no one knew. And except on market day, when the villagers joined together, calling loudly and laughing boldly, the road to Windrush was rarely traveled.

Undisturbed by her presence, a red-winged blackbird watched Phoebe from its perch on a cattail, the rest of the flock hidden. Even things in the marsh weren't normal. East in the direction of Merriton, a dark plume curled upward. Was Lamberton burning behind her? She dared not look.

"I hope you kept to Allyntown yet another day, husband," Phoebe whispered. Poor Giles. What a shock he'd have if he came home and found them gone. More still if Cedric's army was there . . . Cedric's men in Lamberton! What on earth could they want? At least she had the comfort of knowing Jeremy was safe; he would certainly have reached the hermitage by now. All night she'd been afraid of what the day might bring, but now it seemed, they'd been better off locked away. Who knew what might have happened otherwise?

"I'm all questions and no answers, and that's a fact," she said. "I hope my not knowing doesn't bode ill for the outcome. Well, there's naught I can do for anyone but my own boy and those he pledged his help, and little enough for them, except to hope the Marsh King will know what to do, and then will see fit to do it."

The Marsh King was in a foul mood from all she'd heard, and as of late, there'd been gossip enough to satisfy the longest nose. If the High King's messengers weren't coming and going, the Marsh King's were. More than one stopped to rest his horse, and if some had furrowed brows and sealed lips, others were happy enough to sit by the fire and fill her boy's head with tales.

Jeremy had been even more excited by the parade of solemn men on high-spirited horses, who with their squires and knights, rode past without slowing. No one from Lamberton had joined them, but Phoebe saw a few from other villages who had abandoned fields and families for the promise of adventure. The farmer would lose his war with the brush and bramble while he fought the High King's war, and it would be their own fault too. War was no concern for the likes of them; such doings should be left to the highborn.

Every knight and nobleman in the four kingdoms must have ridden through these past months. All but the Marsh King. Some wags said the gout stopped him from riding and accounted for his temper. There were others though, and Phoebe put more faith in them, who said the Marsh King limped less when he thought no one was looking. Now she must knock at his door and ask his help. If only she knew someone at Windrush who might speak for her, or at least tell her what to say. The old bailiff, Simon, would have been just the man, but she'd heard he was dead and buried this past Easter.

All this fuss over a woman. Phoebe would have let a young fowl take its chance on the spit, just for a chance to catch a look at Agatha of Norwood. What a rare woman she must be, for Cedric to go to war because she would not wed him, and for King Reginald to let his sister to have her say. Just last month, one of the messengers told Jeremy all about her. Tall, with red hair that fell to her knees, he had said, with a slow walk and a quick tongue. A King's daughter well fit to be a Queen.

"Is she the most beautiful lady you ever saw?" Jeremy had said.

The man rubbed his chin. "Well," he'd said. "There's beauty that burns and beauty that glows, so it depends on your taste as to which is best. For my part, and for all one differs from the other, I think Agatha of Norwood can't hold a candle to Queen Claire."

It did the King William's man credit to defend his own Queen, whose husband must now fight for the sake of another woman. Queen Claire, mother of three sons and a young daughter; Phoebe had listened to the stories as well. She had said nothing to Jeremy, the idea was unbelievable, but still . . . The question was, what to tell the Marsh King? Would he even see her?

With a shrill cry, a thin-billed bird shot skyward. Phoebe jumped, then blushed, glad no one saw her. The bird perched on a reed a few feet away that swung back and forth with the unaccustomed weight.

"If I am the cause of your distress," Phoebe said, "your nest is safe from me. All the same, you do well to guard your home." She smiled. "I do declare," she said. "I'm more than a bit addle-brained this day. The Marsh King won't care to see me, but I think he'll be glad enough to know what's happened at Lamberton. Once I have his ear, I can tell him what I know and he can decide for himself what it means." She nodded and walked faster.

The road climbed out of the marsh through the stunted remnants of a forgotten orchard, and twisted up the hillside toward Windrush castle. With one step anxious and the next determined, Phoebe began the climb. Near the top of the hill, two boys stood in the road. If they were coming from the castle or going toward it, she could not tell.

"Good day lads," she called out.

They wheeled in unison and stared.

The two were quite a sight, grubby faces and tunics no better. One had a torn legging and carried a small bundle, but other than that, they looked just alike. Phoebe's heart beat faster. "Good day to you," she said.

"Hullo," one said.

When she reached them, the two boys stepped to the side of the road. Beyond them, a woman sat, with her head resting on her knees. A little girl leaned against the woman, patting her on the shoulder and a third, taller boy stood guard over both. Jeremy was nowhere to be seen.

"My goodness!" Phoebe said. "Are you hurt?"

"No." The voice was muffled. Claire raised her head. "No, I don't think so," she said. "It's just that everything began to spin around . . ."

"It's our lady mother," Richard said. "I think she must of fainted or something."

"Fainted and fell flat on her face." There were sturdy legs under the torn leggings, and Phoebe had no doubt he knew a thing or two about taking a tumble.

James watched Phoebe a moment. "And we were scared,"

he said.

"I should think so," Phoebe said.

Claire sat straighter. "I am feeling better now."

But her voice quivered and her face was pale and drawn, with black circles under her eyes that hadn't been caused by a fall. The bottom of her chin was beginning to darken; the youngster hadn't been far wrong in his description of what had happened.

"My name is Phoebe," she said. "Can I help?"

They stared.

"I am Jeremy's mother," she said. "I believe I know who you must be, but where is Jeremy."

"We waited until midmorn," Claire said. "When he hadn't come by then, I thought we should go on without him."

"He was . . . Jeremy was detained through no fault of his own . . ." The children were young and didn't need more to add to their worries. "He left to find you just about midday," Phoebe said. "Jeremy will be worried when he finds you gone, but I'll soon set his mind to ease. That is, as soon as I've seen you safe to the castle." He'd be that worried when he didn't find them at the hermitage, but in the same position, with these young children, like as not she'd have done the same.

"It might be dark," Richard said. "Maybe you should go find him now so he won't be all alone."

Claire nodded. "It can't be far now."

"The wolves might eat him," Edward said.

Phoebe smiled. "Jeremy will be safe enough. As you say, it's only a bit further to the castle and as I've come this far, I'll finish what I've started. Jeremy would never forgive me if I left you now, and as for me, I would never quit worrying if I didn't see you to the door. Besides, the Marsh King . . . I mean King Leveric . . ." Phoebe turned crimson. "The king that is, should know what's happened at home and perhaps . . ." She looked at Claire. "Perhaps you would think such news as I have, might well be of interest to the High King. It's grave news by my way of thinking."

Claire gave Phoebe a sharp glance.

"Did somebody die?" Edward said.

"It's not that kind of grave," Phoebe said. "There's time enough for talking when your mother is some place she can rest, don't you think so?"

"Did you bring us anything to eat?" Edward said.

"I wished I'd thought of it, but then again I didn't know we'd meet. All the more reason to go on though, if your mother's able. Or, maybe I'd better go on alone and fetch help."

"I feel better," Claire said, "but please don't leave us." She held up her hand. "We should go on, all of us."

Phoebe hesitated. Was there a proper way to do these things? No one moved, so she shrugged and helped the High Queen up. Rose petals and children, the small hand put Phoebe in mind of both. Nobody had to say anything, Phoebe knew what she knew, even if she didn't know the why of it. Whatever were they doing all alone in the Brightwood?

"Off you go then," Phoebe said, waving the children forward. She stayed close, ready to offer an arm if needed, and though Claire wobbled a little and seemed to be concentrating on each step, she did not ask for help.

In a low voice, Phoebe said, "I hope I said nothing to cause concern for yourself or your children."

Claire glanced up. "It's just that I am tired and the road grows so steep," she said.

"Well, be assured, my son's oath binds me by my own choosing."

"His oath?"

"To help you."

"He is a good lad, and we were lucky to encounter him."

Phoebe brightened. "He is indeed and he'll be glad to know you think so." She pointed. "You see where the road takes a turn just ahead?"

Claire nodded.

"That's the top of the hill, and from there, it's only a few feet to the castle wall."

"That's good news." A hint of a smile formed, but faded

before reaching Claire's eyes. "I'm glad we got here before dark," she said. "I've been worrying all day that we might get here too late and find the gate closed against us."

"Oh, there's no fear of that, if you'd only known," Phoebe said. "Day or night the way is open. The gate was taken down to make it easier to haul in stone when they built the new castle and was never put back. Besides, there's no need for a gate when there's a dozen ways through the wall itself. If you walk around it, you'll find more than one gap where a log has lost its way and ended up as part of someone's cottage. They like their comfort here, and don't want to work over much to get it."

"What about . . ." Claire smiled. "What about the Marsh King? Doesn't he care?"

"Oh, I'm sure I don't know," Phoebe said. "He might if he noticed, but then again, maybe he has and can't be bothered." Phoebe refrained from adding that from what she heard, no one was less inclined to exert himself than the Marsh King.

Claire nodded, too out of breath to answer.

The children stopped at the crest of the hill.

"Are you waiting to help us old folks up the hill?" Phoebe smiled. They looked to be four motherless mud larks, not children of a cloth merchant, let alone the children of a knight or saints preserve us, a king. Well, a splash of water, some fresh clothes and a warm dinner would make all the difference, and they'd soon have that.

"My toes hurt," Elspeth said.

"Come on Elspeth," Richard said. "I'll carry you pig-a-back."

There was a quiet resolve to the boy. "I'll carry her," Phoebe said. "Likely you're tuckered out yourself . . ."

"It doesn't matter if I'm tired."

"He has carried her more than once this day," Claire said, putting her hand on Richard's shoulder.

"I don't doubt it a bit," Phoebe said. "What I should have said, was that I am more used to the walk, and would be happy to carry the lass. And then son, you would have an arm free if your mother needs it."

"Well . . ." Richard said.

"Bless you lad, but haven't I carried my own Jeremy up this same hill when he was about this age? I don't mind, if the child doesn't."

"She can do it, Richard," Elspeth said, and held up her arms.

The wall stood a hundred feet beyond the last of the fruit trees, a line of pointed spears growing from the top of an earthen embankment. While there were no missing logs within sight of the road, the wall buckled and sagged. A wooden bridge spanned the deep ditch that fronted the wall. The whitewashed keep rose three stories, with a square tower at each corner. Phoebe shifted Elspeth. "There, child, just through the gateway is Windrush castle."

Elspeth stretched for a better view. "There's no door," she said.

"You've got sharp eyes," Phoebe said. "It'll be around the side where the winds aren't so fierce."

Inside the wall, several outbuildings were under construction. A long low building stood on the right, and if the smell of fresh manure did not advertise its purpose, a plaintive moo did. A cobblestone walk led around the building. Two men stood by the door.

They turned. On their surcoats was the yellow shield with black badger. Cedric's men!

Claire moaned. "We must leave before they see us," she said.

Phoebe touched Claire's arm. "Shhh! It's too late now," she whispered. Then she called out, "We ask shelter for the night."

One jerked his head toward the door. "In there," he said.

A flush spread across Claire's pale face. "We are lost," she whispered.

Phoebe pushed the children forward. "We have no choice now."

CHAPTER SEVEN

Inside the keep, the barren stone was bleak after the brilliance of the exterior, and candles did little to dispel the gloom. The small entry was unfurnished and unadorned, except for two carved wooden doors, which were both closed, giving no hint to what lay beyond. A soldier stood by each and like those outside, wore Cedric's emblem.

They should have turned back, Phoebe decided. Asked to see old Simon, then left upon hearing of his demise. Or asked for alms but not shelter. Or . . . or anything that did not trap them in a castle with Cedric's men. Where had the Marsh King gone? "We ask shelter," she said, unable to think of anything else. It was a common enough request and with luck, there would be others besides them. In a larger group, they might pass the night unnoticed. She glanced at the oldest, the lad could scowl until his face froze, if only he held his tongue.

One soldier gave them a long look, shook his head, and opened the door next to him. A dark, narrow staircase led to an open door. They climbed up, stumbled across the threshold and were swallowed by the emptiness of the castle's great room. High above them, tall peaked windows lined one wall. The glazier had been hard at work and all but one still boarded, boasted small squares of greenish glass that glowed in the setting sun. Colorful tapestries hung on the wall opposite, a blurring cacophony of men and horses. In a calmer moment, Phoebe would have noticed the snowy egret rising from a gold-threaded marsh, as well as other symbols capturing the history of the Marsh King's lineage, as he chose to tell it. Empty tables with their attendant benches were abandoned under the tapestries, their usual occupants having ridden to war with the High King. On the far side of the room, a mean fire burned in the bowels of an immense fireplace. Even if she weren't afraid, Phoebe would have found it difficult to breathe in so grand a place.

The Marsh King was not gone, but sat hunched in a chair near the fire, his long spindly legs pressed together, with one foot wrapped around a chair leg. His Queen sat near him, hands folded in her lap, staring at the floor. Next to the Marsh King, a tall man in a green tunic stood with his back to the door. He ignored their arrival and continued talking in a low voice. There were no merchants plying their wares, no pilgrims on their way to the monastery at Fieldthorn or the cathedral at Arent. No scurrying servants. Not even a hunting dog lay by the fire.

Phoebe gave one of the little boy's sleeves a quick tug. "Stand behind me, lad," she whispered.

He stepped back just as the man in green turned. Fine-featured, he did not have the look of a bailiff. His tunic was embroidered in black and gold, but he wore no emblem. No bailiff, but not one of Cedric's men either.

Beside her, Claire shuddered.

"Well?" the Marsh King said. "What do you want?"

Phoebe curtsied. "We seek shelter for the night." She tugged Claire's sleeve, but the High Queen stood fixed. Mercy! Did she even know how to curtsey?

The stranger pointed. "You have ill manners for one seeking favors."

"Beg pardon, my lord," Phoebe said. "But . . ."

"What's happening?" Richard whispered.

The Marsh Queen looked up, red-eyed and a balled-up

handkerchief fell from her hand. She retrieved it, paler for the effort. She leaned forward. "Is your daughter ill, mistress?"

Indeed, Claire's white face and flushed cheeks begged the question.

Phoebe stepped forward so that she stood slightly in front of Claire. Behind her, the boy moved as well. "I'm sure it's not the fever." Phoebe coughed.

The stranger held his arm over his mouth. "Come no closer!"

Had the Marsh Queen nodded? Phoebe coughed again.

"We do not need the likes of you here this day," the stranger said. "Be gone as you have come."

"It is almost dark," the Marsh Queen said, "and there is no other shelter nearby. The castle has more than one empty room in the cellar where they can stay until daylight, and there are many thick walls between here and there."

It would be better if they were turned away. Did Phoebe dare say anything? She cleared her throat.

"That one may grow too ill to leave," the stranger said. "What then?"

Wait . . . perhaps there was still hope.

"There's a smallish boat on the river below," the Marsh Queen said. "Small, but room enough for all of them. The current will carry them farther from here than they can possibly walk, so no matter what course her illness takes, they may easily be removed."

"That might spread sickness down river," the Marsh King said.

The stranger laughed. "What's a little plague among friends, eh? I'm for putting them aboard right now."

"It would be uncharitable, indeed unchristian . . .," the Marsh Queen said.

The Marsh King put his hand on her arm.

The stranger stared at the Marsh Queen. "We risk our lives if they stay in this room," he said, "but you may have your charity for all I care, as long as they're locked well away from me."

The Marsh Queen beckoned and a servant appeared in the doorway. "Follow me," he said.

Not the outcome Phoebe had hoped for, but perhaps it was best. They were all tired and hungry and Claire did seem sick in spite of her earlier protests. Phoebe took Claire gently by the arm and led her toward the door. The children followed.

"I will send someone to see to your needs," the Marsh Queen said, "and again in the morning to make sure you leave. Take care you stay away from all here, so we do not suffer for our kindness." She shook out her handkerchief, covered her mouth and nose, and waved them from the room.

The servant walked quickly, never turning, as if he knew the light of his candle would keep them moth-like in the circle of its glow, with their confused shadows hurrying along the wall behind them. The exhausted group was led from one room to another, down a steep flight of stairs, into a long hall, past closed doors, through a small anteroom and into another hall. There, the servant pushed open the first door and backed away.

"Wait here."

They were barely into the room when he abandoned them to the darkness.

"I'm hungry." Elspeth began to cry.

"Hush child," Phoebe said. "Someone will come and bring us something to eat and if they don't, I'll go find some victuals myself. The wife of an innkeeper can surely smell out a kitchen, even in as great a place as this."

"On your oath?" Richard said.

"Yes, indeed," she said. Fine words. If need be, she would try her best, but trying to find her way to the kitchen was one thing, and finding her way back quite another.

"What's that?" Edward leaned forward. Elspeth's sobs turned to sniffles.

Tap . . . Tap . . . Wood against stone and coming closer. A feeble light grew brighter, then a candle appeared in the doorway. Two dark eyes hung suspended above the flame.

The apparition spoke. "Good eve to all here."

Phoebe crossed herself.

"My lady bid me make you welcome." The woman, bent with age, leaned heavily on her cane. Dressed in a gray wimple and dress, she was nearly invisible in the shadows.

"Better never than now." The old woman held the candle higher. "Still, what's to be done? Do what she wills, do what I can."

Phoebe bit her lip.

"The doors are barred tight, so ye cannot leave tonight," the old woman said.

Claire choked back a cry.

The old woman held her candle toward the High Queen. "One," she muttered. Her hand wavered, then moved a few inches. Richard sat next to Claire.

"Two." The candle moved. "Three . . . Four . . ." She had gotten as far as the twins.

Phoebe could hardly breathe.

"Hm . . . hm . . . three, four . . . hm . . ." The old woman sighed. "These old eyes see all too well, for all I am not to see." Nodding, she raised one elbow and a long loaf of bread slid into view. "Here now, one of you fine boys get up will you, and lend an old woman a hand and rescue this loaf of bread afore it falls."

Richard jumped to his feet, then hesitated.

"There's naught to be afeared of," the old woman said. "Leastways by me. I'm just old Tilda, or what's left of me that is." She grinned, revealing a single jagged tooth.

Keeping an eye on the old woman, Richard pulled the bread free. As he did, the light of a second candle cast Tilda's shadow into the room. Edward and James moved closer to Phoebe.

"Here's the water, Tilda." A much younger woman from the sound of her voice. "If you move, I'll carry it in."

"Nay, nay," Tilda said. "You're not to come near to them, I tell you. Leave it be, we'll manage. Run to the kitchen and see if there aren't some meat pies left over from supper. And get some of that good cheese too, if cook's not looking. I daresay he's snoring afore the fire by now, and you can take what you please. And fetch some bedding, it's too cold down here by half."

"I can't carry it all in one trip."

"Two trips or three, what will it be? I'm sure we don't mind, if the dinner is fine," Tilda sang.

Phoebe frowned. The old woman had clearly lost more than teeth.

"There might be some fowl left. Should I get some of that?"

"The marsh bird is dinner," Tilda said. "While the caged bird is winner. Do as you may, but do it today."

"I'll hurry."

"Quick, now lads," Tilda said. "Come out, come out and haul the bucket in."

Edward and James looked at each other.

"Mother?" Richard said.

Her head turned in his direction.

"Mother?"

"Not to fear, young mother," Tilda said. "If I can't carry a bucket, I can hardly run off with a big boy like one of your tucked under my arm. Hee-hee."

"Go ahead," Claire said softly.

Phoebe took a deep breath. So far so good, but it was too bad the boy had called her mother. Better the castle thinks the children were Phoebe's. Lucky the one boy had caught her drift in the great room and kept out of sight.

Edward and James scrambled to their feet.

"Get the bucket, but don't stray my lambs," Tilda said. "We're all alone but for the guard just arrived in the anteroom, and I can't vouch for him."

The news seemed to have made no impression on Claire.

"A bonus birthing, I see," Tilda said, as the boys returned. "Yes sirree," she said in a loud voice, "they can let old Tilda get the fever. Certain, I'm mostly dried up on this side of the grave instead of the other, and no earthly use to anyone, anymore."

Her voice dropped. "And I my own lady's nurse and her own babe's too."

More nonsense, but at least they'd be fed and better than that, whatever the old woman said elsewhere, would have little merit.

"I'll bring their dinner in, Tilda. It'll be easier." If the young woman wore shoes, the leather left no footsteps.

"Good and well," Tilda said, "and here all this time, I thought you went to the cow barn to see Bob Brinley, but now I find out you just like the cows. Hee-hee."

Her voice grew loud again. "They can sew you a shroud as well as a bride's dress. Go in, go in. We can go to our eternal happiness together, only don't blame me when we get there. I'm only after doing as I'm told."

"I'm only trying to help, but have it your way. I'll fetch the bedding and if you decide you need help, I'll do it when I get back."

"Fine deary, whatever you want," Tilda said. "I'm not partial to shrouds myself. See if you can't find some decent wine hidden away too."

Her voice dropped. "Hidden away like my own lady's babe. Like a brown berry girl, she is too. You'd never recognize her if you hadn't seen her these past years, for she's close on to being a woman."

"Hold a moment." Tilda cocked her head. "Did they have the fever in Oroskree too?" she called.

Phoebe strained, but could not make out the words.

"Well you look like a strong young man," Tilda said, "though they do say that's the type to take it hardest, I dare say you might pull through."

Again, the response was too low to catch.

"Pop out now, boys," Tilda said, "and get your dinner. I dare say you'll be left alone to enjoy it."

"I get the leg," Edward said.

"How do you know there even is one?" Richard said.

"Boys, boys," Tilda said. "You're no heathens I think, for all you're tired. It's your mother who has the first share, and the oldest after that."

"I'm not hungry," Claire said.

Tilda's eyes narrowed. "It's not a fast day."

Phoebe nodded. "If you don't eat, you'll be sick for certain sure, and then what will happen?"

Tilda took a step into the room. "Be you very ill, young mother?" she whispered. "I can fetch the surgeon to bleed you, but truly it would be safer not to."

"You didn't drink the marsh water, did you?" Phoebe said.

"Oh, for sure, that would be bad," Tilda said. "There's true water in the marsh for those who know its secrets, but none near the road."

"I'm not ill," Claire said. "I'm fine."

"If you don't eat," Phoebe said, "you will be. Try some of that cheese. Or maybe you'd rather have a pie?"

Claire closed her eyes and held up one hand. "No pie."

Phoebe tore a small piece of bread from the loaf. "Well, try this at least to start."

Claire broke off a smaller morsel, held it a moment next to her lips, then swallowed. "Let the children eat, Phoebe," she said.

"Here's the blankets and some wine."

Tilda shuffled to the door. "Isn't she a clever girl, to do it all at once? Well, there's naught else to be done. I'll leave my light and you can fetch the things after we go."

"God keep all safe," she said. She grinned, and then put on a most pathetic face. Her voice echoed from the hallway. "I suppose I'll be one of the first," she said, "but at least I'll have a good place in the graveyard."

Phoebe could swear the old woman had started to cry.

"There's only two," Edward said, holding a blanket in each hand.

"I can do without," Phoebe said.

"Thanks to the boys, I have my cloak," Claire said. "They took turns carrying it. The children can share one blanket and you can have the other." The bread seemed to have helped; the room had stopped spinning.

"If you've no objections," Phoebe said, "I can share with the little one and the boys can have the other."

"As you wish."

The food disappeared in silence. When she was finished eating, Elspeth curled up next to Phoebe. "The candle is almost spent," Phoebe said.

"And so are we all," Claire said. She put on her cloak and fastened the brooch that held it. "Pinch it out Phoebe and we'll try to sleep." There was a soft hiss as the flame was extinguished.

"Ow."

"I'm sorry. I didn't mean to."

"Boys."

"We're just fixing the blanket."

"We'll be quiet."

Claire waited, then whispered. "Phoebe?"

"Yes."

"You never asked our names."

"Could be I am wrong," Phoebe said, "but I didn't think I needed to, nor think perhaps it safe to hear them said."

"Do you have special powers then, to know the names of a cloth merchant's family?"

"Jeremy overheard your merchant's name from his perch in the tree," Phoebe said, "and I never heard of a cloth merchant who was a knight. Then there's the children. Three boys and a girl, and two just alike. I may not have noticed one without the other, but there you are. Perhaps though I was wrong."

"We are fortunate," Claire said softly, "that not all share your powers of observation, and that you had the good sense to say nothing. Tell me what message you would have had me send to the High King."

"King Cedric's men were in Lamberton," Phoebe said. "That's why Jeremy couldn't leave. It doesn't seem so important now, since they're here too."

"Worse than that," Claire said. "That was Cedric himself in the great hall."

"It's not my place," Phoebe said, "but you were ill when we

were upstairs. Ill and over-wrought. Perhaps he had a familiar look . . ."

"He was at my wedding feast and has hardly changed these past ten years. I wish I were mistaken. It was providence you were with us, Phoebe. Once I saw him, I could hear nothing for the ringing in my ears, and for a moment, I thought he recognized me. It was all I could do to keep from fainting."

"Like as not you'd have managed."

"You keep too little credit," Claire said.

"The Marsh Queen seemed to recognize you . . . at least I thought she did."

"I saw nothing but Cedric. Don't let his fine looks deceive you, Phoebe. He is an evil man."

"Perhaps he will be gone in the morning."

"Perhaps."

"Try to sleep, My Lady."

"I will." Claire closed her eyes but nothing changed. Even though it was extinguished, the candle had burned a hole in the darkness, with glowing embers around its jagged outline. Morning. In the morning they would learn their fate.

CHAPTER EIGHT

A sword pricked Claire's neck, her silent assailant concealed in the blackness. He touched her arm.

She screamed. Or, did she? Her pounding heart blocked all sound.

"My Lady."

The voice was distant.

"My Lady."

Phoebe . . . It was Phoebe.

"You're having a nightmare."

Claire's hand flew to her throat. "There was a sword." Her skin stung where it had touched.

"There was no one, My Lady. You called out. I do fear it might bring the guard."

"I felt it." Claire rubbed her finger and thumb together. Was that blood? The bile rose in her throat.

"There was something there," she said.

"The door has not opened, I am sure of it."

Claire wrapped her skirt around her ankles; rats needed no open door. Shivering, she reached to pull her cloak closer, but found it had fallen away. Her hand went back to her throat. "It's gone," she said. "Tears streamed down her face. "It was a present and now it's gone."

"What's gone, My Lady?"

"My brooch." The cold penetrated, her bones ached. Claire could not stop shaking. "I have to find it."

Her cloak lay where it had fallen. She ran her hand over the fabric, felt between the folds. Felt along the neckline. Nothing.

"Did you find it?"

"No." She wiped away the tears, but could not stop their flow. No candle at least betrayed her. "It does not matter," she said.

"Let me look." There was a soft grunt, then the sound of Phoebe's hand sweeping across the stone.

"I found it," she said. "Or at least part of it. I'm afraid it's broken."

"Let me see." The half circle was smooth along one side and notched where it had separated. Claire breathed a sigh of relief. "It has come apart, Phoebe, that's all. There should be another half."

"Then it should be easy enough to find," Phoebe said.

"Ow . . . I found it. Be careful of the pin."

Claire held the two irregular sides together, pressed one against the other, and felt them slide into place.

"Is it ruined?" Phoebe said.

The circle was unbroken. "No, I think not. Thank you, Phoebe."

"Come dawn, we'll be away and be safe, I'm sure of it. You'll see him again, just like I'll see my Giles and Jeremy."

"See who?" Claire said.

"Why the King, to be sure."

"Ah." Claire pulled her cloak close and fastened the pin carefully. "I must be tired and overwrought. I cannot think why this seemed so important. The brooch was a present, but not from the King. I got it on my fifteenth name day, pinned to this very cloak in fact, but I never wore either until this journey. The day after it was given to me was my wedding day, and I suppose I put them aside in the excitement and forgot them." In truth, the plain cloak had held little attraction.

"We were all excited when the High King married," Phoebe said. "I still remember the stories. To think, ten thousand people feasted that day. I should have liked to have seen that and tasted a little of the feast."

Claire smiled. "Not nearly so many as that," she said. "Still, there was bread and cheese and pies and ale for all who came. And jugglers and musicians to entertain in the streets." Far better to think of weddings than what the morning might bring. "Did you meet your husband before you got married?" Claire said.

"Mercy, yes. How else could we have gotten married?"

"Very easily, if your father makes the match," Claire said. "It took almost five weeks for me to get to Ambridge after I left home, and I got there three days before I was wed. I should not say this, but I remember I was so relieved the King was not old and bald, and still had all his teeth. And his lady mother was so kind." The room seemed to grow a little warmer.

"Queen Adleah, the Good," Phoebe murmured.

"Indeed," Claire said. "King Owain was dead, of course, so I never met him, but I'm told his son is very like him."

William had been kind as well, as if he'd known how homesick and scared, she was. He'd never even made fun of her when he caught her spying on him, the morning of her name day. She had risen early, awakened by the excited cry of the hounds. From the narrow window slit she could see the High King and a dozen men, all mounted, horses eager to be given the rein. William looked up in the direction of her bedchamber. She jumped back, even as she did, knew the movement betrayed her. When she could not resist a second look, she found him grinning and although she was never sure, thought he had nodded to her before he gave the signal and the horses clattered out of the courtyard.

She dressed quickly, both embarrassed and intrigued, and soon found herself in the great hall. For the first time since her arrival, the room was empty. Garlands had been hung along the blue walls, transforming the room into a woodland bower. Sweet woodruff blossoms had been strewn liberally over the new rush mats, releasing their fragrance as she walked. A merry fire burned in the fireplace. At the high table, she stood behind the High King's chair, then moved to the chair on his right. Beginning tomorrow, this would be her place. She must think of subjects on which they could converse. Hunting anyway, it would be a start.

"Good morrow, Lady Claire."

She jumped.

The man was too tall to be a dwarf, too short to be counted among the men but his voice was too deep to be that of a boy. His garments were simple but both his gray under-tunic and the green over-tunic were of finely woven cloth. Hardly a servant, probably not a knight. She nodded.

"I am Ceonald," he said.

The great bard himself! Whatever could she say to him, the most brilliant of men?

"I beg you to think no less of me for interrupting your thoughts, and yet again, for not waiting for a proper introduction. Had I arrived earlier than this very morning, you would not have found me so wanting, at least in this regard."

"Good morrow, sir," she said. A feeble beginning, her face flushed.

He bowed again, smiling. "At the risk of further injury to my reputation, would you permit me now to give you a gift to celebrate your name-day?"

She nodded once more. I thank you, good sir . . . You are most kind . . . Which would be most correct?

"It is not a gift from me," he said, "but rather from the good people of Soddenwood Forest."

His dark eyes cast a spell and she could not look away. Ceonald examined her as surely as the court physician had, before pronouncing her suitable. She bore one as reluctantly as the other, knew he saw past the thin veneer of her new adulthood. Her new life had many trials.

The gray cloak was dull and serviceable. She felt the fabric. "It looks to be very warm," she said. His face wore a strange look, but he said nothing. Was he laughing at her? Had she somehow insulted him?

The silver brooch had no gems or ornamental enameling, but instead had a smaller circle of gold set into the silver. Concentric lines flowed out from the golden orb and a vine, inset with gold leaves, circled the border. Small marks were etched between the leaves. "It's an interesting brooch," Claire said. "Does the design have a meaning?"

"It is flat and round like mother earth." He stared.

She glanced at his face and looked quickly back to the brooch. A curious statement from an odd man. Did he mean what he said? Still, he was the bard and must not be insulted. Claire tilted the brooch and the gold caught the light, glowing warmly. With her fingertip, she traced the circle within a circle. "If this brooch is like the earth," she said, "is this the sun or the moon?"

"Perhaps it is both, My Lady." Ceonald smiled, but his eyes remained watchful.

"How can it be both?"

"Look carefully." He separated the brooch, which split the golden orb, creating a waxing moon on one half and a waning moon on the other.

"So, it is a moon," she said.

"If My Lady wishes."

"I don't wish it either way," she said. "I want to know which it is, sun or moon."

Ceonald took the brooch, fixed it together and handed it back. "Hold it closer to the flame," he said.

In the firelight, the golden circle glowed brightly.

"It's the sun!"

"Now turn away from the fire, and look again."

The gold paled and shone with a cold glow. "Now it's the moon," Claire said.

"So, it is both," he said. "Things are often more than they seem."

She nodded, this time to humor him. "What are the lines around the sun?"

"Whatever you want them to be."

"You are a most vexing man," she said. "Tell me what you think them to be."

"They could be the ripples from a stone cast into a pond."

"Oh." She brightened. "Or waves along the ocean's shore?"

"That's right."

"Or both," she said laughing.

"Right again." His eyes twinkled.

"The strange marks around the vine, do they have a meaning?"

"I believe they are called runes, My Lady. Very ancient symbols."

"Fine, they're called runes. Can you read their meaning?"

"I believe it is almost a lost art."

A careful answer. "And you do not know it?"

Ceonald shrugged.

"But whoever carved this must have known the meaning," she said, watching the watcher.

"Indeed, I believe he did, as the meaning was given to me in case you asked."

"Tell me then, Bard," the future Queen said.

"It is a poem of sorts. Roughly translated, it goes like this:

'Mist over water
Moon over moor
Keep safe our daughter
From mountain to marshland
And forest to shore.'"

"How can all that fit on something so small?" she said, bending over the brooch.

"Runes are symbols, not letters, and as such, have more meaning," he said.

"May I ask you a question?"

The daydream turned to waking nightmare. Phoebe voice was low in the darkness. "You may, Phoebe," Claire said, "and if I can answer, I will."

"Why didn't you just tell them who you are? Surely you would come to no harm."

"I believe a part of me meant to do just that," Claire said slowly. "But when I saw Cedric, I could not bring myself to speak the words. When I think about it now, I see that we may be in greater danger for my reluctance. Now if anything happens, he can say, and say truthfully, that he did not know who we were."

"There is nothing to prevent you from telling him."

Good, kind, trusting Phoebe. Her voice calmed even though she was wrong. "I could. It may not matter though, unless the right people were there to hear it, and I do not know in this castle who they might be. In truth, it does not matter for if I have the power to stop my lips, I will not tell him, unless to save the children. I am not willing to be hostage to Cedric, for then the High King will have little choice but to sue for peace, and at what cost? And Phoebe, I believe that if Cedric means us evil, he will do it no matter what is said. To give up my secret, I fear, will cost the High King overmuch and save me nothing."

"If you will not tell, My Lady," Phoebe said, "it will not be said, but this is all to naught. Come morning, we'll be gone and he'll be none the wiser."

"I pray you're right." Claire trembled from fear as much as the cold. Had she chosen correctly? Would she have the courage to stand by her words? She ran her finger over the surface of the brooch, feeling for the runes. Holding fast to the brooch, Claire, Queen of Bridland, High Queen of Threbant, mother of small children and make-believe merchant's wife, lay back, and repeated the rhyme.

CHAPTER NINE

High above the storerooms, Cedric stood at the window staring into the darkness. Behind him, his servant, Ivo, lit a third candle and extinguished the torch that had burned away the darkness. Cedric pretended he did not notice, just as its lighting passed each evening without comment. It had been their ritual for as long as he could remember.

The Marsh King's bedchamber had fir wainscoting, but the upper surfaces were still unfinished. The plaster had been whitewashed, and charcoal sketches started, leaving a series of disembodied heads floating mid-wall. Cedric had not noticed the staring eyes the evening before, so had slept soundly, but they would be rubbed out by nightfall.

"This castle is most agreeable," he said. "I would not have thought the Marsh King had it in him to build such a place." There was no response, nor did he expect one. The subject matter was new and Ivo would prefer to put finger to the wind before answering.

Cedric turned. "Think you, it is finer than my castle at Murdstone?"

Ivo sucked in the corner of his upper lip. "Newer," he said. He hesitated. "Yes, better." He had tied back the bed curtains and was straightening the bedding.

Cedric laughed. "You have more courage than some of the carrion that ride with me, old man."

Ivo shrugged. "I have known you longer." He laid two surcoats on the bed, one green, the other, black.

The old man was unduly addled this morning and had done it all wrong. Still, Windrush had exceeded expectations, and even though they were laid too closely together to view properly, either surcoat would complement his new yellow tunic. Cedric decided to overlook the fault.

"The Marsh King keeps his quarry men busy," Cedric said. "Did you notice his stockpile of stone?"

"No, Sire."

"What do you think he's going to build next, old man?"

"I suspect you know, but I will guess if it meets your purpose. A church, maybe?" Ivo glanced down at the bed. The old man's right hand positively twitched. He'd spotted his error but dared not remedy it.

"Ha! I know the man better than you. He'd never part with the coin. The Bishop will build the Marsh King's chapel, and I daresay pay well for the privilege. No, he plans a new wall around his fine new keep, why else let the old one go to ruin?"

"You may be right."

"Of course, I'm right, old fool, he has already begun to dig the foundation. Your hand seems to have developed a tremor, old man. Are you feeling well?" The taunt was irresistible.

Ivo paled. "I am well, Sire."

Normally the reaction would amuse Cedric, but today, when he was in such a temperate mood, it annoyed. Still, once again, he would forgive. "By mid-day," he said, "I want the Marsh King's quarry men, stone masons and engineers assembled. All of them." He smiled. "I am going to put them to work at Murdstone."

"As you like, but they are free men and may not go."

"Offer them double wages."

Ivo's eyes widened. "Double, Your Grace?"

"Do I need repeat myself?"

"No, Sire, my apologies."

"Draw up a contract and have each man make his mark. Make sure a priest is there as witness."

"It's both an arduous trip and a long one," Ivo said. "Many have families and may not want to put them to the hardship."

Cedric frowned. What did he care what they wanted? "A man who refuses an honest offer of work must have a reason, old man."

Ivo's eyes narrowed.

The old man came closer than any to being able to read his master's mind. Besides Ivo's compunction to speak honestly, with little regard to consequence, it was one of the reasons Cedric kept him. Truth be told, Cedric did not know if he valued the honesty as much as the entertainment in punishing it. Ivo, no doubt, might well be able to deduce the answer.

"Not his family then, Sire?"

"A nice excuse," Cedric said. "I would suspect such a man meant to stay and plot behind my back."

"I see." Ivo pointed to the bed. "Which one, Sire?"

"Treason is punishable by death, is it not?" Cedric said.

"Yes, Sire." Ivo picked up the green tunic.

"Not that one!" Cedric turned back to the window. "It's foggy out, but will soon be dawn. Start with the apprentices. Let them teach the lesson, and see how fast their masters learn."

"I believe they'll learn quickly." Ivo held up the black tunic.

"When they have signed, Ivo, levy a tax for each family member who is to make the journey. Make a list of all who say they cannot pay. We'll deduct their debt from future wages."

"You don't want the families in Oroskree then?"

"No, fool, I do. The men will not slack with their family's subject to pay the price, but they are rich men now, with fine wages, while I am the poorer. They can well afford the fee."

"I suspect there will be others."

Cedric laughed. "Greedy men must be taught a lesson. Tell them any family member who stays behind will be under my personal protection, and will travel with my army."

"I congratulate you, Sire. Your reputation, I'm sure, has preceded you and they'll pay the fee gladly. The Marsh King may well complain."

"He's hardly in a position to argue." The Marsh King had been restricted to his Queen's chambers. She had seemed none too pleased with the arrangement, which would be interesting to pursue later.

"I can give him more serious injuries to contemplate," Cedric said, "but for now, unless we are unduly aggravated, we will observe the proprieties." The Marsh Queen was rather limp-eyed for his taste. Still, he had not yet seen the daughter. They had no doubt tucked her away someplace but never mind. In the end, it would all be the same and this way he had the fun of the hunt. The Marsh King had few morals about abandoning the High King, but what would it take to get him to surrender his daughter?

Cedric held out his arms. "How long has it been since that last, most delectable little morsel, old man?"

"A few days, Your Grace."

"Four days, old man. Four days can seem an eternity."

"For her it is."

Cedric laughed. "Ivo, Ivo, you do have a sense of humor after all. Did you let the parents bury her?"

Ivo slipped the surcoat over his head and adjusted the folds so they fell smoothly over the tunic. "If you remember, Sire, the father was dead."

"True, true. I had forgotten." Cedric lifted his tunic a few inches and pointed his foot. His black hose showed off his new red shoes nicely. "For a tanner, he took the sword well, did he not, old man?"

"Yes." Ivo began carefully folding the rejected tunic.

Cedric strolled over to the wall. Was the sketch male or female, saint or sinner? No matter, he would have them destroyed. He studied his foot again. "I must have another pair of red shoes," he said. "These do exceedingly well. Do you think I would do as well as the tanner?"

"No, Sire, you are cunning, but not brave."

Cedric threw his head back and laughed. "Ivo, you amuse me much this morning," he said. "Tell me, did the widow have other children?"

"A young lad. He won't trouble you."

"And he was there?"

"Indeed, Sire, as you may well remember."

Ivo was wrong. Two sets of terrified eyes had watched from the corner shadows. Cedric felt his heart begin to quicken and moistened his lips. "Send the mother a penny . . . no, make it two. I won't have them on my conscience, even if their sister was most impolite."

"It will be done today." Ivo laid the folded tunic into an open leather trunk.

Cedric lay down on the bed and folded his hands across his chest. "What think you, Ivo, if I forego my war, and challenge the High King to a dual instead? Would I win?"

"In a fair fight?"

"Ivo, you are the eternal optimist." Cedric sat up and swung his legs over the bed. "Hmmm . . . Certainly it must have the appearance of a fair fight . . . no, wait . . . let's say it was a fair fight. What then? What does William have that I do not?"

"Besides a wife and an heir?"

The blow was swift. The old fool had deserved it, indeed had been spoiling for it all morning. Now he could wear the mark of master's displeasure, his reddened cheek a small price to pay for such impudence.

"With such an injured look, you play the dog well," Cedric said. "Someday you'll say too much and I'll lock you up with my hounds and let them fight over you."

"Beg pardon, Sire." Ivo bowed.

Cedric returned to the window. "Those two women last night . . ."

"Yes."

"There's something amiss there."

"They are sick, or soon will be."

"No," Cedric said. "Something else. I can't quite put my finger on it, but it will come to me. You were watching, I assume, from some nasty hiding place."

"As you instructed." Ivo straightened.

"And you saw nothing strange?"

"No, Sire."

"The younger one. What think you? Does she have the fever?"

"It was hard to tell from where I was."

"Maybe we'd better check. I may have been over-hasty last night."

"Should I send your physician?"

"Ever the fool, eh Ivo? Go yourself, damn you. I believe I must insist on checking the condition of the younger one. It would be remiss of me to allow her to depart without the benefit of my deep concern."

Ivo bowed.

As he opened the door, Cedric said, "If she is ill, I'll not be over-fussy. You may bring the other."

"Then they're not allowed to leave?"

"Not today, Ivo, not today."

CHAPTER TEN

Caught in the half-world between sleep and wakefulness, where dreams wear the mantle of reality and reality the substance of shadows, Claire did not hear the door open. Throughout the night her nightmares had a common theme, but wrapped themselves in different cloaks. More than once she had jerked awake knowing dawn had come, only to wait disappointed in the darkness. The cold draft was new. Claire opened her eyes. A candle flickered.

"It's time," a voice whispered.

Claire waited, but this new nightmare refused to be banished.

"Good mistresses, stir yourselves."

Who spoke? The room wore an unfamiliar look. Beside Claire, a stranger rolled over, left Elspeth sleeping, and climbed stiffly to her feet.

"Don't be afraid, it's just old Tilda."

Windrush. They were at Windrush, and it must finally and irrevocably be morning. Richard scrambled to his feet, while Phoebe gave Edward a gentle shake. The single touch served for the two, and Edward and James stood, rubbing their eyes. Under the blanket, Elspeth curled into a tighter ball. "Go away," she said.

"Up you go, young mistress, and no nonsense," Phoebe said, peeling away the blanket.

"That's right, that's right," Tilda said. "You must be gone before the dawn's light and light dawns. What the night does not reveal, the day must display."

Claire frowned. The old woman spoke in riddles, her face an enigma, which gave no clue if she knew them. Still, part of her message was clear. The foul Cedric was here, or at the very least, the evil left in his wake.

"You must go by river," Tilda said, "just as My Lady spoke last night. She does suspect Cedric's men now patrol the marsh road and you must avoid him and his men, if you can. My Lady's only wish is to see you safe away."

Charity born of compassion, or of knowledge? "And the Marsh King?" Claire said. "What does he say?"

"He has not been tested with the question."

So, the Marsh Queen recognized them, but chose not to tell her husband? Grave news, but what meaning did it have?

Phoebe flushed. "If the road isn't safe," she said, "there must be a reed cutter who could guide us through the marsh. No one would be able to follow us, and we'd be safe."

"Nay," Tilda said. "The boat is what My Lady did choose. It'd be best, she would know. Hurry now. You've stayed overlong as it is; Cedric was stirring even as I came."

"How will we manage without help?" Claire said. "I cannot row a boat, nor I dare say can Phoebe."

"Not to fear," Tilda said. "The current is strong and will carry you without the effort. Near Allyntown, you should drift close enough to shore to call for help, and there pray Heaven, find safe haven. There are provisions for you by the boat and I brought an extra bundle, as my Lady was not sure if you would continue together."

"Is Jeremy's mother going with us?" Edward said, pointing to Phoebe.

Phoebe nodded solemnly.

Had she hesitated before responding? If she had, Claire would not hold it against her. That they were thus far undiscovered, was surely to Phoebe's credit. But what if they got to Allyntown and Cedric's troops were there as well? The masquerade could not last. "Is there any word of the High King or what's happening to the south?" Claire said.

"None," Tilda said. "You brought more news than I have to give."

"Maybe you should go back by way of the marsh road, Phoebe," Claire said. "Even on that road, if you were by yourself, you'd surely be left alone."

Phoebe smoothed Elspeth's curls. "I swore an oath to help and I'll not leave. My own can wait."

It was the answer Claire prayed for. Phoebe had sworn an oath, and was she not a subject of the High King and duty bound by that as well? Of course, she would attend them. But Claire thought of Jeremy's earnest face. Duty. They all had a duty. Claire would send Phoebe back to her son. She could not. How could she? They weren't yet safe. Did not Phoebe owe a duty to the High King and thus to his family that must override all others? But save for the comfort of her company, what more could Phoebe do?

"You're a good woman, Phoebe," Claire said, "but I must release you from your vow. As it is, we owe more than we can pay, for how does a mother put a value on the lives of her children? We owe Jeremy as well, and the only thanks I can give for now is to send his mother back to him."

"Enough, enough," Tilda said. "Ye must go." She handed the bundle to Phoebe and stepped into the hall.

"I don't know," Phoebe said, rocking back and forth slightly, as if swayed by the force of the argument within her.

"Let go from this vow, but take up another if you will," Claire said.

"Swear or not, but do hurry," Tilda said, taking a step back into the hallway.

Phoebe nodded. "If it is in my power, I will do as you ask."

"My request is simple," Claire said. "Until we reach home, our only safety lies in secrecy. Go to your son, Phoebe, and help us by making sure he tells no one who he met on the road."

"There's nothing to fear from Jeremy. I'm sure he has no idea who he met, and if he did, would only seal his lips more tightly."

"But if he tells the tale in innocence, others may guess what he does not. You did so yourself."

"That's true enough," Phoebe said, nodding.

"There's no time to spare," Tilda said. "Listen well. There's a guard by the door, but he shouldn't trouble you and if he does, I shall give him cause to think of other things." She lifted her right hand, revealing a sharp blade extending from curled fingers, then thrust her hand back into the folds of her skirt.

"When you leave the castle," she said, "you'll be in a courtyard. It's still dark and there's a heavy fog. Hard to see, but hard to be seen as well. Go to the left and follow the castle until you reach the wall. You'll find a gate there, and on the other side of it, there are steps that go down to the river. Do you understand?"

"Yes," Claire said. "Our thanks to you and your Lady, Tilda, and to you, Phoebe, our thanks and gratitude as well." Claire pulled her cloak around her. Richard took Elspeth's hand and Phoebe followed, dabbing at her eyes with the corner of her sleeve.

"My Lady waits to bid you safe journey," Tilda whispered, as Claire left the room.

"There's no way out of the courtyard save by the river stairs," Tilda said, turning to Phoebe. "When we get to the anteroom, stay by the door and wait for me. I don't think your failure to leave will cause comment. The guard who watches was not the one earlier. I'll see you out safely by another door. Do hurry!" She hobbled quickly down the hall.

The Marsh Queen stood by the open door. Above her, a bracketed candle threw dancing shadows across the wall. "I promised to see you leave by dawn," she said, "and I am here to answer my duty. Make haste, before you kill us all."

The guard nodded in agreement.

They hurried across the anteroom. Reaching the door, Claire stepped aside and motioned the children through. The Marsh Queen, her eyes red and face swollen, caught Claire's sleeve.

"My daughter, Ellen, waits by the boat," she whispered. "Pray you, take her with you. Better she is with the hunted than caught in the snare."

Before she could answer, Claire was in the courtyard and the door slammed shut.

Before the door was even closed, Tilda left the anteroom and led Phoebe to a side door. Although Phoebe crowded behind her, Tilda kept the same slow pace, stopping every few feet to peer through the fog, as if as much a stranger to Windrush as Phoebe. The ripe smell that wafted toward them as they walked, pointed to the milking barn as their destination and not the road that led away from the castle, but the old woman had done all she'd promised, and Phoebe trusted her in spite of her peculiarities.

Two horses cantered out of the gray, nearly running Tilda down. Had Phoebe not jumped and pulled Tilda with her, one or both would have been struck. Phoebe shook her fist at their backs. The riders stopped and turned in their saddles. Her heart began to pound. The horses were wet and winded; the men had ridden hard to reach Windrush at dawn. Even in the fog, the scar on one was visible. She shivered. Pray heaven Jeremy was safe! The second pulled his horse around, blocking Phoebe's view of the one called Seth, and rode back, while Seth continued toward the castle. "What're you two up to?" he said.

"Down to see if the cows be poxed," Tilda said, "and if they be clean, bring fresh milk back to the Queen."

"Then don't stand there, lack-about, get to it."

"As you say, sir," Phoebe said. "We've work to do and the day will be done before the work, if we don't get to it. Peace on ye, sir." Mercy! She was beginning to sound like Tilda!

"Aye." Tilda grinned. "A pox on ye, sir. Pox to ye."

He frowned. "Watch your tongue, mistress," he said.

"There's more than one here who'd remove it for such sauciness."

Phoebe curtsied. "Beg pardon, sir. She's a bit addled, but she means no harm."

"No harm, no arms," Tilda said cackling.

"Stop them!" rang out from the direction of the castle.

"Stay with them!" Seth called out. He disappeared into the mist. The other pulled his sword from the scabbard and held it ready.

"No arms, no harm." Tilda began shuffling toward the barn.

The man ignored Tilda and kept his eyes on Phoebe, but little matter since the horse could overtake the old woman in a few strides. Tilda, at least, had the courage to defy him, while Phoebe stood rooted to the spot, her earlier and only defiant act, a raised fist, designed to be unseen. It's not us you want, she wanted to cry, desperate to follow Tilda and at the same time, frantic the old woman seemed oblivious to the threat. Phoebe's face reddened. She had abandoned Jeremy's lady and now, her first thought when challenged was to betray them. "It's someone on the water side," Seth called out.

The man kicked his horse and cantered toward the castle, leaving Phoebe alone in the swirling mist.

.

CHAPTER ELEVEN

In the courtyard, light escaped a window on an upper floor and evaporated into the mist. The fog did not seem to hide them, so much as to hide those watching.

"This way, Mother," Richard whispered.

"Hurry, but stay close to the castle." The cold stone repelled, but held Claire captive, with the need for a guide in the murk. The wall materialized, arched door ajar. They ran.

Once through the doorway, she stopped and took a deep breath. A few steps down to the river and they were safe. Should she close the door or leave it open? Would the Marsh King, who built no gate on one side of his castle, care about one on the other? She pushed it back a little and hoped it looked as it had before. Narrow steps were cut into the hillside, leaving a foggy precipice beneath them.

"Don't go near the edge," Claire said.

"Where is it?" Edward took a step and lurched forward, arms flailing. Then he laughed.

"Edward!! Shhh. Keep your voice down."

He paused, arms midair. "I can't stay away from it if I don't see it."

"Stay close to the hill," Claire said. "You know full well my meaning."

Wind gusts pulled at her skirts and sent her cloak billowing out around her. Picking Elspeth up, she pulled her cloak over the child and clenched the excess fabric in her fist, holding both fast against her.

"I can't see," Elspeth said.

"Shh."

"I can walk by myself." Elspeth squirmed under the cloak.

"Shush." Claire tightened her grip.

"You're supposed to be quiet," Edward said more loudly than his sister.

"Shh," Claire and Richard said in unison.

Heavy timbers anchored each step. Scrub trees clung to the top of the hill; dark sentinels peering down through the mist. With one hand on the cold grit of the scarred bluff, Claire felt her way from one high step to the next. After the fiftieth step she lost count. Finally, tired and winded, they reached a broad platform. Their footsteps echoed on wood as they crossed. Three steps led down to the riverbank.

A movement caught Claire's eye. Ellen stood, unnaturally elongated, looking down at Claire. The girl's dark eyes were startled, but the rest of her face was expressionless, masked by gray. Beginning a strange dance, she jerked right and then left, legs kicking.

The fog thinned. Claire gasped. Ellen hung puppet-like. Below her suspended feet, two more were firmly planted. A gloved hand covered Ellen mouth and a mail-covered arm held her fast. Behind the girl, two eyes stared from under a burnished helmet.

A second knight rushed from the shadows. "Don't scream," he said.

Scream! Claire had lost the possibility of speech. They were everywhere!

Richard leapt down the stairs, and pushed in front of her. "I forbid you to touch her," he said.

His defiance went unchecked. Instead, the man removed his helmet, pulled the mail hood from his head and bowed.

"Forgive me if I startled you, Your Grace," he said.

Elspeth broke loose from her mother's distracted grip and her head popped out from beneath the cloak. "It's Sir Hugh!" she said.

"Indeed, it is," Hugh said, grinning. "It's a good thing I heard your voice on the steps, or I fear you'd have met a much different reception." He looked back at Ellen. Her struggles had ceased. "Now, will you swear to be silent?" he said.

She nodded.

"Well then, Stuart," he said, "you have a chance of saving your fingers, for I swear she'd have bitten them off if she could. It is well we are met, Your Grace. We are sent to bring you back to Ambridge and I did not relish meeting the High King without you."

"A most welcome surprise," Stuart said, "especially since Cedric's standard flies above us." His warm tone matched the relief in his face.

"We thought to relieve the Marsh King of his boat," Hugh said. "Fortunately, the maid here caught our interest, and we decided to wait and see what she was up to, or else we'd have been gone before now."

"I am no lady's maid and I would thank you to remember it. I am Ellen, daughter of Leveric of Morimond, who some call the Marsh King."

"Indeed." Stuart's face darkened. "I will remember that."

"We must hurry," Claire said. "Not only is Cedric's army here, but so is he."

"Then we are in grave danger," Hugh said. "Go ahead, Stuart. I'll bring up the rear."

"What about her?" Stuart jerked his head in Ellen's direction.

"We all go," Claire said.

"The Marsh King is with Cedric, but his daughter goes free?" Hugh said. "Are you sure it's wise to bring her?"

"I need not trouble you with my presence," Ellen said, glaring at Hugh.

"Stop them, idiot," a voice said from the hilltop.

"Hurry!" Hugh held out his arms. "I'll carry Elspeth."

"Run!" Stuart said.

Slipping over the wet rocks, Claire stumbled and slid across the riverbank. Hugh stayed close, while Stuart and Richard took the lead. Halfway to the boat, James tripped and fell. Edward turned and ran back.

"Go on! I'll get him." Hugh thrust Elspeth into Claire's arms. He reached James and pushed Edward toward the boat. "Run!"

"I can hear them!" The voice was closer.

The landing stood out now, a narrow strip jutting out into the river.

"Take the bow, Stuart," Hugh called.

Stuart lifted Richard and Edward into the boat, then stepped into it. Ellen swung after him.

Just ahead of Claire, Hugh reached the boat and lowered James into the stern then swung Elspeth in. "Sit next to James," Hugh said. She scooted back and Hugh dropped down by the empty oarlock.

With one hand steadying the boat, he held out the other to Claire. "Sit between Stuart and I, Your Grace," he said.

The place most shielded by the men's armored bulk. "No," Claire said. "Richard, you sit there."

"Move lad," Hugh said.

Richard scrambled forward.

Hugh held his out hand.

"We'll go as far as Lamberton," Hugh said, as Claire climbed in the boat. "We can put to shore for horses there."

"Not Lamberton," Claire said. "Cedric's army was there yesterday."

"God's blood!" Hugh said. "We must go up river then, and try our luck at Breaham."

The men slipped the mooring lines free, let the boat drift clear and took up the oars. At first, the boat stubbornly maintained its position on the river, but the men evened their strokes and the boat began to inch its way upstream.

Running footsteps sounded, just the dock melted into the

mist. "I can't see them!"

Hugh and Stuart bent over the oars. In the fog, it was hard to tell how far they had gone, but the next voice came from a distance.

"They're gone and there's no other boat."

"Hurry! Maybe we can catch them downriver."

From time to time, dark shapes could be glimpsed along the riverbank, their ghostly branches suspended midair. As the morning lengthened, the fog began to clear, swirling in thick patches, alternating with bright sunlight.

Just as the boat reached a sunny spot, Claire saw a flash on the shore. A second followed. Several lance points broke through the foliage. She placed one hand on Hugh's arm. "Behind you," she mouthed, pointing to the eastern bank.

Hugh turned. As he did so, a soldier stepped into sight. Attached to the end of his lance was a yellow standard. Cedric's black badger advanced and retreated with each gust of wind.

Seeing Claire point, Stuart turned to look. "Let her drift back into the fog," he whispered.

Hugh nodded. They stopped rowing. "We'll head for the other shore," Hugh said. "They may not have seen us."

When the boat was concealed by mist, the men began rowing. The sun broke though again and caught Claire's brooch, sending circles of light dancing on the river.

"You on the river! Name yourselves!"

The fog began to close again, but too late to stop the angry hiss of arrows. Stuart's hands flew to his throat. He gasped and fell forward. The oars fell from his hands. More arrows bit into the side of the boat.

Ellen sprang up, grabbing for an oar as it slipped into the water. With the sudden shift of weight, the boat listed and hung precariously. She teetered off balance. Stuart slid toward the water. The boat dipped lower.

As Claire fell, Elspeth slid from her arms. The bitter cold took her breath away. Claire's skirt held her fast to the boat, pulling her under as it rolled. The swirling cloak caught her arms. She pushed the cloak away; her surcoat took its place. She grabbed the taut fabric. An arrow anchored her skirt to the boat. She grabbed the shank and pulled. It snapped. With fingers growing numb, she pulled. The shank was too short. Lungs screaming, she, she pulled at her skirt. There was a sudden burst of stars and then darkness.

CHAPTER TWELVE

As the man rode toward the castle, Phoebe ran after Tilda. "I need to go back," she said. "They might need me."

"Nay, mistress, it will never do," Tilda said shaking her head emphatically. "Cedric's caught a scent and he may soon learn the smell. The price you'd pay wouldn't buy their freedom."

A truer word was never spoken. Still . . . "Poor lambs," Phoebe whispered.

At the barn, Tilda continued around back and there, the curtain wall had gaping holes not visible from the courtyard. "Say nothing," she whispered. "Hurry on, hurry away."

Phoebe chose the largest opening, and eased her way to freedom. Hard packed and smooth, the narrow path angling down the embankment had obviously been chosen often, and she picked her way down the incline. At the bottom, under a scrub alder, she opened the bundle. Inside was bit of hard bread and cheese. She tucked it under her arm, determined to save it for Jeremy. He'd be worried to death and half-starved by now, and hadn't she gone hungry more than once?

She squeezed through the dense vegetation, holding onto the branches to keep them from rustling. Even in the fog, the movement might be noticed, and the noise serve as an alert.

When the ditch turned in the direction of the bridge, she scrambled up. The hillside below her was broken by low stone walls and at each, Phoebe was forced to search for a spot where the stones had fallen away. Whenever one could not be found, she sat on the stones and swung her legs over. A sprained ankle was the last thing she needed.

The sun began to shine just as she reached the road. Fingers of gray fog lay over the marsh and to the east, a more resolute mist prevented a glimpse of Merriton. Yesterday's smoke was not visible, but an acrid smell remained. The road was empty, and for the first time, Phoebe was more afraid of who might be traveling on it, rather than the marsh's secrets. Although she was anxious for home, she was glad enough for the walk ahead; the recent events were caught in her throat and although she could bide her tongue better than many, she needed to settle it all a little. By the time she reached the Brightwood, the last small pockets of fog were melting rapidly. Phoebe hurried past the sentinel oak, and when she was safe in the Brightwood, looked back. Not a soul was to be seen. "I tried to help," she whispered. "I'm sorry I couldn't do better." With the distance now measured, her impatience to be home increased and Phoebe quickened her pace. Although she had never gone to the hermitage from this direction, she had no fear of getting lost so close to Lamberton and left the road before she reached the village.

The clearing was empty, Jeremy nowhere to be seen. No matter, he must be inside. But he wasn't. She went back outside. No one. She followed the bluff until its slope lessened and climbed up, breathing heavily. No sign of Jeremy in any direction. Maybe he'd gone back to the village and she'd find him with Benjamin. Or maybe Giles was home and had the boy with him. With a heavy heart, she scrambled down the incline and ran toward Lamberton. As she left the forest, Benjamin's Boyo ran to her and jumped up, panting happily.

"Hsst . . ."

The dog retreated back into the trees, his waving tail replaced by a beckoning hand.

"Hsst . . . Phoebe!"

It was Benjamin's mother, Nell. Not the cheerful Nell with the quick grin that never quite matched her appearance, since it didn't stand to reason that someone so relaxed and happy could keep everything so well-scrubbed and orderly, but a Nell with a dirty face, streaked by tears.

"Ye can't go into the village," Nell said, her voice trembling. "We thought you be dead. Did you see they burnt Tom Carpenter's?"

"I need to find Jeremy and Giles," Phoebe said.

Nell caught her arm. "Nay, Phoebe, stay. Ye can't go to the village. Ye've been forbid, like Benjamin. Jim thought you to be dead with your boy; save I told him you couldn't be, if they forbid you come into the village and oh Phoebe! They cut off his ear." Nell covered her face and began to cry.

Phoebe' legs grew weak. "Whose ear, Nell! Was it Jeremy? Nell?"

Nell took a deep shuddering breath and wiped her face on her sleeve. "T'was Benjamin, Phoebe. My Benjamin. It happened so quick like we didn't know it was coming, and both me and Jim standing right there and not able to do a thing."

"Is he . . ."

Nell shook her head. "We were able to stop the bleeding. I need get back to him. I've left him sleeping and come down to see if I could see Jim, though I don't know why, for Jim knows where we be and he'll be back when he can."

"Do you want me to go and fetch him?"

"No, Phoebe." Tears glistened afresh in Nell's eyes. "Like as not, deary, you didn't hear, or maybe I forgot to tell ye, but you can't go into the village, you've been banned. And Jeremy too. He said he'd take his pound of flesh if he saw you once, and if he saw you twice, the priest could have you for his churchyard for that's all the good you'd be. And I daresay he'd a have a good laugh doing it too."

"Who, Nell?"

"Him. The one with the scar."

89

Seth. Seth was at Windrush, but for how long?

"Will ye come with me, Phoebe?" Nell tugged at her arm. "I oughten not to leave my boy so long."

Phoebe shook her head. "I need to find Jeremy."

"Nay, Phoebe. It'll do no good. If you be hurt, you can't help him. And take it from me, if it's meant to be that he be hurt, you can't stop that either."

"Still . . ."

"It's been quiet all day, save for a few strangers, at least from what I can see. Everyone's on the lookout for you and your boy, to warn you away. That was Biddy's idea and heaven knows she's enough to think of what with her Nate, but isn't it just like her to think of everyone? Jim'll be back soon, I know he will. We've naught to eat all day and I can make do, but my poor boy is so pale. Jim's gone to fetch back some victuals."

Phoebe glanced down at her bundle. "I've been keeping this for Jeremy," she said, "but Benjamin might as well have it. We can save part of what Jim brings for Jeremy."

"You'll come then? You'll not leave me? It's just a little ways from here, so they can't find him quite so easy, though he just be banned from the town. They said the tree line. He has to stay in the forest."

Benjamin was sleeping, his head swollen with Nell's bloody apron. Boyo lay beside him, his head on his paws, watching with worried eyes.

"Where's your other boy Toby, Nell?"

"Toby be with his father," Nell said. "Jim's to see if he can stay with Biddy and Nate, or not if them, with all they have to deal with, then with someone else, but they be our first choice if they'll take him."

"What's happened to Biddy and Nate?" Phoebe tried to keep her voice calm, hoping to soothe Nell.

Nell wrung her hands. "They said if Toby came to the forest, he was outlaw with his brother and Jim and me too. He'll come though, if no one will take him. Jim's in between still, first saying he'll come and then not, and I can't decide what's best either. If Jim stays to the village, he can look to

Toby and bring victuals regular to us here, as I can't see how else we'll survive. Like as not we'll be eaten ourselves afore too long, when it comes to that, but if Jim does come, then maybe we can get a shelter together." She burst into tears.

It didn't seem like Nell would take to being hugged, she was far too scattered and still, Phoebe would like to help, but where was Jeremy? She patted Nell on the shoulder. "There, there."

Benjamin sat up, groaned, then brought his hand to the bandage and winced. Boyo licked the boy's face and wagged his tail. "Did Jeremy come?" he said pushing the dog away. Boyo sat tail wagging happily, glad his master had recovered.

"Where is Jeremy?" Nell said. "Why isn't he with you?"

Whatever was said would need to stand up to being talked about. If Jeremy wasn't at the hermitage, and he wasn't in the village, maybe he set out for Windrush. That left only one direction, where it would be safe for someone to look for him and be certain not to find him. "I sent him south," she said. "Giles was to Allyntown and I sent Jeremy to tell him there'd been trouble."

Nell nodded.

"Have you seen Giles?"

"He wasn't there yesterday, that's to be sure. They had us penned like animals all day. Oh, Phoebe, it was awful. They burnt Tom Carpenter's, did I tell you?"

"Yes, did they – ".

"Did you say you had something to eat?"

"Mercy, yes," Phoebe said. "A fine innkeeper's wife I am." She handed the bundle to Benjamin. "I'd start slow, Benjamin, and eat a little bit and make sure it'll stay down."

"That's right," Nell said. "Phoebe, you always did think things through." She opened the bundle, looked inside, shook her head and sat it next to Benjamin.

Benjamin began to pick at the bread.

"Phoebe! Saints preserve us!" It was Jim, or rather, like his wife Nell, an altered version. His body sagged under the weight of his already rounded shoulders. Usually pale from long hours at his bench, his skin had pinked under yesterday's sun. As it was color he was unused to wearing, his face took on an apologetic tone. His hands were empty.

"I thought ye'd be surprised," Nell said. "I was myself, but there you be. I don't see you brought us any supper, husband, but Phoebe here has a bit for the boy, so things aren't so bad. There's naught enough for a sparrow to pick, so there's naught for us or Phoebe either. Hopefully your news will be better than our dinner. How be Nate? Will they take Toby? And here's Phoebe, worried to death about her own. Any news of them?"

Phoebe nodded. Jim would answer as soon as Nell let him, so the less said the better. That anyway had not changed.

Jim squatted down next to Benjamin and patted the boy on the shoulder. "How be you feeling, lad?"

"Oh, my poor boy," Nell said. "But he's been brave through it all, I'll say that."

"Does it hurt awful bad?" Jim said.

"Mostly just if I move my head," Benjamin said, shrugging and then wincing.

"Wish there was somewhat I could do," Jim said.

"It's better," Benjamin said, and tried to smile.

"I didn't tell you yet how it happened, did I Phoebe," Nell said. "I still can't quite take it all in."

"Wife," Jim said. "Sit down here near our boy and rest yourself a bit. You're all done in."

"Well, I won't say no," Nell said. "But we'll hear your news if you'll tell it, won't we, Phoebe."

"Please," Phoebe said.

"First off," Jim said, nodding as Nell sat down near Benjamin. "Him with the scar seems to be gone, but the rest are there and more besides. They be all talking among themselves, and coming and going, but paying no mind to any of us to speak of. Not like yesterday. They've taken over the inn."

Phoebe cried out.

"It's not burnt down, Phoebe dear, think on that," Nell

said.

"I've not seen Giles or Jeremy, nor has anyone else that I know of," Jim said. "I'd have thought your boy be with you, Phoebe."

Phoebe flushed.

"Well, you can see for yourself he's not," Nell said. "She's sent him off to find his father coming back from Allyntown, and quite right too, seeings what's happened to our boy. What about Toby?"

"He's with Nate and Biddy. One more mouth won't put them over the edge and Nate can use the help. The boy's young but he's strong and not afraid of hard work. He'd do worse than to learn to be a smithy and I've a mind to see if Nate'll take him on regular like."

"What's happened to Nate and Biddy?" Phoebe said.

"Biddy's fine," Jim said. "Worried like everybody I guess, but she said she'd see we got our victuals regular. Nate's got a broke arm but it didn't break the skin so that's something. Toby's young but he can help and I warrant he'll learn real good."

"Course he will," Nell said. "Biddy's got a prize rooster that came all the way from Allyntown."

Phoebe smiled in spite of herself. That rooster seemed to be a mark of distinction as far as Nell was concerned and she was as proud of it as if she had owned it herself. Like as not she'd sent more than one hen fluttering in the direction of the smithy. Even with the trauma of the last two days . . .

"As Toby's settled, be you coming with us, husband?"

Jim paused. "I've been thinking on it," he said slowly.

Already old, he had aged overnight. Nell was his second wife and he'd mourned so long after the first, Phoebe never thought he'd marry, and probably wouldn't have either, if Nell hadn't set her cap for him and gone about seeing it through. It had done him a world of good though and he loved his boys. "Is it true what Nell says?" Phoebe said, "that I can't go back into the village or Jeremy either?"

Jim nodded. "They posted it on the church door. Father

Ambrose said it says 'Banned' and then lists your names; Phoebe and Jeremy, late of the inn, and Benjamin with one ear."

Benjamin flushed.

"I'm to tell the priest by sundown today if our names go on it too."

"Don't do it, Jim," Phoebe said.

"What?" Nell frowned.

"It was good of Biddy to say that she'd bring us food since we . . . we aren't able to be to home," Phoebe said. Outlawed! She could not even say the word. And where was Jeremy? "It's up to you of course," she said, "but if you both stayed in town, there'd be more to help. I've got to stay, and Jeremy and Benjamin. That's three already. I can look after both boys, and will gladly, but there's little to be done for food without help."

"She has a point, Nell." Jim already looked more cheerful.

Nell would never be able to stay away from the village with Toby there, let alone Jim, and would be sneaking back within a fortnight. "Biddy could use the help, I'm sure," Phoebe said, "what with Nate laid up."

Nell leaned forward and patted Benjamin's leg. "What would people think if I left my boy?"

"They'd not think anything, knowing he was with Phoebe," Jim said.

"Seems like that scar-faced man was awful mad at you," Nell said, studying Phoebe.

They were only banned to the forest line, but for how long? And what had that Seth meant about Jeremy? "Tell them your boy is dead," Phoebe said. "Tell them Benjamin is dead."

"Phoebe!" Nell crossed herself.

Benjamin put his bread down and stared.

"No one will look for him then Nell, and you won't need to say that you saw me either."

"Then no one would wonder at you leaving him, wife," Jim said.

"Folks would understand if you came to the forest to tend

his grave and grieve in private," Phoebe said. "Then it would be easier to bring food, as no one would be looking for you to do it. Anyway, like as not the High King will soon learn what's happened and set this right."

"Oh, Phoebe," Nell said shaking her head, "as if you know what the High King might do."

"You could take care of Toby and Jim and still see Benjamin," Phoebe said.

Jim nodded.

Nell wiped the corner of her eye. "You'd need a shelter made afore winter, but still there'd be time and we could all help."

"I know a place," Phoebe said.

They stared.

Phoebe nodded. "It's a private place, Nell, kept secret, but not forgotten. Tom Carpenter could do no better."

Nell's mouth opened and closed.

"She's speechless, I can tell you that," Jim said.

"It seems best to me," Phoebe said, "that the fewer that know about it the better."

Her mouth opened, she paused. "Well, I always say," Nell said finally, "that words be welcome, but a secret's meant to be kept."

"That's right," Jim said, nodding encouragement.

Nell meant every word and a more good-hearted woman could not be found. She always had plenty to say, but wouldn't go from house to house like some. All the same . . . "We'd best fix a place to meet and leave things," Phoebe said.

Nell looked at Jim and then nodded slowly.

"It grieves me awful to leave you, son," Jim said, "but you can see that what Phoebe says is true."

Tears ran down Nell's face.

"It won't be long, Benjamin, you'll see," Jim said. "Like Phoebe says, King William will set things right."

"I know, Da." Benjamin kept his head down and his voice low. "I know it's best."

Nell began to sob and Phoebe choked back tears herself.

When the place and time for meetings was decided, Jim put his arms around Nell and led her toward the village.

When they were out of sight, Phoebe held her hand out to Benjamin. "Can you walk, son?" she said.

CHAPTER THIRTEEN

In the Soddenwood, the fog refused to dissipate, thickening instead into a steady drizzle. A hundred yards north of the confluence of the Oberon and Mithray rivers, and midway between the two, lay an uprooted cedar, covered with the latest generation of ferns and mosses to call it home. A number of small trees grew from the rotting trunk, that nursed not only the infant hemlock and fir, but armies of fungi that marched with step like precision, up and down the trunk. A giant cedar, having grown to fill the void left when the other had fallen, stood guard over all. Shielded from view by the decaying trunk and protected under the branches of its successor, Hugh woke and opened his eyes, confused to find himself in the forest and not on the banks of the Oberon.

He moved. An explosion of pain in his shoulder radiated downward. Hugh groaned, then held his breath and waited for the throbbing to subside. The branch had not so much as quivered, but high overhead, a squirrel chattered a warning. When the ache dulled, Hugh lifted his left hand and grimaced. Something amiss there, to be sure. Bent the fingers of his right hand. No pain there. Held it up. Still nothing. He clenched his teeth and touched his left shoulder. The pain was expected, but to his astonishment, his mail shirt had been removed. He raised his head a few inches. A thick bandage covered his shoulder. There was no sign of blood on his tunic, but his left arm had been bound to his chest, explaining its inability to function.

The thick cover of green shut out the sky, and the log obstructed his view of the forest, but shielded him from view as well. He, or his benefactor more likely, had chosen a good shelter. Hugh lay back, then explored the bandage, searching out the damage. When he was done, beads of sweat shone on his forehead, but he was relieved. His collarbone was broken, but appeared to have been set. Painful but not serious. He felt his arm. It was uninjured, bound only to keep the shoulder immobile. That small effort was exhausting.

The tree overhead had a strange look and Hugh needed more than a few moments to discover the reason, but time was inconsequential. He studied the canopy above him. Cedar limbs, along with fir boughs borrowed for the occasion, had been woven through a wooden frame supported by living branches on one side and two wooden posts on the other. A snug shelter, his physician was a woodsman as well. Shelter or not, he must move. The Oberon was cold, with deep undercurrents and swift eddies. He had pushed Richard toward the overturned boat but knew, even as he did so, the gesture was futile. Hugh could only hope the river gave up its victims easily. A grim task waited.

Hugh rolled slightly and swung himself into a sitting position, this time prepared for the pain. He was not alone. A gnarled grandfather of the forest leaned against the fallen cedar. Seeing that he had been seen, his thick eyebrows arched upward. The old man put a finger to his lips, then beckoned and disappeared. Hugh climbed painfully to his feet. The old man had gone only a few steps and when he saw Hugh, turned, and walked briskly into the forest. Hugh hurried after him. Behind them, the cedar boughs shook, as they were worked loose from the frame, and the posts followed, leaving only two faint impressions, to mark Hugh's resting place.

The gray hair deceived; the old man set a hard pace.

Hugh's shoulder throbbed with each step and a sharp pain in his side made breathing difficult. At first, he tried to keep some sense of their route, but within a few feet, he was lost. Just when he thought he must beg for a slower pace or be left behind, the man came to an abrupt stop. Ahead, a jumble of fallen logs rested against the base of a cedar, as if swept there by a flood and abandoned to the care of the tree. One log had been pulled away from the rest, revealing a low opening. Smiling and nodding, the old man pointed.

Hugh debated. If the man meant to make him prisoner, this was a strange way to go about it. But what did it matter now?

Still smiling, the old man made a sweeping motion with his hands.

Hugh walked to the opening and cocked his head. A light flickered inside. Did the old man really mean for him to go in? He looked back. The forest was empty. With his good hand protecting his shoulder, Hugh bent and ducked through the opening.

The small candle cast a feeble light, and he heard the movement as much as saw it. Seated on a low stool, a gray-haired woman turned as he entered and put her finger to her lips. Her hair was parted down the middle and a thick plait hung on each side of her face, while the rest fell unbound to her waist. She bent immediately back to her task, stirring the contents of an iron pot in a slow circular motion, her lips moving to a silent cadence. Acrid steam rose from the pot, but there was no fire beneath it.

Hugh made the sign of the cross and stepped back, banging his shoulder against the wall. When his eyes opened, the woman was standing. "You have no reason for fear," she said softly.

The gentleness of her face calmed him, but did not yet convince. Still, he nodded.

"The fire was outside. Surely you can see that it is hardly safe to light one here."

Inside the seemingly random structure of the woodpile, was

a small irregularly shaped room. While the outside was damp from frequent rains, the inside was tinder dry. Hugh nodded again, unwilling to trust his voice until the pain lessened.

She stepped back. Fresh boughs, covered with thick pelts, had been laid along the far wall and on that makeshift bed, Claire lay covered by her cloak, her face pale and waxen in the candlelight. Her chest rose slightly with each shallow breath, but it moved.

"Thank God," Hugh whispered. "She lives."

"As you see," the woman said, glancing over at her patient. She resumed her seat, stirred the pot once and lifted her stick, pulling out a strip of cloth. With a forked twig, she caught the end of the cloth and twisted. When the liquid stopped running, she gave the cloth a final twist, unwound it, and with a quick snap of her wrist, opened the compress and placed it across Claire's forehead.

"Will she . . ."

Her hand went up. "We must be patient," she said. "It is possible but not yet probable. By tomorrow, we'll know." She repeated the process and laid a second strip over the first.

"There were others in our party," Hugh said. "Do you have news of them?"

She moved the pot to one side and pulled her stool a few inches closer to the bed.

"If you have no news," he said, "I must begin a search while there's still light to see. I'll admit though, I could use some help."

She glanced at him. "You do not offer your name, sir," she said, "but I will give you mine all the same. I am called Breona, and what needs to be done, has been. You are injured and should rest."

"It's not so bad," he said.

She frowned. "What needs done, has been." Then her face softened. "Will you not sit, Sir Knight? I will give you my stool if the ground offends you."

Hugh slumped. The truth was, he had no idea how far they were from the river, or even in what direction it lay. "I have failed my duty," he said, lowly.

But she heard him. "Which was?" Breona watched her patient intently.

The situation required an answer; it must be honest but careful. "To return the woman in your care to her husband's protection," he said.

"He would do well to see to his family," Breona said, "as it seems they are in need of care. It's a pity he did not attend to them earlier."

Hugh flushed. "Do the people of the Soddenwood think so little of the facts of a situation, they do not search them out before they judge?"

Breona's gaze was steady. "Perhaps she is an errant wife, derelict in her duty?"

"Never."

"But as you say, she is not with her husband, nor he with her, and you are sent to fetch her back. There must be a reason."

"As escort, not guard. He seeks only her safety."

"And think you this turn of events would worry him overmuch? Surely, he has important business to attend, and would not want to be bothered with trifles." She smiled, albeit a thin-lipped one.

"Trifles! Indeed lady," Hugh said. "He will be most grieved. He was sorry enough to see her leave and most anxious for her safe return." Hugh knew more than anyone, the truth of that statement. He had not known the Queen left Ambridge until the High King sent him to fetch her back, but he had seen her leave all the same. The night before the High King was to leave Ambridge, he had called Hugh to his chamber.

"Ride with me on the morrow," William had commanded.

They met in the pale, pre-dawn light, but to Hugh's surprise, William turned his horse north instead of east. At the edge of town, the High King guided his horse to the side of the road and stopped. Hugh reined in beside him.

"There is one last duty I must attend," William said.

They had barely gotten to the road when a wagon appeared, and in spite of the driver's costume, Hugh recognized him. William did not appear to notice the wagon. Herbert did not slow the horse or look away from the road. If a gesture of greeting passed between the two, Hugh saw no sign of it. The horses, trained to silence, did not greet their stable mates. After the wagon passed, William sat silently for a moment, then gave a heavy sigh. "It is done," he said. "We will go."

As the first rays of sunlight crept over the horizon, William turned away, eyes glistening, and urged his horse to a gallop. Hugh scrambled to catch up, and when he did, William's face was hard and set. "You will keep secret what you have witnessed this morning," the High King said.

Hugh nodded, knowing he had not seen what William had seen, without looking.

"Swear it."

"I do so swear, Your Grace," he had replied and he had never spoken of that morning again. Nor would he now.

"And does she wish to go?"

"What?"

Nun-like, Breona sat straight-backed, with folded hands. She needed only the beads. "I asked if she wanted to return to her husband."

Hugh shrugged. "It is her duty and she would not shirk it."

"No, the High Queen will do her duty, that is certain."

Hugh started.

"Did you think we did not know who we rescued, young man?"

He did not answer.

"Never mind," she said, brushing some unseen dirt from one of the furs. "It was only at the last minute you were known, when our Lady's brooch caught the sunlight. Only one like that was ever made, and it was fashioned here in the heart of the Soddenwood."

Hugh studied the woman. There was something about her that was familiar. "Did you bring the gift yourself, good lady?" he said.

She smiled. "Where the trees of the Soddenwood stop, so do I. The gift was delivered by my brother, Ceonald."

"Ceonald is your brother! He has always seemed to have been . . ." Hugh felt his face redden.

"Did you think he sprang from the same tree that formed the lute he carries?" she said, eyes twinkling.

"I've never given it any thought," he said. "All men know Ceonald, but it seems no one knows him."

"Sit down, Sir Hugh," Breona said softly. "As you can see, I know you as well. You are injured and must save your strength. I have bad news with the good."

"If there is good news, I would hear it first, gracious lady, to make the sting of the bad less powerful."

Breona leaned over and gently stroked Claire's hair. "We rescued the four children," she said.

His legs grew weak. "Then they are alive! Truly I held no hope. I thought Lady Ellen perhaps may have lived. She grew up on the banks of the river and knows full well its treachery."

"Ah! So, the young woman really is the daughter of the Marsh King," Breona said. "An interesting traveling companion for the High Queen. In fact, I did not believe the child when she told me. I thought she was confused."

"Lady Ellen?"

"No, Mistress Elspeth. A veritable fountain of information once she stopped crying, and now it seems, accurate in all regards, save one. She insisted her mother was a merchant's wife and they were going to find him. But then, she also said the merchant was a knight."

"That merchant was Herbert of Amesly, most foully murdered nearby the village of Lamberton."

Breona's face grew somber. "An able man whose skills are sorely needed." she said. "I am sorry indeed to hear it,"

"Richard?" Hugh said.

"Bruises and a broken rib. Had you not gotten him back to the boat, he would surely have drowned."

"If he told you that, he exaggerates my part. I think at best I could but push him in that direction."

"It is his story and it was well told. My countrymen watched your progress up the river and saw all that happened. There were men in the water to help you before the boat had fully overturned."

"And the others?" Hugh said.

"Edward has a bump on the head, and James a broken arm," she said. "The arm was a nasty break, but has been set now and the boy bore it well. Of Ellen, I have no news."

Hugh looked at her sharply; Ellen had been the first to fall.

"We were few in number," she said. "The High Queen we knew, her children easily deduced. Ellen was swept away before we could reach her. We have a party now, searching the river and its banks."

Hugh nodded. Their choice was clear. So far, the news had been good. He leaned against the wall.

"Sir Stuart was a special friend?" she said gently.

"We were foster brothers together, and I have no brother as close."

"He was a man of bravery and honor," she said.

Was. Hugh focused on the intersection of two logs. They were not special, had not been joined in a special manner and had no particular irregularities, but Hugh knew he would always be able to close his eyes and picture them.

"His injury was beyond our care, even if we could have reached him earlier."

Hugh cleared his throat a few times. "I would like to see him a final time, before he is buried."

"I'm sorry," Breona said. "He is still on the river bank, but one more distant than where he was first found. Your boat rests on a sandbar near him."

"Have you abandoned him to the mercy of the forest and denied him a Christian burial!"

"Do not add to our danger with your raised voice," Breona said. "He is not abandoned, and I swear to you that no beast of the forest will touch him."

"Is he bait then, for some plan of your making?"

Breona smoothed the High Queen's cloak. "If your

assailants seek the results of their attack, they must, in part at least, be satisfied."

"And when that happens?

"I promise you he will be given a proper burial by our customs, and his place of rest remembered. This duty he performs in death, and I do not think he would object if it ensures the High Queen's safety."

Hugh met Breona's eyes and looked deep within them, then caught the shadow of movement behind her. Stuart stood there, smiling. "You would do no less, Hugh," he said. Outside the shelter, someone or something moved. When he looked back, Stuart was gone. "It will be as you say," Hugh said, blinking hard.

"You have my word."

"Then it must satisfy," he said. "I'm sorry if I doubted your intentions. We are truly in your debt and fortunate you happened to be close by."

"It was not luck."

"What?"

"We watch the river and those who travel on it," Breona said. "It is born of an old custom, from a long-ago time, when the world was a dangerous place. We have never given in to new ways and it seems we were right to do so. This is a shelter for those who watch."

"Oh."

She smiled. "Did you think I lived here?"

"Does someone watch the river every day?" Hugh said, once again, crimson-faced.

"Only when there's a need," she said, looking into the distance. "We will watch more closely now."

Claire moaned. Her eyelids flickered.

"Hush daughter," Breona said. "You are safe."

Claire moaned again, then opened her eyes.

Breona dipped a spoon into the pot at her feet and slid one arm under Claire's head. "Drink this," she said. A few drops touched the pale lips. Claire grimaced and turned away. The spoon followed.

"It is bitter, daughter, but you must drink this and more. It will help you and not harm the babe."

Claire's eyes widened and her mouth opened. Before she could speak, the spoon was quickly emptied. For a brief moment she looked up at Breona, then closed her eyes. Breona lowered her gently back onto the bed.

"She is . . ."

"If all goes well, a new life in time for the new year," Breona said, readjusting the cloak. "You see that she is cared for, which was the purpose of bringing you here. That, and to satisfy myself as to your condition. You must leave us now and seek a safer place."

"I will not leave her, except by my death."

"You cannot defend her against illness, that is my province."

"I'll stand watch with you, then."

Breona shook her head. "This place is very near the Oberon," she said. "If it's discovered, we're safer for your absence. You must trust me on this."

"Can we not move her?" he said. "Even injured I can carry one end of a stretcher and I've no doubt the man who led me here could bear the weight of the other."

"It's no good. For the moment, she is more at risk for being moved than for being discovered. And there are the children . . ."

Hugh hesitated. There was truth in what she said. "You will not leave her?"

"She's my patient," Breona said. "For the moment, we are called to different tasks, I to stay and you to go. Your guide waits, and just so you know, he is mute but not deaf. If you speak, he will understand and undertake to answer. But speak softly, if at all. He will signal when it's safe to talk freely."

She began stirring her pot, but when Hugh had gone, she stopped and sat quietly for a few moments. "I think daughter, that we must prepare for company." Breona sighed. "You must not be frightened."

CHAPTER FOURTEEN

Breona stirred slowly, pausing occasionally to lift her stick and watch the drops fall, sending iridescent circles rippling across the surface. A knot had grown between her shoulder blades; it was good the High Queen slept, as it would do her little good to know their danger. She needed a plan. Closing her eyes, Breona took a deep breath and exhaled slowly, then took another, and yet another.

"Start with the obvious." Her voice, but her mother's words. The obvious lay before her; a healer must heal. The High Queen needed more medicine at nightfall and another dose at dawn. Then, if more were warranted, a fresh batch would need to be brewed, since the medicine would have lost its potency. Breona tilted the pot. Two doses left and more besides. She had not miscalculated since she first learned the art, and more than the waste, it troubled her to think she'd made a mistake. What else had she missed?

Two dark spots stained the ground. Breona rubbed one, then sniffed her finger. It was good she had medicine to waste, as it seemed she'd been careless as well. She wiped her finger on her dress, then stared at the silver-sheened smudge. "It seems I brewed the right amount after all," she said, smiling. Where the drops had fallen, Breona dug a small depression and filled the hole with the extra medicine, leaving just the two doses.

Muttering, words unintelligible, Claire threw one arm out from beneath her cloak.

Breona held her hand against Claire's cheek and nodded; for all the High Queen was restless, the fever had lessened. "Rest daughter," she said, "it's the best thing for now and I'll do all I can to keep you safe." She crumbled dirt into the liquid, stirring to form a soft mud. "My wit and my words are my weapons," she said. "Let's pray I have enough of the first, but have no worry about the second. Am I not Ceonald's sister? If I do not have his gift of memory, or his quick hand with the harp, still my tongue is not over shy. Ceonald may be blessed with gifts I do not own, but I am not without."

She dipped two fingers into the mud, drew a circle on one cheek and a triangle on the other. "If you wake, my good Lady Queen," she said, "don't be frightened. I'm going to decorate myself a bit for company, in the event we be discovered. I have it in my mind not to encourage them to stay over long and I trust you'll not object to my lack of hospitality."

On her dress, she drew great circles, spirals and uneven squares. Some symbols she connected with lines, while other lines wandered, disappearing into the fabric. When she was done, Breona stood. Already the mud was beginning to dry, lines of silver on a field of blue. "There be some along the Oberon," she said, "who think the Soddenwood is haunted. We must hope the stories have spread, for it is far easier to frighten a man, when he believes there's something to fear."

Breona pulled a small spray of cedar from the edge of the bed and worked the bits of green into her braids, pulling, so the braids hung askew, disjointed appendages. She tucked two fir sprigs into the top of each braid. "There, that must do." She gave one braid a final jerk.

Breona looked from the bed to the entrance, pulled the stool a few inches from the wall, then went outside and peered back in, from both sides of the opening. It would do. She pulled the stool another inch away from the wall, sat down and pinched out the candle. Outside, the drizzle turned to rain. Only the High Queen's soft breathing punctuated the silence. The gray deepened, and finally, by Breona's reckoning, there was only one hour left until darkness brought its own blanket of safety. It appeared her worries were unfounded.

A twig snapped. Breona tensed. A careless step for one of her countrymen.

"I tell you we're too far north."

A man, but no voice she recognized.

"Maybe, maybe."

Two, and coming closer.

"What's the point in all this? They been carried downstream a longways from here by now."

Was that the first one, or were there three? She closed her eyes. Concentrate.

"I say we turn around and have a look to the south."

Now that sounded like the first one.

"We'll go when I say, and I say they were heading up river, and if they aren't dead that's what they're still about. When we're done here, you can have your turn looking anywhere you want."

"Waste of time."

"What?"

"Nothing."

Claire moaned.

Breona felt for her hand and pressed it. She dared not speak. For a moment there was no response, then Claire returned the gesture. Good, she understood. The men's voices were very close.

"Look at those logs. They'd make a fine bonfire. We ought to give it a light and dry off."

Breona pushed back the fear. She could hear the High Queen's breath quicken.

"You'd never get a spark to catch hold. I swear there's nothing dry enough to burn for miles. This is the Soddenwood all right."

"Did you see that old gaffer's face when we tried to get him to cross the river with us? Old fool. There's nothing I've seen to be afeard of."

"Well, he's a dead fool, isn't he? Still, there's a wildness to this place . . . Give me the mountains any day, I don't like the way the damp here clings to your throat and pushes down at you. This place isn't fit for normal folk, the wet rots everything."

They didn't seem over-serious about their task, their voices now more distant.

"Say, take a look-see over there."

"Where?"

"Those logs. There's an opening. There, on the left."

Breona's chest hurt.

"So?"

"Do you think there's anything in there?"

"Sure, a ten-foot long she-wolf with her cubs. Afraid?"

Laughter. Nervous laughter, she hoped

"Just wondering. Think a person could fit in there?"

"We'd best take a look." It was the one who wouldn't let the men leave.

The undergrowth rustled. Breona dropped Claire's hand and turned to face the entrance. A pair of boots appeared, framed by the opening. The man grunted, his breathing hoarse.

"Can't see anything," he said. "I'll tell you what though, let me climb up and if I can't see anything from the top, let's head back."

"I'm agreed."

As he climbed, the wood creaked. A branch snapped. There was a loud crash, followed by a series of thuds. A rush of cool air filled the hut.

"Don't kill yourself."

"I'm almost there. Damn log was loose."

Ca-chink. Ca-chink. Metal biting wood. A lance probably. He must be testing each log. "The rest feel all right." The wood groaned in protest as he climbed higher. Dust filled the room. Claire choked back a cough.

"Did you hear something?" The voice was directly above them.

Ca-chink. Claire screamed, as a lance hurled down and quivered, a few inches from her head. Outside, a wolf began his mournful howl, answered by a second, then a third.

"I saw it! I saw it!" The shelter shook as the man slid and lurched downward. There was a thud as he hit the ground. "Biggest wolf I ever saw. Had its yellow eye on me and like to froze me to the spot. Took the spear right out of my hand and swallowed it whole."

"Let's get the hell out."

Breona rushed from the shelter. If there were three of them, one had already vanished. "Come back!" she yelled.

One looked back. "It's a sorceress!"

The second looked over his shoulder. "It's the devil himself!" The men crossed themselves and ran faster.

When Breona returned, Claire was on her knees, sobbing, as she tried to pull the lance free. When she saw Breona, she began to pull frantically.

"You've no cause to fear, Your Grace," Breona said, pulling the greenery from her hair and straightening her braids. "There is no sorcery here, and they've gone for now."

Claire shrank back against the wall. "There are wolves!"

Breona smiled. "Unless I'm mistaken, they're the two-legged variety. At least one of them was Garwyn, my mother's brother. He brought Sir Hugh here earlier." Breona frowned. And was to have taken him on.

Claire put one hand on the lance shaft.

Breona smoothed her dress. "Do you like my handiwork? It's just medicine mixed with dirt, but it gave them quite a turn."

The hand dropped.

"Garwyn cannot," Breona said, "or does not, speak in ways we do, but he has other voices and the wolf is one. It takes no great magic to fool a man into hearing what he expects to hear. I suspect Garwyn was close enough to hear them talking about this being a wolf's den, and seized the opportunity."

"It . . . it sounded so real. Are you sure?"

"Sure enough, that I will go outside to talk to him when you are settled." Breona bent down and felt for the pot. It had remained upright. She filled the spoon and held it out. "The medicine is bitter but has sweet effect. Will you take a dose and sleep again? You need rest if we're to move you, and that we must do."

Claire took the spoon, held it to her lips and looked at Breona. "It seems you know me. Do I know you?"

Breona began wiping the mud from her face. "I am Breona," she said, "Ceonald's sister. I am well versed in the healing arts, and you must not fear my potions."

"My children?"

"Safe."

Claire wore a perplexed look. "Did you tell me that before?"

"Yes, but don't worry if you find yourself confused, what with all that's happened and being ill besides. I wonder that you even remember my saying it."

Claire lowered the spoon. "Breona?"

"Yes."

"Breona . . ." Claire studied the spoon, then looked up. "If there comes a time to make a choice . . ."

"You needn't worry—"

"No," Claire said. "Let me say it while I'm able, in case there's a time when I am not. I give my children over to your care, and to Hugh of Tintagel and Stuart of Dalyan, and I charge you all to keep them safe, until they can be reunited with the High King, their father. Above all else, you must do this." Her hand shook slightly and then grew steady.

"We will so do. You have my promise."

"If they are truly safe . . ."

"They are."

"Then," Claire whispered, "send Stuart to warn William, that Cedric is at his back. Beg him make all speed."

"Your Grace . . ."

"And if you have the means, warn Agatha. She is alone at

Redlyham, but may yet flee to Dunraven Castle. Pray its walls may keep her safe."

"I will do all that's within my power," Breona said softly. "Will you not rest now, Your Grace?"

Claire set the empty spoon beside her and lay back on the bed. "The other child . . ."

"Yes, Your Grace, in God's time."

"No. Ellen of Windrush."

"Your Grace?"

"Keep her . . ."

Claire's breathing was shallow but steady. The drug had done its work. What had she meant? Keep Ellen captive? Keep her away? Keep her safe? It would be hours before she could learn the answer. Outside, Garwyn waited.

"Are they gone?"

He nodded.

"And Hugh, Garwyn, what of him?"

Garwyn held up two fingers, tapped himself on the chest and wiggled one finger.

Breona nodded, Hugh and Garwyn.

Garwyn extended his right hand and walked the two fingers toward his chest. At the same time, his other hand walked and met his right. One hand shook the other.

They met with no enemy then.

He reached over and lifted one of Breona's braids, then touched the nape of his neck. His sign for Faythe. Breona frowned.

Garwyn smiled, shook his finger and tapped the back of his hand.

"That's exactly what I'd like to do," Breona said. "The child has no business leaving home. Was she by herself?"

He held up two fingers and made his sign for Peter and Bran. Breona nodded; those two boys would do whatever Faythe asked and worry later for the consequences. She'd have a few words to say to them as well.

He touched his neck again, held up two fingers and pointed north.

"She is going home again, with Hugh?"

He nodded.

"She'd do well to stay there, then. Twelve years old and more headstrong every day. I don't mind telling you that I hardly know what to do with her."

Garwyn grinned, then touched Breona's shoulder, held his arms as if he was cradling an infant, and touched Breona again.

She smiled. "I should pretend not to understand you, Uncle," she said, "but I fear you're telling me my daughter bears some slight resemblance to her mother."

Garwyn nodded and gestured. Faythe had told him her mother needed him, which is why he had returned with the two boys.

"Are you sure?"

He nodded and repeated his earlier gesture.

She must talk to her daughter when there was time. "Did you see how many, Uncle?"

Three. Garwyn pointed south.

The forest was still, layers of black upon black. "I see only their fear," Breona said, finally. "The question is, will they return once they find their bravery?"

Garwyn waited, watching her.

"I think they will," she said. "Do you think they know who they're looking for?"

He shrugged.

"I would wait another day given the choice," she said, "but I think we'd better leave. We'll go just before dawn. Our patient is better than I had any right to expect, and we must take the risk."

Garwyn nodded and held out his arms.

"Yes, she'll need a litter."

He pointed at two different spots in the forest.

"Ah," Breona said. "Peter and Bran, I trust."

Garwyn smiled.

"Do you come with us?"

He shook his head.

"We'll see you then, when we see you. And as we are in

good hands, I'll take what rest I may until this night is done."

Inside, Claire slept soundly. Breona pulled the stool closer to the wall and leaned against it. They had a few hours, anyway.

CHAPTER FIFTEEN

B reona?"
    "Yes, My Lady?"

"Shall we sit here awhile?" Although nearly empty, Claire's basket had grown heavy; her illness had taken its toll. Daisies lay neatly on side of the basket, while a few yellow and purple heartsease smiled shyly on the other.

Breona's taste had been more eclectic, and daisies, violas and red-clover blossoms spilled from her basket. She had chosen coltsfoot, wild carrot, feverfew and boneset as well, naming the leaves and blossoms as she picked them. She took Claire's basket and set it down along with her own. "This is as fine a place as any," she said. "We've walked a goodly while this day, and it would not do to become overtired. The morning sun is gentle and will look kindly on us, while we rest."

A blue trail of prim lupine wound through the meadow where they walked, while daisies nodded with each whispered breeze. The trees of the Soddenwood stood sentinel, their green interrupted by a single thatched roof that stood where the meadowland met forest. Flush from spring rains, the meadow grass provided a soft cushion, most welcome after their morning walk, Claire's longest since Windrush.

"I never asked," Claire said. "How long did it take to get here?"

"Two days." Reaching into her basket, Breona retrieved a small ball of twine and began picking through the flowers, pulling out the daisies.

Two days. It seemed longer. Claire had known only the blurred lurching of the litter, around which boys aged, and then became young again as darkness changed into light and back to darkness. Breona did not change, her voice calm, though her words were garbled. There was a time, after the swaying stopped, when Claire woke to forest, then meadow, then forest again, giving the impression of movement without the sensation. Three days ago, the world came into focus and Claire found herself in a small room, in the same cottage now visible across the meadow. From her bed she could see the meadow from one window and the forest from the other, explaining her earlier confusion. "How long have we been here?" she said.

"In Hopehoven?"

Claire nodded.

"A week tomorrow." Breona tied three daisies together, unwound a few more inches of twine, and tied on another trio.

"So, nine since the river?"

"Yes."

Claire dabbed the unexpected moisture from her eyes. The cottage was not so far, but the walk had tired her. "Your home is very different," she said, "but it reminds me of the place we stayed . . ." Claire wiped her hand on her skirt; Herbert's labored breathing still seemed to call her.

"Do you mean the hermitage?" Breona said.

"Do you know it?"

Breona nodded. "I've seen it in my memories."

Claire looked up, but it only seemed that the sun had gone behind a cloud. She shivered.

"That is to say," Breona said, pulling more daisies from her basket, "I heard it described by my mother, who heard about it from hers, who heard it from hers, and so on until you get back to the one who was there."

"Like the stories Ceonald tells?"

Breona smiled. "Of the same sort. Ceonald holds not only our history, but that of the kings. I know only a few family stories."

"He's a wonderful storyteller," Claire said. "Truly a great Bard. When first I was at Ambridge, I used to plague him to tell me which of the stories he made up and which ones someone else made up, but he would never say."

Breona paused. "How could he answer a question like that?" she said. "A bard may choose the words to tell his tale, but the stories are true, at least to what he knows, or to what was told him."

Claire tried not to smile. "My favorite used to be the story of Drucilla and the dragon," she said.

Breona laughed. "Well, I suppose one or two are really allegories, but even I would not say that to Ceonald. Still, his stories are not told with an intent to deceive, they make no purchase with their conceit."

"And even now, I am no less glad than I was as a bride to listen to his tales," Claire said. How many years ago that seemed. Ambridge was another lifetime. And it would hardly be the same place when she finally returned. "Is James able now, to travel?" she said.

Breona hesitated. "Yes," she said, "but a hard pace would be difficult."

The familiar nausea returned, but Claire could not stop the words from forming. "Then there's no impediment to our travel?"

"None save that." Breona tied the last of the daisies and began sorting leaves.

"Hugh is afire to start for Ambridge," Claire said. "He'd have had us on the road afore now if he could. These last two days his words have been nettle to my skin. Yet, I fear if we don't start, Cedric will have blocked the way entirely." She pulled a daisy from her basket. It had no fragrance. "Is there no news?"

"None save what you know," Breona said. "As for Hugh Tintagel, he has the impatience of his species. It does no good to start a task that can't be finished and there was nothing for it, but to wait until you were all able to finish the journey, before commencing it." She folded her hands. "What of Ellen, Your Grace? If you are loath to take her with you, we can keep her here. The child had a bad night of it alone in the forest, but still, she's lucky to have suffered no injury, and luckier still the wolves can pick and choose this time of year."

"On that," Claire said, "Hugh can have no influence. She comes with us. In truth, Breona, there's a part of me that would have us all stay. Your meadow has much charm. Indeed, there is a whisper in my soul that warns against the south."

Breona looked toward the cottage, then at Claire. "Your words do disquiet me, Your Grace."

Claire flushed. "Don't think badly of me, Breona. I should not have given voice to my fear. It's not the journey. I do not fear the hardships of travel. But will there be a young Jeremy, if we need him? Or a Phoebe? I would, if it were my say, have Hugh go and return with a company of men. I do not like the road with but one against its dangers." Claire smoothed the petals around her finger, then straightened them.

"I am settled that you must stay yet awhile," Breona said, "at least until we have news of Cedric. I don't know if Hugh told you, but I sent three men to see what they could find out. The watchers are still there on the Oberon and Mithray of course, but these three are to go beyond our borders; one in the direction of Windrush, one north to Redlyham and the third to Allyntown."

"I take it you've not heard from them."

"Not yet," Breona said. "There's a change, though, along the river. Garwyn is on the Oberon, and sends word that our watchers now feel they're being watched in turn. What meaning it has, if any, we don't know yet."

"And is there no one else who could cross, to help decipher this new turn?" Claire said.

Breona shook her head. "I fear each man who crosses, steps on a thin thread that sets the web aquiver. The question is, where sits the spider and how hungry is he?"

"Your description of Cedric is apt," Claire said, "but I fear you do impugn the spider. It, at least, have no evil intent. Is there nothing else that can be done?"

"No, I didn't say that," Breona said. "Garwyn may well decide to cross himself. There's nothing to be gained from a man who cannot speak, and much to be gained by one who listens."

"He's your uncle, isn't he, Breona?"

"My mother's brother." Breona smiled. Do you know our history, Your Grace?"

"Of the Soddenwood?"

"Of those who live here. The Soddenwood was not always home."

Had she heard it mentioned? There was the day Ceonald gave her the brooch, but William had never spoken of this area, and Ceonald, who of all people might have, had offered nothing further. Would saying so give offense? "I would be glad to hear your story," Claire said.

"Ah well, Your Grace, I would tell you, if I could tell it well," Breona said. "You must have it from Ceonald, I'm afraid. But know that no matter what course other men may choose, we are loyal to the High King. We do not forget our debts though they be gray-haired and toothless. Besides, there's a closer tie between us than fealty, Your Grace. We have the tie of kinship."

It got worse. Claire's ignorance would give offense where none was intended. "I'm sorry," Claire said, "if you are cousin to William, and if he once spoke of it, I have long ago forgotten the relationship."

"I do not know if he himself knows the tie," Breona said, "but it is there all the same. If you trace his line and mine, and yours as well, the three meet. William is of the house of Aethelstwin, but so too are you and I." Claire started and Breona quickly held up her hand. "You two at such a distance no tie could offend. No clergy could contest your right to marry."

Claire exhaled softly. "I know William is of his line," she said, "indeed, who in Bridland does not, and I do not doubt your own history, but I've never heard anyone in my family make such a claim. I can't believe my father would not, if he knew it to be true. Even in the home of my childhood, we knew the legend of the great King."

"Modern people do not keep their lineage so close," Breona said, "but here in the Soddenwood, we have kept the memories. It is your mother, who is from Aethelstwin, just as it was mine. We can trace all three families back to him, though he be in his grave these eight score years."

Her mother. The daisy Claire held had been joined by others, although she had no memory of taking them from the basket. All had frayed and broken petals, and stared up with their yellow eyes. Her mother, with the gold instead of eyes, and her cold babe. Claire shook her surcoat and brushed away the bruised remains. Would that she survived what her mother did not. Every woman's unspoken prayer. Closing her eyes, Claire tilted her head back, so the sun fell fully on her face. "This warm sun does coax my eyes to close," she said. She wanted no more talk of death and dead people.

"Is she asleep?"

Claire jumped. Hugh's footsteps were silent in the soft grass. "Would that I was," she said, "but what matter now." She could hardly see him with the glare of the sun. "At least have the decency to stand where I can see you."

Hugh looked up, then took two steps, blocking the sun. Waspish words, and his face showed he'd felt their sting. "I beg pardon, Your Grace," he said. "I thought, with just you and Lady Breona here, that it would be a good time for us to talk."

"As you wish." The tone sharper yet. Breona watched her, but whether from concern or as critic, Claire did not know. Well, the words were out. Was she not entitled to a few hours convalescence in this peaceful place?

"Breona tells me that you are now recovered and may travel safely."

It seems the two had discussed much. Claire shaded her eyes with her hand.

"James could do with a few more days rest," Breona said.

Claire nodded. "Breona has told me," she said, "that she sent men to discover where Cedric's troops are. Do you not think it wise to wait for their report, before plans are made?"

Hugh crossed his arms. "As far as James is concerned," he said, "if it's as you say, Breona, we can leave him here, along with the girl, Ellen. He may recover at his leisure, and she can cause no mischief. I would be glad for news, but any report is as old as the journey to bring it, and must therefore be suspect. I have laid my plans. It's time we were gone, indeed, I fear past time."

He stirred what Breona smoothed; it was not for Hugh of Tintagel alone to decide. "James and Ellen travel with us," Claire said.

Hugh looked to Breona and back again. "The boy must be your decision, Your Grace," he said, "but I will not suffer the daughter of a traitor. Given the chance, she may be willing to betray us herself. I will not take the risk."

"She is a child," Breona said softly.

"Hardly a child," Hugh said. "Almost of an age to wed."

"Her age is not relevant," Claire said. "Four or fourteen or forty, it makes no difference. She goes or I stay. Besides, we don't know for certain that the Marsh King is traitor."

He reddened. "By the saints!" Hugh said. "You were there! You said yourself Cedric was there with him and you had to hide in the cellars! What more do you need?"

"Proof," Claire said. Though Hugh did not appear to move, the sun fell again on her face. It was not just the change in light that darkened his.

"William can say if he needs to hear more or not," Hugh said. "For me, I am satisfied."

"You . . ." Claire stopped. The hot words helped only Cedric. She would try to match Breona's tone. "Hugh," she said. "I picked flowers this morning with Breona. Some, which ones and what parts I know not, will go into her good potions. We will all agree, I believe, that she's a wonderful healer and even though today I played a small role, it does not follow that I'm a healer."

"Stuart is dead, Your Grace."

She moved to catch a better look at his face, but he looked away. "I saw the arrow, Hugh," she said. "And I saw his face when it struck. When I close my eyes, I see it yet again."

"I did not mean—"

Claire held up her hand. "The point is, Hugh, I was there at Windrush. The Marsh King may well be traitor. Certainly, it had the look, I can't disagree with that. Let it be as you say, and let William be judge. I do believe though that the Marsh Queen is true. I have as little evidence for that, as you against her husband, save for one thing. She, and she alone, saw that we were hidden in the cellars. And it was the Marsh Queen who saw to it that we were able to leave. Without her help, I don't know what would have happened. Ellen goes with us and you must accord her the respect due her status. We owe the mother her child's safety, and I will pay the debt."

"At what cost to your own?" Hugh said.

How dare he! But Claire bit her lip.

"There's nothing to prevent you from watching her closely," Breona said.

He shrugged. "The decision is yours, Your Grace. You must answer the High King, for what befalls from your choice."

"As must we all," she said.

He bowed stiffly. "We will leave at first light," he said.

"What is your plan, Hugh?" Claire said.

"You need not concern yourself with details," he said. "You must only do as I say . . ."

Claire frowned.

"On matters of the journey anyway," he said, "and I will see you safe back to Ambridge."

She stood. "You are neither my sovereign nor my Lord,

Hugh Tintagel, and in his absence, I will book no commands. I was ordered out of Ambridge, sent packing to Windrush, and to what avail? I tell you, Sir Hugh, whatever you think I must do, you need tell me first, and then convince me of its wisdom."

He sighed. "Your Grace, I was commanded by your husband, the King . . ."

He could sigh, and sigh again. "You were commanded, I believe, to see me safe back to Ambridge. Surely that does not preclude discussing with me the method and means of its accomplishment. Do you think me such a simpleton I cannot grasp the situation?"

"I don't want Your Grace to worry overmuch, that's all."

"I'd be the fool if I did not," Claire said. "Surely evil brought into the light is less fearsome than left lurking in the shadows."

"I have my duty."

"And I do not?" Hugh's face was red and her own warm. She must cool this heat before the damage was beyond repair; she had learned that much these last weeks. "I appreciate your dedication to duty, and service to William," Claire said. "I do not ask you, Hugh of Tintagel, to forswear your oath."

"Nor would I, no matter what cost to me."

She took a deep breath. "We are not enemies, Hugh, and I would not have us so."

His eyes shifted. His hand went to his sword. "Your Grace," he said quietly. "Don't move."

"Stay your hand!" Breona said. "Don't draw your sword or the dog will attack."

Hugh's face paled. "Edward! Stay there!"

Claire turned. Ten paces behind her, a giant brindled dog stood stiff-legged, fixated, Hugh, the object of his interest. Behind the dog, Edward ran straight toward them, the dog directly in his path.

The dog growled.

"Hugh, don't move!" Breona rose with deliberate care.

Edward reached the dog and threw his arms around it. The

dog did not flinch. "What a great dog, you are," Edward said, panting. "Isn't he great? We ran all the way from the cottage and he beat me good."

"Vim," Breona said. "Where are your manners?" She stepped closer to the dog. "These are our guests."

The dog glanced at her and resumed his stare.

"Where's your master?" Breona said. "Where's Ceonald?" She walked quietly over to him, and took hold of his collar. Keeping a firm grip, she stroked the dog slowly. "Vim is Ceonald's dog," she said. "He loves children and is quite protective of me. It seems he means to extend his protection to you as well, Your Grace."

Claire held out her hand. The dog's tail began a cautious wag. "I thank you, Master Vim," she said. "I'm honored that you should watch me and mine while we're here."

"Ceonald is here!" Edward said, letting go of the dog. "He's here at Hopehoven."

The dog glanced back at the boy, and his tail wagged faster.

"Vim," Breona said, "these are our guests. Sir Hugh is friend as well." The dog sat, and looked from Breona to Hugh, then back again. "That's right," she said.

Claire laughed. "I trust our disagreement is at end, Hugh," she said, "else it seems I have a new ally."

Hugh smiled, let his hands fall to his side, then bowed slowly. "I am your servant, Your Grace."

"Nay servant, Hugh," she said. "Better protector, guardian, guide or friend."

Hugh nodded. "I would be all," he said. "My words were over-hasty. Would that I could call them back."

She nodded.

"Where is Ceonald?" Breona said.

Edward flushed. "I'm sorry," he said. "I forgot. I'm supposed to tell you that he's fa . . . fa . . .something and he's waiting at the cottage."

"Fatigued?" Breona said.

Edward nodded.

"Ceonald was with the King, when I left," Hugh said.

"Let's hope he has news."

"He said he would tell us a story." The boy's eyes shone.

"After we sup, perhaps," Claire said. Ceonald was no longer a young man and the journey must have tired him.

"He promised."

"If, he's not too tired."

The boy's chin jutted out, the echo of the father in the son. "He won't be," Edward said.

And he wasn't, or claimed not to be, though they had supped without him. Ceonald slept through the meal, but not before they'd heard his news. What there was of it had not been good.

"I started north not more than two days after you, Hugh," Ceonald told them. "William had word by then that Cedric was on the move. He thought I could get a message to you as well as anyone, if not better than some, and I daresay, he was loath to lose another fighting man before the battle was joined. We all know I would be no help to him there."

Breona nodded.

"William thought Cedric had crossed into Bridland just above Mullendown, then headed north instead of south to escape detection. I was to tell you to stay at Windrush rather than risk the journey home."

Claire felt sick. William was no warrior king, and not half so cunning as the treacherous Cedric.

"When I found the wagon just below Lamberton," Ceonald said, "I took it as a sign. I waited until dark to get near the village, and it's a good thing I did, although a blind man could probably smell the army there. The devil knows how they did it, but my guess is they came down the Lisage, and as near as I could tell, the whole valley was rotten with them. I decided then for the ferry to Allyntown. My plan was to go north from there, and cross back above Windrush, then sneak in by the waterside. I was there at first light, the ferryman glum as you please, and not a word to me about anything. The whole way across, I congratulated myself on catching the ferry while it still ran unmolested, but as it turned out, why guard a trip between one rotten stench and another?"

"They've crossed the river then," Hugh said.

"Aye," Ceonald said. "I don't know if they're there in large numbers, but I had to answer for my business when I was not five feet from the landing. I made up a pretty tale and it served, but the man was over-keen to my liking, and I'd not want to test my luck again."

"This is bad news," Hugh said. "We must get word to William."

Claire nodded.

"We're of a like mind there," Ceonald said. "I had meant to do just that, as soon as I'd seen you. I was headed for Windrush, when I passed old John's son, Tom atte Well, without even knowing him. It's good the lad had his wits about him when I did not, but who'd ever think to see a man of the Soddenwood across the river? You did well to send him, Breona."

"I had expected his return before now, and have been worried," she said. "It seems he did well though, to stay as long as he did."

"T'was he who told me that Windrush had been taken," Ceonald said. "Otherwise, I'd no doubt be there as unwilling guest. He didn't tell me about your guests, Breona, but was most insistent I talk to you before heading back."

"It's not common knowledge, even here," Breona said. "He did not know."

"He did well even so," Ceonald said. "He said he'd had tested the forest west of Allyntown, and found Cedric's men there too, but he thinks in smaller numbers the further west you go. The boy's no dull wit. I sent him south to tell William what he'd seen."

"So, if we go far enough west, before we turn south," Hugh said, "do you think we could pass undetected?"

Ceonald's eyes met Claire's. Did he read their fear?

He shook his head. "To my way of thinking, it's a bit like a field after a snowstorm, Hugh. The snow doesn't have to have much depth to it, but you can't cross without leaving footsteps.

It might be worth a try if it's just you, or maybe you and Richard, but a larger party, well . . ."

He had given her William's small signet ring then, and excused himself. Used only for William's especially private papers, a seal marked with this ring would be recognized only by the High King and a select few. Through her dress, Claire fingered the ring that now hung near her heart. She turned her chair slightly, to catch more of the fire's warmth.

Ceonald had wakened and now sat on the other side of the fire, lost in thought, his chin cupped in his hand. A cup and pitcher rested on a small table next to his chair. The four children and Ellen sat on the floor, Richard at the bard's feet. Ellen had chosen the spot closest to Claire, but when Hugh picked a seat next to the High Queen, the girl had looked around the room for another spot. All had been taken and she sat now, head bowed slightly, cheeks flushed in the firelight, but her straight back told a different story.

Faythe stood leaning on the back of Ceonald's chair. "Do you want for anything, Uncle?" she said.

Ceonald blinked and looked around, as if surprised by the company assembled, then peered into the cup. He took a sip, cleared his throat, then another, and held out the cup. Faythe replenished the drink. When he still did not move, she took the cup and set it on the table.

Ceonald nodded, rested his hands on the arms of the chair and leaned forward.

"I will tell you children this night," he said, "a story of Wolphard, grandfather to your grandfather."

"Good," Richard said. "Tell us how he killed all the Fersians and got to be High King."

James and Edward wiggled a few inches closer. "Tell the part where he sent the bad King's head around so everybody could see it," Edward said.

Ceonald threw up his hands. "You know the story over well."

"No, we don't," Richard said. "Tell us again."

"I'll tell you of Wolphard," Ceonald said, "but a story

128

you've not heard, the story of his mother, Winifred, wife to
Cormith, and how Wolphard came to be King."

He waited until the room was silent, and then said,

"In the days before your father,
In the days before your father's father,
Cormith, King of Bridland,
Took Winifred as his Queen.
Seven strong sons she bore him,
Five fair daughters graced his hearth,
Fat cattle grazed his meadows,
And fine wool fell from his sheep.
Laughter lit the chambers,
Of Cormith the King.
An eighth son was born him,
To be named Wolphard on his name day,
When his name day was named.
On a dark night of the new moon,
Winifred rose to nurse the babe,
Found the night deadly cold,
Saw across the hilltops,
A burning river flowed.
Hoof beats echoed in the valley,
Of Cormith the King.
The dread came upon her,
A chill seized her heart.
Only Fersian mounts belched fire,
Half horse and half dragon,
Gifts from the Prince of Darkness,
To Evil, their King.
She took Cormith's small dagger,
Cut off one of her braids,
Stole a lock of her husband's hair,
Wrapped Wolphard in his father's cloak,
And tucked in the burnished curl and amber braid.
Stepped over her sleeping daughters,
Stepped past her sleeping sons,

Out of the house and across the fields,
Into the woods, to the great oak tree.
Her legs grew and grew and carried her up,
Up to a hollow high in the tree.
An owl blinked, then swallowed,
Who disturbs my dinner,' he said.
'Whoo? Who?'
'This is the son of Cormith,
Wolphard, newest son to the King.'
'I need leave him to your keeping,' she cried.
'And only look north to know the reason why.'
'Who will pay my price?' he said.
'Whoo? Who?'
Winifred held up her finger,
Swollen from the birth of the boy.
Her gold ring glittered.
'Ah yesss,' the great owl hissed.
Cormith's dagger was sharp,
Winifred's finger small.
She walked out of the forest,
Back across the fields,
Stepped past her sleeping sons,
Stepped over her sleeping daughters,
Back to the bed of her husband,
Cormith the King.
Her head touched the pillow, an ax the door.
When daylight banished darkness,
The kill lay in the courtyard.
Cormith lay headless,
Winifred as well.
Seven strong sons lay silent,
Five fair daughters lay still.
By all who counted, and all did,
The line of Cormith lay dead.
A great owl swept over the courtyard,
Glided silently back to the oak.
'Who knew?' he said. 'Who could tell?

Who will right this wrong?
Who will avenge this day?
Whoo? Who?'

Ceonald picked up the cup and swallowed noisily. When it was empty, he sat back in his chair.

"What happened next?" Richard said.

"Did he make Wolphard the king?" Edward said.

James nodded, wide-eyed.

"You know the answer, yourself." Ceonald leaned back and closed his eyes.

"But how exactly?" Richard said.

His eyes did not open. "That is another story for another time."

"And another day," Breona said. "It's time you were abed."

Ceonald snorted, then began to snore. The children waited. Richard leaned closer and peeked up at him. Finally, they rose and tiptoed from the room. Claire stood.

"Bide awhile, Your Grace," Breona said. "And you too, Hugh. We must hold council. This story of Ceonald's has given me an idea."

The snoring stopped.

CHAPTER SIXTEEN

Breona's plan was adopted, but not without debate. Hugh had vehemently opposed a separation of the party, while Breona had insisted. Claire wavered, anxious to keep the fragile truce between she and Hugh, but ultimately casting her vote in favor of Breona, all the while worrying she voted because it was Breona's idea, rather than because she agreed with the plan. Claire was hard pressed to like either. Still, what did it matter, as long as the other two agreed?

She left Hopehoven with the same reluctance she left Ambridge, but with none of the anger. Breona could assemble no army to protect them, while William had chosen not to. The Soddenwood, perhaps, could have kept them hidden and if Claire had been without the children, she might have been tempted, but no son of the High King could skulk from tree to tree.

Ellen, Elspeth and James took one route, with four men to accompany them. Before they set out, Hugh pulled one of the men aside and when they left, Ellen was in the middle of the party. She'd do nothing and say nothing without the men's knowledge. Once again Hugh presumed overmuch, but Claire let the moment pass. She had expected James to be chagrined when told he would be separated from his brothers, but Hugh had prepared him for the moment and it passed without difficulty. When James explained to his brothers that one of the men of the family must go along to protect Elspeth, blessedly, neither Richard or Edward pointed out that he was still too weak to take their more difficult route. Hugh had done his work well. As soon as the first party was out of sight, Richard and Edward left with Hugh, their route the longest, with Ceonald as guide. Breona and Claire took the middling route with Garwyn, who had appeared in Hopehoven the night before. Whether he had been summoned or had come on his own, Claire did not know.

Garwyn set a gentle but steady pace, unperturbed by the bundle on his back or the small nosegay of heartsease, Faythe had tucked under one of the ropes. He had grimaced and groaned when she approached with it, but winked and bent slightly so she could fasten it where she liked. Overhead, an ashen sky sobered the day, and by contrast, the blossoms grinned cheerfully. There were undoubtedly trails and roads through the forest, but Garwyn chose a path, barely discernable, that wound between the cedar and the fir. I will tell you a story of Wolphard, Ceonald had said. Claire meant to ask him to tell it to her again but had forgotten in the flurry of activity. Still, she had a decent memory. Sons and daughters and sheep and cattle . . . Nothing in Breona's plan put Claire in mind of the poem. "Breona?"

"Yes?"

Claire changed her mind. If it was a riddle, she meant to solve it herself. "Were you able to send a message about Cedric to Agatha?" she said.

"Yes," Breona said. "I hope when I get back to Hopehoven, I'll have word as to whether or not it reached her."

"I wish you could get word to me, as well," Claire said.

There was no answer, nor was there any conversation to pass the time as they walked. Breona seemed disinclined to talk, but the day did not pass as disagreeably as Claire had feared. She was stronger than she thought, but by the time they reached the Mithray River, she was glad Garwyn set up a camp, rather than untying the boat that waited on the riverbank. Even though she was tired, Claire slept restlessly. In the morning, the boat trip passed without incident and they plunged back into the dappled world of cedar and fir. Claire's legs began to hurt and her need to rest grew more frequent. Breona was, as always, solicitous, but she glanced overhead frequently, as if to check the steady progress of the sun in its orbit.

"I'm sorry, Breona," Claire said when they stopped to rest in a small clearing.

"It's not an easy trip," Breona said, "especially for someone who's been ill. I'm a little tired myself."

It was the only lie Claire had known her to tell. Claire sat on a mossy log and closed her eyes. She fingered her wedding ring. Would she have been as brave as Winifred? Would her mother, with the gold coins where her eyes ought to be, have been? Something brushed against her cheek. A whisper of grey. She started! Screamed.

"My Lady!" Breona jumped to her feet.

"It was a ghost!" Claire said, her heartbeat muffling the words. "Winifred's ghost," she whispered.

Garwyn tugged Breona's sleeve and pointed.

Breona nodded. "It's no ghost, Your Grace. We are safe. Listen a moment and see if he would speak."

"Whoo."

Claire jumped up.

"Whoo-hoo-hoo."

Breona pointed. High above them, a great rounded head stared with yellow eyes. "Not Winifred, Your Grace, but certainly of a noble race. He is one of the greatest of all the owls and to my way of thinking, if an owl did safeguard young Wolphard, it must have been an ancestor of those who live here. Of all the owls in the forest, these seem most to claim some kinship with those who walk here."

The bird preened its breast feathers.

"Is it ill?"

"It doesn't appear so to me, Your Grace."

"But surely it's not so near night?" Claire said.

"These owls hunt by day and night, as they please," Breona said. "Another reason I think they must be of the line of Wolphard's protectors. How does it go? A great owl swept over the courtyard . . ."

Claire shivered and the old nausea returned. "Do you think he's trying to tell us the others are . . ."

"They're safe, Your Grace," Breona said. "I'm confident of the Soddenwood. Our separation was a precaution, that's all. There will come a day I fear, when there will be a search, and those searching must not find a number that matches those they search. Sometimes there's safety in numbers, and other times the number endangers the safety."

Garwyn nodded, put his finger to his lips, then curled a lock of hair around his finger and set his hand to flapping.

Claire curled the end of one braid around her finger. "Does that stand for Elspeth?"

He grinned.

"Then are you saying that there are times there's safety in silence?"

Garwyn nodded and repeated the last sign.

"And sometimes safety lies in speaking," Breona said. "The difficulty is in discerning the difference."

Whoo-hoo-hoo.

Breona glanced up. "The great owl hunts where he has the best of both meadowland and forest, Your Grace, and the time has come for me to leave you. Garwyn will see you safe from here on."

"Do you never go beyond the Soddenwood, Breona?" Claire said.

Breona hesitated. "I have not, but there is nothing to stay me from leaving, if I must."

Deserted. Claire knew it would come. She blinked back the tears. "I don't have words adequate . . ." She bit her lip. "I – ".

Breona held up her hand. "It was nothing," she said. "A

duty with a light yoke. Would that I could do more. If there comes a time you have need of me, say it to Ceonald, or to anyone of the Soddenwood, or within its green canopy, and I will come."

Garwyn motioned.

"Go with God."

"And you."

They had gone only a few feet when Breona called out, "Your Grace!"

Claire turned.

"About Gregory of Elstow . . ."

"Yes?"

Breona shook her head. "Never mind, Your Grace. I'm sorry to have stayed you."

"You were going to say something."

"It was born of an ancient prejudice," Breona said, "before the time of Wolphard even. I'm sorry I spoke."

Was it a memory of the past or a premonition the future?

Garwyn tapped her gently on the arm. Her eyes met Breona's, but Claire could not will herself to ask more. All had agreed. They needed Gregory's help. Claire turned and followed Garwyn.

"Whoo-hoo-hoo."

She looked back. Breona stood with one hand raised to wave them on. The owl had flown to a lower branch, as if ready now to start conversing. When Claire stole a second look, both were gone. If anything, Garwyn set a slower pace, but even so, more than once, Claire was forced to ask for a rest before he was ready to give one. Today, he did not sit when she did, but stood patiently watching her, smiling when she rose, and once patting her arm in his enthusiasm, or encouragement, or both.

By nightfall, the trees thinned and so did the undergrowth. The night was warm and a friendly moon peeked coyly from behind soft clouds. The surface under her feet became more regular and finally the path left the forest. The ground began to climb gradually as they crossed a newly washed meadow, still fragrant after a recent rain.

"Whoo-hoo-hoo."

An owl glided over the meadow, dipped down and rose heavily.

"Whoo."

"Whoo."

The answering calls came from east and west.

"Garwyn," she whispered.

He shook his head and pointed to the top of a hill just ahead.

Claire nodded. She wanted to ask him about the owls more than she needed to stop. By the time they reached the hilltop though, she was well winded and glad to rest. Garwyn pointed. Ahead, a black ribbon wound through grasses silvered in the moonlight and on the other side, the great Elstowian plateau rose against the twilight.

"Are they there?" she whispered.

He shook his head and made a sweeping arch with his hand.

Claire nodded, understanding his no, but not the hand motion. With their goal in sight, she found a new energy even though the rest was short. An occasional small footprint in the softer dirt at the edge of the path was still flooded with rainwater, leaving a trail of small moonlit footsteps. Garwyn pointed and smiled. The rainwater had escaped one print, but in the middle was a smaller moon print. Claire laughed and her fear washed away.

Finally, the plateau towered above them. Its rock walls scarred the land from the Muchelney Mountains in the north, to the Kusshi Mountains in the south. By land, there were only two ways onto the plateau. To the north, a narrow road wound through a gap in the Muchelneys into Norvik. In the south, the western fork of the Oberon had, over the course of centuries, succeeded into carving a path through the rocks, and there a road climbed beside the river. Both roads were well traveled.

Garwyn looked up at the plateau, then back at the meadow,

and began walking north, disappearing quickly where the wall turned. Claire waited, having no intention of taking a single step that needed to be retraced. Their route had not been discussed, but it was obvious they must go south to the lesser Oberon to gain the plateau. She crossed her arms against the night air and if he took it for her displeasure, so be it. But when Garwyn did not return, she relented and hurried after him.

He had not gone far and stood waiting.

"Aren't we going in the wrong direction?" she said.

He put his finger to his lips.

"Sorry," she mouthed.

He held out her cloak. When she took it, he put on his own, pulling the hood low over his face. She did the same. They walked in silence another hundred yards, gray ghosts in a black world. Claire suppressed a giggle at the thought, then felt like crying; it had been a long day. Garwyn stopped near a narrow ledge that angled up the cliff side and held out his hand.

She stepped back and shook her head. This had not been part of the plan.

He pantomimed. The ledge was narrow to start, but became wider. A little higher yet and it widened into a broad area. He tilted his head, folded his hands together and placed them under his head. They would sleep there.

"I will not." The ledge could widen or not and Garwyn could risk life and limb, but she had the sense to stay where she was.

He held out his hand again, refusing to look away when she glared at him. Garwyn stepped onto the ledge, and offered his hand again.

"I can't," she whispered, but took his hand.

Backs pressed to the cliff wall, they inched their way. The ledge was broad enough for her foot but not for his, and the sight of his boots hanging out over the abyss made her stomach churn, but she was mesmerized all the same. He stepped confidently, but it was all she could do to slide one foot up and drag the other after it. The ledge slowly widened. His boots fit. Then had room to spare. Garwyn pressed her hand and stopped. He turned slowly and motioned for her to do the same.

She shook her head.

He patted her arm and climbed two steps higher.

She took a deep breath, turned and pressed her face against the wall, feeling its coolness. Garwyn climbed a few more feet, then stopped and pointed. Ahead, the ledge disappeared into the empty night. Her knees grew weak. He motioned; the path continued around the rock. She was powerless to move. Garwyn grabbed her arm and jumped.

They landed on a broad platform between the wall and a large outcropping. Had there not been a need for silence, she would have told him how vile he was – or cried – or both. Claire leaned against the rock wall and tried to stop her legs from shaking. A large basket-like contraption occupied the bulk of the space, its bottom wooden, but the rest metal, with small loops at intervals along the top. Garwyn put one foot on the bottom rung, swung his other leg over, then stepped out and motioned. Claire nodded. It looked to be an uncomfortable bed, but had the decided advantage of security, since once in it, you could not fall. Besides, even if she obliged him, neither had room to stretch out comfortably.

"It's a strange bed," she whispered, as she climbed into it. Inside, and midway down the sides, there were two additional iron loops, one across from the other. She wished Breona was here to tell her about it and how it had gotten onto the ledge.

Garwyn nodded.

Claire arranged her cloak, but more to humor Garwyn than for comfort. With the unhappy prospect of the ledge come morning, she knew she would not sleep.

"Whoo-hoo."

She started, then looked up, sure the owl must be just overhead. Garwyn looked up and hooted softly, answered by a shower of small pebbles and dirt. He waited. A small rope slid into view, with a single feather attached. Garwyn fumbled under his cloak, bent over the rope, then gave it two quick tugs. Waited a moment and gave it a third. The rope retreated, with two feathers where there had been one. A second shower followed, larger than the first.

Was it their supper? Claire smiled; she was hungry after all. Leave it to Breona to devise some unorthodox method to see to their comfort.

A jumble of ropes slid into view, stopping a few feet above the ledge. Garwyn pulled at them, and when the lines were untangled, he picked one up and began tying it to the iron frame.

"What are you doing?" she whispered.

He ignored her, tying on a second rope.

"What are the ropes for?"

Deaf now as well as mute, he tied on the last of the ropes, touched one of the inner loops, and then tapped her hand.

"I'm—"

He cautioned her to silence and touched the loop again.

Claire took hold of one. He pointed. She took the other. Fine, she would humor him.

He smiled, head nodding in approval and patted her shoulder. He jerked one rope. The basket moved.

She started to stand.

Frowning, Garwyn motioned to sit. The ropes groaned. The basket began to rise.

"No," she whispered. "Wait . . ." Her head was even now with his. She gripped both handles. Garwyn slid from view. Disappeared. She closed her eyes. The basket bumped against the rock, sending it swaying. Stones slid down the hillside. She hardly dared breath. The upward movement stopped. Once again, the ropes complained. The basket lurched. Stopped. Swayed wildly. Claire slid toward one side of the basket, then the other. All movement but her shaking stopped. Had the ropes fouled? She dared not look. I'm sending you north to safety, William had said. She hated them all.

CHAPTER SEVENTEEN

Your Grace." He spoke in the faintest of whispers.

Hugh of Tintagel! She might have known.

"Our voices carry too well here," he said. "Sit for a moment while I undo these ropes. When I'm done, and you're able, we'll go where we can talk more freely."

When you're able. As if she could move, let alone walk. But Claire nodded.

"You can let go."

Her hands were locked around the handles, just as Garwyn had instructed. And she had wondered what they were for. Before she was ready, the ropes were untied. Hugh held out his hand. "Let me help you."

She pulled herself up. Got one leg over the side. It was then merely a question of which direction to fall. To her surprise and relief, she slid as much as fell, and managed to remain upright. Claire leaned against the basket and hoped Hugh couldn't tell how much her legs shook.

"Take my arm, Your Grace," he said. "'Twill help. We don't have far to go."

Of course, he lied.

The basket had come to rest on a broad ledge below the top of the cliff. Crumbling boulders, some as tall as Hugh,

141

balanced delicately, and blocked their final ascent. Others had sheared away, and the shards and half submerged remnants littered what some might call a path, now barely visible in the moonlight. Hugh made no further offer of assistance, but glanced back frequently as they climbed upward, still along the cliff edge. When they reached a small, shallow stream that flowed across the path and fell hissing over the precipice, Hugh turned aside. They followed the stream and climbed up a final hillside, finally reaching the plateau. Claire remained silent still. Heaven forbid she expose them to danger or give Hugh a defense against her anger, which was the one thing that kept her walking. It seemed an eternity before they reached a small valley where a campfire burned brightly.

"Welcome to Elstow, Your Grace." Hugh pointed. "We'll camp here tonight. I've got some sup—"

"Did you know about this before we left!"

"Your—"

"Did you know!"

He flushed.

"How dare you, Hugh Tintagel!"

He put his finger to his lips.

"I will say what I please. How dare you!"

"Mother?"

She spun around. Richard clambered up from a small ravine, hidden in the darkness. "I suppose you knew about this as well," she said.

He shook his head, no, but Claire wasn't sure she believed him. Then felt guilty. Richard was guileless, his face innocent.

"I will not be schemed about, and played with behind my back," she said, "and you can make your mind up to it right now. I am so angry I could . . . I could . . ." Her legs began to shake. She sat down.

Hugh stood nervously, giving the appearance of shuffling his feet without actually doing so.

"Where are the others?" she said. Did Hugh intend to parade them out one by one to stay her anger?

"They've gone on ahead. It was not planned," he said

hurriedly, "but Ceonald devised the scheme on the way, thinking it better to arrive at our destination separately and I, for my part, agreed. I had thought to send Richard too, but he would not go, and convinced me of the wisdom of letting him stay."

Claire frowned. Hugh's face was all politeness. Who had done the calculating, and had the scheming been done before they left, or was it as Hugh said? She could not read his face and wanted to slap him. But he was an honorable man, and he wouldn't lie, at least hadn't up until now, and if Ceonald thought it best . . .

Richard filled a cup with Breona's best wine and handed it to Claire, before sitting down next to her.

"Weren't you frightened?" she said.

He grinned. "It was fun. Elspeth never even cried, but Ellen threw up."

Hugh nodded and looked rather pleased.

"And got much sympathy, I'm sure," Claire said. "If I'd known, I'd have chosen another option."

"There was no other," Hugh said.

"I know." She did know, but it made her angry anyway.

They ate in silence. Even with the fire, the night air was cold, and when Claire lay down next to Richard, she was glad for his added warmth. He was asleep before she arranged her cloak. Had the lad always worn such a mantle of worry?

The sun rose without ceremony. The folded hills surrounding the valley differed only in the degree to which the withered grasses had vanquished the rocks. On some, only a few rocky outcroppings were visible, while others were layers of rocky ledges with sparse vegetation that clung to the patches of barren soil. They scrambled up hillsides and slid down into gullies, and on those few occasions the ground was level, the rocks multiplied and dozens of small burrows hid between them. Without trees, the sun burned fiercely, sending sharp rays that fractured on the rocks and reflected back.

They had stopped to rest infrequently, and as the sun began to flirt with the horizon, they came to a small valley. It was not the broadest valley at the eastern edge of the Elstowian plateau, nor the hills surrounding it as gentle as could be found in other locations, but it had the only true river in the area, flowing at the same rate and at the same depth, no matter how hot the summer or how dry the spring. Grey-green trees marked the river's course, interrupted only by the walls of a monastery situated in the middle of the valley. A few trees nestled in the contours of the hillsides, as if seeking safety in their folds.

"I hope that's Oakrose," Claire said. If there weren't blisters on her feet, there should be. Her back hurt and her legs ached.

Hugh wore a sympathetic look. "We'll rest the night, whether it is or not. In fact, we can rest longer if need be. I could be tempted to see if any fish in this river want catching. Do you think the good sisters would object to a taste, if I caught some?"

"Can I help, Sir Hugh?" Richard said.

"If your mother has no complaint, I don't see why not. Seeing to your supper is a good skill to learn, and I've no objection to providing you a few lessons."

"I wish you'd mentioned that earlier, Hugh," Claire said. "I'm sure Richard has missed his tutor these past weeks."

Hugh winked.

Richard grinned. "It's not very big," he said, nodding in the direction of the monastery.

The buildings did look small from this distance, but the abbey complex was larger than Claire expected. Larger, and something about it was different. "Big enough," she said. "We're lucky that some are called to serve in such desolate places. There's safety in its location."

"I'll set you a lesson of sorts, Richard," Hugh said. "Tell me what you see ahead."

"I see a church."

"And?"

"There's the abbey and . . . and . . . up there on the hill, there's some sheep."

Claire shielded her eyes against the setting sun. The flock

was good sized and she hadn't even noticed it.

Hugh nodded. "Very good. What else?"

"They grow things in those fields."

"That's right. What else?"

Richard frowned. "There's some trees . . ."

"Think about what you don't see, lad," Hugh said, "For example, there's naught to keep those sheep on the hillside, so there must be a shepherd, or shepherdess, as would be the case here. We can't see them, but likely they can see us. And look opposite. There's a small vineyard there. Some of the vines look newer than the rest, so either the flock here has grown or they make wine good enough to market."

Richard laughed. "Sheep don't drink wine."

Hugh smiled. "That wasn't the flock I was thinking of. My bet is they sell some, or mean to. There's no sign of any construction and they'd not neglect the church if a larger one was wanted."

"How come you know so much?" Richard said.

"A lord looks to his manor and lands, just as a king looks to his country," Hugh said. "My father paid attention to such matters and saw that his sons did as well. He did not set us to master the plow, Richard, but to understand how a field should be plowed and how often the plow must be sharpened and how much a man can plow in a day."

Richard nodded. "When you go away," he said, "I could go with you. I could be your page."

"Even if your Mother would allow it," Hugh said, "I would need say no. There's a price to be paid for safety, lad. It may be the price of a sword, or chain mail, or the cost of a wall around a castle, or being someplace you don't want to be, but the price must be paid. As for being my page, I'd be lucky to have you, but that's a matter for your father and he'd not see much wisdom in it."

Claire nodded. Hugh was right—and wrong at the same time. William was fortunate in his choice of hunting companions.

Richard flushed. "My father was Sir Herbert's page," he

said.

Claire looked sharply at her son. A fanciful tale—

"That's right," Hugh said. "Herbert of Amesly was the last of a very old and noble family, and as a knight had no peer. He was a suitable choice for your father."

Richard looked down. "But he got killed."

Hugh picked up a pebble and threw it.

"You could get killed," Richard said.

"I believe I'll have an objection to it, if I do," Hugh said grinning. Then his face sobered. "It's not a risk that hasn't been thought of, lad."

Claire stopped. "If something does happen, Richard, and we pray it does not, I will come back, and if for some unforeseen reason I cannot, Breona will watch out for you."

"How will she know?" Richard kicked at the dirt.

Hugh looked at Claire and shrugged. "Someone will tell her."

"Who?" Richard said.

"I don't know," Hugh said, "but if Breona says she'll know, then I'm sure she will. Breona would not say what she could not do."

She and Breona had agreed some things were to be kept private, but surely Richard's furrowed brows would have persuaded Breona of the necessity of answering the boy's question. Claire bent down and put her hand on his shoulder. "I will tell you, son," she said, "because you are the oldest, because you will worry overmuch if you don't know, and because maybe one of you should know. But you must swear first, to hold what I tell you, and not to tell your secret to your brothers, or to your sister, or to Ellen, or to anyone."

Richard nodded.

"Say it."

"I swear I won't tell anyone."

"Breona will know," Claire said, "because the Abbess is her Aunt."

Richard looked at Hugh.

Hugh shrugged. "It's news to me, too, but it makes sense

after what Ceonald said."

"It's not a plan without risks," Claire said, "but it was the best we could devise on short notice. Now, let us continue and say no more."

Now that there was a decent path, Hugh walked beside Claire, and Richard walked a few steps ahead, as if to lead the way. Claire had always thought Edward was most like his father, with an embrace of all things physical, a love of action and a boisterous spirit. William was ever on the move, hunting or traveling throughout the country, and often gone months at a time, leaving her at Ambridge, as she was so often with child or in confinement after the birth of one.

Today, as she watched Richard, she saw William in him as well. They both walked with the same self-assurance and the same measured, steady stride. While Richard had never seemed to have the need to be active, the long day did not seem to faze him, and she sensed a resoluteness about the boy, so recently seen in his father.

Next to the abbey, a well-tended orchard was beginning to show its promise. The stone church, with its square bell tower, and the roofs of several buildings could be seen from behind the whitewashed walls. Buildings on both sides of the church. How strange.

An elderly monk opened the gate before Hugh could ring the bell. The hair on his tonsured head was whiter than his robe, but his eyes were lively. "Welcome, travelers," he said. "My name is Brother Cuthbert. How may I be of service?"

A monk! Claire wanted to cry. This was not Breona's nunnery. Hugh had led them in the wrong direction and now she would have another day of walking, or maybe even more, to reach the right abbey.

Hugh stepped forward. "Thank you, brother," he said. "Could we rest here tonight?"

"You are most welcome. We're a simple order, but will share our fare, and gladly, as we do with all who travel our way."

The outer court had the usual assortment of abbey

buildings, but the day's work had ended, so Claire could not tell which was the bakery or which the granary, or to what purpose any of the others served. Beyond the outbuildings, was the church. The building on its right undoubtedly housed the monks, but unlike other abbeys she had seen, there was a similar building to the left. Both had arched windows, like so many hands pressed together in prayer.

"Do you have many guests?" Hugh said.

"A few, a few. It's a busy world and some find their way to our door. Why just yesterday, another party arrived. We've never had so many guests in so short a time, but all are welcome."

Claire grew lightheaded.

Brother Cuthbert closed the gate. "Have you traveled far?"

"Far enough to be glad for rest," Hugh said, "but not as far as we need."

"We'll sup soon—"

Two puppies scampered from behind the closest building, followed closely by Elspeth. She looked toward the gate. "Mo—"

Before she could finish, Ellen appeared and swooped her up. "Mind your manners, young mistress," she said, carrying her away. Elspeth giggled. One of the puppies followed, and the other began to whimper. Edward peeked around the corner, then walked grinning into the courtyard, studiously ignoring the group at the gate.

"Hsst!" James leaned out. Edward held out his hand to the puppy, then scooped it up and ran back to his brother.

"That's the guest house," Brother Cuthbert said, nodding.

"Whose puppies?" Richard said.

"Ah well," Brother Cuthbert said. "They belong to the abbey. We have dogs to help with the sheep."

"This abbey is of unusual design, I think." Hugh said.

Brother Cuthbert smiled. "You're very observant, My Lord. The design is not that common. This is a double monastery." He pointed. "North of the church is the nunnery and the buildings on this side are for the monks. Other than that, each part is built as they all are. We lead separate lives but are united in prayer."

"You have children here as well, I see," Hugh said.

"Only since yesterday," Brother Cuthbert said. "They're part of the party I spoke of. Why it was just a few days ago the Abbess let it be known that she meant to start a school, and here we already have its first students. It's something we've done from time to time over the years. Indeed, many of our members came here as children and stayed, or later returned to us."

"Perhaps she'd take on another," Hugh said. "His mother and I must travel some distance but will return this way. Schooling would be good for the lad."

"But I won't stay," Richard said, sizing up Brother Cuthbert and waiting for his response.

Brother Cuthbert scratched his head. "Well," he said, "I can't answer that as the school is the nun's affair and none of mine, but I'll see that a message is sent to the Abbess and you may ask her yourself." He looked at Richard. "We hold no prisoners," he said, smiling.

"Does your abbey have a name?" Claire whispered. The lightheadedness had gone, but still, she found it difficult to talk.

Hugh put his hand on Claire's arm. "My Lady is very tired from her journey," he said.

She jerked away. For a man who could deduce shepherdesses who couldn't be seen, it had taken him the whole day to see how tired she was.

Brother Cuthbert nodded sympathetically. "Then it's most providential we are here. You must tell the Abbess if you are unwell. Oakrose has a fine medicinal garden and she is very wise in the use of its bounty."

Richard was directed to the guest house to join the other children, while Claire and Hugh were escorted to see the Abbess. The Abbess Maud had Breona's capable hands, but other than that, resembled Ceonald, with dark eyes that took in everything, and deep lines that showed evidence of a smile even when one was not present. She greeted them alone, in a small room in the chapter house, seated at a wooden table that served as her desk. An empty chair sat across from her, and two wooden chests stood along the back wall, with a ledger-lined shelf above them. With the exception of a single lit candle, the desktop was empty.

"God's peace," the Abbess said. She rose, came around the table and moved the chair away from the desk, so Claire could sit down.

Claire nodded and took the seat.

"You must be very tired from traveling," the Abbess said. "Is there anything special you require?"

"Thank you, no," Claire said.

"Richard is with the other children?"

Claire smiled. "He is, but with more interest in seeing the puppies, I suspect than his brothers or sister."

The Abbess turned. "And you, Sir Hugh?"

"Forgive me for staring, Mother," he said. "I find it hard to believe Breona has an aunt who is an Abbess."

She smiled. "There are some here, who if they knew her, would find it strange that an Abbess has a niece like Breona."

As tired as she was, Claire was restless and walked to the window. Even in the gathering twilight, she could see the finely carved stone pillars that supported the cloister. The walkway surrounded what appeared to be a rectangular space with a tall stone cross in the middle. The garden itself was a mass of color. Like the embroidered border of a fine tunic, ribbons of purple and white, yellow and pink, twisted over and under each other, spilling over their formal borders of green and gray and they were now deepening into shades of mauve and gray.

"You have a beautiful garden," Claire said. "One Breona would enjoy."

The Abbess smiled. "She would appreciate its benefits, no doubt. You're welcome to dine with me in the refectory, Your Grace, and the Abbott, I know, will extend the same invitation to you, Sir Hugh."

"Thank you," Claire said, then hesitated. "Would you

extend the same invitation to all who sought shelter."

"No," the Abbess said, "and your caution no doubt is wise, but here we have both the habit of obedience and of silence. You are free to choose."

Claire turned away from the window. "I don't believe I could embrace a life of silence," she said.

"It is only the external voice that is quiet," the Abbess said," so that the inner voice may be heard. For most, it does take a period of adjustment."

"We'll sup in the guest house," Claire said. "We too must make an adjustment." Hugh frowned, but said nothing.

"Very well," the Abbess said. "Before you go, we must discuss the care of your children, and of Lady Ellen."

"I must speak to you about Ellen," Hugh said.

The Abbess nodded. "As I have already listened to her complaints against you, I can do no less than listen to yours."

"Her complaints!" Hugh said.

"Do you think she could have none?"

"What said she?"

"I said only that I listened, Hugh of Tintagel, not that what she said would be repeated, no more than what you say will leave this room. If you have given her no cause for complaint, I have heard only the prattling of an angry young woman. But, if you search within yourself and find you may have done her wrong, it is between you and her to remedy. I have no role either way."

Hugh flushed. "She might do well to take the veil here and now," he said.

The Abbess tucked her hands into her sleeves. "We do not see that as a punishment," she said quietly.

"Forgive me," Hugh said. "But I would that she swore to your habit of silence. Her father—"

Claire coughed and smoothed her dress.

"Cedric's banner files from Windrush," Hugh said. "Did she tell you that?"

"Breona sent word to that effect," the Abbess said. "While you're gone, I'll see what the poor child says of her father and how Cedric came to be there. I will not condemn her, though, for her father's actions."

"Many will," Hugh said.

"Yes," the Abbess said, "that's true. If her father is traitor, she'll be glad enough for the nunnery, as there will no place else for her to go."

"We've agreed," Claire said, "to let William be judge of the matter."

The Abbess nodded. "When do you plan to leave for Mellifont?"

"As soon as Her Grace is able," Hugh said. "For my part, I'm anxious to get started."

"I'm very tired," Claire said, "but I think it's only the distance we've walked. I am fixed that we leave on the morrow. Our pace must be slow, but hopefully the habit of it will settle on us, and we'll do better as we progress."

"I can help there," the Abbess said. "We have three middling palfrey mares and will lend you the use of two. One especially is quite gentle, and as she is mine, is used to a side mounted rider."

"We'll leave early, then," Hugh said, "so we can travel in the cool of the morning."

The Abbess nodded. "If you agree, we'll settle the rest after we sup, each in our own place, as it were. When the meal is done, I'll send for you again, for I do not plan to see you tomorrow and we must fix today, what is to happen."

"Very well," Claire said.

Hugh bowed.

CHAPTER EIGHTEEN

The mare, Buttercup, was as good as promised, ambling slowly and picking her way over the rocks. Claire held the reins only out of courtesy to the horse, who was content to follow her stable mate, stopping and starting at the same time, although at the slightest urging, would follow Claire's direction gladly. She and Hugh rode away from the Abbey, just as the office of Prime began, the deeper voices of the monks lingering in the early dawn. When they crested the hill south of the valley, Hugh turned his horse east.

The two mares maintained the same pace, but Claire's kept two steps behind the other. Hugh's mare, Fern, was as even tempered as Buttercup, except that she had, when they started, stubbornly insisted on walking just ahead and to the right of Buttercup. Since the foot rest on Claire's saddle hung to the left, she thus rode with her back to Hugh and two paces behind, making conversation difficult. Twice, Hugh circled his horse behind and came up on Claire's left. Both times the mare obliged, but by the time they'd gone fifty paces, Buttercup slowed and Fern quickened, so Fern could cross ahead and take her accustomed place.

"It's no good arguing with such intractability," Hugh said after the second attempt, and made no further demands on his horse.

As Hugh was too good a horseman to be ruled by such a gentle mare, Claire suspected that he, like the Abbott whose horse it was, preferred the silence that resulted. Already the night air had lost its edge. "It is a pleasant morning," she said, finally breaking the silence.

Hugh turned. "Are you tired? Do you need to rest?" He was, as always, most polite, but it was clear by his tone, the effort cost.

"No," she said. "If I'd wanted to rest, I would have said so. It was merely a pleasantry, which you may choose to ignore." She turned back to the side.

"Oh." A frosty tone.

They rode on in silence.

"It's going to get hot today," he said.

She bit back her first reply. "Yes," she said, "I am sure you're correct."

Hugh reined in his horse. "It's not too late to change our plans," he said.

She twisted around. "How so, Hugh?" she said. "We were all agreed."

"I do not like to separate the party."

He didn't like the separation! Weren't those her children sleeping so soundly they didn't feel her kiss? She had caressed each small head and been tempted to cut a lock from each, but had resisted, afraid the children would notice the loss and misinterpret its meaning. "I can't see that we had any other choice," she said, "and now is not the time to reason another."

"We could go back. You could stay at Oakrose while I ride for Mellifont, or better yet, for William."

"For how long, Hugh? Their resources will be strained as it is and we cannot supplement them, even if we had the funds, which I do not and I don't believe you do either. It was remiss of me I know, but when I left Ambridge, I did not think to include a chest of silver. I have the clothes I wear, the loan of this horse, the gift from the Abbess of a used gown to exchange for this travel stained one, when we meet with

Gregory, and the hope, but not expectation, of charity from others. Besides, your plan still does separate us."

"It need not be for long."

"If you can reach William," Claire said. "If you can get back."

"It shouldn't be that difficult. I can cross the plateau and cut down the upper Oberon."

"If it's so easy," Claire said, "let's go back at once to Oakrose, get the children and we can all go on together."

Hugh rubbed his shoulder. He was not conscious of the act and had never mentioned the injury sustained on the Oberon. Claire knew of it only because Breona told her. "Does the break still bother you?" she said.

"Yes . . . no . . . not really . . . it would be hard to carry my shield over long." He sighed. "I am of little use now to the High King."

"It will heal," Claire said gently, "and I think, while William will be glad for your sword when you return, he will be equally glad if his children are safe. He did not think it too small a task for Herbert of Amesly."

"He was an abler man than I, and still could not protect you."

Claire could not refute the first part of his statement. Although much older, Herbert had lost none of his strength and had years of training to supplement his natural skill. Hugh was still young, probably closer to her own age than William, who was nine years older than Claire, but showed no signs yet of aging.

"I must differ with you, Hugh Tintagel," she said. "Herbert did protect us and you must agree. We still have our liberty and we're in no immediate danger. Herbert of Amesly paid for our safety with his life, as did Stuart. Both good men and true. You will do what you can, Hugh. It's the best anyone can do."

Hugh bent over his horse, then straightened. "Thank you, Your Grace. We should continue or else take a true rest if you're tired."

"Lead on, Hugh," she said. The silence between them

seemed more comfortable now. They reached the top of another hill and Hugh reined in.

"Perhaps we should go back and avail ourselves of the Abbess Maud's offer," he said. "I could tolerate the company of two nuns and it might be good to have them accompany us."

"Why would we do that?" Claire said. "We've already declined."

He jumped down and adjusted his saddle. "Is it seemly that we travel alone, Your Grace?"

She stiffened. "Whose honor do you impinge, Hugh of Tintagel? Do you think William believes his wife has so little honor that she cannot travel safely in the company of an honorable man?"

"No, Your Grace. I did not mean to imply—"

"Unless you meant to smear your own good name, you do smear mine."

He looked up. "My only thought was to protect it. There are those who may later, put this to a different light."

"What has changed since yesterday?" she said. "Have the number of nunneries on the Elstow doubled, or even trebled, so that if someone recognizes us in the company of two nuns, he may have trouble finding the abbey they come from?"

"Still . . ."

"Perhaps I should take special care to be difficult, Hugh of Tintagel, and then you may complain loudly of me later."

He shrugged. "And, I do not like to leave that Ellen."

"I have had enough of Ellen! I forbid you say her name henceforth. But undoubtedly, you're right. I am sure that even as we left, she did sneak out of the guest house, steal their remaining horse, the most decrepit mare I ever did see, and ride like the wind for Cedric. I am sure she meant to. Of course, she would be in her chemise as they took her dress to mend it. Can you just picture the scene when she rides into Windrush clad such? Maybe she stole a monk's habit as well, I wouldn't put it past her. She could not yet fill out a nun's."

"She would do better in that regard than you think."

"How come you to know that Hugh Tintagel?" Claire said. "Perhaps we do require the company of the good nuns."

He flushed. "You have no reason for disquiet," he said, "nor does she. I spoke overmuch. I did need to grab her in a hurry when we were at Windrush and my only thought then was to keep her silent. The result, well, was inadvertent."

"Very well," Claire said. "I am satisfied that her honor has not been besmirched. If we have disagreed enough for the moment, let us proceed."

Hugh mounted and nudged his horse. Buttercup followed.

"One last thing, if you please," Claire said. "Please tell me why we travel east, when Mellifont is to the west."

Hugh's horse did not break her stride. "Breona bade me do it," he said coldly. "She did forswear me to countenance no one at the Abbey, but to turn east as soon as we were out of the valley."

"To what end?"

"In truth, Your Grace, I know not. I now regret to having agreed to it. It will add at least a half day to our travels."

He was in an especially irritable mood this day. "She must have had a good reason," Claire said, "but she would know best. I'm sure you must agree, since once again you did not consult me on the matter."

Hugh looked over his shoulder, his face hard. "She didn't know Oakrose was a double monastery," Hugh said. "She may not be so knowledgeable or so sound a council as I thought."

"Perhaps she thought it insignificant."

"Perhaps."

The sun grew hot and the rhythmic swish of the horses' tails hypnotic, so that as long as their path was fairly level, Claire rested. Hugh had done well to see that the straps of her footrest were shortened. The Abbess was taller and had the straps been longer, Claire's feet would not have reached the footrest comfortably.

"Your Grace."

She opened one eye, but ignored him.

He wheeled his horse around and came up on the other

side of her. "Your Grace," he said. "Just ahead is a large oak grove. Breona told me to turn into the grove. The shade would provide a good resting spot, if you are agreed."

"I was not planning on being agreeable," she said and opened her eyes.

He kept his horse even with hers and his face passive. Then he grinned.

"I sound like my children do at times, do I not, Hugh?" she said, laughing. "I confess to being out of sorts and you must do the same, then let's have peace."

"I must agree to being disagreeable," he said, chuckling. "For to disagree about being agreeable would mean that I was disagreeable." They rode into the grove laughing. Hugh reined up sharply and grabbed Buttercup's reins. "Hold, Your Grace," he said. "We're not alone."

A gray mare stood under one of the oaks, her reins looped over a branch. "It's a good thing, Hugh," Ceonald said, straightening up from behind the horse, "that we three are very much alone. I must try to dissuade you from addressing Lady Claire so, as it will do her no service here on the Elstow."

"By the saints!" Hugh said. "It's good to see you. It seems more than two days since we are met."

Ceonald bowed. "My Lady is well, I hope."

"I am," she said, "and you're a welcome surprise."

"You've had more than one of late, I think," Ceonald said.

Claire laughed. "And not all so welcome. You must tell Breona that I'm wise to her ways now, and the next time she sends me off with someone who cannot describe what lays ahead, I will ask for more details first."

Ceonald bowed again. "It was coincidence I assure you."

"What brings you here, Ceonald?" Hugh said.

"In good time. This grove is on the edge of a bluff that overlooks a small valley. Let us go where we may have the benefit of the view and take our rest."

He had been there earlier. A blanket had been spread out, and on it, a noonday meal waited. The valley below was small, formed by steep-walled rocks. Oaks crowded near the edge on all sides, so from a distance, the place was hidden. Across the valley, a waterfall plunged into the verdant green. On the valley floor, red roses arched skyward, their stone foundations barely visible, but here and there the broken arch of a window hinted at the broader outline of buildings that once graced the valley.

"My Aunt is well, I hope," Ceonald said.

"The Abbess Maud is very well, I believe," Claire said. "She has set about to start a school it seems. That is very providential for us."

"I believe, My Lady," Ceonald said, "that her interest may be short lived, and may ebb and flow from time to time, as is her whim."

"This seems a special place," Claire said, "and is very beautiful. Is there a path down into it? There must have been at one time, but I can't make it out."

Ceonald shook his head. "The path has been lost," he said.

"Who lived here?" Hugh said. "Do you know?"

"It was after Aethelstwin, in the time of Cormith, that the people here were forced from their homes. It's said the earth groaned and shuddered when they left, crying for her children, and blocked the way until they return."

"That must have been over a hundred years ago," Hugh said. "I think the wait is in vain."

"Will you tell us more about it?" Claire said.

Ceonald sighed. "Another time," he said. "I have not my singing voice with me today."

They ate in silence. When Hugh finished, Ceonald said, "There's a small brook not a hundred paces from here, Hugh. Would you be so kind to water my horse with yours?"

"Gladly," Hugh said and jumped up.

Ceonald looked out into the valley, his face wistful.

"Ceonald," Claire said softly.

"Yes."

"Breona sent us here, didn't she?"

"Yes, Your Grace. She wanted you to see this place."

"Why?"

"It's a beautiful place."

"One she has not seen." Or a place she had seen in her memories, like the hermitage.

He nodded.

"It was your home, wasn't it, Ceonald? Yours and Breona's and the people of the Soddenwood?"

"Breona thought you might guess."

"And Hugh is not to know."

"Not now. Later, perhaps."

He pointed. "Do you see that opening in the rocks there? About half way down the cliff?"

"Yes."

"My mother is there, and Breona will be too, in her time, until the way into the valley is free and they may go home."

She could not read his look, so only asked part of her question. "And the Abbess Maud?" she said.

"No, not Maud. She will rest at Oakrose."

"Oak . . . rose. The name seems more of this place, than that."

Ceonald smiled. "The history of how the abbey came to be named, Maud perhaps can tell you. But there is more than one monk there, and nuns too, who grew up in the Soddenwood. We keep the memories."

"What memories?" Hugh led the horses into the clearing.

"There's a rhyme about this place," Ceonald said. "I have just remembered it. It begins:

> The oak sings of Eiryn's cries for her lover,
> The rose sings of her cries for the King,
> The water sings of her cries for her lover,
> The people mourn for their Queen."

Ceonald picked up the remnants of their meal. "I'm glad you could be here on a nice day," he said. "When it storms, the wind whistles through the glade and echoes in the valley. It is a desolate, mournful cry."

"But it was not always so, I think," Claire said. "Desolate, that is. Is there more to your poem, Ceonald? It starts off very sadly, but I would like to hear it."

Hugh patted Fern on the neck. "We have many miles ahead," he said.

"Indeed," Ceonald said. "The story can wait."

"You've not told us how you came to meet us here, Ceonald," Hugh said.

"I came to join you if I might. Breona thought you might want the company. I'll ride with you until you reach the road to Mellifont and then we must go our separate ways. There'll be many travelers on the road no doubt, and they can entertain you until you reach the city."

"Breona is a wise woman," Hugh said. "We welcome the company."

Claire frowned and both men pretended not to notice.

Ceonald folded the blanket. "It's good I'm here, Hugh, if for no other reason than to remind you to say your new lines now. Words must serve where you once used your sword."

Hugh turned so he spoke directly to Ceonald. "I mean no offense when I say this," he said, "but this deceit is hard. The lies do not spring quickly to my lips. The sword, at least, is direct."

"True," Ceonald said, "but I think, Hugh, the sword is direct but swordplay is not. In open battle, it's a test of strength and quickness both for one man and an army. Blade meets blade."

"I would rather an honorable defeat, than a dishonorable victory," Hugh said.

Ceonald walked to the edge of the bluff, then turned. "If you were backed into a corner, Hugh, or fighting at the edge of a precipice, would you not use all the tricks you could conjure? Anything to help you gain advantage, especially if you knew your opponent was wont to do the same."

"Suicide is a sin against God," Hugh said. "There's no dishonor in saving yourself, save you do it by harming someone innocent to the conflict."

Claire put her hand on his arm, then dropped it quickly,

surprised her touch met with such warmth. "The story we concoct, Hugh," she said, "is much the same as the swordplay. As Ceonald says, our backs are at the cliff's edge and we must fight with every trick at our disposal." Her words were like a nursery maid's to an errant child. Hadn't Ceonald said the same thing? She blushed. The heat and the strain of traveling were creating such confusion. Hugh . . . and Ceonald . . . must overlook it.

"It is merely a different form of warfare," Ceonald said. "And as my mother used to say, if it sticks in your throat but it's all you have to eat, best swallow."

Hugh gulped loudly and grinned. "If My Lady sister is ready," he said bowing deeply, "let us ride on. I am resolved to my duty."

Although she had mounted her horse earlier without help, Hugh now helped boost her up. Her face grew warm. "I'm glad you've joined us, Ceonald," she said. "No doubt it's better to travel in a group, especially in these dangerous times." Claire always enjoyed Ceonald's company. She was glad. She almost believed what she said. Hugh's touch still warm.

When they were mounted, Ceonald rode to the edge of the bluff and looked out over the valley. "Say what you will, Hugh, but the people will return and the four sons of Aethelstwin will lead them.

The child yet to be born, the child that would join the three sons of the line of Aethelstwin, moved deep within her.

CHAPTER NINETEEN

A cheerful companion, Ceonald rode with them even after they reached the road to Mellifont, but if he had a hidden purpose, Claire could not discover it. After they left the oak grove, the hills grew gentler, the valleys broadened and more trees dotted the landscape. Small communities clustered along the hilltops, with fields of rye and wheat and hay ripening in the valleys below. By day, Hugh's mare, Fern, took her accustomed place, while Ceonald rode next to Claire, pointing out things that caught his interest.

They slept in the open if there was no monastery and in the monk's guesthouse if one was available. As they neared Mellifont, the road grew increasingly crowded, and Ceonald rode more often with the other travelers than with Claire, as if their acquaintance was one of the road. People of every class traveled to Mellifont for the summer market, noblemen and their ladies, a few clergy, and peasants, who herded gaggles of geese or carried covered baskets filled with cackling chickens or clucking ducks. Sheep, too old to lamb, bleated with sad eyes. Men carried sacks or pushed carts or pulled larger wagons, all swollen with wool.

Ceonald left them without explanation or warning, saying only that he had business to the north before he rode away. As he'd undoubtedly known, the city of Mellifont could be seen when they crested the next hill. Their fellow travelers, sharing Ceonald's knowledge, or perhaps the source of it, had risen before dawn that morning, and hurried toward the city, leaving Claire and Hugh alone on the road.

Claire had changed from her travel stained dress the night before, and wore a yellow dress with a brown tunic that had been given to her by the Abbess. The linen was finely woven, with a broad band of red, yellow and green embroidery along the neckband and sleeve edges. As it had belonged to a widow of more ample proportions, it fit more comfortably and her pregnancy was less noticeable. Hugh wore the same dark green under tunic Breona had given him, but had a new gray surcoat that fell below his knees. Like the buff one he'd worn earlier, it was split in front, making it easier to ride. With a black leather purse hung across his chest, he looked the very image of a prosperous merchant. As their horses began to climb up toward the city, the deep peal of the cathedral bell was answered by the thinner clang of the market bell. God's business was over and the business of the city had begun.

"Hugh?"

He wheeled Fern around and circled back. "My Lady?"

"Do you think Gregory will help?"

"I don't know much about him," Hugh said, "but there's every reason that he should. It's the honorable thing to do. Cedric is a base king and Gregory has no guarantee Cedric's evil will not spill over into his own borders. Besides, we do not seek an ally in arms, but only help for you and your children."

"I've been thinking," she said.

"Yes, My Lady?"

He pretended to listen. That, at least, was an improvement. "Reflect a bit on what I say," she said, "and see if there's not some sense to it."

He nodded.

"Mighten it make sense to stable the horses and make arrangements for our accommodation, in the event it should be warranted?" Claire said. "We have no guarantee we can gain an audience today, even if it is the King's Assize."

Hugh rubbed his chin. "I cannot think it necessary," he said.

Her face flushed.

He shook his head. "But I find I can no longer rely on what I might once have said was certain. I'm sure there will be a priory or two and we'll find one before we approach the castle."

"Rather an inn, I think, Hugh."

He looked shocked. "My Lady, even a woman of your supposed station would certainly seek a priory rather than an inn."

"I know this to be true," she said, "but think on it. When we met with company on the road these past days, did not the tradesman and the merchant talk freely, but say little to you and less to me? And though we were not dressed the part, the lord and his lady from Feldfield were all questions and conversation. Had it not been that Ceonald so easily distracted them, I fear that even if they could not guess our identities, they must know our roles to be false." Their clothes had been indeterminate, good for a peasant, acceptable for a merchant and poor for the nobility. The two mares meant they weren't peasants, and it was only when they neared Mellifont, she realized what made them stand out. She was the only one, save the lady from Feldfield, who rode side mounted. It did not fit with their clothing, she decided, and made them the object of curiosity.

"I think an inn would be worse," Hugh said. "Our presence would only cause curiosity and attract attention. And, I mean no offense, but I don't think you could ever be taken for type of person that might choose an inn."

She smiled. "I did speak freely to Phoebe," she said, "but she saw through me at once and I have no delusions that my artifice has improved. I thought instead that you might say that we were on a pilgrimage to seek safety for my family . . . that's true, is it not, Hugh?"

"It is, My Lady."

"And further, you could say that I had sworn to say nothing of my circumstance except to those few who might be in a position to help, and that I have forsworn my comfortable life until my pilgrimage has ended. I will swear it now, if you wish."

"It's not necessary, Your Grace," he whispered. "I know it to be true. Your plan has merit. We'll find an inn."

Hugh kept his mare next to Buttercup and they rode in silence until they reached the city gates. Claire looked up as the horses entered the gatehouse and shuddered. The iron-studded teeth of the portcullis above her seemed more a trap than protection. The gate was guarded by two men in mail, and a taxman stood just inside, ready to collect his due. Claire and Hugh passed into the city unmolested by either.

Hugh leaned over and took her reins. "Let me lead her, My Lady," he said. "I don't know how Buttercup will fare in this place, with all its strange noises and smells."

The horses' hooves clattered on the cobblestones, and although they made no move to bolt, Fern kept one ear back, and Buttercup crowded close to her stable mate. They rode up the main street leading into the city and paused at each intersection until Hugh found one he liked, where they turned, following a narrow street that twisted over the hillside.

Fern paused at the first inn, as if she recognized the sign. Hugh urged her on but at the second, he did not. The inn's green sign was freshly painted, but instead of an unadorned bush, the sign painter had added roses. A young Phoebe in the making was busily sweeping the cobblestones in front of the building. She leaned her broom against the door jam and curtsied.

"That is the sign for an inn, I believe," Hugh said.

She blushed and curtsied again. "Yes, My Lord."

"Have you accommodations for my sister and myself?"

"My Lord?"

"Have you room for us to stay?"

Her face reddened further. "You mean yourselves?"

"Provided you have room for the horses," he said.

"We be honored, My Lord," she said, "but . . ."

"If you have no room," Hugh said, "you need only to say so. Perhaps you can suggest another place."

"No, My Lord . . . I mean, yes, My Lord . . . I mean we do have room and for the horses as well, around to the back." She picked up the broom and began sweeping the immaculate cobblestones. "It's just that my husband just hung this sign this very day and you be our first cust . . . er . . . guests and, well, I don't know if we should do things right by what you expect." She took a deep breath. "I am called Bet." She curtsied.

Hugh looked at Claire, who nodded. He helped her dismount. "Begin by inviting my Lady sister inside," Hugh said, "while I see to the horses. Then we'll settle the price."

The arrangements were made and money paid to procure a chicken for their dinner, then Hugh and Claire started up the hill to the castle.

"Do you think he'll see us?" Claire said.

"Today is the King's Assize," Hugh said. "Ceonald told me King Gregory hears petitions all day, whether they are on appeal from a previous proceeding or not. If he keeps an honest day, we stand a decent chance, and if not, we must fall back on our second plan."

"I don't relish the idea of announcing myself to the court," Claire said. "Today would be better."

"In the end it is the same."

"I hope so."

As the castle stood at the highest spot on the hillside, there was no need for a map. They kept to the side streets, avoiding the market, but the smell of foreign spices, cooked meat pies and sheep dung mixed, wafting down the side streets. The castle walls were the same height as the city walls and had a similar gatehouse. Two men stood guard.

Hugh bowed. "We wish to avail ourselves of the King's Assize."

"Have you a written petition?" one of the men said. "If

you don't, there's a street of scribes not far from here, and they can set the matter down on paper for you."

Hugh opened the black purse and pulled out a corner of the vellum they'd composed and written at Oakrose. "It's here."

The man held out his hand.

Hugh pushed it back into the pouch. "I will give it to the King, with my own hands."

The guard was unimpressed, his companion bored. "The petition first. You do not proceed elsewhere."

Hugh hesitated, then opened the pouch. "Let only King Gregory break the seal," he said. The honey colored wax had been sealed with a thumbprint.

The guard ran a fingernail under the seal and popped it free. "I see no seal," he said.

The second turned toward the castle and shouted. "You . . . boy!"

A young boy of twelve or thirteen ran out.

"Take this to your master."

He took the petition and disappeared. It wasn't long before he reappeared and motioned. The men stepped aside. Hugh and Claire followed the boy to a side entrance, down a hallway and into a small room. What purpose the room normally served was unclear, the stone walls had not been plastered and bore no decoration. The room was empty save but for a single chair. Behind the chair, an open door revealed a handsomely furnished room. Claire turned the chair around, sat down and arranged her skirts, then removed her wimple and folded it. Checking for a vagrant curl, she smoothed her hair. The braids had been easy, but without help, pulling them back and weaving them as she was accustomed to wearing them, had taken a great deal of time and had been the source of some irritation on Hugh's part that morning.

She caught a flash of scarlet. Was there whispering?

A tall, florid man filled the doorway, then strolled into the room. Although he was dressed in a dull brown gown with a black under-tunic and might have been mistaken for a servant, the gold circlet on his head left no doubt this was Gregory.

Behind him, the pinch-nosed man in scarlet looked familiar. He bowed, "My Lord, Gregory," he said. "Allow me the honor of introducing you to Queen Claire of Bridland, High Queen of Threbant."

Gregory bowed.

"This is His Highness, Gregory, King of Elstow."

Claire inclined her head.

"Sir Thomas is not mistaken, then?" Gregory said.

Thomas. Of course, Thomas of Jarrow. He had been frequent messenger to William these past years, emissary of Gregory, who did not, as far as she knew, leave his plateau.

"You must forgive the slight subterfuge," Claire said. "These are perilous times and we traveled in both secrecy and haste." She held her hand out toward Hugh. "This is Sir Hugh of Tintagel. He does accompany me at the High King, my husband's request. Sir Hugh, you may well remember Sir Thomas of Jarrow. He has been visitor to Ambridge more than once."

Hugh bowed.

Either flattered to be remembered or disappointed he no longer had the advantage, Thomas pursed his lips and returned the bow.

"This is a mean room to receive you, My Lady," Gregory said, "but of course I didn't know it was you until Sir Thomas spied you out. You are a most honored guest. Do come and we'll move to a more comfortable furnishing." He had a genial face, rather like a favorite uncle.

"This seems a good place for a private exchange," Claire said, "Let us speak closely here and after we've had our discourse, decide between us our course of action."

Gregory inclined his head. "Sir Thomas, you've told me of the High Queen's beauty, but had I known she was wise as well, I might have been tempted from my plateau before now." He raised his hands and started to snap his fingers, then stopped. "My Lord, Thomas," he said, "be so kind as to have my man fetch another chair and a flagon of my best wine, but see that you bring them in yourself. We will have the secrecy Her Ladyship does desire."

When his deliveries had been made, Thomas bowed and left the room.

The wine had a delicate sweetness.

"My Lady," Gregory said, "I must tell you how relieved we are to see you safe. It was not two days hence that we heard Cedric was at Ambridge and I did assume you to be an unfortunate hostage." He slapped his knee. "By the saints! I did expect to see the High King come to borrow a ransom rather than to see his Queen here. This is good news and we must have a celebration. What's this! Be you ill?"

She shook her head, but found it difficult to breath. "Your news is sudden, that's all."

"You had not heard . . . Well, it was thoughtless of me to mention Ambridge so, without warning, but never mind. Of course, you left before it happened. Or else, it is that it's worse than that? What of your children?"

"They are safe."

"That is excellent. Cedric is a blackguard and a villain and I would fear if you had daughters."

"I have one, but she is only three."

"Ah well, then there is naught to fear."

Hugh shifted behind her. "Your Grace."

"Ah, Sir Hugh," Gregory said. "Does the wine not suit? Go on man, speak up."

"It's an excellent wine, Your Majesty."

Gregory put one hand on his chest and nodded in agreement. "It is, it is, if I do say so myself and I do. You are kind to notice."

"If I may be so bold," Hugh said. "Even in our haste, we have been several days in travel. What news, pray, do you have of the High King?"

"Of course, of course," Gregory said smiling, the perfect host. "You must be keen for news. He has left Mullendown . . . you knew he was there?"

Claire nodded. "Cedric challenged him to do battle at

Mullendown."

"Challenged? At Mullendown?" Gregory frowned. "Humph. He is a blackguard for sure. I must remember this deceit."

"And the High King?" Hugh said.

"Ah yes, to be sure. Left Mullendown and shifted his army northward but there had, as of yet, been no battle. At least as far as we've heard."

Claire pressed her hands together to stop the trembling. No battle yet, nothing resolved.

"By the saints," Gregory said. "I can't see what he's waiting for. Cedric's like a tick under the skin. Every day in Bridland he burrows deeper." He shook his head. "So, the High King sent you to me, did he?"

"Well . . ." Hugh said.

"We've come," Claire said, "to ask your help."

"And you shall have it, My Lady," Gregory said. "Cedric is a blackguard, a disgrace to his own. Tell us what you need and if it's within our power, we will see you have it."

A glimmer of hope flickered. Claire chose her words carefully. "It was decided," she said, "that since Ambridge has no natural defenses, that the children and I should relocate to a safer environ until this unpleasantness is over."

Gregory nodded. "Indeed, indeed. An excellent plan."

"Circumstances have effected a change in our original plan," Claire said, "and we've fixed upon another."

"And I am to be an instrument of help," Gregory said, smiling. "Excellent."

"With Cedric on the move," Hugh said, "we felt the need of an additional force to serve as escort for Her Grace. Purely precautionary, of course. With the High King so near to battle, we did think to appeal to you in this regard."

"Consider it done," Gregory said. "But name the number of the escort and I will order them ready."

"Thomas," he yelled. "Have two dozen men be made ready to ride . . . no make it a hundred."

"On behalf of my husband and Lord, William, we thank

you," Claire said. "The request, I fear, must go deeper than that and is the source of some slight embarrassment."

"My Lady?"

Claire held up her hands. "We have nothing to pay the keep of an escort, nor as it happens, for ourselves, save but for the kindness of others and the promise of a purse when we are a position to pay it. I can only mark my seal on behalf of My Lord husband that it will be done."

"Feel no discomfort, My Lady," Gregory said, looking a little less jovial. "We are no less inclined to help in the matter, but I must ask, how many men do you feel you require, and for what duration. And we must know your plan. I do not like Cedric, but I do nevertheless have no sentiment for making war with him."

"You tell me that Cedric's army is at Ambridge," Claire said, "and we understood his men were north of the city as well." Even in this room, the less revealed the better. The door was open for all Gregory's offer of privacy. "William did think this to be a matter easily settled," she said, "but I am fixed now that it will be a matter of some duration and may indeed last past this harvest. We have determined to make our way to Denholm, which is both remote from these troubles and more readily defended than any locale in Bridland. If your men could serve as escort, and some small portion remain until William can send a like contingent, I would be grateful. As to the number of men, I leave that to your good judgment, save that Sir Hugh be consulted in all arrangements."

"By all the Saints!" Gregory said, pacing about the room. "I do not like it, not at all. Begging your pardon, My Lady, but I cannot accede to such a plan. It's clear to me that it is insufficient. I have naught against the city of Denholm, but their King is with the High King and as you say, you have neither the men to protect you or the means to pay them. Besides, it's a lengthy trip and must inconvenience you to make it, as it does me to prepare for such an undertaking. It plainly will not satisfy." He stopped and turned toward her. "You must stay here instead. Then we shall have no more discomfort than having a chamber got ready."

"Thomas," he yelled, "see that a chamber is prepared for Her Grace."

"And for her children!" He walked to the door, peered into the room and returned. "You must tell me where they may be found and I will send for them. We have grandchildren in all sorts of various ages and I will have my lady wife send for some to keep company with yours."

"My Lord—"

"It is of no consequence. Their parents see far too much of them and I, far too little."

"My Lord, you're most gracious indeed to—"

"It's nothing. I wonder that the High King did not think of himself. I met him once, you know."

"My Lord?"

"William, I mean, "Gregory said. "He was just a young lad, and having a grand tour. He was page to Herbert of Amesly and they spent the better part of two months here. On his way to Denholm as well, if I recollect correctly, or just back."

Herbert of Amesly. Her hands trembled slightly and she bit her lip. She had heard about the tour more than once; but strangely it seemed now, not who accompanied William on his journey. They had been gone more than a year, she knew, traveling to every place of importance in the four kingdoms. She didn't remember William mentioning Elstow, but he had talked once of a summer in Amadee, so must have traveled through Elstow. It was not so strange then, that William should have chosen dear gruff Herbert to accompany her.

"William is a keen man with hawk and hound," Gregory was saying. "He will have better quarry now I trust."

"There is no better huntsman," Hugh said.

"He'd have done better to build a wall or two, eh, my Lady?"

Claire flushed.

"Never mind. I'll send him my best architects when this nonsense is over. Cedric's is not the only court with an avaricious mouth. What say you, My Lady? Will you not direct me to your children, so we may quit this room and find one with more suitable furnishings?"

"My Lord, Gregory," Claire said. "In truth, I did not expect such generosity and know not what to say in the absence of my Lord, William. I do believe we should stay to our plan, however much I appreciate your offer."

Gregory stiffened. "There's no city so well fortified as Mellifont," he said, "and while you're here, no man may remove you without my say so."

There was too much truth in what he said. The walls did serve as a barrier to invasion, but also to escape. "I believe the High King does expect that we go on," she said, careful to keep her tone pleasant and unconcerned.

"Nonsense. I can appreciate, however, that this places you in a difficult situation in regard to the High King's wishes and I do not wish to come between you and him. Let us agree to bring your children to the castle and we will each send a message to the High King and beg him decide his preference."

"My Lord . . ."

His brows arched in indignation. "We are not inclined to further discussion. We have stated what we are willing to do."

Claire would have preferred a private conversation with Hugh, but even with that, it seemed the outcome must be the same. They must be glad for so generous an offer. Indeed, if it were not that she felt William would prefer she not be an exile, she would prefer staying here to a lengthy journey. "You are exceedingly kind, My Lord," she said, "and have discovered in part my reason for reluctance. We will do as you suggest, with one small exception and that only from necessity."

He did not smile so freely now.

"It is only in the matter of the children," she said. "We did not expect such generosity and did leave them in a place where they are safe and well hidden from discovery. We did give instructions that they be given up only to myself, on my return."

Hugh choked on his wine and coughed.

"Indeed, My Lady," Gregory said. "Had you no

alternative? Did you not think that perhaps something might prevent your return and give directions thus?"

Claire sighed. "It was short sighted," she said. "I see that now, but at the time I did think it best. I am unused to such travails." She lowered her head and dabbed at her eyes. "Now I must pay the penalty and make the trip back instead of enjoying the comfort of your hospitality."

"Then it seems I must ready an escort," Gregory said.

"With your consent," Claire said, "we will go as we came. I fear a larger escort would only call attention to our mission and a man with evil intent could easily deduce our destination and ride ahead to his own purpose. There is not so strong a body of men with the children as I would like, and I think our best safety is in secrecy. Besides, however much your escort would be welcome, we do not know how close Cedric's army has come to our hiding place. Such an escort outside your borders must certainly give offense to Cedric." She could not bring herself to stay.

"Even so, that's no plan," Gregory said. "Once you have reunited with your children, you will be more at risk."

"Your Highness," Hugh said. "Might I suggest we adopt a form of both plans since I think both have merit. Let us leave as we came, and we will travel at a gentle pace, while you, Sire, do prepare a force to act as escort. In say, two weeks, we will meet at the border near Hedridge and will welcome your escort. Perhaps you might send a litter for Her Grace, so that she may travel in more comfort. Then, as you say, a message to William can resolve his intent, once all are safe."

"Well," Gregory said. "I don't like the first part overmuch, but I can see that it might make sense. 'Tis most unfortunate you are in this position to begin with, and I will tell the High King so myself." He walked back to the door. "I am agreed to the plan. You must stay at the castle tonight and start fresh tomorrow."

Claire smiled. "It would then be much harder to leave, My Lord, and would not help us pass unnoticed. We've made arrangements in advance for lodging in your excellent city."

Gregory hesitated and fingered the folds of fabric across one knee. He rose suddenly, and bowed. "In two weeks then, my men will be waiting near the border."

Claire stood and smiled prettily.

"Cedric is a blackguard and a scoundrel," Gregory said. "He has a slippery way about him and did even as a boy. I always did say that I did not like him and I say so still, even though he is my lady wife's nephew."

CHAPTER TWENTY

Gregory a relative of the foul Cedric! Hugh took her arm and for once, Claire did not object. Her vision blurred. Lights appeared where there were no candles and only changed color when she closed her eyes. They had an escort, at least she thought they did. Hugh spoke to someone but his words had no meaning. Gregory and Cedric! Gregory's smile now seemed an artifice, his offers of help a trap. Did he really mean to let them go? Was that what Breona was going to warn them about? But surely, she would not have advanced their plan if she knew of the relationship. Had she known? They stepped into the sunshine and the castle door closed convincingly behind them.

"Do you think—" Claire said.

"The King is most generous, "Hugh said, pressing her elbow.

He leaned forward and whispered, "Don't speak until I bid you."

The sun hurt Claire's eyes, but her vision cleared. Their escort was the same boy who led them into the castle. Full of his role, he walked quickly and although he seemed oblivious to what had been said, Claire noticed he kept his head turned slightly. A quirk, perhaps, but it made eavesdropping easier should he be so inclined. At the gatehouse, Hugh turned to one of the guards. "Can you give us directions to the street of the scribes?"

The guard pointed. "Go right. The first street is the street of the gold and silver merchants and the next one is the one you want." He looked around, then said in a low voice, "If you go to the third place on your left and tell them I sent you, you'll get a fair price."

Hugh continued to grasp Claire's arm and propelled her firmly, holding her back when she walked too fast, and pushing her when she slowed. Well into the street of the scribes, he released his hold and nodded toward the door of one of the smaller establishments. "That will do," he said.

Inside, a portly man sat at a writing table, copying a text. Rolls of vellum were laid out neatly on a small table next to him. He stood and bowed. "Good morrow to ye, My Lord," he said.

"Have you some vellum and a sharp quill for sale?" Hugh said.

He looked disappointed. "I'll be happy to take down whatever you wish, My Lord, and as any man'll tell you, keep the matter betwixt us, save that it be against King or country."

Hugh was not interested. The scribe had only his service for sale. The haggling began. The scribe lowered his price, not once but twice and in the end, the cost was as much as if the scribe had been employed, but the quill was new and Hugh had gotten a small bottle of ink as well. When they had turned into the street, Claire whispered. "Do you mean to send a message to William?"

"In truth, My Lady," Hugh said, "I don't have any use in mind. It seemed a good thing to acquire and more than that, gave us a reason to delay our return to the inn." He looked in the direction of the castle and took her arm. "The market is near. Let's go and take in the sights."

"I have absolutely no interest—"

His hand tightened.

"What is it?"

"Perhaps nothing. Just act normal."

She choked back a laugh. Normal. There was no such thing. Normal had been left in Ambridge. "I wonder if there'll be mummers," she said finally.

"I should not doubt it," Hugh said, and it looked like there had been, but the actors were gone and their elevated platform empty. The serious business of the day had been done and now the crowd milled from one entertainment to another. Nearby an unseen man plucked a harp and sang a bawdy song to the delight of the crowd. Somewhere in the square there would be acrobats and a trained bear or trained dogs, or both. Hugh pushed her forward.

"This is a good place to talk," he said.

"There are too many people," she whispered.

"If you talk and walk normally, whatever you say will be noticed less than if we whispered in some quiet corner."

Normal. There was that word again. From across the square, a dog yelped and the nearby crowd roared. Neither the tradesman selling felt near Claire, nor his patron looked up.

"I had my hopes pinned on Gregory," Claire said. "But now . . ."

"I was surprised that you seemed so distrustful," Hugh said, "especially without knowing his connections. Why did you say you must return? I had thought the offer generous and there was no arrangement in regard to your return that I was told."

She shrugged. He sighed. "I'd gladly welcome such council as we had these days past and I'm sorry our companion of late has left us."

The felt merchant began packing up his goods, attracting a last-minute shopper. "I felt much relief at his words," Claire said, "and spoke to thank him, but found my mouth forming words I did not recognize. I have, I suppose, formed a new habit of caution. One lie soon followed another. I did regret each falsehood, but now I wonder what influence might have persuaded my tongue, and do thank it. His uncle!" She shivered.

"He sounded sincere," Hugh said, "but does not the enemy

present himself with glib tongue and false smile? The part of me that welcomed his words would say that if he were false, he would not have mentioned his relationship, but sought instead to deceive us. Still, I don't think I can be persuaded to leave you to his mercy." Hugh paused near a table piled high with brightly woven wool in shades of blue and yellow and green and red.

The tradesman picked up a length of fabric and held it out. "You'll not find so fine a cloth anywhere in Elstow," he said, running his hand under the top layer. "This is of the finest wool, gotten only from sheep raised in Amadee." He put down the blue and held up the yellow. "Feel the softness, My Lord and Lady. This will take the needle well." He held it out. "You can buy no finer. Test its strength."

Hugh caught the edge between his thumb and forefinger and gave the fabric a fainthearted tug, looking around the market as he did so.

The tradesman's wife stepped forward and held out a bolt of the blue. "Perhaps My Lady prefers another color," she said.

Claire ran her hand over the fabric. "It is very fine," she said, "but we're not in the market for fabric this day."

"We'll be here until noon tomorrow," the man said, bowing.

"We only come once a year," the woman said, bobbing behind him.

"Come, My Lady," Hugh said. "We've seen only a little of the attractions and must continue." He bent close to Claire and smiled broadly. "Don't look now, but there's a large crowd just across from us. When we reach it, I'll push a way into it and once we're inside, I want you to continue. As soon as you're able, go as directly as you can to the cathedral and wait for me there."

"Separate!"

"Hsst," he said. "I'll explain when we meet."

They continued as before, pausing at a few of the tables that still displayed goods, and once to watch a juggler. When they reached the crowd, it parted politely. At its heart, a magician held up a small leather bag to the delight of the crowd and the red-faced embarrassment of a buxom young woman. Claire did as Hugh instructed. Just as she left the crowd, two women broke away as well, walking in the direction of the cathedral. Although their gowns were finer than the one Claire wore, they seemed ill suited.

"He had quick hands," the taller one said.

"Aye, and lots hidden beneath his tunic, I'll warrant," the other said, laughing.

"I'd like to show him what I have hidden under mine," the taller one said.

They chortled, and then noticing Claire, bowed and laughed again.

"Are you alone, My Lady?" the shorter one said.

"I'm only going to the cathedral," Claire said. "It doesn't seem a place where company is required."

"Ah," the taller one said. "Sometimes it is exactly what's required." They laughed again.

The conversation brought them to the arched doors of the cathedral. Inside, the shaded interior was cool after the heat of the afternoon sun. A pilgrim's path led toward the altar and a handful of petitioners prayed silently at intervals along the path. Tradesman mingled with peasants and pilgrims, each undoubtedly offering prayers to their favorite patron saint, perhaps of the cathedral or perhaps of their guild. Benches had been placed at intervals along the walls. Claire chose one near a side door and folded her hands in her lap. The accustomed quiet did not come. Cedric's uncle! She should never have left Hugh. She wiped the corner of her eye.

"My Lady?"

He was alone.

"Let us leave directly," he said, "I have, more than once, seen a flash of red beneath a cloak that's too warm to wear."

Thomas! He had no need to tell her to choose the side door. They hurried into the afternoon brilliance and turned away from the square.

"Take the first side street," Hugh said in a low voice. "Don't run unless I tell you."

She nodded. Twenty paces. Thirty. A small lane appeared. Forty. A few more steps. She turned into the side street.

"Turn left at the next street," Hugh said. "Don't look back."

The lane was straight, offering a full view down its length to anyone who cared to notice. A hundred and twenty-three steps to the corner. As they turned, she glanced up the street and saw Hugh did the same.

"Did you see anyone?"

"No," he said.

"Do you know where we are?" Claire said.

"Yes."

They turned twice more, before Hugh slowed the pace. "I may have been mistaken," he said, "but I thought it better to take no chances."

She nodded. What could be said? Betrayal—it had a familiar smell.

When they reached the inn, the street behind them was empty. They hurried inside. A fat chicken browned on the spit and their hostess stirred a bubbling pot. Claire sank down on a bench in the small common room.

"Oh, My Lady!" Bet said. "Be ye ill? You've no color to your face at all."

"Some ale, Mistress," Hugh said.

Claire's hand shook as she took the flagon. Bet stood hesitantly. "Should I fetch someone?"

The door opened. A dark-haired man of about Hugh's age entered and bowed. "Good day to ye," he said.

"Jack," Bet said. "We've our first guests, but I do fear My Lady is taken ill."

"No, not ill," Hugh said. He turned to Claire. "You aren't ill, are you?"

She shook her head. "It's just . . ."

"She's had a terrible fright," Hugh said. "Some man did follow her and we did think he meant some mischief. We were able to give him the slip and hurried back as fast as we could."

It didn't ring true, even to Claire. If she had been accosted, wouldn't Bet and Jack wonder why hadn't Hugh taken care of the situation?

"I'll fetch one of the sheriff's men," Jack said. "If you can describe him, they can find and question him."

"No!" Claire's voice betrayed her.

"Thank you," Hugh said. "While we're concerned, I don't think it's a matter for the authorities."

Jack and Bet exchanged glances.

"It's a family matter," Claire said.

Hugh nodded. "We could have been mistaken," he said, "and if we are, it would be a source of great embarrassment."

"But what if you weren't?" Bet said.

"To escalate this would only make it worse," Hugh said. "We must try to leave the city without being noticed and seek refuge until this matter can be resolved. You know how family situations can be."

The cathedral bells began to toll.

Jack nodded. "Ye cannot leave today," he said. "That's the bell for the gates being closed for the night."

The iron portcullis was being lowered, the drawbridge raised. They were trapped.

"How many gates are there?" Hugh said.

"Four," Jack said, "but one is closed for repair."

Three. Hugh did not need to explain the significance. It would be an easy matter to post a watch.

Their dinner was ready. In spite of herself, Claire found she was ravenously hungry. Her body made its own demands.

"We'll leave at dawn," Hugh said, picking the last of the meat off a chicken bone. "The only question is, which gate to take. The question is, which one wouldn't be watched?"

Bet pushed her husband forward. "My Lord," Jack said, "I've been thinking and thinking and it seems to me, I have an idea."

"Go on," Hugh said.

"Even if you pick a gate that's not being watched, or pass

unnoticed, once you leave the city, the roads are visible for miles. I'd wait for the market to end and go when the traders leave, but that would work only if you left your horses."

Hugh frowned.

"I can't ride," Jack said, "but I have a cousin who can. You could name the place and he could bring the horses to you. He stands night watch on the walls so has his days free, but must be back before the gates close."

"Thank you," Hugh said, "but the fewer people involved the better. There is the question of the family honor, you know."

Again, Jack nodded. Family feuds were a nasty business. And here was a woman who looked to be in the family way and a man who said he was her brother . . . Still, he wouldn't judge.

"What if we were wrong?" Claire said.

"Then we will have worried for naught," Hugh said.

"I wish we could know," Claire said, "whether or not we were followed." She sighed.

"We're caught in a dilemma, that's certain," Hugh said. "The only way we'd know for sure is if we leave and keep a sharp eye out. Even then, unless we catch him out, we won't know the truth of it." He turned toward Jack. "We don't want any confrontations," Hugh said. "we only need to resolve some things and pray to do it without conflict."

"I could watch to see," Jack said, "but that would be no help since I'd have no way to get word to you."

"What if My Lord and Lady could watch themselves?" Bet said.

"That makes no sense," Jack said. He stared, puzzled. Bet must have decided to take a side in the matter. They'd had a time convincing her own father to let them marry so maybe she felt particularly sympathetic. She was a good judge of people, Jack knew.

Bet looked at Claire. "What if whoever was following you saw what he wanted to see?" she said. "A man and a woman, dressed as you're dressed now, as he last saw you, leaving the city. Jack and I could go in your stead."

"It might work," Hugh said.

"I could dab at my eyes from time to time and keep my head down."

"No," Claire said.

Jack looked from one to the other. "There's a monastery not far from here," he said. "We could meet there and return your clothes, or leave them there for you to collect if you'd rather."

"It's too dangerous," Claire said.

"Dangerous for you," Bet said, "but not for us."

"Unless you've committed a crime and we've helped you get away," Jack said. He laughed but his eyes grew wary.

"Jack, bide your tongue," Bet said, "as if My Lady looked the sort. I never!"

"Upon my oath before all the saints," Claire said, "we have done no wrong, but it's too dangerous. You don't know who you might anger and I'd put you at greater risk if I told you."

Hugh rubbed his chin. "Still," he said, "it might work. And, if the deception is discovered, what's the harm?"

"No."

Hugh shrugged. "You're probably right," he said. "Besides, if we were followed today, and if he falls for the ruse, and follows Bet and Jack here, how would we know? I don't see that it solves overmuch."

"Let me think on that part," Jack said.

Bet cleared the table and Jack disappeared in the direction of the stable. But the proposal hung in the air and by nightfall, after hearing Jack's new ideas, and when she could think of no other alternative, Claire relented. "You may keep the gown, if you like," she said, finally. "The cloth is good. Perhaps you'd like to recut it."

"Begging your pardon, My Lady," Bet said, "but I can't keep so fine a gift. We have oft spoken of that monastery and wished to make a pilgrimage. This gives us the reason."

"Keep the gown," Claire said, "or else see if the monks can find someone to use it."

Bet blushed and curtsied. "I will keep it then, My Lady, and gladly."

"Where is this monastery?" Hugh said.

"A half day's walk east of Mellifont," Jack said.

"Go as far as the monastery you spoke of," Hugh said, "and when you've sufficiently rested, and at a time of your choosing, return. We'll travel at our own pace and may or may not meet with you on the road. If we do, best act as if we'd never met."

Claire shook her head. "I hope I do you no disservice by giving you the dress. You must promise—swear to me and to My Lord—that if anyone asks you about it, or about either of us, that you do answer each question truthfully."

"My Lady . . .", Hugh said.

"It cannot be otherwise," Claire said. "We've done no wrong, but only suffered some anxiety, some misapprehension about what lay before us that we seek to resolve by our actions. I will not have what we do made wrong by a lie. It gains too little and does sully us all."

Jack left to make the arrangements. Claire heard him return but when he said nothing to Hugh, she stayed behind her curtain and closed her eyes. When she woke, no new plan had presented itself and there'd been no new inspiration. She'd changed into her old gown the night before and given the other to Bet, so now there was nothing to do but pull on her over-tunic and splash water on her face. The snug fabric told more than she cared and Claire felt Bet's eyes on her, but nothing was said.

"It'd be better not to speak too plainly after we've left the house," Hugh said, "so I'll thank you now and wish you safe journey to the monastery and back again."

"I add my thanks," Claire said. "Would that we could give you more as a token of our gratitude, but we can offer nothing else save our thanks."

Bet fingered the yellow dress, smiling. "This dress is far finer than we could ever hope to afford," she said.

When they left the inn, the sun was not up yet, but the sky

had begun to lighten. Claire wore her cloak even though Hugh had offered to carry it, and soon wished she'd left it with the horses. The morning was not a cool as she had expected. She pushed the fabric back over her shoulders and resolved to say nothing. Jack and Bet took the lead; they were but two couples about their business. Here and there a shutter was thrown open, the morning routines of the occupants intruding into the quiet. Soon other townspeople would join them on the street, and the din of the city would swallow the intimate sounds of morning. Their route led through meaner streets than the ones Hugh and Claire had taken into the city and as they descended the hill, the streets narrowed.

Jack stopped at an intersection. Pointing to his left, he said in a low voice, "You need only follow this street.

"Go with God," Bet said quietly. They turned in the opposite direction and walked quickly away.

"Look for a cat carved into the house," Hugh whispered. So, Jack had spoken to him last night, it was only that she hadn't heard them.

The buildings had a mean uniformity, except for gargoyles carved high on the corner of each, guardians against evil. They watched the intruders, grimacing and laughing, as Claire studied each in the early light. The cat was on the last house on the left. Claire pointed.

Hugh nodded. "We wait here," he said. Across from them, narrow steps climbed up to the wall walk.

A mail-clad figure appeared. He motioned.

"Go ahead," Hugh whispered.

"I'll wait here," Claire said.

"He thinks it you that wants to go up," Hugh said.

She shook her head.

"Jack told him I've promised you a look from the wall and then you will consider my offer of marriage."

Her face reddened. Claire jerked at her tunic. "I'm obviously married."

"Or needing to marry," Hugh said, smiling.

She frowned.

"Jack did the best he could."

The guard motioned again.

At the bottom step, Claire pulled her skirts close. The steps were steep and hardly seemed large enough for a woman, let alone an armed man. She pressed against the wall as she climbed. At the next to last step she stopped. The wall walk was wide enough for two abreast, but the wall itself was only a couple of feet higher than the wall walk. Her stomach churned.

The guard held out his hand. "There's naught to fear," he said. His voice was low enough so that it wouldn't carry, but not so low as to arouse suspicion should anyone see them. "Just don't go too near the edge if you feel light-headed," he said.

She took his hand. One step. Then the second. She was powerless to move forward.

"Ye can turn around and go back down, if ye've a mind to," the guard said, "but if you take only three steps, ye'll have gone as far as ye need and can kneel down. It's a sight less fearful that way and once ye've gotten used to it, ye'll see that the view of the valley is grand. Besides, from here ye can see who comes in and out of this gate, and it's a sight that's most interesting, especially at market time."

Claire held out both hands. He clasped them firmly and took one step back. It took two steps to equal his one. He took another and another. "That's good," he said.

She sank to her knees. Hugh came up quickly and knelt beside her. Below them was a broad valley they would have crossed had they come from the direction of Hedridge. A group of about twenty waited outside the wall. One of the sheep bleated occasionally but the small flock was docile. If there were ducks and chickens in the baskets, they waited quietly for their impending demise. As the sun slid over the horizon, the cathedral bells tolled. The ropes creaked as the portcullis was raised, and chains clattered as the drawbridge was lowered. She put one hand on the wall and leaned closer.

The tableau in front of the gate sprang to life and

disappeared by twos and threes. They waited. An over-sized monk on an under-sized donkey was the first to leave, followed by two merchants on horseback and after a few moments, Jack and Bet appeared. The two stopped for a moment as if to get their bearings, then began down the road to Hedridge. Late to arrive, a goat herder urged his flock forward, eager to reach the city before the market bell chimed.

"It looks—" Claire whispered.

"Wait," Hugh said.

The goat herder and his flock gained the city and disappeared. The yellow dress was halfway down the hillside.

"Ye must go, now," the guard said, casting an eye over his shoulder.

Hugh held up a finger. "When the market bell rings," he said.

The guard looked back toward the tower behind him. "No longer."

Jack and Bet reached the valley floor. Behind Claire, the city sprang to life. A dog barked, a child laughed, a man shouted. The cathedral bell tolled again, services were over. The market bell clanged. Hugh did not move.

"Go on with ye," the guard said,

Hugh stood, then stooped down and held out his hand to Claire. She grasped it but found it limp.

"I'm afraid," she said, releasing Hugh's hand. His eyes narrowed and he nodded almost imperceptivity in the direction of the gate. She turned to the guard. "Will you be so kind as to help me," she said. "We are neither one used to such heights and I fear must both feel its effects." She fluttered her eyes.

Hugh stepped back along the wall walk to give them room, gaining a few more moments. The guard held out his hand. Claire held on tightly and got clumsily to her feet. She took one step back, then another. She reached the steps.

"Ye—" the guard said.

"Hsst," Hugh said.

The guard stopped and Claire crouched down. Just outside

the wall, a man on horseback appeared from the shadows. There'd been no hoof beats on the drawbridge, so the rider had either been outside the city all night, or had left it by another gate. He followed the wall, riding toward them. A traveler, perhaps, who eschewed the roadway. He drew near the gate, stopped and looked out over the valley. Bet, in her yellow dress had begun to cross. Claire held her breath.

The rider tugged at one rein. Thomas of Jarrow nudged his horse forward, and rode toward Hedridge.

CHAPTER TWENTY-ONE

Cedric stabbed at the fish on his plate and watched it crumble away from the bone. It had an odd taste, coming from the waters of the Oberon, rather than the mountain rivers in Oroskree. His army was encamped all around Ambridge, but he had chosen a spot north of the city. Rather Ivo did. Cedric didn't mind the smell of blood on the battlefield, but he disliked the aftermath; men rotting with infection waiting to die, corpses waiting to be buried, and the lingering smell of the inevitable fires, whenever a town was taken. He should have been pleased with events these past weeks but he wasn't. At least not completely.

It began in Windrush. First, there were the two women who had left earlier than he had anticipated, and spoiled what had started out as a good morning. With his man, Seth's, arrival to report on the army's progress, Cedric put it out of his mind as a minor annoyance, but not before he ordered no one else be allowed to leave the castle grounds. He should have done it when he arrived, and for that he blamed Ivo. Like a small sliver that couldn't be pulled out, it continued to annoy and then fester just beneath the surface. As soon as Seth had finished, another came to make his report and yet another after him. The Marsh King had drifted in and out of the great hall all day, fussing about any number of nuisances. "Is the fire to your liking?" he said. Then he checked to see if Cedric wanted fresh floor reeds spread. Or if he was hungry, or thirsty. The last frustration was the Marsh King's instance that the candles be replaced with new ones, claiming the wicks on the ones burning hadn't been properly trimmed.

"Ivo!" Cedric yelled, even though he was sure Ivo was close by. The old man's spritely steps annoyed Cedric. "Lock him up with his family," he said, waving his hand toward the Marsh King. "I don't know if he plays the spy or sycophant or fool, but I've seen more of him today than suits."

The Marsh King started to protest but quickly shut his mouth. Cedric was sure Ivo had warned him off somehow. That would bear food for thought. Before he could pursue it further, his men returned to report that the two women had indeed left the castle and had not been found. His annoyance grew, but still, there was ample entertainment at hand in the castle. Did not the Marsh King have a daughter? Another arrived with a report, and Cedric began to wonder if Ivo had arranged things to keep him occupied. The number of small irritations dampened his enthusiasm for his army's successes.

The Marsh's King's daughter. Or rather, the lack, was the second thing to go wrong. He had decided to wait until the next day to pursue matters, and then to reward himself with a day of entertainment after all his hard work. He looked forward to meeting her.

Early the next morning he went to the great hall and called for Ivo.

"What's her name?"

"Who, sire?".

Cedric toyed with his small knife and wondered if the old man would duck if it was thrown at him. He sighed. Cedric didn't have the appetite or energy for games. Well, not that kind of game. "The daughter, fool. The Marsh King's daughter."

"Is her father not your ally?"

Cedric threw the knife without thinking. It came closer to

the old man's head than he had really intended. All the same, Ivo had barely reacted, and if he had flinched, Cedric did not see it. An interesting tidbit to file away. Did the old man have a death wish, or was he confident in his safety? Did Cedric wish him dead? Probably not, he decided. For all his annoyances, Ivo had his usefulness. "The Marsh King was not over-zealous in his fealty to the High King. His lack of action was in fact, a betrayal of his oath. I'd not trust such a man with any oath sworn to me and he's not yet made it anyway. He has merely acquiesced to our presence."

"If you want him, even as a bad ally, this is a poor way to start."

"The name." His words were sharp. He stared at Ivo and finally the old man paled.

"Ellen."

"Bring her here. It's time I got acquainted."

But she was nowhere to be found. After a quick search, Ivo brought her parents to Cedric, while castle was searched more thoroughly. The Marsh King was pale but the Queen seemed quite resolute. Cedric ignored them while the search was being conducted, and played with his small knife, retrieved from the floor after Ivo first left him. He was almost blind with rage. How dare they! He would ferret her out. If the search ended badly, which of the two would he start with? And what means would he use? It had to make them talk, and it had to satisfy him if their daughter would not. He wet his lips. There were so many ways . . .

"She's not in the castle." Ivo looked slightly palsied. It was not like him. "I have men checking the grounds."

Cedric decided to start with the Marsh Queen. She needed to be put in her place. He didn't get a chance.

"She's not here," she said.

The March King stared at his wife.

"I sent her away, the day after you came," she said.

Cedric began to hear the rushing sounds that always blotted out everything. "Don't take me for a fool! There's been no one allowed to leave, and I know there's been no traffic on the road in either direction, save for my own men." He began stabbing the knife into the arm of his chair, watching the wood splinter and fall away. He stopped and pointed the knife toward the Marsh King. "You will tell me what I want to know." And if he did tell, it wouldn't matter, Cedric would still exact a toll. He nodded to the guards at the doorway. They grabbed the Marsh King. Forced him to his knees.

"I don't know where she is," the Marsh King said. He was flushed and looked wildly over at his Queen.

Cedric rose and wiped the small splinters from his knife.

"You are a fool." The Marsh Queen stood defiantly.

Cedric stopped. The rushing grew louder.

"You say no one left," she laughed. "but you know they did, save not by the road. I sent Ellen by boat."

Cedric didn't remember exactly what happened next. He's hit her, he knew that. Backhanded her and cut his hand on her teeth. He thought he'd kicked one of them. Or maybe both. When his head had cleared, the meddlesome Bishop had arrived and was mopping up some blood from the floor in the empty room. Not much blood, though. Apparently, he'd arrived just as things had gotten started. Even in his rage, Cedric would not war against the church. He needed them. He needed to be able to tell them . . . It was probably the only thing that could have stopped him.

Cedric knew the Marsh Queen's words were true. She had thrown the words at him and had smirked as she did so, he remembered that at least. Something still didn't ring true about it, but he'd had no time to pursue it further. He had assumed William would move north against him, but his scouts arrived with the news that the way to Ambridge appeared to be clear. Cedric left enough troops to secure his conquests, and hurried his army south. The High Queen was a much better prize than a puling child.

For the most part, the villages and hamlets all capitulated, as he'd known they would, and already his coffers were beginning to swell. The small attempts at resistance were easily overcome, but the further south they went, the more meager the pickings, with the villagers hiding what they could. More annoyances, but there was time to remedy the deficiencies later.

When they arrived at Ambridge, Cedric was stunned to see the city completely defenseless, with no walls or fortifications. He'd heard rumors to that effect, but didn't credit their truthfulness. Even, William, whom he had no use for even as a child, could not be that foolhardy. But he had been, and the few barricades hastily put into place did little to stop Cedric's men. It had almost been a disappointment. He lusted after the bloodshed, especially after Windrush.

"Where is she!'.

Ivo did not mistake his meaning this time. He removed the platter of fish and put one with a roast hare on it in its place. "She isn't here," he said. "No one even knows when she left."

It had been the same answer yesterday. The wind shifted and the smell of stale smoke drifted through the tent. Cedric frowned and then shrugged. The smoke was a minor inconvenience that resulted from his necessary actions, and could have been worse. He had spared most of the city, save the castle which was meager and would need to be rebuilt for his purposes, and a few sections of town, to serve as a lesson. Situated at the mouth of the Oberon, Ambridge had a fine harbor and would serve him well, or he would have destroyed it just to spite William. But the High Queen . . .

"Bring it to me."

As he had several times over the past few days, Ivo hurried to the chest and took out the small likeness of the High Queen, found when the castle was pillaged before the fires were set. Cedric himself had gone through the castle room by room. The High King had hidden his gold or taken it with him. Cedric cared little for the rest. In the Queen chambers, he demanded to be left alone. He found one of her tunics and stroked the soft fabric as he looked at the painting he'd found. He would slay William and have his queen. He'd get children on her and her own would be hostage until he did. He thought to bring her tunic back with him to his tent but in the end, took only her likeness.

Ivo unwrapped it and handed it to Cedric.

Cedric wondered when it had been painted. She didn't appear to have been much changed since her wedding. Still, she'd had a child, or children, so perhaps it wasn't recent. He stopped toying with the food and sat up straighter. It should be easy — easier — to trace a woman with a child. Far easier than finding one woman and her servants. A child would mean a much larger household, especially a royal child and heir to the throne. She'd have a retinue, with servants and guards, and that large a group would leave a trail. He hadn't been thinking clearly. "Tell me about the High Queen," he said. "She has gotten her husband an heir, you told me."

"Yes, Sire."

"Well, speak up. If the High King has a brat, I must find it and its mother as well. I WILL have them."

"There is more than one," Ivo said carefully. "It should make them easier to find."

Cedric waited.

"I'm told there are four children," Ivo said, finally. "Three boys and a girl."

'Hmm," Cedric said. "A large group will be even easier to find."

"Two of the boys are twins."

Cedric's eyes narrowed. The older woman at Windrush. He could picture her pulling one of the brats behind her. Why? He hadn't paid them that much attention. Something about that whole night hadn't been right, but he hadn't had time to tease it out. They'd been gone that next morning, when he sent Ivo to find them. And were to go by boat, if he remembered correctly. By boat . . . The Marsh Queen said her daughter had gone by boat. How many boats did the Marsh King have? "Tell me about our first night at Windrush," he said.

"In what regard?" Ivo said. For once he looked perplexed.

The two woman and children," Cedric said. "What of them? In specific, what do you remember about the children."

"Three boys and a girl," Ivo whispered.

Cedric pushed the likeness of Claire toward Ivo. "Was she there!"

Ivo fell to his knees. "It might have been her, I'm not sure."

When the rushing stopped, Cedric found Ivo slumped over, covered in blood. Cedric knelt; tried to put things back, but they wouldn't go. He'd put one thing in and something else slid out. Cedric's hands and tunic were covered in blood before he gave up. Or maybe they had been before he started. He cradled the old man in his arms, and rocked back and forth, sobbing. He couldn't remember a time without Ivo. Ivo, who picked him up when he was learning to ride, Ivo, who came to his chambers when Cedric was little and things came out of the darkness. Ivo, who kept the candles lit even now . . .

Cedric shuddered and stopped suddenly. He lowered Ivo carefully. William had done this as surely as if he'd been there. And his Queen. They would pay. Both of them. He would scour the earth if that's what it took.

CHAPTER TWENTY-TWO

He's a perfidious, lying weasel," Claire said, when they were safely away from the wall. "Gregory may be of noble birth, but I consider him to be one of the lowest of creatures. I don't doubt he is uncle to the badger."

They walked quickly. Claire had no sense of the direction they took, only that it was away from the gate.

"We only know what we see, not the meaning," Hugh said.

She stopped. "Do you believe what you just said, Hugh Tintagel?"

He turned toward her. Reddened. "Not really. This has a bad feel to it."

"Then do not utter such banalities. I have not the patience. We must fix on another plan."

"Let's go on," Hugh said. "I'll feel better when we've gained the inn."

"It's no safe haven, now."

"No, perhaps it isn't, but we have to get the horses before we can leave."

"To go where?"

"We have only one choice, as I see it," Hugh said, "and must to William. If we travel fast, we may yet gain his camp without discovery."

"And the children?"

He shrugged. "There're as safe where they are now, as anywhere."

"Do you believe that, upon your oath, Hugh of Tintagel?" she said.

He shook his head slowly. "I hope it to be true."

She burst into tears.

His face reddened and he put one hand on her shoulder. "Your Grace . . ."

She jerked away and began walking. He hurried after her.

"You do forget yourself, Sir Hugh," she said.

He looked her into her eyes for a brief moment. "My most abject apology, My Lady."

She wiped her eyes.

"I believe," Hugh said, "that Thomas will not stay them from their journey, but rather seek to find where it ends, as there lies the total prize. He'll not discover his error until they turn back toward the city, and Jack has promised to wait until the morrow. If we're cautious, I believe we're reasonably safe for the moment. Let's get some victuals at the market. You'll feel better after you've eaten and when we are provisioned, we'll get the horses. That should have been our plan all along."

"There must be a better plan," she said.

"Than eating?"

"No," she smiled. "That, I'm convinced, is an excellent idea. It's what we undertake after. We did fix, these many days ago, that to travel to join William was a path with great peril."

"Perhaps there will not be as great a risk when we approach from this direction."

"Perhaps."

"I'm sorry, My Lady," Hugh said. "I can only think that we have two choices, to go forward as we now discuss, or to go back from whence we came."

"If it was safe there," Claire said, "we would not have been counseled to leave. I cannot think that to be a choice."

"I agree. You must have high walls or a strong army. That has neither."

The street emptied into the crowded market, and business everywhere was brisk. Claire had taken only two steps when a bald-headed man backed into her, nearly knocking her over.

"Hey there!" Hugh said.

The man wheeled around. Above the black badger on his tunic, a deep scar divided his chin and mimicked the snarl of his mouth. He raised one fist.

The black badger. She did not know the man, but she knew the badge. Claire began to shake. Hugh pushed his way in front of her.

"Begging your pardon, Sire." The taller of the two women from yesterday appeared suddenly. A shorter man of about twenty stood beside her, holding a red rose. "I met this woman yesterday," she said to the scar-faced man, nodding toward Claire. "She is fresh from the country, I can tell you, and does not know city ways." The young man held up his rose and inhaled deeply, watching the scar-faced man out of the corner of his eye, then waved the rose in his direction.

Seth glanced the young man's way, then stared.

"My brother, My Lord," the woman said.

Seth looked from one to the other and snickered. "You seem to know city ways," he said.

"Indeed," the woman said. "Perhaps my brother can show you some interesting sights while I see this poor woman to her destination. I'm sure she's most sorry."

Claire nodded, but kept her head averted.

"My Lord is new to Mellifont?" the young man said. He fingered the rose and ripped off a few petals, crushing them before he let them fall.

Seth reached out and took the rose.

The woman took Claire by the arm and pulled her away. "No need to tarry now, Mistress. We all have work to be done." The crowd milled around them. Claire dared not turn to see if Hugh was behind her.

The woman glanced back. "I believe the scar-faced one is

safely occupied, but the man who stepped forward for you follows. Should we lose him in the crowd?"

"No," Claire said. "We are together."

"Ah," the woman said. "I thought as much. Pity."

Claire looked up.

The woman smiled. "Don't worry Mistress. I have a bad habit, among many I'm afraid, of thinking out loud. Since I said I would deliver you to your destination, tell me where it is and I will see you safe, then be on my way."

"But why? Why step in when I am but a stranger to you? Not that I'm not grateful . . ."

The woman chuckled. "Why indeed," she said. "God's truth, I hardly know myself Maybe because it's been a profitable market for us, maybe just to amuse, and maybe, because I was once a stranger here and in need of a friend. And partly out of curiosity, too. You were rather a lost soul yesterday and now you're here again, but much changed in dress. I'd hear your tale, but better we work our way to wherever it is you want to go. My brother may not be overlong." She laughed again.

"I don't know where to go," Claire said, and felt tears begin to form.

The woman frowned.

Claire shook her head. "We meant to buy something to eat," she said. "And then what, I don't know."

The woman looked at Claire more closely. "You look pale, and seem today, to have a reason to keep up your strength. I'll take you to the place with the finest meat pies in Mellifont. They do delight the tongue."

How much coin did Hugh have left? Claire flushed. "I believe we must watch the cost."

The woman looked behind them and back again at Claire. "Sometimes, I suppose," she said, "it's best not to be too curious." She sighed. "I'll take you to another place then. I buy from there myself frequently and have no complaint. They make a good pie for the price."

The stalls of the bakers and food vendors were alongside

each other, jointly advertising with smells of freshly baked bread and pies. When they stopped at a large stall, Claire looked back. The scar-faced man had disappeared and Hugh was about ten feet behind, trying to edge his way through the crowd. He nodded. She was pushed forward, coming to a stop at the vendor's table. When she turned back, her escort had disappeared.

"Here, Mistress," the vendor said, "look lively now, I'm a busy man." He shoved a pie at her.

She looked around, trying to find out who he was talking to.

"Hold out your hand."

Confused, she held her hand out, as if to shake his. He shook his head, turned her hand and placed a pie in it.

She opened her mouth.

He held out the second. "Take this one as well. It's paid for and I'm an honest man."

She stood bewildered, a warm pie in each hand.

"Next!"

A large woman nudged her, then took her place at the table. Claire stepped back, holding her pies above the crowd who jostled good-naturedly, all eager to fill the void.

She turned slowly, almost running into Hugh.

He grinned. "Should I ask how you managed that?"

She smiled. "You may well ask, but I don't know myself. It seems the woman who took me to the stall must have paid as well, but I have no idea why we merited such kindness." She held out a pie.

"Let's stand away from the crowd," Hugh said. "I mean to buy some cheese and bread, but I'd rather see the inside of this first."

She nodded. At the edge of the square, they found a shady spot. The crust gave way readily and the filling was warm and well-seasoned. Claire sighed when she finished; she had meant to give part to Hugh, who could probably have eaten two or three with no compliant, but each mouthful begged another. Several fingers were covered with pastry crumbs and brown gravy.

Hugh grinned and held out his hands. His pie had disappeared in a few mouthfuls and his fingers were clean. "Lick them as best you can," he said, "then you can use the corner of my tunic to finish the job."

She shook her head slowly, but smiled. As he watched, she tentatively licked one finger. Her face grew warm. She averted her head, then looked past him. "Do you see a good place to get some cheese?" she said. Her heart beat strangely. It seemed very quiet.

He turned towards the square. "No," he said. "I must pay better mind to my duty."

"I can have no compliant of that, Hugh," she said softly.

The muscles in his jaw contracted, but he remained silent. They both studied the market, while she hastily wiped her fingers on the hem of her skirt. Diagonally across the square were the cloth traders from the day before.

"I wager they'd not be so eager to show us their wares today," she said.

"My Lady?"

She nodded.

His eyes searched the crowd, then stopped. "If I had enough," Hugh said, "I'd buy some of the blue. The one the color of cornflowers. It would suit you well and since you've given the other away, it seems to me you'll need something else soon."

She blushed, then looked directly at Hugh. "My Lord Husband will be happy with this news at least," she said.

"Yes, My Lady."

She looked back at the cloth merchant and frowned. Amadee. William had loved that place but never spoke of it. That made no sense. "William was there for a summer once."

"Where?"

She nodded. "On his tour."

"I believe you must be mistaken," Hugh said. "His father and King Ulric were at odds with one another. I believe one felt the jilted suitor, but I don't know the details, or who lost the contest. Owain would have never allowed his son the visit."

"I must be mistaken." But was she? Who then was Aldwin and why did his name come to mind? Aldwin of Amadee. There was no one near to hear her. "Who followed Ulric, Hugh?"

"No one, he's still alive."

"Ah . . . has he sons?"

"One. Aldwin."

Aldwin. William had been there, but he never spoke of it. Who had? She tried to remember where she'd heard it. Not in the great hall. And it hadn't been from Ceonald . . . it was in Claire's own chambers.

"He's a bonny lad," William's mother, Adleah, had said, holding Richard not long after his birth. "He's very like his father. William had the same habit of fixing on your face as if he understood everything you said. T'was just yesterday it seems, and now he's a father and I a grandmother. The years go by too quickly, Claire. You must begin to make arrangements to foster him."

"Surely that's for the High King to arrange," Claire said. "My poor boy can't even support the weight of his own head yet, and you want me to plan on sending him away."

"Seven years go by quickly," Adleah said, "and there is much to be considered. It's not only who will train him to become a knight, but also who serves as foster brother with him. You can forge new friendships, mend fences, and disarm your enemies all at one time if it's done correctly. He may be the future High King, but in the need to be fostered, he's the same as any noble lad."

"I'm sure you're right," Claire said. "I'll speak to William about it." But she hadn't, or at least not successfully, the hunting had been exceptionally fine that year.

"And you must plan a tour for him," Adleah had added.

It hadn't been William that told her the story, but his mother. And he had visited Amadee at her urging, and kept it secret.

"Of all the people William met," Adleah said, "he formed the greatest friendship with Aldwin of Amadee. They have a bond now, as foster brothers, and William told me they swore a special oath of eternal friendship. Owain would not have cared for it, but it pleased me greatly."

Foster brothers and eternal friends. Her heart skipped a beat. "Let's resume a tour of the market, Hugh," she said. "We can get the cheese you spoke of and while we walk, hear what I have to say. I beg you, do no reject my idea until I have gotten it all out."

They began a slow circuit, moving ever closer to the traders from Amadee. Her plan came out a bit at a time, which suited her, since much of it was made up as they walked. When she was finished, she stopped. Hugh chose the closest stall to buy cheese, even though there looked to be a better place two tables down. He asked about every kind on the table, and then bought a small piece of the cheapest, much to the disgust of the merchant.

"I don't like it," he said, when they continued. "But I dislike it less than I do the alternative. And even though it's not without risk, it would be so unexpected that it has a fair chance of success. The risk is yours. If you choose to undertake it, I say yes."

Claire nodded. Her legs felt like they had when she first saw the black badge at Windrush, only now she had no Phoebe. Hugh might agree, but he would never push her into it. By the time they reached the traders from Amadee, they had worked out the details. She stopped and Hugh continued. He would find a place to watch from a distance.

"Good morrow to you," Claire said.

The cloth merchant nodded politely and sidled down the table, as his wife stepped into his place.

"Good morrow, Mistress," she said, keeping an eye on the crowd.

She was their only customer, but this was a far different greeting than yesterday.

"We spoke yesterday," Claire said, "perhaps you

remember."

The woman stopped watching the crowd.

"You showed me a lovely piece of blue."

Her stare missed nothing.

Claire blushed. "I wore a yellow gown," she said. "It had a fuller cut."

"Ah."

Her husband moved closer. "It has not sold, My Lady. The color is just right for you."

"It is not the cloth I came for," Claire said.

The two exchanged looks.

"My Lady?" the woman said.

"I've come to ask your help," Claire said. "I do ask, no beseech you, to allow me to go with you upon your return to Amadee, so that I may have private council with Aldwin, son of Ulric."

The man flushed and the woman grew pale. "My Lady . . ." she said.

Claire held up her hand. "Is he not an honorable man?" she said. "He did, once upon a time, swear an oath, and I would see if he will honor it. I cannot offer you recompense for your aid, but you have my word that I will seek to have such redress as is due you, paid, if not by Aldwin or Ulric, than by another who will also be beholden to you, but is not here to lend the weight of his word to mine."

"It's not that, My Lady," the cloth merchant said. "I am sorry . . ."

"Husband. Before you speak further, let us talk in private."

Claire pretended to debate between two small pieces of fabric. The merchant gesticulated; his wife shook her finger. He nodded in what seemed agreement; she threw up her hands. She whispered in his ear and pointed. He stared. Claire smoothed her tunic over her rounding belly. Hopefully that helped argue her case.

It was the wife who spoke. "We are part of a larger party," she said, "and all must be agreed, but my husband is the Master Weaver, and his say will have an influence. We will both speak in favor of it."

"Can you be ready by midday?" he said. "We want to leave no later than that."

"I'm ready now," Claire said.

"Very well," he said. "Come back then."

"I've no place to go," Claire said. "I can wait in the cathedral if you wish, but I'd rather not."

The weaver's wife nodded. "Come around to this side of the table then, if you like."

Claire hesitated. "Before I do, I must in faith tell you that I believe that whatever happens between Aldwin and me, he will not fault you for your kindness. There are others though, here in Elstow, in this very city, who would seek to stop you if they knew, and you must understand there is some danger."

The two looked at one another. The weaver shrugged. "Life is dangerous," he said, "but that might sway the others."

Claire nodded. "It's only fair that they know. There's one other thing. You may call me by any name of your choosing, but I cannot divulge my true identity until I've spoken to Aldwin."

"That's a small matter," the weaver said. "Pick your own name if you like."

"Best decide it now," his wife said. "I think it's better to keep this part betwixt the three of us. No sense making things more complicated."

Claire smiled. "I will be Phoebe then," she said.

The number of shoppers dwindled, but the crowd increased. If this market fair was like those at Ambridge, the day would increasingly be given over to entertainment and revelry. It was harder than she thought to find Hugh in the milling sea of people. When their eyes met, he nodded to his left. The scar-faced man would soon reach the weaver's table.

"I think I must leave," Claire said.

"Be ye ill, Mistress Phoebe," the weaver's wife said.

"No." Claire turned her back to the crowd. "There's a man coming this way I do not want to meet with."

"Who, Mistress?" the master weaver said.

The one with the scar! She bit back the words before they could out. "I do not know his name," she said.

He studied her face, as if the man's reflection might still be there, and looked at the crowd. "I could manage by myself, wife," he said finally. "You can go on ahead."

Claire resisted the temptation to look again at Hugh; she had no desire to see how close the other one was. The weaver's wife led her into a part of the city she had not seen. To her surprise, they continued through one of the gates to a large encampment. A few people lingered here and there, but for the most part it was empty. At the far edge, two horses stood tied next to a merchant's wagon. The weaver's wife pulled aside the cloth covering the back of the wagon. "Best wait in here," she said.

CHAPTER TWENTY-THREE

Not only was the wagon smaller than the one in the Brightwood, most of it was filled. The weaver's wife pushed one barrel back and turned one basket, leaving just enough room to shove two smaller bundles between a basket and a crate. "There," she said. "That's better."

And it was. Claire rolled her cloak into a pillow for her back and climbed into the wagon. With only fear to comfort her, the silence was worse than the heat. Her plan was daring, Hugh said as much. Her plan was ill conceived, born of desperation, and Hugh's reluctant consent now seemed more designed to please her than true agreement. Worse yet, like her supposed arrangements for her children, they had devised no backup. If the weaver couldn't convince his party to include her, how would she find her way to the rendezvous place where Hugh was to wait for word from Amadee? She should have asked him to wait until he was sure she'd left. If the weaver succeeded, and if Aldwin agreed to help her, would his oath of more than a decade, induce him to send an escort for her children, or had she abandoned them to their fate, just as she'd been abandoned? The man with Cedric's badge. What was he doing in Mellifont? She shivered.

Slivers of sunlight pierced the darkness where the flap did

not quite meet, and like glowing cinders, radiated heat. Removing the wimple didn't help and Claire reluctantly put it back on. The sunshine might be cooler. She pushed the edge of the flap and peeked outside. The weaver's wife was gone.

Across from the wagon, a burly man wrapped his arms around a barrel and hefted it on to a cart. Claire lowered the flap back into place. We're part of a larger group the weaver said, but was he one of the party? From mountain to marshland and forest to shore. Claire touched her brooch, felt William's ring against her breastbone and leaned back. When the wagon lurched and began to creep out of Mellifont, she woke. A corner of the flap had been tied up and the weaver's wife walked behind the wagon, smiling.

"We don't go far, today," she said. "It's too hot to travel too long and there's a nice grove of trees and a stream ahead."

Claire waited, but the weaver's wife was apparently not one for gossip and there would be no report of the discussion about whether or not to include Claire. No report of what went on in the market after she left. An early stop, and Thomas of Jarrow on the hunt. "That will be nice," Claire said.

The weaver's wife nodded. We can leave the flap as it is and be safe, but best not to raise it too much more today," she said. T'would be best if you not meet with the group until after tomorrow's travels. My husband has discussed your presence with all concerned, and has given out that you are exhausted and must rest. Tomorrow two groups will split off and go their own ways. After that, it will be just family. The cart behind us is my brother, then my daughter's husband after that, and then some cousins."

"What explanation did he give for my presence, that I am to be hidden away?"

"Only that you were a young woman, on your own and in trouble, and that you hoped to return to your home, before your time. And that he thought you were loath to appear in public until you knew your parents would give you welcome, because you did not want to shame them."

Claire flushed. She had not thought she was to play a harlot.

The weaver's wife smiled. "In affairs of the heart, things don't always go as we hope or plan, and there's been many an early birth after a marriage. Some would judge your 'situation' harshly, but I'll wage more would understand – the women anyway." She left Claire and walked at the side of the road away from the dust.

Every day was the same. The long-suffering horses did not complain, but the wheels groaned a protest as they rumbled over the parched grassland. The bright light of the unrelenting sun hurt her eyes, the darkness suffocated and the fear pressed against her, whispering in her solitude. After the first day, besides the weaver and his wife, the party consisted of six men, any one of whom might be the brother or the son-in-law, and four women, one of whom looked too young to be the weaver's daughter and the others too old. They rose early and were on the road before daybreak, taking only a few short breaks during the day and stopping only when the heat exhausted them all.

No one attempted to engage her in conversation and "Good morrow, Mistress," was as lengthy a dialogue as Claire heard. Still, they were polite, and although the women measured her with their eyes and whispered, they shared their meals willingly. That they kept their distance, so Claire was not forced to fabricate polite conversation, was welcome, still her face was stiff with politeness and she would have suffered a discourse to know what they said behind their hands. Had they met with the scar-faced man? What induced them to help her in the first place? Claire was afraid to ask.

A half day out of Cotterstock, they reached the foothills of the Kusshi Mountains where the shimmering brown grassland gave way to bright meadows, pungent pine and proud fir, their green, peaceful after the Elstow. Their pace slowed as the grade increased and the cooler air brought relief. The breaks lessened, but increased in duration, and occasionally Claire joined the group, walking beside the wagon. As much as she tried though, she could not match their pace and soon went back.

When the wagon stopped midmorning on the fifth day, the master weaver pointed. "This valley," he said, "is Amadee. By nightfall, we'll be to Siftdun Castle. Like as not there'll be quite a crowd. Mellifont is not the only summer market and it's custom, you see, for all of us to stop on the way back to see how everyone fared, doing a little trading amongst ourselves and pay the tax man." His eyes twinkled. "Bit of a celebration before the work of harvest." He turned serious again. "In the old days, King Ulric himself would be there, riding the camps with a glad word for everyone and catching up on the news. These past years, it's more likely to have been Prince Aldwin." His face dropped. "This year . . . I don't know, but there'll be somebody who'll know where the King is."

It was the most anyone had said in days. She nodded.

"There's a nice stream up ahead with some good size pools."

Did he mean to fish? "Indeed," she said.

"The road is very dry this time of year."

"It is."

"Dusty, you might say,"

"You might."

"Well, we could stop if you like," he said, "there's places you'd have privacy and the woman folk could make sure you're not disturbed."

"Stop?"

He reddened. "No matter, My Lady."

"You mean so I can wash off the dust?"

He nodded.

It would not repair to rip in her tunic, or ease the fabric, but her hands were stained beyond recognition and no doubt her face was no better. Claire smiled. "That is an excellent idea."

At their next stop, the weaver's wife pulled a bundle from one of the carts and led her down a grassy path to a winding creek. At the creek's edge, Claire hesitated. There was a pool of sorts, but no vegetation on either bank and unless she was mistaken, the water was no deeper than her knees.

The weaver's wife beckoned. "The men'll have a bit of a splash here," she said. "There's a better spot upstream."

She was right. The pool was deeper and the water crystal clear. Tall trees lined both banks, offering a fair amount of privacy and the dappled light played with the currents. Claire pulled her surcoat over her head and looked around. Not completely private. She stripped off the remaining tunic, leaving her chemise on; she'd wash it as she washed herself. It would dry quickly in the sun.

"Mistress Phoebe." The weaver's wife held out her hand.

So, the weaver's wife would be lady's maid. Claire took off her wimple, handed her the garments, then sat on the bank and began to unbraid her hair. Her gown would still be dirty, but she, at least, would be clean.

The weaver's wife draped the clothing over her arm. "Beg pardon, Mistress."

Claire paused. "Yes?"

"I hope you'll not take offense, but this is in need of more than a shake."

Claire smiled. "I can't take offense at the truth, Mistress Weaver," she said.

"We discussed it amongst us," the weaver's wife said. "Plain and simple, you'll never get King Ulric to see you dressed like that. Tis a pity you don't have the yellow, but that's as it is and naught to be done."

Claire paused. "I will not need to see the King, only Aldwin."

"Aye." The weaver's wife sobered. "But, well, we voted on it, and decided best to do somewhat to help." She laid Claire's clothing on the grass and unfolded her bundle. In addition to a fawn colored under-tunic and a blue over-tunic made from the cloth Hugh had admired, there was a new chemise. "The fabric's ours, you see. Ours to do with what we will."

Claire blinked in the sunlight, and tried not to cry.

"Best hurry. There may be others along before you know it."

Just as Claire slipped into the water, one of the women bustled up with a pot of soft soap, then hurried on upstream. For all it was summer, the water was cold, so Claire did not linger and dressed quickly when she was done. The whispers were forgiven, the women's close scrutiny paid off and the garments fit as well as if they had marked off the measurements. They must have cut the fabric by moonlight and stitched it by turns on the wagon seat. Claire divided her hair and braided each section, then wrapped one braid into a circle crowning her head and looped one at each ear. When she returned to the wagon, Claire knew her reflection was accurate and she'd undergone a transformation. The weaver's wife bobbed, blushing and beaming. "Oh, My Lady!" The weaver harrumphed an I-told-you-so and stood proudly as if he alone was responsible. In a sense, he was.

Claire looked at each. "I cannot tell you," she said, "how much I appreciate your kindness. This gift did bring me close to tears." Her voice quivered and she coughed. "It is only a small part for which I'm grateful. I don't know what brought you to help me, save it be from true charity, but I would ask one final favor."

The weaver's eyes narrowed and he pretended not to notice that one of his neighbors elbowed another.

"I ask," Claire said, "that from the moment we part, you do endeavor to forget me and to never speak about these days, save only to King Ulric or Prince Aldwin. The consequence to me and mine, of even one mislaid word, even long after this child is born, may have grave effect. But as I ask this, I tell you that I will not forget what you have done, and when the day comes that it is safe to speak, or events have taken such a turn that it no longer matters, I will speak of it and endeavor to thank you as best I can."

The weaver relaxed. All wore nodding smiles.

"Best be going," the weaver said, ending the festive moment.

When the wagon stopped again, the weaver's wife lifted the flap. "We be at Siftdun, My Lady. Best stay where you be, if you will. It's almost dark. T'will be safer then."

"Can you leave the flap open a little?" Claire said, but she had disappeared. It was just as well. Claire slipped off the chain Ceonald brought her in the Soddenwood and put William's ring on her right forefinger, then wove the chain through the braid around her head.

"My Lady?"

It was the weaver. Apparently, there was no need to whisper. "Yes," she said.

He helped her from the wagon and stood open-mouthed. A waning moon lit the encampment and the ring glimmered in the moonlight, as must the gold circle on her head. Next to the weaver, a fresh-faced squire with an unfamiliar badge held the reins of two horses.

"King Ulric does comman . . . the King wishes to see you," the squire said.

"I asked to see Sir Aldwin," she said.

He and the weaver exchanged looks. "Yes, My Lady. Do you ride?"

She pulled her cloak close and fastened the brooch, then swung neatly into the saddle. The days on horseback had their effect; William would have been surprised to see it. Across the encampment, small figures danced by the bonfire and a late arrival raised a trail of dust as he approached. The squire took her reins and led her away from the gathering. She turned back into the darkness, pulled the cloak's hood against the moonlight and sat very straight in the saddle.

Their path curved over a low hill and back again toward Siftdun. Near the gates, but far enough away to escape the noise and smell of the city, a large tent had been erected and a half dozen smaller tents circled the larger, their campfires smaller echoes of the earlier bonfire, without the levity. "The King is there," the squire said, pointing.

The camp had a relaxed feel, so there appeared to be no enmity between Ulric and the lord of Siftdun. When they reached the largest tent, a small boy ran out and when they had dismounted, trotted off with both horses. The squire disappeared into the tent, then held open the flap and beckoned.

Rush mats covered the ground, and a dark ornate desk sat in the middle. A thin-lipped man was seated behind it, his shock of silver hair in argument with dark, whiskered brows. Two chairs sat in front of the desk. He appraised her openly, and there was both curiosity and anger in his stare. No man at Ambridge would dare look at her so.

Her face grew warm. Claire pushed back her hood and inclined her head slightly. She may be supplicant but she was also the High Queen.

A tonsured monk, who had not suffered overmuch from fasting, leaned forward out of the darkness and whispered a few words.

Ulric frowned. "You," he said, "are not who you pretend to be."

"I do not pretend to be any one person in particular," Claire said. "I do admit to be pretending to be someone other than who I am."

"So then, who are you?" the monk said.

"I've had a long journey," she said, "and I would prefer to sit." Standing had been a relief, but she had a point to make. Ulric frowned. Claire turned. The squire stood behind her. "The chair on the left will do," she said, "but I fear it's in a draft. Pray be so kind as to move it a foot to the left."

The squire's eyes widened. He looked past her, then hurried in. The chair was not exactly where she'd specified, but close enough. She unfastened her cloak and let it fall, then stepped across it, sat down and arranged her skirts.

"You take great liberties with my furniture," Ulric said.

"And with the King," the monk said. "State your business."

"My business is with Sir Aldwin," she said, "and my words for him are private."

"Aldwin is dead," the monk said.

The blood rushed from her head and she pressed her hands together. "I didn't know," she said. Prayed she wouldn't faint.

Ulric leaned forward, his face mottled. "And that's all? You claim to have known him, to lay some claim on him and that's all you can say?"

"But I never met him," Claire said. "Nor did I claim to. If you were told so, it was in error."

Ulric pointed. "Then that is not his?"

Claire kept her hands from going to her rounding belly, but her face flushed. "There has been a grave error, My Lord," she said, "and save if it were not for that, I would countenance my lord husband to challenge any man who dare say so."

"You claimed Aldwin swore you an oath," the monk said, "or is the weaver mistaken?"

"I spoke of an oath, but it was not to me. I can reason, though, that the weaver might have deduced incorrectly."

Ulric stood. "I need hear no more," he said. "If it's charity you seek, Wido here is the man for it."

"Sire," Claire said. "I came to ask your son's help. I do ask it now in his name and in his memory and I do request a private audience." Had William's mother told her anything that might give him reason? She'd said he was a fine horseman and had a hint of the old ways. No, the monk behind him bespoke that. Or did it? "You are my only hope," she said.

"Your hope, Mistress," the monk said, "is in the Almighty, and you would do well to beseech him."

There was a look of irritation on Ulric's face. "His Christian ways are too thin for my father's liking," Adleah had told her.

"In Amadee, I do appeal to both Kings," she said. The monk flushed and Ulric's eyes narrowed.

It was a delicate dance she'd begun.

"I am done with games," Ulric said. "There will be no private speech, I see no reason for it."

Thea. They had played their own games once, Adleah and Ulric, and he had called her Thea. "Sometimes a pretense is necessary, Sire," she said. "Sometimes it's only for pleasure, but you are right, I do digress overmuch. I come to you, because of my memories of a woman called Thea, whom I once did love, and whose memory did prompt me to think of Amadee."

Ulric stared.

"The King has said all that's required," Wido said.

"No," Ulric said. "Leave us. We will hear her, and then we'll decide."

The monk sidled toward the tent flap.

"Now."

He scurried out.

"You, boy," Ulric said. "See that no one disturbs us, and no one hears what we speak."

The squire bowed and backed from the tent.

"What of this Thea, then?" Ulric said, hard-eyed.

"More than a score of years ago," Claire said, "a woman you once called Thea did send her son to you and he did stay some months in Amadee."

"Perhaps."

"Her son and yours did forge a true friendship beyond that of foster brothers and did swear to each other an oath of eternal friendship."

"Aldwin, is not alive to confirm or deny it, and even if it was true, his oath does not bind me."

"William, King of Bridland, High King of Threbant, can vouchsafe for its veracity," she said. "But it was not from him that I heard it, but from his Lady Mother, Queen Adleah."

Ulric rubbed his chin. "You," he said slowly, "are Queen Claire."

She held out her hand. "The seal you may know. This ring is all I have as proof of my identity."

"You do not need it," Ulric said. "I believe you. There has been such a hue and cry to discover you that its echoes rang even here. The High King did send out such men as he could spare to search along the Oberon, but you had vanished. I did hear that once his search was mounted, another one began as well."

Cedric. Claire shuddered.

"Yes. You did well to escape that net."

Of their journey before Mellifont, she told him only what she'd told Gregory, but she left out nothing of what had transpired in Mellifont, save that she did not say who left the city in their place.

Ulric sat quietly after she finished. "So," he said, "you trust me more than Gregory."

"No," she said. "I trusted in Aldwin's oath and his friendship to William, and thus sought his help. I do not know if you will deliver me, or deliver me to Cedric. I can only pray that if you do, you will not betray my children unto him as well."

He picked up a quill and played with it, pulling the feather through his fingers. "I should not like to make war with Cedric," he said.

"You are of like mind with Elstow, then," she said.

He put the quill down. "I will not send an escort into Norvik."

She stood. "I see. Perhaps you can give me the use of a middling horse if I am to make my own way, or does that offend your sense of what you might be willing to do?"

"And where would you go?"

"First, back to my children."

"And then?"

"I am no mouse, king cat," she said. "I don't know what I am to do, but rest assured, I will do what I can."

His eyes twinkled. "It is not often that I am abused to my face by the very person who has so recently asked for my assistance."

"And was declined."

His brows arched. "No indeed, Your Grace. I only said that I would not send men into Norvik. I did not say that I would not help. It's a poor plan, that's all."

"I can assure you—"

"It's a brave plan, and I like it better than Gregory's idea of staying in Mellifont, especially if, as you say, he meant to deceive you."

"You mistake my words, Sire," Claire said. "I only meant

that we believed we were followed, and that the one who followed us was from Gregory's court, and close to the King. I do not accuse him or anyone, only say that it had the appearance of some untoward movement that went against our understanding with him."

"It is very close to the same thing."

"It is, but it is not the same. In truth, as I stand here, I tell you that I do not know what to believe, except that I was afraid to trust in his help, especially since Cedric is his wife's nephew."

"But surely you knew that."

She flushed. "I did not, nor do I even now recall hearing it. Gregory himself mentioned it, else I would not know it now." She sniffed and dabbed at the corner of her eyes.

Ulric stood and leaned forward. "Nay, nay. Dinna cry, My Lady." he said. "In truth, I will help you, but it must suit me as to the plan. I cannot send an army across Elstow, and you would need that to reach Denholm. Besides, my men would not know the way through the Muchelneys."

"But . . ."

"Even if you reached it safely, the High King would have no choice but to split his force and send men north to protect you, and if he does not, Cedric has only to make a feint in your direction and it will force the High King's hand. Once William's army is split, Cedric can . . . Well, it would have been a different matter altogether if it had been planned in advance. In a well-fortified place, well provisioned, with a small force known to be loyal, unlike Gregory's men who must obey their King and have no allegiance to the High King, you could have withstood a siege while the High King did battle and did rout his enemy. It's too late for that, to my way of thinking."

Claire sank down. "Is there no hope then?"

"Aye," Ulric said. "Until the High King has prevailed, you must continue as you have, living in secrecy. That is your best defense, and Amadee is a place well suited to harbor secrets."

"Then you will help?" The tears this time were real and not so easily checked.

Ulric came over to her and reached out tentatively as if to pat her on the shoulder. "You have spoken true that Aldwin and William forged a bond. He often spoke of the visit and wished it could be returned."

The next morning, the traders woke to find King Ulric had broken camp and left Siftdun. Few wondered at his absence, the surprise had been in his arrival.

CHAPTER TWENTY-FOUR

In spite of the approaching darkness, Hugh urged his horse forward. The mare stumbled frequently now, turning apologetically to look at him, perhaps asking if now he would be willing to slacken the pace.

"A bit more," he whispered. They were both tired and a less stouthearted horse would have flagged long before now. He had hardly slept in days, but he meant to reach the flanks of the Mullendown hills before he rested.

It had been two weeks since he'd reunited the High Queen with her children, leaving them at a small monastery in the foothills of the Kusshi Mountains, just inside the border of Amadee. The High Queen had changed in the three weeks since he'd seen her at Mellifont, her pregnancy unmistakable now. Although she smiled, her face looked drawn, and if it had been up to him, he'd have ridden for the Soddenwood and Breona first.

Instead, he had ridden further into Amadee. Armed by Ulric, and given a better horse and a sword, he had crossed the Kusshis through a secret pass into Bridland. Cedric's army was said to be assembled south of the Brightwood, somewhere near the Falkirk River, while William's was now thought to be just north of the Mullendowns or perhaps still camped there.

Hugh crossed the Oberon just above Ambridge and rode east. He meant to follow the Merry River into the Mullendowns and come up behind the High King's army. After having negotiated the Kusshis, a stranger might assume the hills of Mullendown to be of little consequence, but Hugh knew they held their own secrets.

He heard the Merry before he saw it. When he reached the river, he let the horse have a taste and urged her on. The ground began to slope upward and the terrain grew rockier until finally, he came to the Ruins. Two tall monoliths marked the entrance, silhouetted by the moonlight against a dimming sky. It was said that ancient runes were carved at the tops of the rocks, but that anyone finding them would be rendered senseless, so as to keep their secrets. Perhaps Ceonald knew what they said, but even he never spoke of it.

The horse shied, refusing to pass between them, but Hugh urged her on, into the giants' rubble, rocks that towered over Hugh even on horseback. The river, and the path beside it, were constricted into an ever-narrower channel until finally, the path was blocked. Hugh clucked to the horse and urged her forward. She hesitated at the bank, then stepped hesitantly into the water. He dismounted. She was a good horse, but she was tired and didn't know, as he did, that a firm ledge lay under the water for about a hundred yards, long enough to bypass the obstruction. Keeping her on a short lead, he led the horse upstream, patting her encouragingly on the neck. They fought the current and the cold, but finally, the ledge climbed up out of the water. When they reached a small patch of grass a few hundred feet upriver, he put a soft hobble on the horse and leaned against a rock.

When he woke, the morning dew had already dried. Hugh untied the satchel on the back of his saddle and pulled out the blue tunic Breona sent, by way of the Abbess Maud. He stripped and pulled it on. By the Saints, he was glad to be wearing William's badge again. Divided into fourths, each quadrant of the field represented one of the four kingdoms. Two diagonal fields were white and the others a pale blue. An oak leaf was stitched in gold thread over the whole field, the leaf a sign he was from Bridland, and the gold that he was of the High King's household.

By mid-day, he'd left the Ruins behind, and traversed through the heart of the Mullendowns, riding over the hills, rather than keeping to the valleys, in search of the High King. At the top of one, he spied the encampment below. Just beyond, lay the Falkirk River. Hugh rode slowly, letting his horse pick the way. A sentry above him whistled, and two riders thundered up from the valley. He pulled up and waited. One of the two was Percival.

"Name yourself," the other said. He was from Norvik, by his badge. Percival remained silent.

"I am Hugh of Tintagel," he said. "In service of the High King."

"Give the word."

"God save King William," Hugh said, "but I do not know the word to pass."

The stranger's sword leapt out of his scabbard. His horse lunged forward. The blade rested an inch from Hugh's neck.

Hugh flushed. "God's blood!" he said. "Hold up. I have been away these many months and only now return. If Percival here does not know me, I know him."

Percival grinned. "So, Hugh," he said, "you're no ghost then."

"Do I look like a blasted apparition!"

Percival signaled and the sword came down. "Andrew of Blanblow, meet Hugh of Tintagel."

Andrew touched his sword to his forehead. "My Lord."

Hugh nodded.

"It's a good thing you held steady, Hugh," Percival said. "Andrew takes this business seriously."

"No more than Percival, here," Andrew said. "It's just that it was my turn to greet a visitor."

Percival nodded. "I'll ride into camp with you." He looked past Hugh. "Are we to expect anyone else?"

Their eyes met. Hugh shook his head.

"He seemed a bit eager with the blade," Hugh said, when he and Percival were alone.

Percival grinned. "He's a good man. I had you spotted, but I admit I didn't know you myself for a bit, probably because I'd given both you and Stuart up for dead."

Hugh nodded. "I'd silence your sentry," he said. "It'd be easy to fix his place."

"Oh that. You were spotted some miles back and watched all along the way. If you'd been one of Cedric's vermin, you'd never have gotten this close and would have had a more silent greeting. As it was, you wore William's badge and aroused curiosity."

Hugh clapped Percival on the arm. "How goes the war, Percival? I've been out of touch these months and have heard nothing but rumors and lies. I even heard that William had been defeated at Grafton."

"We very nearly were, Hugh," Percival said quietly. "Cedric got a good part of his army behind us and nearly closed the trap. Then, for some reason known only to Cedric, and probably to the devil, he withdrew from the field. It was a draw at best."

"I must speak to the King," Hugh said.

Percival shook his head. "I doubt he'll see you today. He's been in conference these past two days and it's just broken up. I suspect you've arrived just in time for some blood sport, my friend."

"Then I must see him today, at all costs," Hugh said, and it was as easy as asking. The High King was pacing his tent, dictating to a scribe seated at a small writing table, when Hugh was announced. Physically William looked fit, he was always a man who thrived on days in the saddle, but the ready smile was absent and his eyes dull. Hugh bowed.

"Hugh of Tintagel," William said, smiling thinly. "We did not believe our ears at first, when your name was announced. We had not thought to see you this side of hell, but you are welcome, even if you're sent from the devil himself. You are long overdue. I would have the reason, but I've had Percival's report and that is sufficient for now. Save that you know something of Cedric's army, keep your story for another day. Where's Stuart? Looking to your horses? You're hardly one without the other."

"A word in private if you please, Sire."

"There's no need Hugh. Percival brought the boy back and I've heard his tale. You did what you could and I have not the heart to speak of it further. Leave us in peace now, but come again in the morning as we ride out to meet Cedric. You will ride with me."

Hugh did not move. "I must insist, Sire," he said. "I've been gone these months and owe you the reason."

"Very well." William sighed. "We will speak of it once and then it will truly be dead. Do we wait for Stuart?"

Hugh glanced at the scribe. "Stuart is dead, Sire. Killed on the Oberon, near to Breaham."

"Breaham! That was far north of your goal." William raised his hand. "Say no more, Hugh. The tent walls seem much closer to their neighbor as late. Let us ride out from camp and you must begin again and tell us all."

When William reined in his horse, Hugh began. "We found ourselves escort, Sire, to a woman and her children. Late the widow of a cloth merchant, or so she would say."

"By the Heavens, Hugh, is it true! Children too you say? All safe of life and limb?"

"Safe enough. We were attack without cause, Sire, and two of the boys injured. Richard has already shed the effect of the injury and the other is mending well. My Lady was ill, but thanks to time and the care of Breona of the Soddenwood, has grown much stronger." Hugh chuckled. Grown indeed. "I am charged with many messages, Sire, but must start with the first. My Lady bid me to remind you of her efforts to stay in her home."

William reddened. "Even from a distance she does chide me, but the mark is well met."

Hugh paused. To be messenger between husband and wife was difficult enough, but to be messenger between this husband and this wife was as hard a task as he'd found. He had sworn to the King, but now, would lay down his life for either. "I do not know the full meaning of her words, Sire," he said, "but they were said without malice. I am charged to tell you that first, and then to say, that if you would see her now, you would find her much changed."

"How changed, Hugh? Was the illness a pox? Quick man answer . . . no it is of no mind. No illness can change her beyond my care."

"My Lady grows as she grows stronger, Sire." Hugh motioned. "By the new year, you and she will count five where once four would answer."

"By the Saints! And she is well? Good, good. And safe with Lady Breona? That's a good a news as I have heard these many months."

"She was both safe and well when last we met, Sire, but no longer with Breona. There is much more to tell."

When they rode back into camp, men nudged their neighbors and Hugh did not blame them. The High King sat straighter, and although his face was still sober, looked around him with an air of enthusiasm that had been absent on his departure.

"Mind trim them well," William called to one man, who had arrows laid out neatly on the grass. "Give your arm a good rest tonight," he called to another, who had just launched one spear at a target, and was reaching for another.

"Rest yourself, Hugh," William added. "Percival will fit you out. Heaven willing, this time tomorrow, Cedric will be dead. You and Percival will ride in my company."

"I am honored, Sire, and at your disposal. I have only the one thing that we spoke of left to do this day."

"Let it wait, man, you're near to dropping."

"I don't want him to see me and say something he shouldn't," Hugh said. "If I have your leave?"

William shrugged. "After tomorrow, it will not matter."

"But today it does."

"As you will then, Hugh. It's your idea, and I trust your

judgment in the matter."

Hugh rode to the kitchen tents. News had traveled fast, and the cook came out personally to greet him. "I am Hugh of Tintagel," he said. "I'm told you have a kitchen boy named Jeremy."

"Yes, my lord."

"I require his service this day."

"As you will, My Lord," the cook said bowing. "Jeremy!"

The boy was taller than Hugh remembered, and thinner in the face. The patched tunic had been replaced by the High King's livery.

"You are to attend, Sir Hugh," the cook said, "until he has no further need of you."

"Can you ride, boy?"

"No." The boy wore a cautious look.

"But I'm told you can keep to the back of a horse."

Jeremy nodded.

"Then climb on." Hugh held out his hand.

Jeremy looked around.

"Don't stand there gaping like you've got a head filled with sausage, boy," the cook said. "Do as you're told."

The encampment was lost behind the hillside when Hugh reined in. "This is as good a place as any," Hugh said. "Get down, boy."

Jeremy slid from the horse and stood with his hands to his side.

Hugh swung one leg over and jumped down. "Do you remember me, Jeremy?" he said. "Truth, now."

Jeremy nodded.

"And will you tell me now, what you refused to then?"

"No, My Lord."

Jeremy looked as ready to bolt as he had in the Brightwood. "But you told King William."

"It was his right to know."

"But not mine?"

Jeremy was silent.

"But you know my role in the matter, do you not?"

"Yes, My Lord, I do now."

Hugh smiled. "Good boy, you do well to keep your secret close. We will not speak of it, nor of where I've been. If someone asks, say only that I was in service of the King. Understand?"

Jeremy nodded, then flushed. "No, My Lord, I don't understand, not exactly."

"Good, lad, never lie to me."

"No, sir."

Hugh ruffled Jeremy's hair. "You've learned some manners since last we met, young Jeremy. Tell me, do you have a special affinity for kitchen work?"

"Affinity, My Lord?"

"Do you like it?"

Jeremy wrinkled his nose. "Not especially, but I do my best."

"So I was told. It seems, young Jeremy, that I find myself a knight in need of a page. You must have your ear to the camp, do you know anyone who might fit the job?"

"I know no one of high birth, My Lord."

"There are exceptions at times," Hugh said. "Perhaps now, you can think of someone."

"I do not know what is required of a page, My Lord, so do not know what name to suggest."

Hugh chuckled. "Let me tell you then, Jeremy. A page must be brave and must be truthful. He must learn polite manners and to serve his lord to the best of his ability."

Jeremy nodded.

"Then he must learn to ride and care for the horses and eventually to wield a sword so that he may defend his lord and his King. Courage, honor and honesty cannot be taught. Are you willing, Jeremy, to undertake the rest?"

"Me, My Lord?" Jeremy whispered.

"I can think of no one better. You're a bit old as most pages go, and I cannot promise that you will be knighted, but I'd be glad for your service."

Excitement lit Jeremy's face and disappeared as quickly.

"But the King told me to work in the kitchen."

"I'd not have spoken of it if I did not have his agreement. I would have spoken to your parents too, if I were able."

Jeremy looked down. "My father is dead. We found him along the road, like . . ."

An innocent unarmed man. And he was not the only one. Truly evil had been unloosed when Cedric put his foot in the stirrup. "The King tells me you witnessed the attack on Sir Herbert."

Jeremy looked up. "Yes, My Lord."

"It was more than likely the same men."

Jeremy nodded and swallowed.

"Herbert of Amesly was good friend to the King and to me as well." Herbert and Stuart and how many others? On the morrow, his sword would sing their names.

"And Queen Claire." Jeremy's eyes shone.

"Indeed, he was that," Hugh said. "I will swear an oath to you, lad. If it is within my power, I will see these men brought to the King's justice and they will answer for their crimes."

Jeremy nodded, solemn faced.

"That justice may be long in coming," Hugh said, "but I will not forget. My first duty though, is to the King's business. What say you lad, are you to be cook's helper or page?"

Jeremy knelt down. "I will do your biding, My Lord, and serve you as best I can, unto my life if it's required."

Hugh smiled. He was right, the boy learned quickly. Who knows, he might surprise them all and become knighted someday. "What was your father's name, Jeremy?"

"Giles, My Lord."

Hugh put his hand on Jeremy's shoulder. "Do you, Jeremy, son of Phoebe of the village of Lamberton, and son of Giles, late of the village of Lamberton, undertake this of your own free will?"

"Oh, yes!" Jeremy grinned, bright-eyed.

"Well then, we must get back to camp. I'm tired and hungry, so you have your first work to do in my service."

Once mounted, Hugh held out his hand and Jeremy

scrambled up.

"What about the cook?"

"I believe I heard him say that you were to attend me until I had no further need of you, did he not?"

Jeremy laughed. "He did so say."

"Then I'll drop you off at the cooking tent and you must tell him that I have need of you for these next few years, God willing."

"The King and Sir Percival had given you up for dead," Jeremy said.

Hugh glanced over his shoulder. "So, you're in the King's confidence. It seems I made a fortunate choice in a page."

"No. People in the camp say that he had," Jeremy said in a small voice.

"I'll be glad to hear what you've heard, Jeremy. In fact, your ears may catch what mine do not. But never confuse the source of the information when telling me. Sometimes it's as important as the information itself."

"I'm sorry."

Was there a quiver in his voice? Hugh was careful not to look. "Never mind, lad, there's a lot for you to learn. What say the camp of our Lady Queen and her children, Jeremy?"

"Some say that they are hidden away by magic."

"And the rest?"

"Most people think they're dead."

"And you?"

"I don't know. I thought they must of been, but now you're here, so I'm not so sure anymore."

"Never bring the subject up, Jeremy, or show overmuch interest if it is, but if any speak of it, I want to know what was said."

"Yes, My Lord."

"No matter how small or far-fetched it seems."

"I'll remember everything."

They rode in silence until they reached the camp. "Do you know where Sir Percival is camped?" Hugh said.

"There." Jeremy pointed.

Hugh recognized the standard. "I'll let you down here, lad," he said. "Run to the cook and tell him that you are to serve me and that I am monstrously hungry and require some providence from his kitchen."

Jeremy slipped off the horse and looked up. "My Lord?"

"Food, lad. I have not eaten this day."

The boy ran and Hugh turned toward Percival's tent. He'd need the loan of equipment and a warhorse come morning. He had just dismounted when the call came.

"To arms! To arms! Cedric is upon us!" The thunder of hoofbeats was heard to the north.

CHAPTER TWENTY-FIVE

Fat crumbling flakes drifted down and disappeared into the white and Claire pulled her cloak closer. Behind her, the baby began to cry and his wet nurse fussed over the cradle. He had not been named, nor had the other who had been washed, sewn into the small white shroud and sealed in an iron casket to sleep alone, in a dark place of Ulric's choosing. But both had cried, she was sure of it.

"Leave us," Claire said, but she knew the wet nurse wouldn't. Her prison was one of the tower rooms, the walls as empty as she was, her gown the same gray. It was meanly furnished, a small bed, a cradle, a pallet for the nurse, two chairs and a small table. Still, the fire was kept well fueled and only during the bitterest cold, when the wind screamed and scoured the hillside, did the hoarfrost creep along the walls. Claire reached through the narrow window opening and watched the snowflakes accumulate on her hand.

"Your Grace."

She pulled her hand back, but did not turn around. The wet nurse did double duty. Claire could not decide if Ulric really thought her mad, or merely wanted to drive her to it. If she worried about her sanity, did that mean she was still sane?

She circled the room, one hand trailing along the wall until she reached the fire, where she leaned over the cradle. The wet nurse stiffened. Claire continued her circuit and stopped again at the window, blinking back the tears. She had never held him. To be absolutely correct, she had no memory of holding him. The days since his birth were faded and dull, rubbed out by the gray and numbed by the cold.

She returned to the fire, forcing herself to walk across the room rather than along the wall, and sank into the empty chair. Careful to keep her hands in her lap, she leaned forward slightly and watched the baby. He was solidly built, with blue eyes and fine wisps of baby hair showing a hint of ginger in the firelight.

"Do you think his hair will stay that color, nurse?" she said.

The wet nurse started, her ruddy cheeks reddened further. She looked into the cradle as if she hadn't seen him every waking minute these past weeks. "I believe so, Your Grace."

Claire leaned back. "Of all my children," Claire said sighing, "he is the most like his father." Her eyes teared and for once, she did not walk back to the window. William had been routed at Falkirk, gained the field at Wythe, but was wounded and unable to finish the kill. Both armies had retired for the winter, Cedric to Windrush and William . . . William's army was last near Ambridge.

"Is there any news of the High King?" Claire said.

The nurse sat back and her face closed. "No, Your Grace."

Claire twisted the edge of her cloak. "Do you have children?" It was a stupid question. No, it wasn't, didn't the woman nurse her child? Claire was so tired; none of the other babies had been like this. "I mean aliv . . . I'm sorry. Perhaps I pry."

"Never mind, Your Grace."

They were the first kind words she'd heard since her confinement. A sob escaped and she covered her face with her hands.

"Nay, nay, dinna cry, Your Grace."

It seemed every choked back tear from these many months must now out. The wet nurse came over, rested on the arm of the chair and put her arms around Claire. "There, there, you mustn't take it so hard."

Her sobbing increased.

"Well then, have a good cry, deary, perhaps that's just what you need. I know I'd cry myself if I was you and that's for certain."

If she were mad, she would stab the nurse with her brooch and steal the baby. But she wasn't. Would it work? She cried anew.

When she woke, sunlight streamed in through the window. The wet nurse was feeding the baby and humming a low song. Whatever else she was, she was a good nurse.

"Good morrow, Your Grace."

It was the same every day, but today, instead of rolling away from the voice, Claire sat up. "Good morrow, nurse." Her voice still sounded shaky but today, at least, she could claim it as her own.

The wet nurse approved of it as well, smiling and nodding as she sat the baby up and began rubbing his back. The baby belched. Claire attempted a smile. "I'm hungry myself this day."

"As well you might be. You slept straight through your supper."

A key rattled in the lock. As the door swung open, Claire lay back down and turned toward the wall. The nurse was enough.

"Any change, nurse?" A deep voice, the court physician.

"No, sir. She is much the same."

Lies and more lies. He should know it from the wet nurse's voice.

"I'll not disturb her then," he said. "We must give it time."

Time for what? To eat at least, their breakfast had been delivered and she could smell the bread.

"Yes, sir."

"You will let me know if you need anything."

"Indeed sir."

"I'll check back in a few days." The door closed.

Claire should have said something, exposed the woman for the fraud she was, and freed herself from her jailer. But she was a good wet nurse. It was all very confusing. Claire sat up slowly. The wet nurse was already busy arranging the breakfast things on the table. As was usual, she kept out one portion for herself and ate after Claire finished. Only their drink was different; the nurse drank thick ale and a flagon of honey-colored wine was sent up daily for Claire.

"How did you sleep, Your Grace? It did not seem to me that you were quite as restless."

"No." The wet nurse did not deserve a better response. Still, she was right. For the first time in a long time, there had been no nightmares. No vision of William lost in a foggy wood, with black sores, some crusted, other split and oozing, and her mother following with gold coins instead of eyes.

Claire took her accustomed seat and held up her empty cup.

The nurse picked up the flagon, hesitated, hurried to the window and flung out its contents, then put her hand over mouth, as if surprised by her actions. "Forgive me, Your Grace. I should not have done that."

Had the physician some new torment? Claire turned her head, wishing the wet nurse would stop staring.

"You did not take your supper last night," the wet nurse said.

So, her wine was forfeit today? "No, as you say, I slept."

"I did a very wicked thing." The nurse's face was flushed.

"Wasteful perhaps, I don't call it wicked."

"No, not that," the nurse nodded toward the window. "Last night, very late, I was thirsty, and it seemed a shame to waste such fine wine . . . so, well, I had a little sip."

Claire shrugged. "It doesn't matter."

"It had a strange taste to my way of thinking."

Claire held up one hand, then dropped it. That a wet nurse should criticize the king's wine!

"I am no stranger to wine, Your Grace. Do you not think the wine has an especially bitter taste?"

"Yes. It must be the soil. Or, the way it's made."

"Or what was added."

Their eyes met. From then on, the wine was thrown out and they prayed for fresh snowfall. The restless pacing stopped, Claire's appetite improved and she slowly gained strength. While the wet nurse still kept a careful eye, Claire held the baby a little each day. On the morning of the fifth day, she was standing near the window when the key turned and the physician appeared. She watched him from the corner of her eye, pretending to watch the interminable snow.

He bowed. "Your Grace."

He was all solicitude, but must either be a poor physician to fail to see the cause of her illness, or must play a broader role. Was he ally or enemy?

"Little change, I see, Nurse."

"As you say, sir."

"She seems tractable. Does she eat and drink what is sent?"

Who poured the wine, Claire screamed silently. Who carries it here?

The wet nurse picked up the baby and pressed him to her breast. "I see she has what's required."

"Very good. Do you think she can comprehend me?"

"Indeed, sir, I do."

"Very well." He put his hands behind his back. "Your Grace, I am charged to tell you that King Ulric will return to the castle this day and does require to see you on the morrow."

Claire turned, staring.

"He is most anxious for a favorable report."

Was he? The physician had small beads of sweat on his forehead. What price did he pay if Ulric was not satisfied? And what would satisfy? Still, the prospect of a visit was not unforeseen. Would the nurse remember her role?

"If it please, sir?"

"Yes."

"She is hardly dressed in a manner to see the King."

"He will not mind."

"No, sir, as you say, but mightn't she? Might there be

something else more suitable?"

The physician squinted as if to see her better. "I'll see."

"And perhaps the young woman who came with her might help as lady's maid."

"You can't manage by yourself?"

"I was only after thinking the other might know better what was required."

"Hmmm . . . I will see about a better gown, but you'll have to manage by yourself."

Claire stifled a sob. The clean clothes were welcome, but she was desperate to know if her children were still in the castle and Ellen would have had the answer.

The dun and blue from Siftdun were returned, along buckets of warm water, a wooden tub and an invitation to dine with Ulric. After she's bathed, she dried her hair by the fire and the wet nurse helped braid it. Claire's arms tired easily and she contented herself with weaving the braids at the back of her neck. She finished just as the servant knocked at the door. By the time she'd walked down one flight of stairs, her legs were tired and after the second, shaking; she'd been prisoner overlong. Her escort led her to a small chamber. Ulric was alone, standing by the fire. She hesitated. There were three chairs at the table. Good.

"Sire."

He studied her carefully. This was ever a castle for scrutiny. "Your Grace."

She walked into the room.

"You do me honor by accepting my invitation to dine," he said, inclining his head.

She nodded in turn. "The flattery was in the invitation, Sire," she said. "I am afraid I was not myself, when last we met and I must give you explanation."

He scowled. "Your words were very clear. We require nothing further, but that does not preclude an obligation to me, as your host."

"Am I a guest with the courtesy of discourse, or am I prisoner?"

Again, the mottled face and tight jaw Claire had seen more than once. "You are no prisoner, Your Grace." He waved his hand toward the door. "You are free, if you wish, to leave at any time."

"Forgive me, Sire. Even as a child my father did chide me to mind my temper. I have perhaps been shut up too long for polite company."

"I have taken the liberty of asking one other," he said, frostily. "I am certain that you will not find his company repugnant."

She flushed. Had Hugh returned?

"Your Grace."

Claire turned. The bard bowed, smiling.

"Ceonald! You're a most welcome sight." She wanted to cry and laugh at the same time. Still, even with him here there was much to sort out. "What news?"

"Sire." He bowed to Ulric.

"You must sit here, Lady Claire," Ulric said, pulling out a chair. He chose the one opposite.

When Ceonald had joined them, Ulric said, "Ceonald is late from the High King and does assure me your lord husband is well."

Ceonald nodded.

"I assume," Ulric said through clenched teeth, "that he has some amount of private messages for you. I must reassure you that he, like yourself, is guest as long as you desire, so you will have ample time for conversation."

"The High King is most anxious for your health, My Lady. Sir Hugh did come to us at Falkirk, and the King has been most concerned about you and the outcome of your condition."

Had Ulric had not told him? She looked at her hands, raw from the window, then full into Ceonald's face. "The High King has another son. There was a girl child. She is dead."

"The table is not the place for things that cause distress. We will talk of other things," Ulric said.

The silence changed nothing. "I have not named the boy,"

Claire said, "as the High King did always wish to make that choice. I would mark the girl child's casket after my mother, if that is his want."

"I cannot think he would have objection," Ceonald said, "and I have come with a suggestion for a name if it were to be a boy. But what of yourself, My Lady? I'm told you've been ill."

She smoothed the blue wool and wished the touch would stop her legs from shaking. "A return, I believe," she said, "of the illness I had in June, brought on in no small part by the news Ulric brought me, of the battle at Wythe. I am much recovered."

"We must toast to your continued health." Ulric beckoned. A manservant carried in a tray, set a goblet in front of each and poured a ruby wine for Ceonald and Ulric. Claire's was already full.

Ulric raised his goblet. "To your health, Lady Claire."

Ceonald raised his and they both drank. "And yours, Sire," Ceonald said.

Claire sat silently.

The muscles twitched along Ulric's jaw. "Do you refuse my wine, or is it that the toast is not to your liking?"

"I would prefer the toast, if you drank from my goblet and I from yours," Claire said.

Ceonald gasped.

Ulric's face went white. He grabbed her goblet and swallowed. Flung the contents hissing into the fire, swept the other two from the table and stalked from the room. The servant hurried after his master.

"This is a bad business, My Lady," Ceonald said quietly.

"Indeed, it is," she said. "You are well come." She dropped her voice. "I did begin to fear that I would meet that same dark angel that did take my last born, and like her, wait eternity in an unmarked casket, gone from sight and thus from mind."

The sililoguioius bard was silent, his dark eyes more darkened.

"Well bard? Why look at me so? Did the King poison your mind against me, just as I am poisoned?"

"I understand you've been ill, Your Grace," Ceonald said gently. "Still, you do level a serious charge against Ulric."

"I level a charge against no one in particular, bard," she said, "only charge that the wine is drugged and further, that it is the cause of my illness, not the cure."

Ceonald shook his head slowly. "It seems to me that Ulric has done all he could to keep you safe. Two men from William did seek to find you and were repulsed. The King's acquaintance with my craft did give me access where others could not."

Claire folded her arms. "That only proves we are well hidden, but does not answer if we are really but helpless pawns in a scheme Ulric has yet to unfold."

Ceonald stood and paced slowly around the room. "You are still recovering, Your Grace," he said, "and should not distress yourself. If Ulric has some untoward purpose, he would not have let me to see you, even unto accompanying me himself."

She smirked. "Pray he will let you go as readily."

"Ulric does offer the best hope for your safety in these difficult times," Ceonald said. "The High King was delighted that you did devise this plan."

"You must not lecture me bard," she said, "or wear such a troubled brow. Have I not journeyed half the length and breathe of the four Kingdoms in search of such a place?" She sighed, looked down and said softly. "It does seem that the stars that aligned these dark forces are as fixed above me, as the north star in the heavens."

Ceonald pulled a chair close and sat down. "Breona always did say that the day seemed darker when you were unable to go out to greet the day."

"I wish she was here."

"I too, so that she may comfort you. She would tell you herself that she has prepared many a good medicine with foul taste and odd effect, but all to good end."

Claire shook her head. He refused to understand. "Her potions did bring gentle sleep, but this did bring the terror of darkness and did stupefy me when awake. Better fresh tears to wash away the sorrow than to seal it inside."

"The physician who sees to your care, did the same for Ulric's own Queen."

"She is long buried, so he must be glad for the employment."

He stared, and while she read frustration, she also saw worry. "I'm sorry, Ceonald. My tongue is over-sharp and it is well I'm shut away, lest I injure someone."

"It would seem you've been rather too near Ulric," he said.

She flushed. "In truth, Ceonald, there is too much truth in what you say for rebuke. I am not even sure how I came to offend him. I was taken ill before my confinement and he was all solicitude. I did not see him after that until they had wrapped my dead child in her burial cloth and laid her in her casket. He came then and did wait until they took her. After that, I remember his outstretched hand and that I did push it away, but nothing else."

Ceonald paled. "He did accost you?"

"No. He offered the cost of the ferryman, a gold coin for each eye, but I was so distraught, all I could think was that they were too large for the babe's eyes and besides, she had been taken from the room, so I did think that he meant that I was to die as well. I got hysterical. I may have said things. I might have screamed, truly I don't know, but ever after that he has been vexed, and until this day, I have been prisoner in a tower room, drugged each day and night. When I did ask for my children, they were, all save the baby, forbidden to me, so that all I know are platitudes and reassurances but not their true fate. By Divine Providence, some days hence I did come to suspect the wine and took care to throw it out through the window opening when the wet nurse was busy." The nurse had happily agreed to the lie.

"Only now, when I'm more myself," Claire said, "did I begin to wonder if I confused the sequence of events or did come to think wrongly of them."

The servant appeared with a tray of food, three new goblets and a flagon of wine. Setting it on the table, he said, "King Ulric is now otherwise occupied so will not rejoin you. He has said to tell you that he personally did taste and drink of everything on this platter, and I am to do the same in your presence."

"It's not necessary," Ceonald said.

He hadn't been there. Claire watched each piece that was sampled. When he was finished, the servant bowed and withdrew. Claire sipped her wine. "A better year, bard," she said.

"My art is not that of a statesman," Ceonald said, "but it seems I must fill the need. I would beg Your Grace, not to make the role more difficult."

"It seems the pain must out, even though it cause pain anew," Claire said. "I will try to curb my tongue, but grant me one wish, Ceonald, and consider that my fear does come from without and not within. Reflect on the King's actions. Ulric did not rush from the room by my insults, but from the taste of the wine. If you see only a rabbit in its warren, you do not see that danger that lurks for it in the forest."

Ceonald rubbed his chin. "I'm a man made to tell a tale and tell it well," he said. "Breona would do better than I to see to the heart of this matter, but I can see that there's much to consider."

"I can ask no more," Claire said, "and your words do breathe the promise of spring into this winter of my soul. I have waited over long, Ceonald. What news of My Lord husband? I did hear that he was wounded at Wythe. Is he much recovered?"

"He is better. Had he received the same wound before Hugh came to us at Falkirk, I must doubt the outcome, but now, with that happy news, the High King makes plans for spring in spite of his wounds. Wythe was well fought, and had he not been wounded, they would have carried the day."

Claire lifted her cup. "To a speedy resolution and

successful outcome. It will be good to be home." She traced a line on the table. "I know there must be some empty spots in the great hall. Herbert, Stuart . . ."

Ceonald took her hand. "At Falkirk, much as before, we were caught unaware and did must flee after some resistance, as the chance to group and fight was lost ere the battle began. At Wythe, the armies did meet fairly; the arrows did fly thick and the swords and lances and maces compete to see who was the most lethal. John of Ravenswood clings to life, even as I left, but has no arm to wield a sword for William. Ralf of Piermont was blinded and addled as well. There were many wounded, more than I can recount, but the number pales next to those who did die. Simon of Trenchton, Ian of Ardmont, James of Collinswood, with his brothers, Nathan and Peter . . ."

Each name a fresh wound. She shrank from the news but did not silence him. When he was finished, she pulled her hand away and folded them on her lap. "And Cedric's army?"

"We cannot count his wounded but did count many dead. They too have felt the sting of war."

"I would see William, Ceonald, before he rides again."

"It would not be safe, Your Grace."

"You must convey my wish to him in this regard."

Again, the piercing eyes, but it did not matter. Claire did not know herself why she felt compelled to go.

"First things first, My Lady. We must treat with Ulric and resolve this difference between you."

She smiled. "You are ever the optimist, Ceonald. I don't know how this may be remedied, although I agree to the attempt. We must decipher his intent so that we may act accordingly. And I must, at the least, be allowed to return to my children and Ellen, or they returned to me."

In the next room, Ulric lowered the tapestry hiding the small peephole and left the room.

CHAPTER TWENTY-SIX

Although Ceonald lingered with Claire over their supper, one might have thought they were strangers from the dearth of conversation. Still, it was a relief to spend time with someone from home, even if he did measure her words and weigh their reason. To Claire's surprise, when the meal ended, she was led to another part of the castle and up one flight of stairs, to a door guarded by two of Ulric's men. One knocked lightly, then pushed the door open.

The wet nurse curtsied and somewhere behind her, the baby fussed. Her escort held out a large key. "King Ulric has a key to this room and you are to have the other. He asks that for this night, at least, or until he does meet with you again, that you keep the door locked."

Her hand shook, as she took the key.

"The guards outside are for your protection. If you require anything, you have only to send the wet nurse or your lady's maid." Her lady's maid! He backed bowing from the room and the door swung closed. She turned the key. Ellen stood by the wet nurse, curtseying. The room swayed. Somehow Elspeth was on her lap and the little boys crowded close, talking, arms waving, jumping.

"Mistress Elspeth," Ellen said. "Do get down. Your Lady

Mother has been ill."

Elspeth threw her arms around Claire's neck and began to cry.

The tears and pandemonium were better medicine than any she'd had of late. She stroked Elspeth's hair. "It's all right, don't cry."

The sobs lessened, but the baby began to cry. Elspeth wiped her eyes, slid down and ran over to the cradle.

"What's his name?" Richard said.

"Can I play with him?" Elspeth reached over and tried to grab one of the baby's waving arms.

"Does he always do that?" Edward said. "He's worse than Elspeth."

Elspeth stuck out her tongue.

"How come he's all red?" James said.

The wet nurse threw up her hands. "Mercy! Let your poor Mother recover."

"You may all help," Claire said, "and watch to see that he is neither too hot nor too cold and when he begins to walk, you can watch to see that he doesn't go where he shouldn't."

"Are you better, now?" Richard said. He wore his worry face and stood a little behind the others.

Claire held out her hand. "I don't yet have all my strength, but that improves each day and will get even better now that we're together." He hugged her stiffly, with a semblance of contact, and stepped back out of her reach, all the time watching.

"Are you going to stay here?" Edward said.

"There's a chamber beyond the next one," Ellen said. "The door was only just unlocked and a bed brought in."

"Behind you, my lady," the wet nurse whispered.

An open door led to another chamber. Both chambers had white washed wainscoting and above that, the walls had been painted with red lines resembling masonry. Both rooms were comfortably furnished.

"What about him?" Elspeth said, trying to pat the baby's head.

The questions were answered, and between Ellen and the wet nurse, order established.

To the delight of the children, Ceonald came to visit the next day, but she did not see Ulric for three days. His visit was timed when the children were out playing in the snow and Ceonald who served as escort. There were dark circles under the King's eyes and a furrow on his brow. Both men were subdued. She was vindicated, the suspicion proved baseless; Claire read it in their eyes and saw it in their carriage, Ceonald pale but otherwise his old self, and Ulric sober, but with his jaw still tight. She took no pleasure in her victory, only relief the ordeal had ended.

"When I did ask my physician to care for you," Ulric said stiffly, "I had no thought but to your safety and continued health. When he did describe to me your temperament, I did ascribe it with all the color he gave, but had little thought that it was the bearer of the news who bore watching, rather than the subject. I have now interviewed the man at length. He did believe the necessity of his potions through some altered understanding. After some . . . prodding . . . I am led to believe that he had an idea of sparing you the necessity of further childbirth, but if he meant to take it to the ultimate end, I do not know. Ceonald did witness my interrogation, and can say for himself if he believes what I say is accurate."

Ceonald nodded.

"You must interview the bard privately," Ulric said. "He will not tell you tales, I believe, in this regard."

Ceonald moved as if to speak, but checked himself. Claire nodded.

"The man did physick my own lady," Ulric said. "You must trust that he has had his justice." He stood. "You will regard Condleath castle as your home for the time being. It's a summer residence, which is why it's so poorly furnished. Aldwin had given over to a redecoration but, well . . . Its isolation does afford the best privacy, which is why I choose it. It must do for the present." He withdrew, leaving her alone with Ceonald.

"Well, bard," Claire said. "You have been messenger and statesman and now I ask another role, advisor to your Queen."

Ceonald bowed. "I am your servant in all matters, Your Grace. I fear though, that I make a poor advisor; I know more of the past than the present, very little, it seems, of the present and nothing of the future. Still, I will venture forth an opinion, however ill-advised it may turn out to be."

"Do you believe Ulric innocent of any attempt to cause harm?" she said. "He has a hard edge of anger about him and I do wonder if the anger is at the medic, or because the medic was discovered."

"If he is actor," Ceonald said, "he is better player than King. I have talked to him much and as he said, did witness the interrogation . . ." Ceonald paled and walked to the window. "The physician was mad and did confess to his act. Ulric is innocent, I believe, of any ill intent. His anger is cold beyond the warmth of rage." He returned and sat down again. "He has buried two Queens, Your Grace, at least one I have discovered, in similar circumstance to your own."

Claire shivered. "Then you would advise us to stay?"

"I can't see any other alternative at present."

"William had no other plan?"

"He did not."

Of course not. Still, the High King had much to occupy him. "When do you go back?"

Ceonald drummed his fingers on the arm of the chair. "As this seems to have been resolved, I'll make arrangements at once and leave on the morrow, if possible. The day after, if not."

"What will you tell William when you see him?"

"That you were ill, but now are well. That he has a new son. That his children are well."

Claire put her hand over Ceonald's, stifling the restlessness. "Do not tell him about the physician."

The bard paused. "You think not?"

"He has much to consider. There was a danger. It is past. He must focus on what is ahead. I would see him before the season of battle is at hand. I will tell him then."

"He will not agree to a visit," Ceonald said.

"Deliver the message, Bard," Claire said. "Let him decide."

By late afternoon, the wind blew in fierce eddies that slammed into the castle and thunder and lightning shook the mountaintop. Ceonald had no option but to delay. The next afternoon, they all gathered in the great room, waiting out the storm. Even Ulric joined them, forgoing his dais and taking a seat near the group.

"This reminds me of the story of Aethelstwin and Quivil," Ceonald said.

"Tell us about Wolphard again," Edward said.

Ceonald slipped his hands into his tunic sleeves and sat back. "I do not recollect saying I would tell a story," he said, eyes twinkling, "only that this weather did put me in mind of one. Besides, my throat is raw from the cold and I've not been invited to recite by my host."

Ulric nodded. Claire motioned and Ellen filled his cup with spiced wine warmed at the fire. Ceonald took a sip, swirled the contents, and stared as if mesmerized.

Ulric cleared his throat. "Of Aethelstwin, I know," he said. "Who is this Quivil?"

Ceonald looked up. "Quivil," he said, "was a perfectly fine specimen of dragon, and for the life of me, I cannot understand why you don't want to hear about him."

"We do, we do," the children said.

"Sire?"

Ulric smiled and waved his consent.

"Well," Ceonald said shaking his finger, "as your education has been remiss in this regard, let me preface my remarks by saying that Quivil was not one of your ordinary dragons, but one of the ancient race of Nunraw dragons, a giant among giants. He lived, once upon a time, where now stand the Muchelney Mountains, and some say the lakes near Elbottle are really his footprints and the mountains merely hills, until he walked among them and when he walked, the earth trembled." Ceonald leaned forward and whispered, "Quivil could cook a whole village in a single breath."

The boys shivered. Elspeth ran to Ulric and climbed onto the surprised King's lap. The wet nurse hurried forward, but Ulric shrugged and patted Elspeth's back awkwardly. Elspeth tugged at his sleeve until his arm came up. She found the hem of his sleeve, plopped her thumb into her mouth and leaned back.

"If My Lady is quite comfortable . . .," Ceonald said.

Elspeth giggled.

Ceonald cleared his throat. "As I was saying, Quivil was a fierce dragon, with scales that glowed gold in the sunlight and silver in the moonlight and his chest shone like rubies. When he belched, as he was apt to do after an especially fine meal, he set the whole sky ablaze. And, like all the Nunraw dragons, Quivil could see into the future, but like all his brethren, never did, in case he saw his own death, which was considered very bad luck, or another dragon's, which was bad manners. At any rate, as you can imagine, after two or three hundred years, he had eaten just about everyone and everything worth eating in his vicinity and he decided to try his luck to the south, in what's now Bridland. That is where he met Aethelstwin."

Richard shifted and sat straighter.

"The land shook, the rivers boiled and ran dry, so all men knew somewhere upriver Quivil had drunk his fill. The sky turned red. Quivil was coming. A boy named Aethelstwin, put on his sword. By coincidence, he found the dragon just after Quivil had eaten heartily and had drunk a whole lake dry. The dragon was on his way to feeling full, the fire within him partially quenched and he had settled down for a nap. Of course, this doesn't make Aethelstwin less brave, since he had no way of knowing the state of the dragon. Aethelstwin walked to within a few hundred yards of the dragon, and pulled out his sword.

Quivil opened one eye."

Ceonald paused for a drink, his eyes twinkling. The children sat breathlessly, and he continued,

"Aethelstwin bowed. 'I am Aethelstwin,' he said, 'and this

is my sword.'

Quivil yawned. 'I am Quivil,' he said, 'and I need no swords.' He was full and secretly pleased at the boy's fine manners.

'I, Aethelstwin, do come to tell you, Quivil, of the Nunraw's, that you may come no further.'

The dragon snorted. 'And who is to stop me?'

'I am,' Aethelstwin said. 'My sword is very sharp.'

'Bah. I have met many swords. The swordsmen are a little stringy for my taste.'

Aethelstwin bowed again. 'I hope this meal met with your liking, since if you don't leave, it must be your last.'

'An excellent repast,' Quivil said, smacking his dragon lips. 'It should last a day or two.'

'Then you must leave before you feel the pangs of hunger,' Aethelstwin said, 'for I have sworn to save Bridland.'

'Bah,' Quivil said. His tail twitched, leveling some dozen full-grown oaks.

Aethelstwin ran forward, leapt up, and struck the dragon across the snout.

Quivil snorted and blew the boy back a hundred yards.

Aethelstwin climbed to his feet and raised his sword. 'I did not want it to come to this,' he said, 'but I can see I must declare a state of war between us.'

Quivil squinted and said nothing.

Aethelstwin hurled himself at the dragon. By the twelfth charge, Quivil had grown irritated. By the fortieth, he was annoyed. On the forty-first, he opened his mouth to blow the boy back and accidentally swallowed him.

Aethelstwin continued in the darkness of the dragon's belly, thrusting again and again.

Quivil blinked. The sword thrusts tickled. The boy did not give up. Finally, Quivil could stand it no longer and began to laugh. Aethelstwin seized the moment and escaped, stopping a few feet from the dragon.

'If all men of Bridland are like you,' Quivil said, 'I should not enjoy my meals for laughing.'

'Every man, woman and child will do the same,' Aethelstwin said.

Quivil wasn't born yesterday but decided not to contradict. 'You are brave, Aethelstwin, O mightiest of warriors,' the dragon said. 'I could kill you but I admire your spirit. Still, I will not leave, a dragon must eat.'

'You have come upon us too suddenly,' Aethelstwin said, 'or else we would have had a proper tribute ready. Surely you do not think a guest in our house goes hungry?'

Quivil arched his brow. "You do not seek to bribe me with fat cattle, do you?' he said, wishing he'd thought to include a few sheep as well.

'One does not bribe such a formidable foe,' Aethelstwin said. 'One might negotiate. One might give gifts to an ally.'

Forty fat cattle were forfeit; forty fat sheep filled the bill.

'I accept your gifts,' Quivil said. 'I must give you one in return.' He closed his eyes and lay silent. A week passed before he moved.

'I will give you your future, Aethelstwin,' Quivil said. 'You will be King of Bridland and High King too. Your kingdom will be prosperous and peaceful, but when a time comes that it's threatened, your four sons will raise up their swords as you have done and deliver their people.'"

Ceonald lifted his cup, then wiped his mouth and sat back. "And so, it will be," he said.

"I like the one about Wolphard better," Edward said.

"It was a fine story," Richard said. "Thank you, bard."

Claire touched the back of her neck. In his cradle, the baby began to fuss. That night, her nightmare about William returned.

The next morning dawned a dazzling white, releasing Ceonald. Two weeks passed before Ulric requested Claire join him. She took Richard with her. The monk, Wido, stood near Ulric.

"The boy was not summoned," Ulric said.

Claire bit back her first reply; the truce between them was still tenuous. "I did ask him, Sire," she said. "Though he is still a boy, he should have left my skirts before now, and been set as page to some goodly knight, who could teach him the manly arts. I did think, that to see how a King does have discourse with his guests would prove some small lesson. And, what does concern me, is in all ways of concern to him." In truth, she was never without either Ellen or Richard, hoping that if she was made a prisoner again, those two at least might disbelieve what was said of her and somehow come to her defense. She believed Ulric, but could not bring herself to fully trust him yet. It should have been one and the same, but somehow it wasn't. She seated herself across from the King, smoothed her skirts and smiled. "I do crave your indulgence," she said softly. Beside her, Richard bowed.

Ulric looked at Claire and then behind her to Richard. He nodded. "The High King will undoubtedly break camp when winter is done," he said. "I did think to send a messenger to him, before he joined again in battle and did think you might want to compose some few lines of your own. Wido here can write them for you, and has sworn to keep private what message you do dictate."

"Your intentions do cheer me, Sire," she said, "but I need write no lines. I intend to go to My Lord and can accompany your man." If the news she was safe could cheer William through winter, how much more would her presence do? Surely, he could not agree she was unable to withstand the rigors of camp life after all she'd endured, and with the army, she would be a safe as anywhere. Ceonald had said it himself, one more battle and it would be over. Time then to send for the children.

"It's too arduous a journey, My Lady," Ulric said. "I cannot allow it." But his words were without the force of conviction.

"That is not your province, Sire, unless you do think to take my key from me and entomb me in your tower. That I go, if left to mine own free will, is not a question. But I do agree with you as to its danger, and it's not a journey to which I can willing subject my children or Lady Ellen."

"I have no lady who can travel with you," he said. "It would not be proper."

"I will have the baby's wet nurse," she said.

Wido gasped. "It's far too dangerous for an infant," he said.

"The High King must see his new son," Claire said.

"At grave risk to the child," Wido protested. Still, Ulric was silent.

"It's the child I'm thinking of."

Ulric's eyes narrowed, but he nodded. "My Lady is right," he said. "This untimely separation between man and wife must be put in its proper place on the calendar. It does secure the boy's future, and stop the chance of tongues wagging should the war stretch overlong and it be years until the father meets his son."

"I would leave Lady Ellen and the other children in your care," she said.

Richard opened his mouth, then stopped himself.

"What about this young man?" Ulric said. "Do you take him with you as well?"

Richard looked up at her.

"It will be a difficult journey, son," she said, "with many risks."

"I would go with you," Richard said. "if a baby can go, I can as well."

Ulric's face was passive.

"How think you this war will end, Ulric?" she said.

He shrugged, as indeed he might. He was no truth-teller any more than she. The war would end when either Cedric or William was dead.

"Richard will go with me," she said.

The boy exhaled loudly and grinned.

"I will see that preparations are made," Ulric said. "Best be ready to leave within the week."

Wido waited until Claire and Richard were well out of the room. "You were right, Sire," he said, "but I can't concede the bet in its entirety, since it was you that planted the idea of bringing the boy."

"I'd wager she's debated the subject already," Ulric said, "and she'd have come to it all the same. It's harder for her to admit the need though. By taking Richard, she establishes that the High King's heir lives, but that will only matter when the High King dies."

"She's a strong-willed woman."

"She's a strong woman," Ulric said, "there's a difference. It's not altogether a bad thing for a woman, especially if the man she marries knows how to handle her."

"And is the High King such a man?"

"William was an affable boy," Ulric said. "I sense that he has not much changed."

"You did not answer when she asked how you thought the war would end."

"She didn't really want an answer," Ulric said. "Besides, I am no soothsayer. Cedric is more treacherous than I would have thought, but the High King more resolved than I would have given him credit."

"But you have resolved on the side of the High King?" Wido said.

Ulric laughed. "I have resolved for Amadee," he said. "Be prepared to leave the day after the High Queen."

"And the children?"

"Ah," Ulric said. "The sound of little voices. I was quite coming to admire it. Come spring I will, as is my usual want, bring the court here. These halls must show no signs of their present occupants. A pity, but nevertheless necessary. I need to work out the details and we will speak upon it later."

CHAPTER TWENTY-SEVEN

Willwell Abbey was nestled in a small valley on the eastern flanks of the Kusshi. Abbott Neely had no particular ambitions, having accepted his position as head of the community when the old Abbott died, only after it became clear that it was the unanimous will of their small community. The monks grew their crops successfully enough, so that neither the Bishop nor their chapter house worried about needing to supplement their meager needs, but nor was there enough surplus to arouse envy.

The Abbey buildings were old, but had been well built under the patronage, a century earlier, of Queen Edwina, who endowed the abbey after her husband, Wolphard, died. A modest apartment had been included in the complex for the Queen, who had intended to retire to the seclusion of its four walls, but never had, dying only four years after the King and before the Abbey had been completed. As she was preceded in death by her only son, leaving one-year old Owain as heir to the throne, the existence of Willwell Abbey passed from royal consciousness and faded into obscurity, attracting only the pious, who were content with their isolation.

Like all monasteries, they had a small guesthouse and an infirmary for travelers. The rooms were swept and aired monthly, and a fire build at intervals during the colder months to keep the wood dry, but only on rare occasions, were they occupied. The presence of smoke coming from the guesthouse chimney one day in late February, would therefore have attracted little attention, even if the monks had close neighbors, which they did not. The arrival, at dusk, of a man and boy, both on horseback and leading a string of four palfrey mares, would have been of considerably more interest.

The royal apartment had been occupied for two days, the occupants arriving in mid-day, sliding and picking their way through a narrow gap, passable only in winter, when deep snows evened the rock-filled ravines, and the waterfalls that kept the ridge walls slick, were frozen into cathedrals of ice. Although the route was known, few ever chose it. There was little if any reason to cross the mountains; the people on both sides living in similar circumstance, with little in the way of novelty or opportunity to induce a visit. The bitter weather that made the pass accessible, substituted one set of dangers for another. Even if the traveler didn't freeze or slip to his death, the trip must be perfectly timed so that blizzards didn't block the way and the snow had a firm enough crust to support the horses, but was not so icy as to send them careening down the mountain. Ideally, there was also enough new powder so the horses' hooves penetrated and had a footing, but not so much that caused them to flounder.

The monks had been hard at their prayers when their latest guests arrived, tired but little worse for the wear, just as a storm whistled up the ravines and swirling snow hid the path. As he had with the arrival of his previous guests, Abbott Neely hurried out. "My lord," he said. "God's welcome."

Hugh of Tintagel swung down. "Thank you, Abbott," he said. "Peace to all here."

A broad faced monk hurried forward and took his reins.

"Brother Martin will see to your horses," Abbott Neely said. "The victualer has kept some supper for you, so come and refresh yourself."

"Any news?"

"Arrived two days hence, with God's help. All safe. They were blessed with perfect conditions for travel."

Hugh grinned.

"She'll see you after you've supped," the Abbott said.

Hugh turned to the small figure still mounted. "Go with Brother Martin, lad. When the horses are cared for, he'll no doubt show you to the guest house and find you something to eat."

"Yes, My Lord," Jeremy said, jumping down.

"All in good time, lad," Hugh said.

Brother Martin clucked and led the horses away, with Jeremy close behind.

"You've aroused his curiosity, Abbott," Hugh said. "He knows nothing of our mission, save that we serve William."

"As do we all. God keep him safe."

"Amen to that," Hugh said. "If you could spare the water to bathe, I'd be beholden, and the boy could do with a bath as well. It's been months for us both. Camp life is fine for rougher company, but I would present Her Grace with a less fragrant guide."

"The pot is steaming even as we speak," Abbott Neely said. "I'll send word to Brother Martin to see to the boy."

Hugh scratched his head. "Have him put on his other tunic."

It took time to satisfy the Abbott with news from the outside world, and when Hugh reached the guesthouse, Jeremy stood red-legged in front of the fire, drying his hair. A steaming tub sat near him and Brother Martin waited with two buckets, ready to assist.

"You did well to be ready, Jeremy," Hugh said. "Are you satisfied with the accommodations for our horses?"

"Yes, My Lord," Jeremy said. "They're brushed, fed and bedded down. Brother Martin helped."

"And you've eaten?"

"Yes, sir."

Hugh left his clothes where they fell and climbed into the tub. They'd not been over-sparing with the water, but at least it was clean. The tub must have been emptied after Jeremy was done. The boy reached for Hugh's clothes.

"Leave them for the moment," Hugh said. "You're freshly clean and they're overripe."

Bother Martin picked up the clothes and disappeared.

"Can't he talk?" Jeremy said.

"Most monks live in silence," Hugh said, "though they have a set time to talk within the community and no doubt Brother Martin takes advantage of it."

"The Abbott talked."

"Only because we're special guests, here on the King's business. Besides, he's in charge so probably does not have the same requirement for silence as the others."

"Oh."

Hugh waited, but Jeremy gazed into the fire and said nothing. The boy had a good head about him and missed very little. He'd been full of questions before Wythe, but now mulled things over by himself first. In truth, the carnage on the field of battle changed them all.

Brother Martin returned in time to dump the contents of two buckets over Hugh's soapy head and hand him a towel. Jeremy had laid out his green wool tunic.

"I have an important meeting, Jeremy," Hugh said when he'd finished. "You may attend me, and take care to remember all that you've learned."

Jeremy grinned and bowed. "Yes, My Lord," he said.

It was approaching twilight when they left the guesthouse. Hugh was afire to see her and wished he were a hundred miles away. How would he find words to tell her . . .

"How did you know he was the Abbott?"

Hugh smiled. "I've been here before."

Jeremy nodded.

They reached the Queen's apartment and Hugh knocked.

A ruddy-faced woman curtsied. "My lord."

"Hugh of Tintagel to see—"

"Come in, Sir Hugh."

Her voice was as soft and melodious as he remembered.

Claire sat a few feet from the fire, situated so her face was not in its direct light, and he could not read her look.

Jeremy gasped.

Hugh took a few steps and bowed. "Your Grace."

Richard stepped from the shadows.

Hugh bowed again. "My Lord, Richard. This is a surprise."

"I see you have company," she said.

"My page, Your Grace. I will dismiss him if you desire."

"You have chosen well, my lord," she said.

Jeremy flushed and stood straighter.

Claire held out her hand. "Come and sit near the fire, Sir Hugh. Then, if you will, tell me the news of my lord husband."

Sir Hugh. She did not refuse to meet his glance, or look away too readily, but neither did her eyes linger. She was exactly as she should be, High Queen and mother of a future king. Hugh nodded slightly. What might have begun at Elstow was dead, as it should be.

The wet nurse bustled over a low wooden box, lifted out a bundle and handed the baby to Claire. Save for the bright eyes that were so like the High Queen's, the baby looked like a small version of his father, with the same round face and satisfied smile. That is, like the High King before Wythe. One might meet him now and had they not known him before, miss the similarity.

"He is named Warin," Claire said, looking down at the baby.

She wore a new blue tunic, that looked as well as he'd thought it would, so many months ago on the Elstow. Hugh had been with the High King, when Ceonald returned from Amadee, and so had heard most of what transpired there. On first glance, he thought she'd been untouched by the ordeal, but now, with closer inspection, could see that her face was thinner and had a more resolute look.

"He's a fine baby," Hugh said. "Very much in appearance like the High King, his father."

She flushed. "I think so as well." Claire looked up. "What news, Sir Hugh?"

"Richard," Hugh said. "Would you like to go and see the horses we brought? You can pick out the one you'd like to ride and one for your mother."

Richard gave him a quizzical look. "Mother?"

"Don't be overlong and don't leave the Abbey."

"Can I pick any one?"

"All save my own," Hugh said. "Jeremy will take you and show you which one is it."

Jeremy bowed, opened the door, and followed Richard out.

"You're Jeremy from the Brightwood, aren't you?" Richard said. The door closed behind them.

The baby squirmed. "He's no doubt hungry," Claire said. "Take him, nurse, and feed him in the other room." When the wet nurse had gone, Claire smoothed her tunic. "Tell me what you hold so close, Sir Hugh. What news of the High King?"

"There was an accident, Your Grace," Hugh said, hoping his voice was calm. "The King was hunting and his horse fell. He was not injured in the fall, save that his wounds from Wythe re-opened. One has refused to heal. Ceonald has gone for Lady Breona, and we hope to see her any time."

Claire folded her hands in her lap, then stood and looked into the fire. "But he is alive?" He thought for a moment she had shivered, but her voice was low and steady.

"Yes. He has a very strong constitution, Your Grace."

"We will leave on the morrow," she said. Her hands trembled slightly and she tucked them nun-like into her sleeves.

"He is much changed in appearance, My Lady," he said. "I thought you should be prepared, and Richard as well. I can talk to him if you wish."

"Thank you. It will not be necessary . . . How long is the journey?" she said.

"Jeremy and I made it in one day, but with few stops. We won't push so hard going back, so we'll plan on two."

"One will be sufficient."

He bowed. "Very well, Your Grace." They could still stop where he'd made arrangements, whether she agreed to it now or not. "We should plan on leaving early, then."

"We'll be ready at first light." She turned. "Please excuse me now. I have some preparations to make before we leave."

Hugh had thought to be with the High Queen when Richard returned, and as that was not the case, he went instead to the barn. Oblivious to the cold, the boys were perched on top of the stone wall.

"Weren't you scared?" Richard was saying.

"Mostly, yes," Jeremy said. "But I pretended I wasn't."

"Then what happened?"

"I'm sorry to interrupt," Hugh said, "but we leave at dawn tomorrow. Your mother, Richard, did say that she had some preparations to make. Perhaps she has need of you."

Richard swung his legs over the wall and dropped down, with Jeremy right behind him.

"Go on to the guest house, Jeremy," Hugh said. "I'll see Richard back to his quarters."

"I know the way, Sir Hugh," Richard said. "You don't need to come."

"But I will, lad, else I'll not sleep as well as I'd like."

"Where's his mother?" Richard said, when Jeremy was out of earshot.

"Hopefully safe in her own home," Hugh said. "We've never had troops close enough to Lamberton to find out. His father was killed. Probably by the same men who killed Sir Herbert."

"Is that why you made him your page? Because you felt sorry for him?"

"I do feel bad for Jeremy, but that's not the reason." Hugh put his hand on Richard's shoulder. "He's a bright lad, quick to learn, and he did you and yours a great service."

"He's really brave," Richard said. "Braver than me."

"This from the boy who was all set to fight me at Windrush?"

"He is braver, 'cause he had to be brave lots of times and

not just for a few minutes. Can a knight have two pages?"

Hugh ruffled the boy's hair.

"When I saw my father, I thought . . ."

"You've been a comfort to your mother these past weeks," Hugh said.

Richard bit his lips. "Does the King, my father, know about . . ."

"About what, lad?"

Richard looked down. "About my mother."

Hugh stopped. "What about her, Richard?"

Richard flushed.

"Best tell me, lad."

Richard scuffed at the snow. "About when she was sick."

"In the Soddenwood?"

"No."

"Your father knows about your new brother. He's most anxious to see him."

"No, not that."

"What then?"

"Well . . . well . . . after the baby, then they locked her . . ."

Hugh bent down and looked Richard full in the eye. "The High King has had a report from Ceonald and a letter from King Ulric as well."

"Is she going to be like that anymore?" Richard said in a low voice.

"What do you think was wrong with her, Richard?"

His eyes filled. "They said . . . they said she'd gone . . ."

Hugh took his arm. "Mad? Lost her mind?"

A tear ran down the boy's face. "But she's all better, isn't she?"

Hugh nodded. "Indeed, she is lad, but you should know the whole truth of what happened."

Richard wiped his face.

"She was given a poison, Richard, that's why she acted so strangely. She was able somehow to figure out what'd happened and then pretend to take it. She was very brave and very strong."

"Did he do it?"

"Who?"

"King Ulric." Richard jerked away from Hugh. "He'd better not hurt my brothers and Elspeth."

"It was not the King, but his physician. Ulric knew nothing of it, and I tell you this part, Richard, but upon your oath, you must not repeat it . . ."

Richard nodded.

"It appears that the physician was most likely mad himself and probably killed Ulric's own Queen. Ceonald was there when the physician confessed and did see the King mete out the punishment."

"Did he die?"

"Yes."

"Good."

"You can talk to your father about it if you wish. Better yet, talk to Ceonald. He was there." Hugh would like to have been there himself. Not that he didn't trust what Ceonald said, but he would have liked to look Ulric in the face and judge for himself. Under the right circumstances a man might confess to anything. And a dead man could not recant.

"Is Ceonald going to be with my father?"

"I hope so, lad. I certainly hope so."

After he left Richard, Hugh went directly to the guesthouse. There was no need to leave a message for the Abbott. They'd already discussed the possibility of a departure the next morning and besides, the monks would be up and at their prayers long before sunrise. It was not all bad. The High Queen appeared to have recovered and Hugh had no doubt he would see her safely to the care of her husband. The High King had been ill to be sure, but hadn't Hugh seen for himself, Breona's curative powers? There was no need for this unease. The monk's low-throated prayers calmed the night, but failed to soothe him.

CHAPTER TWENTY-EIGHT

When they left the abbey, a thin sun shone overhead with little effect, leaving the ground still frozen. A recent thaw after the last snowfall left the trees strangely barren, without summer finery or winter mantle. The breath of the travelers and their horses, appeared in puffs and snorts, accompanied by the crunch of hooves in the tired snow.

Jeremy had taken the lead, prearranged presumably with Hugh, who said nothing when the boy set out. Not well versed in the route, he'd hesitated once or twice, but never turned back to Hugh to confirm the direction. Richard rode at his side, his excitement evident in his questions and commentary on their surroundings. Claire followed, keeping close to Richard, while Hugh and the wet nurse, with baby Warin peeking up from a long, conical basket tied at the side of the horse, brought up the rear. The baby was warmly swaddled and firmly supported by the layers of fabric and fur that shielded him from the cold.

Dressing with special care, Claire had chosen a light taupe tunic with a white wool under dress. Her gray cloak was packed away and she wore a dark blue one lined with ermine. Ulric had been a generous host. That he arrived with Cedric bearing such gifts, helped her believe his innocence in any acts against her. He would not have taken the time, nor spent so much, if he had expected to find her dead.

Although they stopped infrequently, and the rests were short in duration, they still had not reached the High King's encampment when the sun slipped down over the horizon. Richard's excitement waned as the day grew longer, so by afternoon, except for the baby who cried when he was hungry, they rode in silence, bypassing the villages and small hamlets. A bright moon shone among glittering stars, when Hugh urged his horse forward and motioned Jeremy to stop.

"We're almost upon our goal, Your Grace," he said.

"Let us to it, then," she said. Two months ago, she might have been annoyed by his pronouncement. It was not, after all, as if she had any reason to delay their arrival, or any method to prepare for the meeting. Now though, she wondered if his words were meant kindly, his attempt at an encouragement at the end of a tiring day. In truth, he had changed since last she saw him. As had she.

Hugh reached into a bag tied to his saddle. "His Majesty, King William did think to send you this," he said, holding out a gold circlet. "The High King removed this from Ambridge, along with those other possessions set to follow you to Windrush, and did secret them upon your safe return."

Although it was the smaller of the two crowns she wore, it felt strangely heavy upon her head.

"The High King is at Heston Grange," Hugh said, "his winter army camped around it. We should see some of their campfires over the next ridge and no doubt they'll see us at the same time, if they've not already."

When they resumed their journey, Claire, with Hugh riding beside her, took the lead. Either the sentinels did not see them or let them pass by some pre-arranged signal. They were not challenged as they mounted the ridge or when they started down into the valley. A few dozen campfires twinkled in the twilight.

"There are so few," she whispered.

"It is a small guard, Your Grace," Hugh said. "The

majority are assembled to the south and east, and those who could winter at home unmolested, have long departed." As they reached the valley floor, a half dozen or so men rode to meet them. Hugh reined in his horse. They waited.

The first was Reginald of Norwood, the King's red hair a beacon in the twilight. The next was Jon of Langeston, his gray hair gone white, but otherwise, in spite of his advanced years, unchanged. Then Morgan of Ilyarod and Percival. Two were of William's council and Percival, like Hugh, was a favorite hunting companion. The others she did not recognize. The husband did not come to meet his wife.

"Welcome to the Lithnot Valley, Your Grace." Reginald bowed from atop his horse, as ever the graceful courtier. He nodded toward one of the strangers. "Allow me to present Sir Nyls of Heston Grange, our host." Nyls nodded and bowed.

She nodded to them all. "King Reginald . . . My Lords."

"Your Grace." The men bowed.

"His Majesty, the High King, did wish that you have a proper escort, Your Grace. We were most honored to oblige him." Morgan stared past her, craning his head.

So, he knew to expect her, but not the children. "How far to Heston Grange?" she said.

He straightened in his saddle and looked at her again. Still, she could see his eyes look past her, as did others.

"If it were daylight, Your Grace," Jon of Langeston said, "you'd see the castle from here. If you'll allow me, I'll lead the way."

Behind him, a torch flared into life, followed by another and yet another. It was to be no quiet arrival. Claire urged her horse forward. As she rode past Percival, he bowed and handed her a large bouquet of winter daphne, the pale pink blossoms jewels among the white edged green. Jon of Langeston turned his horse and Reginald pulled in beside her. The rest fell in behind, save for the men with torches, who flanked the riders, spacing themselves along the length of the party. Rather than skirting the valley, Jon of Langeston led them toward the campfires. Within the hour, the whole camp would know who rode toward Heston Grange castle. They would know, and no doubt Cedric would learn of it too. She shuddered.

Reginald leaned in her direction. "I am at your service, Your Grace, if you do require anything."

She shook her head and smiled. If the game must be played, she would play it well. She pushed back the hood of her cloak, letting the torchlight play on the gold, and straightened, ignoring the protest that began to grow in the small of her back. Her companion nodded. "My Lord of Norwood," Claire said, "you do us great honor by meeting us. I trust Lady Agatha is both safe and well. She has been much on my mind these past months." Indeed, if his sister had refused anyone but Cedric . . .

"You are most kind to inquire," Reginald said. "She is safe in Dunraven Castle. There is no army that can take it and they have ample supply to last them for at least two years if they husband it well. Enough to resolve this present danger."

Dunraven was what Windrush was not, Agatha was fortunate to have a protector who cared so well.

The camp was well roused by the time they reached the first campfire. Reginald left her then, joining Jon of Langeston, and Richard took his place. Mother and son rode together through the camp, their names going from lip to lip. As she rode by William's troops, some bowed, others knelt. Hugh told her later, he had seen tears in more than one man's eyes. She would remember it as a river of golden light and the sweet smell of daphne that lingered in the night air. As they neared the castle, a gust of wind touched her cheek. She looked up, half expecting to see the King of Owls, but the sky was empty. So, to all purposes, was the castle, as she learned upon her arrival. The High King had ridden out that morning and so far, had not returned, his illness, it seemed more convenient than debilitating.

Claire was warming her hands at the fireplace, when Hugh came to serve as escort. She'd risen early and dressed in the gown she least liked, a dark one that put her in mind of the cloisters. At the last moment, she pulled it off and pulled on the clothes she had worn the day before. The High King could hardly object to the faint scent of horse, as he seemed to prefer it to all others.

Hugh bowed. "His Majesty is with his council and does bid you come."

She walked over and sat down on the nearest chair, her face warm. The High King was no doubt punishing her for the trouble between them when last they met. Well, two could play that game and she had her own set of grievances. He had caused her much hardship these past months, put her life at risk as well as her children's and now did insult her by this casual summons. "I believe I am fatigued," she said.

Hugh cast a wary glance, which she ignored. "Your Grace—"

"That is all, Hugh of Tintagel," she said.

He bowed.

"Sir Hugh."

He stopped at the door.

"I have overmuch to discuss with my lord, husband. A wife might prefer to meet with her husband, before the Queen meets King and council." He hesitated, then bowed again and withdrew. She did not trust her tongue to silence, even in the presence of the entire court, save the King's council alone. Better that she and William meet first.

Hugh returned almost immediately. She followed him in silence down a long corridor and into a small anteroom. Hugh knocked at the closed door. "Hugh," she said in a low voice, "give us a few moments, then bring the High King's sons." He pushed the door open.

Claire hardly knew him. William's face was furrowed with anxious lines that spread across his pale brow and down his gaunt cheeks. His hair was likewise streaked with gray and as he sat watching her, his body shook with a slight palsy. She curtsied. "Your Majesty." Her voice shook slightly. He frowned and she took a deep breath. "It is overlong since we have met, My Lord." Good her voice was even now. "You have been much in my thoughts these past months and I did pray most earnestly for your safety and success on the field of battle." There was no lie in what she said, and no trace of what she felt.

He lifted a trembling hand and motioned her closer.

She must kiss this old man who had taken the High King's place. Even with Hugh's warning, she had not expected this.

"Sit there where I can see you," he said.

She sank into the chair, glad her legs had not betrayed her, then sprang up, knelt quickly by his chair and pressed her face into his thin hand. "My Lord, Husband," she whispered. She felt his hand lightly caress her hair before she returned to her seat.

"I see you—" He hesitated, then began again in a softer tone. "You were right to be angry with me last spring, My Lady," he said. "I have heard an outline, at least, of what has happened to you since. You have more right to be angry now, as I am to blame for your many hardships. If I could go back, I would have had you stay in Ambridge and I would have had Ambridge made safe."

Fine words. Agatha of Norwood was safe at Dunraven, while she and her children had been subjected to much hardship and even now were at Ulric's mercy. Had it been anyone but Agatha, William would not have gone to war so quickly. Still, there was a conciliatory tone she could not ignore. "Nay, My Lord husband, it is I who have the fault," Claire said. "You were right to send us. Ambridge was no safer than Windrush, and even fortified may not have fared any better."

He watched her closely and she met his look in full now. "In truth, Sire, I have been angry and did privately rail against you as the source of my tribulations these past months."

"I do not feel that anger now," she said. It was true. It had vanished with his youth. "The truth is, the person who must answer to all our difficulties is the most foul Cedric, and I was wrong to place his blame on you. Had things not transpired as they did after we left Ambridge, the children and I might well have been his captives. I would endure all again and more, rather than be hostage to your kingdom." She smiled. "Far better to be hidden than hostage."

"Had it been anyone but Cedric," William said, "I would have told Reginald to hold firm with his sister, and Agatha would long be wed and we at peace."

Claire glanced up. William's face had a firmness to it not usually found. "She is strong-headed, over-indulged and petted from birth," he said. "By rights she should have been wed years ago and by a husband who could curb this unfortunate tendency."

William inhaled loudly and seemed to hold his breathe. She reached over touched his hand gently. "For all she ought to have done, and for all Reginald might have done, it would not answer that she marry Cedric." Her knees shook slightly. "I had such a fear of him at Windrush that I feel it must arise from some evil deep within him. Perhaps it's Heaven's providence that he chose the one woman who dared renounce his offer, and thus may meet the fate he so deserves."

"She had . . . has . . . the right to refuse him, with her brother's consent, and it is my duty to defend that right."

"I know."

He nodded, eyes tearing.

If she had any doubt he was ill, she could not have now, seeing this. William had always been both jovial and affable, but without deep emotion. Or at least none that was shown, or shared.

"Still," William said, "I have a duty to mine own family. It must have seemed to you that I embraced the one with little thought to the other."

Claire shook her head. She wanted to cry but held back the tears. It would do William no good to see them. "We must be done with regrets. In truth, I think we shared a similar view of the matter, but with different conclusions as to what needed to be done"

William smiled and the tension between them vanished. "I am glad you are not hidden from my eyes now, my lady, Claire.

I don't know what our futures hold, but if I go to my death, I would have peace between us."

She held up her hand.

"In truth," he said, "I did not want you to come but I am glad now that you have."

A knock sounded.

Richard stepped in, with Sir Hugh behind him. holding the baby.

"You have grown, son." William's voice sounded stronger and she was glad of it for the boy's sake.

"Yes, Sire," Richard said, his face pale.

"What have you got in your arms, Sir Hugh?"

"It is a matter of what you have got, Sire," Hugh said.

The High King held the baby at arms' length and studied his latest offspring. "He's a fine boy."

"He has your likeness, Your Grace," Hugh said.

"Does he?" The High King held the baby out to Claire. "You take him. I can observe him better thus."

It was clear Warin's weight taxed his father's strength. How was the man to wield a sword and hold a shield like this? She held the baby, so he faced his father.

"So, what think you, Richard, of your new brother?" the High King said.

"He's not so bad for a baby."

"Look how well he holds his head," the High King said. "And look at him watch me. He has the making of a fine huntsman, I can tell that already. Have someone fetch Langeston, Hugh. Let's see what he has to say."

Sir Jon had perhaps anticipated the summons and arrived almost immediately. "He is certainly a strong child," Sir Jon said. "The very picture of you Sire, at that age."

The High King showed off his son for a bit longer, and Claire soon sensed that he had grown tired. Jon of Langeston felt the same, trying several times to excuse himself. The baby continued as good naturedly as ever, so there was nothing, finally, to do but lie. "You must have important duties to attend, husband," Claire said, "and the baby must to his wet nurse before long, or you will see how strong his lungs are when he's vexed."

"Sir Jon," the High King said. "You must call my council to meet this afternoon. My Lady will return with my sons at that time. It is past time to have made arrangements for Richard to serve as page and I might as well arrange for the other three when their time comes, as well."

Jon of Langeston hesitated. "As you wish, Sire," he said. "I'm pleased you've had time to consider the matter and confer with those you have chosen. I'm far too old, of course, but I know the men you've selected are honored, even at such a perilous time."

The High King flushed. Hugh looked uncomfortable.

"Do you imply, Jon Langeston," the High King said, "that I need ask? By the saints, it's an honor!"

"It is both honor and responsibility, Sire. One not to be undertaken lightly, especially since we are at war."

"Bah, that will end soon."

"Richard," Claire said. "Take your brother to his wet nurse."

"He may stay." It was the William of old in tone. He had been ill . . . was ill . . . but he was still the King. For once, she was glad to be countermanded.

"My Lord, husband," Claire said. "You know full well I have encouraged you to place our son with some goodly knight—"

William nodded.

"But is now such a time for him to take up this new role?"

"Who said anything about making such a change now," William said, his cheeks slightly flushed. "I will not encumber any man with this charge at such a time."

Richard flushed and looked down.

"This summer, when things are resolved, will do. But I suppose some preparations must be made on both sides. Hugh, you must pick out two good horses. I'll not see my son ill-mounted."

Hugh bowed.

"But for Lady Claire, I would have all of you leave," the High King said. "There's much that needs my attention, however pleasant it would be to spend time with my sons."

Claire handed the baby to Hugh. The High King leaned against his chair and closed his eyes. The tremor, which had been barely visible before, was more pronounced, his face chalky. After a few moments, and with apparent effort, the High King opened his eyes.

"Sit near to me, wife," he said.

She debated about pulling her chair over next to him, but sat instead, on the floor near his feet. She had never done so before, but neither had she had such a request. He touched the top of her head and began to stroke her hair. "Do you remember the day we met, my lady?"

Did she remember how terrified she was? She would never forget. Still, he had been kind. "It's not so long ago as all that, my lord."

"It seems both yesterday and yet another lifetime," he said. "You seemed such a delicate, fragile thing."

She looked up. His eyes were still closed.

"I had not planned to marry for several more years, save that my mother and Ceonald convinced me of my duty . . ."

She stiffened.

"The moment I saw you," he said, "I blessed them for it and cursed myself for not learning better how to be courtier, so I could sing love songs to the woman I cherished from the first moment I saw her."

"My lord." Her voice shook.

"I cared you from that moment, and every day more, My Lady. I thought you should know it in case . . ."

She pulled away, then took his hand in hers. "You must not speak this way. Breona will be here any day . . ."

He nodded and managed a wan smile. "I met her once, did I ever tell you that? It was the year of my great tour, the same year I met Aldwin. She is my distant cousin, I believe."

"She told me. Of us both, it seems."

He opened his eyes and struggled to sit straighter. "How

so, my lady?"

"It's a distant connection between us, my lord. Not one which would bother the bishops, nor be near so close as many royal marriages we both could name."

"But what connection?"

He would not leave it and would be at her until it was answered. She sighed. "If Breona is correct, and knows true of such a foreign line as my own, my mother's family came down from Aethelstwin. I've never heard the connection, myself."

He stared for a moment and leaned back. Did he know the legend of Quivil? She hoped not.

He pressed her hand. "I'm sorry about the girl child. We may yet again, Heaven willing, have another."

She prayed not. She had done her duty. What did a man know of the terrors of childbirth save he lost a wife to it? "Cedric has cost many good lives," she said finally, "and the price of his folly is not yet paid."

The High King was silent.

"Who knows what may befall even your best knights, even those you have selected for some later endeavors or intended as mentors for our sons . . ."

"You have never meddled in affairs that don't concern you, Claire," he said, "but as it seems you have some point to make, pray continue."

As if the future of her sons was not her business. "I was only thinking, husband," she said, keeping her voice even and the inflection warm, "if the men you have chosen to send your sons to, are killed or incapacitated in battle, the men who then take their places will always remember they were a second choice."

"It will be an honor, none the less."

"Of course, and I know you certainly know better than I, in such affairs. But, if it were me asked to take on such a task, as second, I may feel complimented, but at the same time, insulted. Not that I would say so."

"It's an interesting perspective. I will consider it. Is there anything else?"

"Since you do ask, husband, it has occurred to me this castle seems well provided. And the walls around it go higher every day, I'm told. Rather than be here for a short visit, what say you if instead, I stay until this is at an end. By spring, the wall will have grown enough to suffice."

He pulled his hand away slowly. "I meant to tell you this after . . . later tonight . . .," he said. "You must leave straight away, on the morrow, in fact. Cedric is beginning to stir his forces. It's the reason I was away yesterday."

"My lord . . ."

"I fear the walls grow too slowly," the High King said. "I cannot risk it. You must return whence you came." He took her hand. "I would rather it was not so, but there's no alternative."

"Let me go only to the Abbey then, husband," she said, "and I may yet see you again before this thing is launched. Even Cedric would not defile a monastery, I think."

"No. There is no compromise here, My Lady. No gentle art of persuasion that might alter me."

She could not leave this time with rancor between them. In truth, she felt none. The anger she had nursed so carefully these past months had died when she saw him, and refused to be resurrected. "As you will, My Lord," she said. There was even the promise of something new between them. Something beyond their duties.

"I will rest, then, My Lady, and see you anon."

"Very well." She blinked back the tears, took a deep breath, and left the room.

CHAPTER TWENTY-NINE

They left Heston Grange just before dawn. It had snowed earlier, but the sky had cleared and a three-quarter moon shone brightly. Claire had not slept, but lie awake, waiting for the summons.

"Your Grace."

The wet nurse stood near Claire's bed, silhouetted in the darkness. There were to be no candles, no telltale glimpse of life stirring in the castle. She held up a garment, lady's maid now as well as wet nurse; accepting her new role with little comment. The gown, invisible in the darkness, was the same dark one Claire rejected the day before.

"This gown smells of long chants and fat candles," Claire said. She did not expect a reply, but stood and pulled it over her head. A sensible choice from a sensible woman. They had arrived with great bravado, but would leave in secrecy, that much of the plan had been discussed when the council met, and although the High King was pressed more than once for her destination, he had demurred, saying only he would divulge it when he had learned she had reached it in safety.

But for the High King's reticence, and the change in composition of the council, the meeting went much as she expected. Jon of Langeston was the most senior member, having served Owain before William; he had seemed an old man when Claire first came to Bridland. Dreu of Codwell and Keith of Falkirk were also long-time fixtures, the bald-headed Keith very little changed, while the thin-faced Dreu Codwell had grown more pinched, his thick gray hair undisturbed by the process. Nyls of Heston Grange was her first surprise, there not only as host, but as newly appointed member to replace Ian of Ardmont, who had fallen at Wythe. Hugh of Tintagel was the other surprise, there not as permanent member, but to fill in for Edward of Collinswood who had gone home to bury his three sons and persuade his wife to part with the two youngest.

They were assembled, when she and the children joined them, standing separately, as if unfamiliar with their roles. Still, they bowed in unison and Jon Langeston stepped forward. "On behalf of the King's Council, Your Grace, I bid you most welcome. May I also congratulate both Your Majesties on the birth of your son."

"Hear, hear," Keith of Falkirk, as reticent as ever.

"So, it's a boy, is it?" Dreu of Codwell said. "I can now understand why the King kept your location so close."

Nyls, lord of the manor, bowed again. "I hope your accommodations are to your satisfaction, My Lady. We had very little time to prepare." There was a flash of irritation on Jon Langeston's face and a look of surprise on the faces of the other two senior members. They had not, she guessed, been told of her impending arrival, while the most junior member had been taken into the King's confidence. Still he was their host and needed to be told. Why the discomfort?

She smiled and nodded. "Thank you, my lords, for your kind greeting." She took the chair near William. The wet nurse handed her the baby, curtsied and left.

Jon of Langeston carried a small table into the middle of the room. "Summon the King's physician," he called out.

Rhys Bent-Back was waiting, as she had known he would be. A handsome-faced man, the right side of his body gave an indication of the man he might have been, had not the left betrayed him, shrunken and largely useless. While he did not have Breona's way with herbs, he could set a bone better than any other, and had a ready smile and a gentle touch. He bowed, cradled the baby in his good hand and placed him on the table, deftly undressing him. The council members shifted for a view of the proceeding, while their host fussed nervously as Rhys lifted one limb and then another atop the fine table.

"A fine boy." Rhys stepped back so they could all see more clearly. "Close to three months, is he not, My Lady?"

"December fifth," she said.

"He's the image of the High King at that age," Jon Langeston said, as if he'd not already made the proclamation earlier. The others nodded and the High King smiled.

"You have a fine brother, My Lord, Richard," Keith of Falkirk said.

"I don't see he's any finer than the other two," Richard said, "just littler."

"Your sister thinks so," Claire said, watching the council for their reaction.

"She's just a girl," Richard said.

They were, except Hugh and the High King, surprised. Hugh had returned to his spot at the periphery of the group, so more than likely, the others did not notice his lack of expression.

"Your Majesties." Dreu of Codwell bowed. "I take it then the other children are both safe and well? I confess when I did not see them, I feared the worse, but thought to ask privately rather than mar this happy occasion."

"They are all well," Claire said, "or at least, were when I left them. Altogether we make rather too large a party to travel in these troubled times, even though the distance be short."

Richard's mouth opened and quickly shut again.

Rhys Bent-Back took the occasion to summon the wet nurse, who frowned when she saw her charge naked. She snatched up the baby, along with his apparel and disappeared.

"I had hoped that once here, they would soon follow," Claire said, "but my Lord husband does think they are better where they are, and I to rejoin them."

Except for Nyls, they nodded. Her host frowned. "Surely you will stay, Your Grace," he said. "My walls grow higher every day and my troops will fight to the death to protect you."

His walls. His troops. As if they weren't all pledged to the High King. Her host did either seek to curry favor, or to attain some distant advantage. She had become such a cynic.

"Treachery blooms with the jonquils," Jon Langeston said. "Even now we hear Cedric has begun to stir his forces. We must rouse ourselves from this slumber and plan our plans." Although the pleasantries continued, more than one cast an eye at the door. She left them then, plotting their successes, and retired from the scene, catalogued and taken care of, but her purpose satisfied. Although none witnessed his birth, Warin was acknowledged by all as William's son.

There had been no final meeting with the High King, although whether by design or circumstance, she did not know. He was there to see them off, but accompanied by Keith of Falkirk and Jon Langeston, and she had no private words. It was better perhaps. There was peace between them; each had their role and knew it well. Yet there was a new closeness she would have explored, some private words she would whisper. They must wait upon his plans, the seeds planted, to lay dormant until peace came.

She wore her old gray cloak, the fur-lined one packed away in a carrying trunk and strapped, she supposed, to one of the horses. Their escort was double the one which had escorted them to Heston Grange, undoubtedly due to whatever new circumstance kept the High King and his council secreted all afternoon. The men wore mail and were well armed, and in the early morning gloom, Claire saw not one familiar face.

One dismounted and bowed before the High King. "To your service in this endeavor, Sire, we pledge our lives." He looked very like the dark beetle-shaped man she'd seen leaving the council chamber the day before.

"You have your instructions," William said.

The man bowed.

"God speed to all here." William helped her mount, an unusual gesture. "Your escort is from your host," he whispered. "It is better so."

Ulric! He did take his role very seriously. Before she could respond, the beetle man spurred his horse, jolting hers into motion, and they cantered out of the courtyard. When they were full away from the castle, he slowed the pace, but kept the horses at a brisk walk. He chose a path to the south, away from Willwell Abbey and away from the pass across the Kusshi, across snow covered fields, and over the gentle swell of the southwestern plains of Bridland.

As they did on their journey to Heston Grange, they avoided the small villages, where whispers of smoke rose from the chimneys and an occasional dog barked. The guards kept their distance and the pace was such it was difficult to converse. When it was barely full light, they stopped in the private recess between two small hills.

"We will rest here," the beetle man said.

"We can continue along awhile," Claire said. "We are well used to travel." She smiled. And was ignored.

One held her reins, while another offered his hand. A blanket was spread on the snow, and bread and cheese placed upon it. Men held the reins of their horses while she, Richard and the wet nurse broke their fast in silence. The others stayed near their horses, while the beetle man stayed mounted, watching the proceedings carefully. When they had eaten, and baby Warin fed, the men held the reins of their horses, and one helped her into the saddle. Richard needed no help climbing into the saddle and was offered none, while the wet nurse was left to cope on her own. Once they were ready, the beetle man rode over to the wet nurse and checked Warin in his nest. When he was satisfied, he gave the signal to continue. The men handed over their reins, and climbed into their saddles. The second stop differed little from the first, except no food was brought out and only Warin was fed. After a short rest, they continued southward.

The third stop was in a small glade and much the same as

the others, except the rest was longer. The beetle man watched the sky carefully, as if waiting. When he gave the signal to leave, the soldier who had been designated to help Claire had disappeared behind a tree. Although she did not really need his help, she waited out of habit. It was easier in the snow. By the time he reappeared, the wet nurse and Richard were in their saddles.

The beetle man urged his horse forward, stopping near Claire. "By the King's command," he said. "I do now tell you, my lady, the course of action that will be taken. This party must to different paths, the boy to one, the baby and his nurse to another, and you, My Lady, to a third."

Claire stiffened. "I know nothing of this and cannot consent. I will not—"

The men acted in concert. They urged their horses forward. Each set of slackened reins went to a rider. The horses peeled away, pulling their captives with them. Along with the beetle man, three men remained, no hint of mercy in any face.

Her children disappeared before she could scream their names.

CHAPTER THIRTY

In the same room that had served as council chamber the day before, William handed Jon Langeston an unrolled parchment. The two were alone; King and advisor of kings, the white-haired advisor the last of William's childhood, the last man to have served both William's father and William. Jon Langeston carried the parchment to the window and bent over it, squinting, while William sat near the fireplace where a blazing fire threw off heat.

"It would be my advice not to trust him, sire," Jon Langeston said. "Cedric was false at Mullendown, and I see no reason why he would have suffered a conscience now. There can be no treaty with him that would vouchsafe peace."

"I grant you he was false on that score," William said. "I further grant you that Cedric is impulsive and intemperate."

"I would hardly call it intemperate to declare war sorely because one's suit is rejected. Even a King, if he is civilized, must realize he cannot marry whoever he wants solely because he wants it."

William looked up sharply.

"Oh, in his own country he could compel the issue, of course," Jon Langeston said, "but Lady Agatha is not his subject and over-more, is the sister of a King and under his protection and yours as well. If her brother had consented, then it would be different, but Cedric insults two sovereign Kings as well as the lady. It is shameful."

William held up his hand. "I have the given the messenger my response and he is already gone. You've read Cedric's missive. The tone was conciliatory. At best, there is a chance much may be gained. At worst, it keeps Cedric fixed in his location while My Lady and my sons put some distance between us."

Jon Langeston strode to the fireplace and held out his hands to warm them. The King wanted his council, but if it was not on whether or not to meet with Cedric then what? "About Lady Claire," he said. "I do not ask the locale of her refuge, but are you satisfied as to its safety? Is there something I can do to help with in that respect?"

William brightened, still a ghost of his former self. "She has found as good a place as I could hope for under the circumstances. I know she gave it out when she was here that it was a plan of my devise, but I tell you Jon Langeston, it is of her choosing and has more merit than my ill-fated plans." He sobered. "I thought I did everything I could for their safety, but I did less than I ought and I suppose Claire knew that full well, which is why she railed so much against my plan."

Jon Langeston nodded slightly. William was not a man given to introspection and he had no compass to guide his response. He may have been there when the King was brought red-faced and bawling into the world, but William was still the High King. His King. Advice must be honest but well-tempered and that much, Jon Langeston was good at. He had no intention of wading in these other waters.

"She has forgiven me," William said. "For the children's sake, I am glad they will not grow up with her anger to nurse them."

Jon Langeston waited, hoping William would continue his introspection, but a response appeared to be required. "It will make for a happier reunion than otherwise, I suppose."

William held out a palsied hand. "The old wounds still

fester," he said slowly. "I fear I rot from within." He shook his head. "I do not look for a good outcome of it, unless Breona can conjure what my physicians cannot. Still, My Lady's smile did give me a reason to hope." He pulled himself up and walked stiffly to the window. "Soon the trees will leaf out and the roses bud. My children will ride their ponies in the sunshine and Claire will take her embroidery threads into the garden to sort them. I would be there . . ."

Jon Langeston strode over to the window and placed his hand on the thin shoulder and pressed it firmly. "And so, you shall, Sire, you'll see."

William's eyes met his. "It is in heaven's hands," he said, "and those of the Lady Breona. Whatever the outcome, Jon Langeston, there are things I still control. Tasks to fulfill. I must defeat Cedric. I must give my lady security and my children their future. And I must face that I may not. In that event . . . I name you, Jon Langeston, and Hugh Tintagel and my good Lady Claire as co-regents."

Jon Langeston bowed. "I am honored, Sire, and pray it is a role I never fill."

William managed a smile. "I join you in that prayer," he said. "You have no concerns about my selections, I hope. I want no scheming discord. I wanted to apprise you of my decision before I told the council."

"Hugh loves you both," Jon Langeston said, "and I have come to respect his judgment. He is young, but I am old so we will balance each other. As you said earlier, Lady Claire has made good decisions herself, regarding her safety."

William's hand shook slightly. "She may wish to remarry."

Jon Langeston shook his head. "She has no passion for Hugh Tintagel, Sire."

William flushed and shook his head. "I didn't mean—"

"She may marry," Jon Langeston said. "She has been raised to do what is necessary and the situation may warrant it." He smiled. "Your lady has her wits about her and a mind of her own. She bends her will to you out of love and duty, but I think she will not so easily bend it to another."

William smiled. "I have come to learn of her spirit only lately, or perhaps it is that she has changed with what has transpired. You may well be right. We will rely on her judgment, and the advice of the council, should the situation arise."

Jon Langeston nodded and wished he could call for the King's physician to see if the flushed face was due to fever. Still, he did not judge lightly the cost it took William to say what he had.

William returned to his chair. "I must meet Cedric," he said. "If I can broker an honorable peace I will, for I had no appetite for this war and have even less now. He will be false eventually I suppose, but it may buy a few years. If I survive these putrefying sores, I can use the time to fortify my kingdom. Peace now, would give Richard time to grow into his own. If I do not . . . ." He sighed and held up his hands. "At worst, it buys some days or perhaps weeks for Lady Claire to gain her retreat, and for my army to gather."

"Should I send word, Sire, to call the men to back to camp?"

"I did so this morning," William said. "I also had word Breona is but a days' ride away. We will give her two or maybe three at the most, and then ride for Cedric."

CHAPTER THIRTY-ONE

You may have questions," the beetle man said, "but I have my instructions, and nothing else, so save your breath. We are, all four of us, resolved in our mission, and I would prefer you join us without restraint, My Lady. I am sure my companions do not care how you accompany us though, and we will do what musts."

Claire was stunned. This trickery had been worse than any small conceit of Hugh or Breona on the Elstow. She could not take in its meaning. What of her sons? She struggled to check the tears. Even if she knew where she was, and even if she could escape, how would she find them? And then what? Did William know? Where were Cedric's men? She must try to collect herself and see if she could come up with a plan, when she wasn't so numb. When she didn't feel as if she'd been kicked. It would serve her better, if these ruffians had no window on her private feelings. "I do not care for deceit," she said, her tone angry. They deserved that much at least. "You would do better with reason and logic."

The beetle man ignored her dark look, and urged his horse forward. Without restraint. Had he meant to infer he would restrain her? Claire allowed her horse to follow his. As if she had a choice. They rode at the same steady pace, and did not stop so frequently now, or for so long a time. Her anger carried her for much of the day, but by late afternoon, she was exhausted, and when the beetle man led them to the gate of a small monastery, she was relieved. She caught a glimpse of a tonsured head as the gate opened, but saw no other sign of its inhabitants. The guesthouse was a mean room with low benches, a table in the center and a few gray coals struggling in the fireplace. The beetle man brought her supper, a thin soup of dried pea and loaf of coarse bread. Her other escorts did not join her, and since the monk had apparently made no objections to their arms, her escorts perhaps had an objection to the monks, but she could not see why, they were as quiet and churchish as the monks.

"The brothers have closed the gate for the night," the beetle man said, "so you'll have this room alone. I'll be just outside the door, so if you become alarmed for any reason, you need only call out. My men will take turn as sentry."

So, there would be no chance to seek help. "You are very diligent."

"As you say, My Lady."

As always polite, his voice a monotone, his face expressionless.

"Why travel south?" she said.

"Those were my instructions."

"Is there a better . . ."

He put his finger to his lips and nodded toward the wall. However unlikely it was someone was listening, or could benefit from what they heard, he was right, she could not take a chance. But was it just a way to silence her?

It had begun raining during the night, but otherwise the next day was much like the one before. They stopped earlier though, at another small monastery. This time, the beetle man brought in dry wood and built up the fire before bringing her something to eat. Once again, she had no glimpse of any of the monks, but then they hadn't seen her either. Perhaps it was better.

Claire started a campaign to make one of her captors speak,

being careful to thank them, asking what they thought of the weather, asking if they spent the night well. To a man they rebuffed her attempts and stayed silent and flat-faced. The beetle man watched but did not interfere. On the third morning, the one who always helped her mount, smiled shyly and flushed after she'd greeted him.

The beetle man let one of the others take the lead and rode beside her. "They do not speak, My Lady."

"What?" Her face grew warm.

"I mean they cannot speak. They have not the means."

"Surely . . ."

"They have no tongues."

She stared.

"I will save you the question. They were cut out."

"All of them? On purpose?" Her face grew warm and she felt sick. It could hardly have been an accident. She drew away from the beetle man.

"They have a common enemy," the beetle man said. "I can assure you it is not me."

"I hardly thought so," she said, although it was her first thought. "You might have told me." Her voice grew icy. "I've been made fool of, and insulted them at the same time."

"They've taken no offense. They understand you didn't know."

"Still, you might have had the courtesy to tell me."

"There was no need. The men have sworn to their duty and as they cannot read nor write nor speak, they will never disclose it to others."

"But how? And by whose hand?"

"Each man has his story, My Lady, but as they will not say it, neither will I." He spurred his horse and retook the lead, leaving the impression of a smirk hanging in the air behind him.

By midday the rain stopped and the clouds cleared. The sun soon dried her cloak and Claire grew warm. When they stopped, she pushed it back over her shoulders and enjoyed the first taste of spring's warmth. The men appeared to be immune to the improvement in the temperature, as they had to everything else. An occasional gull laughed overhead, their white-grey a sign lands-end was near. Ahead she could see a low cluster of buildings and the round cupola of a large church. It would be the cathedral of St. Jerome, she guessed, and around it the town of Highdell.

They circled to the east and stopped in a small ravine. The usual blanket was spread and the usual fare provided. This time, they seemed in no hurry and allowed the horses to graze. She fell asleep waiting, and when she awakened, it was late afternoon. The men jumped up when they saw her stir.

"You should have wakened me," Claire said.

"The horses needed a rest." The beetle man had discarded his cloak. They all had. Cedric's yellow badge was on his tunic. And on another. And on the others.

She ran, scrambling over the rocks and reached the top of the ravine, then ran north along the edge. She had only to gain some distance, climb down again, and hide until nightfall. The church at Highdell was a cathedral, and would offer sanctuary, if she could outwit her pursuers.

Two horsemen rode across the valley from the south. William's men! She ran toward them. They saw her, turned their horses and broke into a gallop. One of her pursuers broke out of the ravine. She looked back. Her foot caught and she fell. The strangers grew closer. Both wore the yellow badge.

The beetle man reached her just when they did. Claire scrambled to her feet and winced. The sharp pain in her ankle made it difficult to stand.

"Well, well," a scar-faced man said. "What have we here?"

The man from Mellifont. Claire averted her face, hoping he didn't recognize her. But then why would he?

"It's naught that concerns you," the beetle man said.

The strangers dismounted. One circled and came up behind the beetle man, as one of her escort galloped toward them.

"But I'm interested all the same," the scar-faced man said.

"Very interested." He laughed. "We're among friends, are we not? Share and share alike, I always say."

The beetle man shrugged. "I've no real objection," he said, "provided you remember who was here first."

"Oh, I'm a patient man, as long as I don't lose sight of the prize," the scar-faced man said. "In fact, I believe patience has certain virtues." He winked and laughed again.

"She's a comely wench," the other said. "Cedric will be generous."

"A good wine steward samples the wine," the beetle man said, "but you can choose to abstain. I choose different." He put his hand on his sword.

"No need to be over hasty," the scar-faced man said.

"There's a ravine yonder," the beetle man said, nodding his head in its direction. "Might be less of a chance of anyone else wandering by, and we'd have a bit more leisure if undisturbed."

The scar-faced man rubbed his chin.

"Might as well take her there now," the beetle man said.

"Suits me," the other stranger said.

The beetle man signaled. His man urged his horse forward and grabbed Claire, hoisting her onto his horse and holding onto her tightly. He galloped for the ravine, followed by the others. At the edge, instead of continuing, her captor turned his horse, spurred him, and raced south, just as his two other companions burst out of the ravine. He whipped the horse forward. The thundering hoofbeats blocked any sound of what was happening behind them.

CHAPTER THIRTY-TWO

The horse plunged down an embankment and stopped, foam flecked and quivering. Gasping and unable to catch her breath, Claire slid from the horse, stumbled and fell. Her captor jumped down and stood over her. Daylight had already abandoned the ravine, and behind him, black-fingered branches were outlined against a leaden sky. It was the one who had smiled earlier, his dark eyes now burning. Was there any hope? "Good sir," she said hoarsely.

He threw himself at her and pressed his hand over her mouth. Slid the sword from its scabbard. She pushed at his hand, but that only seemed to tighten his hold. As if a scream was defense against the blade. Everything but his face and the sword blurred. His breathing grew hoarse and ragged. Or was it hers? Letting her hand fall, Claire fixed her eyes on his and felt for a rock or a stick. He frowned. Had he seen her hand move? She must wake from this nightmare! She bit him, but tasted only his glove.

He lifted the sword, the blade glimmering in the last of the light. She found only a few tufts of coarse grass and the powdery remnants of last year's leaves on the hard-packed soil beneath her right hand. On her left, more of the same. Claire looked away, then back. Let him see her face and remember.

Let him tell the loathsome Cedric that William's Queen met death without flinching. Her children, at least, were spared the sight and would have no nightmares of the journeyman's coins. If only she had an opening . . .

He kept one hand over her mouth, but lay his sword next to him and crossed himself with his free hand, then pointed to the hated badge. He covered it with his hand and smiled. Then repeated the gestures. Taking up the sword again, he nodded and touched the sword to his forehead. A salute, perchance a pledge. He put a finger to his lips and watched her. He wanted silence. So far, he hadn't hurt her.

She nodded, shaking, the slender hint of hope stealing the last of her courage.

He sheathed his sword, and motioned. They should go on. He held out his hand.

Claire pulled herself up. Took a small hop. He helped her mount and once in the saddle, she burst into tears. He had saved her. Almost killed her and changed his mind. Or had he? The man with no tongue had not Garwyn's gift to say what he meant.

He led the horse, picking their way along the ravine in the growing darkness. A thin bow of light climbed slowly overhead and one by one the stars were kindled as the clouds cleared, leaving the night air the colder for it. Claire pulled her cloak closer. Her ankle still throbbed, but the sharp pain in her side eased. She had only to grab the reins back and kick the horse to escape, but to what end? Claire pushed aside the thought of Richard's eager face and Warin's soft grunts as he nursed. She could not help them even if she knew where they were.

When the dark scent of rotting sea kelp could no longer be ignored, her captor led the horse up into the open. Although the ocean remained hidden, the crash of waves was constant, the sound neither increasing nor diminishing as they traveled. Think about what you don't see, Hugh had said. Claire guessed their path paralleled the shoreline, which meant they must have been traveling east. East, toward Oroskree. East toward a rocky kingdom where there would be no rescue. No escape. But to what end, if Cedric was in Bridland?

Coming to a creek, the man turned and urged the horse upstream. Within a couple dozen yards, they crossed and continued until they came to a larger river. Was it the Oberon? She couldn't be sure in the darkness. If it was, they were probably very near Cedric's camp. He moved closer to her, pointed to his badge and put his finger to his lips. She nodded.

Tying the horse to a low hanging branch, her captor eased himself quietly into the river and swam quietly upstream. A gull screeched in the darkness and Claire patted the horse nervously. An empty boat drifted into view. No, not empty, two men rowed quietly, while her captor swam beside it. They maneuvered the boat so it came to rest just below the horse. Even in the darkness, their yellow badges were visible. Her captor stood, dripping darkly, pulled her from the horse and lifted her into the boat, between the two men. They took up their oars. As the boat began to drift downstream, her escort mounted and rode silently from sight.

The oarsman facing her was thick-handed and thick-chested, with small legs, as if he had been formed for the boat or it had formed him as he grew. The yellow-badged tunic was ill fit, pulling tautly as he rowed. He leaned forward and whispered. "The worst part will be breasting the surf. Dinna worry. It's old hat to the likes of us and we've never lost a cargo yet." He grinned.

So, this one talked. A smuggler most likely, in spite of the tunic, but then Cedric was hardly particular who did his dirty work. Her eyes watered. There was no point is asking him anything, he would only lie. "Who are you?" she said, anyway.

"I've no name that matters, Mistress," he said. "I know yours and that's all what counts." He was honest at least.

As they rowed, the boat began to dip and rise and dip again, the motion at first gentle and then more pitched. "We're in the harbor," he said. "The tide will have well-turned when we reach the mouth. It's there we run the most risk, but it's a calm night."

The blackened bluffs embracing the harbor receded from view. A wall of water blocked their passage. The boat climbed frantically and fell back with a sickening thud, throwing Claire back and then forward. "Hang on!" The oarsman bent over, pulling grimly. The next wave was higher. And the next. Just when she thought all was lost, the swells lessened. Ahead, just beyond the bay, a small, masted ship waited. The men rowed alongside. A rope flew out, caught neatly by the oarsman and a rope ladder slid down the side. Another rope was thrown. The oarsman pulled their boat closer.

"Stand up slow," he said. "When the swell pushes us against the boat, step onto the ladder."

"I can't," she said.

"There's no time to rig a sling," he said. "I can carry you on my back if you'd rather, but it's a harder maneuver."

She shook her head.

He nodded encouragingly. "When I say now, stand up. When I say go, catch the ladder." He held out his hand. "Now!"

The boat rolled beneath her, then steadied.

"Go."

She took a half step and faltered. The gap widened.

"Not to fear," he said. "Watch the waves. On the third, I'll signal."

The boat bobbed.

"Go."

She stepped into the abyss. Felt the rope ladder under her foot. The smaller boat rocked, threatening to rip her in two.

"Step away!"

She pulled as hard as she could. Gained a precarious foothold. Pulled herself up to the next step, her ankle a torment. Then the next. And another. When she neared the top, two strong hands clasped her arms and helped pull her over the side. As she reached the deck, men sprang into action and the sail began to rise against the night sky.

One of the men pointed to a low cabin in the stern. "There's dry clothes and blankets," he said. "Best have some ale too, to take off the chill."

She hobbled slowly, stopping as the ship groaned and shuddered. "That's the sail catching the wind," a sailor said, as he pulled at the ropes, urging the sail ever higher. "There's naught to fear. We've calm seas, fair winds and good omens."

Good omens. For whom? She pushed the door open. And fainted.

CHAPTER THIRTY-THREE

When Claire woke, Richard was still there, sitting cross legged on the floor near her, with a worried look. "Is it really you?" she said.

"It's me. We're on a boat."

She nodded. Save for Richard, and the narrow cot she lay on, the room was empty. Warin must be in another such room with his wet nurse.

She held out her hand. "Are you all right?"

He nodded. "Did they . . . you couldn't hardly walk and then you fell . . ."

"I'm fine," She said, forcing a smile. "I twisted my ankle when I wasn't watching where I was going, that's all. And I fell when it happened, so I am a little bruised and battered, but none the worse for it." In truth, her ankle throbbed and she ached all over, but it would not help Richard to know of it, or the real cause.

"Warin?"

Richard's concerned look grew. "He's not here."

He was just a baby! The old feeling of panic and helplessness returned. Why were they separated and then not all reunited? The winter days after the baby's birth still haunted her.

"Is my brother going to be alright?"

Richard seemed almost on the verge of tears. Claire took a deep breath. It would not do to lie to Richard, but she didn't want to worry him any more than he already was. "As of this moment," she said, "we have no reason to believe otherwise. He may join us very soon, much as we have been brought here separately. We must be grateful we are together and will pray we will all be together soon." Above all else, let her children be safe.

Richard looked at her and few moments and then nodded. "You've been asleep a long time," he said. "Do you want something to eat? They said maybe you would, and I was to see to you."

"No, nothing."

"I'll get you something." He trotted out, returning with some coarse bread and cold porridge smelling slightly of sea salt.

To satisfy him, she nibbled at it, but soon gave up the effort, and fell into a fitful, nightmare-filled sleep. When she woke, the ship was rolling gently, with occasional creaks from the timbers. She was tired, as if she'd run a race, but did not ache so much. The door was ajar and Richard was sitting in the doorway, watching the men on deck, but still available should she need him.

"Good morrow," she said.

He turned and nodded happily. "Are you hungry?"

It seems he had been assigned one task and took it very seriously. She wasn't, but hated to disappoint him. "Perhaps just a little," she said, "and we'll see how it goes. The rocking doesn't bother you?"

He shook his head, no. "I've got sea legs now."

She tried not to smile. "When you go get the food, could you ask their leader to come here." What purpose it would serve to talk to one of them, she did not know, but she must learn what she could. If Richard was here, where was little Warin?

"He's busy," was the response. The food was the same as

the day before and as it would be every day. Richard spent most of the time on deck, running back and forth to bring her the dreaded meal or to share the news. The crew wore Cedric's badge, she had ascertained that much from him. To her surprise, Richard didn't seem concerned about it, and had the freedom to move about at will. She didn't press the subject, fearing to alarm him, when nothing could be done anyway. From his reports, it seemed the men were willing to answer his questions about the ship and how to sail it, but not about where they were heading. Claire's ankle healed quickly, supported her weight, and allowed her to walk tentatively in the small room.

"There's a storm out at sea," Richard said one morning. "You can see the rain." He swaggered slightly. "It's headed away from us but we'll get a few good winds from it." Claire was sure the boat began to rock more violently. From forests to shore . . . had Breona cured the High King? Was she with him now?

The next day dawned clear. Richard burst into the cabin. "They said to tell you to please come on deck." He held out his hand. "We're going to land!" She pinned on her cloak and smoothed her hair.

When she reached the deck, one of the sailors bowed. "We're men of the sea, Your Grace," he said, "and have not the words of those noble born, but even so, we too serve our King. T'was at his instruction we did deliver you unto this place, even though it be known only unto a small number and its secrets most jealously guarded."

The ship tacked near high cliffs, spattered with white droppings from the nesting terns. Waves pounded the rocks, sea foam sprayed up and slid back into the swirling sea, while sea lions bellowed below. The sailor glanced skyward. "The tide'll soon turn and as it goes out, you'll see a cave in the rocks there. That's where we be going." He pointed.

She stared, but the cliff remained inviolate.

He signaled and the men hoisted up a sling. "It's safe, you'll see," he said, but if he was referring to the sling or their destination, Claire did not know.

Nothing could be as bad as the Elstow and it wasn't. The one oarsman already aboard helped her and then Richard, who was swung over and lowered after Claire, his face a little pale beneath the ruddy tan. She squeezed his hand. The sailor who had addressed her, climbed into the stern and untied the rope. As they rowed closer to land, a hint of the promised cave appeared where the waves struck less resolutely. Finally, a dark line appeared at the water edge. The slit grew wider and higher. The small boat would manage the width, but there was hardly room to clear the rocks.

"Get down as low as ye can," the sailor said. "Dinna raise your heads until we say or the rocks'll have ye."

The bottom of the boat reeked of pine tar and seaweed. Claire pulled Richard closer and put her hand on his head. The thunder grew louder. The men rowed furiously. One shouted and they bent over. The sunlight turned to darkness. The boat groaned as it ground against the rocks. The men grunted and used their oars to push against the rock overhead. The boat shifted, as each wave drove it further under the rock and pulled it back again. On the fourth wave, they shot free.

"Stay down." His voice echoed. Hunched over their oars, the men began rowing,

"Ye can sit up now."

Claire sat up weakly. Two fissures in the rocks overhead sent rays of light spilling into the cavern and reflecting on the wet rocks. Behind her, a thin strip of sunlight marked their entry point. The men rowed toward the light farthest from the entrance. One swung a rope with a hook fixed to it, caught an iron ring barely visible on the wall above, and pulled the boat closer.

"We'll rest here until the tide turns," he said. Finally, the other oarsman eased himself out of the boat and began to climb a series of rock ledges, which led up the side of the cave toward the sunlight. Halfway up, he stopped, shuffled a few feet to his right and leaned forward, his head and shoulders disappearing from view.

He coughed, and coughed again, the sound reverberating. A think trickle of smoke drifted across his back. Holding a lighted torch, he climbed back down. "You can mind the torch, lad," he said, handing it to Richard and climbed up again, returning with two unlit torches.

The cave opening, which had widened as the torches were gotten, now began to narrow again. "When I say the word, keep you silent," one said. "We know the way by a song we say unto ourselves and it tells us when we are to turn into the difference passages. Much like a healer sings a chant to know how long to steep her medicines."

"Tis a wonderous sight you'll be seeing, but say naught for now," the other said. One unhooked the rope, and they pushed away and began rowing deeper into the cavern. The passage narrowed. The men locked their oars and grabbed the rocks, easing the boat through the gap and into a shimmering cathedral of rock, rising up from the water. Rock formations hung down from the ceiling and projected up from the water and the narrow shore. With the waves no longer an influence, the surface was glassy, broken only by the oar strokes and an occasional ripple where unseen fish nibbled prey.

"Quivil's gullet," the sailor whispered. "Silence now." He shrank against his oar as if afraid to waken the giant, and he was right, the formations looked like ancient teeth. If Richard heard the remark, he did not react, but sat mesmerized, hardly seeming to breath. The cold penetrated. Claire had no thought of escape, no hope of freedom, no resolution to fight. Quivil had conquered.

Just as the first torch began to sputter, the second torch was lit and the men returned to their rhythmic strokes. Tall pinnacles of rock began to appear in the lakebed, some now touching the downward growths and fusing into large columns transecting the chamber. Smaller caverns appeared at random intervals, some lit by the torchlight, while others remained black, higher perhaps than the lake or shuttered by something unseen.

"Give me the light now, lad," one of the oarsmen said. The

other rowed on in silence as the first became more agitated, holding the torch to one side and then the other. He signaled finally, and at the next watery offshoot, the men rowed into the narrow chamber. Rock projections hung lower in this chamber, and although the men did not react, more than once Claire fought the impulse to duck as they went under an especially low outcropping. The cavern twisted and split into branches, then gave the impression of reforming again, although she could not be sure of it. The second torch began to smoke. Ahead, a solid wall blocked their path. A dead end. On one side a small ledge was lined with good-sized rocks.

They stopped rowing. "To know the belly of Quivil," one of the men said, "is given only unto a few who have guarded its secret from one generation to the next."

Claire nodded.

"On your honor, daughter of Aethelstwin, swear you to tell no one of your passage, save that Quivil give you leave to speak of it."

They would live! She had thought it may have been but a watery grave. She nodded. "I, Claire, Queen of Bridland, High Queen of Threbant, do so swear."

"And you, lad?"

"I, Richard, son of William, son of Owain . . ." He faltered, then his voice grew stronger. "I Richard, of the house of William, known to all as a man of honor, do so swear by his honor and mine that I will not besmirch it."

The sailor plunged the torch into the water, where it sizzled briefly, sending up a small puff of steam. The cave was blacker than any night, but ahead, against the wall, the water glowed. One of the men eased himself over the side, disappeared under the water and reappeared moments later, snorting and shaking the water from his face.

"All set."

"Look where the rocks meet the water, lad, and tell me what you see."

"A light."

"Just that?"

Richard squinted. "The water doesn't touch."

"Ye've sharp eyes, lad, and I believe ye're brave as well. Are ye?"

"Sometimes I get afraid," Richard said.

"Ah then, it takes a brave man to admit it."

She was sure Richard grinned.

"We've the worst behind us," he said. "Only one small thing left."

"Left until what?" Richard leaned forward, rocking the boat.

"Let me explain what'll happen," he said. "The water here is very deep and has a strong undertow, so you and your Mother are to stay in the boat. You need to lie down. We're going to put rocks in with you, until the boat almost, but not quite, takes in water."

"Why?"

"Ye must be very still or the boat'll tip."

"But why?"

"You'll see. Lay still now." He eased himself into the water.

The men worked quickly, but carefully, alternating the placement of each stone so the boat stayed level as it was lowered. "We're two fingers width above the water line," one said. The other grunted and the boat moved slightly. Claire started.

"Stay very still," he said. "We're going to slide you under."

Under? She heard a splash and the boat began to wobble. Under! The boat ground against rock. Sand filtered down. She closed her eyes. "Richard?"

"I'm all right."

"Close your eyes."

The groaning continued. Then stopped.

CHAPTER THIRTY-FOUR

In the welcome warmth of unexpected sunshine, Claire blinked and then closed her eyes, not daring to move enough to shield them with her hand. The blinding light did not seem to affect the men, who splashed nosily as they removed the rocks, causing the boat to bob in the water. Knowing they were out of the darkness, the movement was no longer terrifying.

"Ye can sit up now if ye're of a mind to," one said.

It was as much an order as request. Claire sat up slowly. Richard sat up and rubbed his eyes. The boat was in a lagoon, seemingly carved from rock. At the far end, a waterfall ruptured and spilled into thin columns that cascaded into the pool. Overhead a few white clouds drifted across a blue sky.

"Where are we?" she said.

"Why you be in Amadee," one of the men said, grinning.

Amadee. Ulric had kept his promise. Still, there was Cedric's badge. Had he aligned himself with the dark force? Claire shivered. Richard's clothing was soaked, as was her own. "We'll need to dry our clothes," she said.

"Yes, My Lady. In good time."

The sun was warm and the pool sheltered. When all the rocks had been removed and stacked at the side of the lagoon, the men climbed in as they left, easing themselves over the side. Without comment, they took their old places and began rowing, puddles of water forming under each. Near the base of the waterfall, one climbed out and pulled the boat onto the shore. "If you please, Your Grace, we must disembark now."

She stood nervously. Richard scrambled from the boat and held out his hand. It was good to have solid footing again, but the ground still swayed. She stumbled.

"Takes a bit to adjust," the oarsman said, reaching to steady her. "Sit a bit."

The rocks were warm and the fresh air welcome. The men squatted near her. "We've a bit of a walk," one said finally. "Best we continue while it's light. We can carry you, if you haven't gotten your land legs yet."

She stood slowly and took a step. "I believe I'll be fine," she said, "but I see only rock walls and know I couldn't climb them, if I rested a week of days."

"Ah well," he said grinning, "there's no need to scale the walls or we'd all be in trouble. Follow me and you'll soon see a better route. Call out if you need help." He turned and started up a narrow path near the waterfall. The rocks were wet from the spray but the path climbed gradually. When he reached the waterfall, the oarsman disappeared behind it. Claire followed him into a small cave, dimly lit from the light on the other side of the cascading water.

Away from the waterfall, the cave was dry, the floor spongy. In its dark shadows, her wet clothes clung with icy hands. Claire began to shake. The cave did not end where she suspected, but turned instead, and the end was obvious. A broad swath of sunshine streamed in.

An old woman, with a halo of white hair, sat near the mouth of the cave. A half-dozen men sat near her and just beyond them, a dozen or so palfrey mares worried the remnants of last year's grass. The woman walked to meet them.

"I am Lady Gwyneth of the house of Ridrow," she said, "cousin by marriage to Ulric. On behalf of the King, and of my own house of Ridrow, I bid you welcome. The King himself had thought to meet you, but decided it was improvident, should someone someday connect you to him."

She signaled, and one of the men came forward. "The King did send some articles of wardrobe for Your Grace," Gwyneth said.

Claire retreated to the privacy of the cave and shed her wet clothes. Finely woven, the clothing smelled slightly of lavender, which seemed a good sign. When she emerged, Richard was also freshly attired.

"The King does assure me you are well mounted and do not require a litter," Gwyneth said. "Still, I had one brought. It is one thing to ride when you're rested, but another, I think, after a voyage such as yours."

Claire made no objection. Richard had at first been reluctant, looking past the litter to the horses, but cheered up when Gwyneth said she expected he would prefer to ride on the morrow. The litter had both furs and blankets, and both Richard and Claire were asleep before the party was well out of the valley. They traveled for several days, camping at night in round stone buildings, neatly thatched, with an opening in the center of the roof to let the smoke escape.

"They're built after the old way," Gwyneth said, but if they served any modern purpose other than as occasional refuge for travelers, she did not say. Richard rode every day, no matter what the weather, which true to the season, changed capriciously, hot one day and snowing the next. Claire rode when the weather was temperate, but kept to the litter a good portion of the time. Gwyneth rode most of the time, joining her in the litter occasionally, but snoring almost immediately upon entering, so they had no real conversation. From her earlier questions, Claire knew Gwyneth could not tell her anything she was desperate to know.

Claire rode with the others as they entered Mowcop, a small village situated in a narrow valley. In the fashion of Oakrose Abbey, vineyards grew in terraces along one hillside, while the other side was given over to sheep. Mowcop sheltered in the shade of tall trees, which grew in a wandering line marking the course of the river. Above the village, arbors surrounded a cluster of buildings. Although it was early in the season, carefully tended fields showed signs of recent cultivation. If the travelers' arrival sparked excitement, Claire could not tell. Lady Gwyneth could have told her, but did not, that the scene was unusually busy. Everyone had a mission, some excuse to catch a glimpse of the new arrivals. They rode through the village and started up the hill. Two ponies cantered down to meet them.

"Hello, Mother!" Edward called out. "Richard, look at our ponies! We can ride whenever we want."

"Welcome to Mowcop, my Lady Mother," James said, then kicked his horse to catch up with Edward who had cantered past and was circling back.

Claire waved and smiled, trying not to cry.

"Come see the new colts, Richard," Edward said, coming up behind them.

"Mother?"

"Go on, if you wish." The three cantered up the hillside. Two figures waved from the doorway. The smaller, with long curls.

Gwyneth's home was large, built around two courtyards, much like the cloisters but without the abundance of flowers. She occupied one section and gave the other over to Claire. There had been no word of the baby, but Claire found a small pair of leather shoes in one of the trunks Ulric sent, and she kept them in her sewing basket, pulling them out when Ellen was busy elsewhere. The days were long, with no household duties to oversee and no company. Claire and Ellen spent long hours at their needlework, both watching the valley for a hoped arrival.

The spring rains in the upper Amadee were brief but ample, turning the hills a velvet green. Ewes dropped their lambs and disappeared into the hills with their offspring, leaving mountains of wool behind, some to be cleaned, carded, spun and woven and the rest to be bundled and taken to the wool markets for sale. The fields had been tilled and the crops planted, when Ulric's banner appeared. Had Claire noticed Gwyneth's face was unusually flushed, she would no doubt have attributed it to the bustle in the household occasioned by the sight of the King's party. In fact, Ulric sent his itinerary some days before, as was his wont, a courtesy so his host could prepare for the visit. Part of his spring progression, he came with his taxman to measure the wool and count the acreage tilled. The taxman would reappear in the fall and assess the final duties, knowing full well what had been planted. The route of the progression differed each year, so the King visited every part of his kingdom every three years. This year, a covered wagon accompanied the King.

A guest in the household, Claire waited in her chambers so Gwyneth could welcome the King. He had barely arrived when a servant announced him. He wore a kindly look, "I do not stay, Your Grace. I must first to Lady Gwyneth and then we must converse, but I did think to bring you something to occupy yourself." He motioned.

It was not the same wet nurse, but there was no mistaking the baby she carried. Warin had been fed and kissed and was asleep in a cradle near Claire's chair, when Ulric was announced a second time. He was alone.

"Your Grace." He bowed.

"Your Majesty." She nodded.

"You are well?" He seemed nervous, a residual perhaps of their last encounter.

Claire smiled. "I am. I must profess my gratitude to you Sire, for the safe return of my youngest child and the continued safety of myself and my children. I do pray you bring news that relieves you of this burden and sends us homeward."

His face grew solemn. "I thought to give you a moment of joy, Lady Claire, but I must now tell you something I wish I did not have to impart. There was a battle at a place called Nettlerue." He pulled his hand over his eyes, then stroked his chin. "If the bard lives, he must sing a long lament of battle axe and sword, of falling back and then rallying against all hope, only to find there was no hope."

No hope . . . "The High King was routed?" Her chest tightened. She coughed. She had not known Ulric could wear so gentle a countenance.

"His most noble knights did create a litter from his shield and place the King upon it and carry him from the field of battle. Thus, they honored their King, who lived well and died nobly."

Lies. It must be. The strange lights from Mellifont returned, blurring Ulric.

He sat, folded his hands, then stood and paced the room. "I know this is bitter news, Your Grace. There has been no formal message, but few would know where to send one and I don't know who else fell that day. I had my own spies, the very men who did attend you, and more besides. There's no mistake. The priest has sprinkled his water and so that Cedric could not defile the body, it was taken to some hidden burial."

"A ruse perhaps, so that an injured man could recover," she whispered.

Ulric shook his head slowly. "I had no men at the battle, Your Grace, but everyone my men talked to, had the same tale. William's army was not only defeated but the men disbanded. They would not have done so if there was hope."

Claire sat very straight, hands folded in her lap, face pale but composed. "I see." Her voice was low, but steady.

"I'll leave you now," he said. "We'll talk again when you've had some time."

She did not remember Ulric leaving, or summoning the children, but suddenly they were there, standing by her chair with anxious faces. The High King was dead, she told them. They nodded, as if appraised by others. "Your father is dead."

"Can we go home now?" Edward said.

She stared, then shook her head slowly.

"When can we?"

"Can't we ever go?" James said.

Just as she did not summon them, she did not dismiss

them, but they left all the same, answering perhaps to a call she did not hear. From her seat near the window, she watched them spill into the sunshine.

The three youngest disappeared from view, lured by some unseen attraction. Ulric walked from the same direction. She couldn't hear what was said, but he put his hand on Richard's shoulder and they walked up onto the hillside. When Richard reappeared, his eyes were red but his face composed. "Am I King now?" he said, when he rejoined her.

"The army was defeated," Claire said. "We are exiles now, but yes, you are the rightful King."

"And when I say things, will people have to do them?"

"You are the King of Bridland," she said, "but Ulric is King here. If we were home, the council would meet and declare a regent, who is to act in your name until you are of age. When you are, and are crowned King, then people must obey you. You will then have rights, my son, but you will have greater responsibilities, and they will temper your rights."

"Who gets picked?"

She sighed. "If your father named a regent before he died, the council would declare for him." Hopefully.

"Did he? Did he pick one?"

"I don't know." She waited, but he didn't ask how one would be selected otherwise. It was just as well. Each man would most likely vote for himself, and if there was no appetite for his candidacy, for the person he thought he could most easily influence and baring that, the person least likely to dissuade the young King from any loyalty to his own interests. In normal times, there would have been vast holdings to control, royal licenses to be issued, an army to command . . .

Claire waited all the next day, but Ulric did not reappear. Gwyneth came to offer her condolences and left again. The next morning, the steward appeared and handed her a letter. She broke Ulric's seal. "I am called away," it said. "Know that I do not forget my vow."

"Mowcop and all the upper Amadee were Aldwin's," the steward said. "Lady Gwyneth did reside here first upon his favor and then upon the King's. He has had a message that the woman who claimed Aldwin's late favors, and had been purported to have married him, has been located, along with her child. Ulric does so value my Lady Gwyneth, that he takes her with him. She has a long association with him, but no view to the inheritance of the crown for herself or her line, so may offer such help as the King desires, without encumbrance. For the time being, Your Grace, His Majesty does give you this residence and the proceeds of the rents and leases and harvests of Mowcop, and of this valley, and also of the village and valley of Longgreen, so your daily expense is met. The portion not required for your keep, should there be any, is to revert to the King and he will examine your accounts as he requires."

She had not asked him about Cedric's badge. It seemed it no longer mattered.

CHAPTER THIRTY-FIVE

The hills had bronzed and the crops harvested and stored safely away, when a small party rode into the valley. Although none were recognized by the inhabitants of Mowcop, they rode to the residence on the hillside, as if they knew the way. Other visitors had occasionally come to the valley in the last year, a few staying, but most traveling on.

At first, with each visitor making his way up the hillside, Claire's heart had raced, but then she remembered anew. William was dead, his hearty laugh to be heard no more. As much as she grieved his loss, both for herself and for her children, what caused the sharpest pain, was the memory of Heston Grange and the hint of what might have been. She soon stopped watching the hillside and stopped waiting for news. Still she was grateful for each person sent by Ulric. He had been generous, sending a tutor for the children and a knight of his own household, to train the boys in hunting and in combat.

Claire was sewing with Ellen, when a visitor was announced.

"Sir Hugh of Tintagel, Your Grace."

Her hand went to her throat. No news that he lived, and now he was here.

He walked with a limp, a gaunt reflection of his former self. He bowed. "Your Grace."

"Hugh." Her eyes filled. She held out her hand.

He came closer and bowed again. "Lady Ellen."

Ellen nodded, her face pale.

"King Ulric told me where to find you," he said. "By his word, I know you have heard about Nettlerue."

She nodded. "Is it true?" But she knew it was, by his face. Hugh would be able to put details to the day, to put names to the carnage. She was glad he'd come . . . and sorry.

"Yes, I'm sorry, Your Grace. William is dead."

"There's no chance he was just wounded and he lives?" she whispered.

"I'd be with him, if that was the case." Hugh's voice softened. "I was with him at the end, Your Grace. He did suffer more than one mortal wound and all beyond even the care of Lady Breona. There was naught to repair what spilled that day. With his death, the army was shattered and Cedric declared victory, and there were none who can naysay him."

She walked to the window, where the view had not changed. William had died in battle. He would have been glad for it. Had he seen his future that day in Heston Grange?

"The old wounds still festered," Hugh said. "They drained and filled and drained again, for all Breona did. No one dare say what they feared, but he weakened daily. Then at Nettlerue, it was if he had the strength of his youth . . . you could believe . . ."

She'd known it was true, the loss a constant companion these many months, but his words now put a fresh face to her pain. "Sit down, Hugh," Claire said. "We will sup within the hour, but if you're hungry, I'll call to the kitchens now."

He shook his head no. "There is much to tell and much to discuss," he said. "but first and most important, how fare Richard and the rest of the children?"

She smiled. "They all do well, Hugh. I dare say they thrive, considering all that has happened."

He pulled a chair nearer and sat down.

"We've had no word about anyone save the High King," Claire said, her voice not as steady as she would have liked. "Whatever your opinion, this child does wait for news of her parents. What know you of the Marsh King and Queen?"

Hugh looked down at his hands and spoke in a low voice. "Your mother, Lady Ellen, was prisoner at Windrush, but I'm told she will take the veil and even now may be shorn."

Ellen gasped.

He need not say it, but did anyway. "I'm sorry. Your father, the Marsh King, is dead."

Ellen fled from the room.

Hugh stood, took a step in the direction she'd taken, then sank down again. "There are other losses, of which I can tell you as you can bear them, Your Grace."

She nodded. "What of you, Hugh?" she said. "You've been wounded."

"I am much recovered," he said, brushing aside her concern. "My lands are forfeit and I come to you, now, as a supplicant for your providence." He knelt. "Whatever your answer, I pledge to you and to the King, my fidelity and my life."

"Thank you, Hugh," Claire said. "I don't think Ulric will make objection to the increase in my household. It would not matter if he did. You are most welcome."

"We are three, Your Grace," he said. "If it please you, I have come with my page."

"Young Jeremy!"

"The same."

"He is welcome as well." Glad news for a somber day.

"He is tending to the horses," Hugh said, "There's one other person I hope you'll not object to seeing."

Breona?

". . . and who does also ask for you providence."

Ceonald?

"I'll tell you the details later," he said, "but the other in my party is Jeremy's mother."

"Phoebe is here!" Claire smiled. "She is welcome."

"She was in dire straits, declared outlaw -"

"Outlaw! What an outrage. Phoebe is a goodly woman. She has paid dearly for helping us . . ."

"T'was Cedric's men, although I don't know if they discovered her role in your escape. I believe it was her own earlier escape with Jeremy that angered them. At any rate, she was not the only one to be outcast. There was a young boy too, Benjamin by name. We found them at a hermitage in the forest, which I'm told you also know."

Claire nodded.

"The villagers tried to leave them provisions, but it had become increasingly difficult and I don't suppose they could have lasted another winter. I met with Benjamin's father secretly, and with his consent, we took him, the boy that is, to a monastery, and the monks agreed to see to his education. I didn't think Mistress Phoebe would like that choice for herself, so brought her here. She proposes to find some employment—"

"Have her come in, Hugh."

Like Hugh, Phoebe was gaunt, her face lined. She curtsied shyly.

"You're welcome to this household, Phoebe," Claire said. "I had hoped someday we would meet again, and I thought then, there'd be more I could do to repay you and Jeremy for your kindness."

Phoebe blushed. "To have my boy safe is enough, Your Grace."

It wasn't, but there was little else Claire could offer. "I exist on King Ulric's charity," Claire said, "but I am mistress of my own household. Would you consider a further kindness, Phoebe? Would you consider taking a position in this household to help care for my children? There are five now and each seems to have the energy of three. Or perhaps this is another role you'd prefer . . ."

Phoebe smiled. "I would be happy with anything," she said.

"Save for food and clothing for you and Jeremy," Claire said, "I can offer little else. Of course, I expect Hugh might still wish to keep Jeremy in his service, and you must speak to that."

"I've already consented," Phoebe said, "but will have the decision unmade if it be your wish."

"No," Claire said. "It's a good place for him, if it suits you, Phoebe. Sir Hugh serves this household now and although he may travel from it, you will still see Jeremy."

They left her then, Phoebe to get situated, and Hugh to find Jeremy, and then both to greet the children.

When Hugh reached the stables, Jeremy jumped to his feet, eager for the news. The horses had been unsaddled and brushed. The boy's face was still damp from a recent scrubbing and he had dusted most of the dirt from his clothes. "You've done well, lad," Hugh said. "The horses look well cared for."

Jeremy nodded. He hesitated but then could no longer contain himself. "Are they here?"

Hugh smiled. "They are, and all are well."

Jeremy grinned. "Can we stay then, for a little while, before we move on?"

Hugh nodded. "We will make our home here, Jeremy, as long as they are here, and we can be of service. I serve both the Queen and the young King and you will continue as my page, if it suits you."

"It does," Jeremy said, "but I must see to my mother first."

"She is to have a place in the household," Hugh said, "so we are all settled."

Jeremy whooped and startled the horses. He caught himself and reddened. "I'm sorry, Sir Hugh."

Hugh reached over the nearest stall door and began slowly stroking one of the horses. The horses settled down immediately and began working at the hay Jeremy had spread for them. "There's no harm done," Hugh said.

"I don't know how to act here," Jeremy whispered. "I've never lived anywhere but Lamberton."

"Aye, it will be an adjustment and you'll have much to learn," Hugh said.

Jeremy scuffed at the dirt and sighed.

"I was much like you once upon a time," Hugh said.

Jeremy brightened and looked up.

"I was about your age," Hugh said, "when I was sent to live with the High King. It was Owain, then, William's father."

"I'd have been scared," Jeremy said.

"I was," Hugh said, "and homesick too. I'd left my father and mother and two little brothers behind. I was lucky though, because Stuart and Percival joined the household when I did and we were all new together. We were a few years younger than William but he didn't seem to mind and he let us tag along wherever he went. We were never one without the other. When he had lessons, we did as well and when he trained in the martial arts, so too did we. At first, he was far better than any of us, but as we got older, we began to catch up, and he always seemed excited when one of us could best him."

"In one of the villages," Jeremy said slowly, "they called him William the Unready."

Hugh nodded. He understood the name. How many people had cautioned the King? Apparently, including his Lady, Claire. "Let's stretch our legs, lad, and see what's over the hill. We've been on horseback far too long" The ground was dusty, the dried grasses rustling as they walked. "It's an unfortunate title," Hugh said, when they were far enough away to speak without being overheard. "Partly because there is some truth to it. Most people don't think too highly of the vanquished and it's easy to criticize."

"But he was a good King, wasn't he," Jeremy said, "and your friend . . . if a King can have friends."

"Aye," Hugh said. "To both." Even his marriage had not put a dent in the number of hunts and tournaments and tours. Which was probably William's other flaw. Life at Ambridge must have been lonely for the Queen, who was invariably left behind, either waiting to have a baby or just recovering from the birth of one. Hugh shook his head. "I think maybe one of William's strengths was also a weakness," he said. "He loved people and he loved life. He thought everyone was good and I don't think he could believe anyone, even Cedric, could be truly treacherous and evil. I don't think he really believed he needed to prepare for war." Hadn't believed it or hadn't wanted to.

"But he was wrong," Jeremy said, looking up a Hugh. "There are bad men. Like Cedric and that man . . . who killed Sir Herbert and my father."

Hugh put his hand on Jeremy's shoulder. "There are indeed, Jeremy. There are some who are truly evil and some who are truly good. I'd like to think the good outweighs the evil but at times it's hard to think so."

"I think he should be called William the Good," Jeremy said, "because he was good, and if he wasn't so good, he would have known about the bad things."

Hugh smiled. "I like that."

In the distance the mountains were purple in the late afternoon sun, their flanks golden where trees climbed up the narrow ravines. Below them, the crimson and orange-leaved oaks crowded the river and danced their way across the valley. It was if the summer's sun had hidden in amongst the leaves, and now burst forth, the last sign of its radiance before the winter snows.

"Do you think Benjamin could come here?" Jeremy said. "He doesn't know anyone where he is and we can be new here together."

Hugh looked down at Jeremy. "I don't really know what the situation is here, lad, and whether or not they can support more in the household. But I can't say what the future holds. For now, Benjamin is safe where he is and he will be warm and well fed. That's something."

For all Phoebe had tried to do, Hugh recognized the signs of slow wasting. The boy would not be able to withstand an illness in the shape he was in, and Hugh wasn't sure he would have survived a long journey. Hadn't he seen the same thin limbs on his littler brother, at about that age? It hadn't been that many years ago, when they got word of the crop failure and famine at Tintagel. He'd ridden north right away, with William sending supply wagons as quickly as they could be filled. The graves of his mother and the older of his two little brothers were still fresh when he got home, and he knew by looking, it was already too late for the other. Hugh had watched him sicken and die in a matter of two short days, helpless against the fever and ague. Only his father had survived.

A startled pheasant burst out of the grasses and flew skyward. "I wonder if anyone in the neighborhood keeps hawks," Hugh said. "A pheasant dinner would be nice."

He looked at Jeremy. "What with the war, I'd venture there will be many new boys at the monastery. When you think about it, Jeremy, you aren't the only new boy here."

Jeremy furrowed his brow. "I'm not?"

"No," Hugh said. "Richard and James and Edward are new to this life, just like you are. In some ways, it may be harder for them, for Richard anyway, because he must pretend to be someone he is not, while he studies and plans for the man he would become. I don't know if he'll want a friend right now, Jeremy, but I hope you'll be one to him. For all he's the heir to his father's throne, he's lost his father just like you. You must let him take the lead on this, but I think he'll be glad for your company. You can learn a lot from him, and he from you."

Jeremy nodded. "I will pledge to Richard," he said, with a bright face. "I hope he will think me worthy to be his friend."

Hugh smiled. "Best go back now and greet them."

CHAPTER THIRTY-SIX

Claire dreaded the news of death and destruction Hugh brought with him, but she requested he join her the next morning. They exchanged pleasantries much as strangers might. "What other news, Hugh? As you said yesterday, there is much to tell."

He stared into the fire. "When the battle was done, and the surrender given, I did meet with those of the King's council, both great and small, whom I could seek out. We did agree, separately and then together, we would not forswear our allegiance to Richard, but we had no means to support him, and none of us had any idea where he might be. I knew about your time with Ulric, but I chose to bide my tongue, since the King's discovery would not raise the dead nor repair the wounded, and it seemed to me have little consequence or benefit. You, Your Grace, and I and Sir Jon of Langeston, are named coregents . . ."

Claire wiped the tears from her eyes. William did pronounce that at least before the battle.

"Sir Jon and I met privately and he was agreed with me that I should seek you out and discover your wishes for us and such others as are prepared for exile."

Exile. She'd said the words herself, but they took on a new

finality. "We're at Ulric's mercy now," she said, "and must treat with him before sending word."

He nodded.

"Hugh, you said, Ulric, told you where we were. Do you think . . ."

Hugh held up his hand. "There is naught to fear on his account, Your Grace. I had the papers with William's seal naming me co-regent, which I meant to give you yesterday, and even then, I had a hard time persuading him to tell his secrets. For a time, I wasn't sure he knew where you were. I'm glad he did, because he was my last hope, for all the stories I'd heard."

"I would hear those stories, Hugh." Richard had come quietly into the room.

Hugh started to stand, but Richard motioned him to remain seated.

"After the council," Hugh said, "I resolved to make my way to you, but to leave such a long path behind me that it would be hard to unravel, and since I didn't know where to find you, that, at least, was an easy task. I thought first to meet again with my Lady Breona, and then do what I could to reunite Jeremy with his mother."

Claire smiled. "Both wise."

"Lady Breona was not in the Soddenwood from what I determine at a distance, nor was Ceonald. I knew Ceonald had accompanied the men who cared for the High King and I suspect Lady Breona had gone to him."

"How did you find us?" Richard said.

"I went back to Heston Grange," Hugh said. "They had fled, so I started in the direction you'd taken and asked at every village and monastery, seeking news. There was one sighting, I believe, not far from Heston Grange, but then you disappeared. If it was just a woman, I was told, or just a baby, or just a man and his son, or a man with two sons and a donkey . . ." Hugh smiled and then frowned. "I believe others had asked before me, so I'm glad the tracks were well hidden."

Richard looked at Claire. She'd been on the verge of telling Hugh how the party had been split up, but now hesitated. She trusted him with her life, with all their lives, but did it serve for him to know?

Hugh seemed not to notice. "I'd not stopped at many places, when I could see Ceonald's hand at play. I was told you'd been carried away on the wings of giant owls, that you'd sailed on a magic ship to an enchanted island and were hidden by a magic spell. I even heard Cedric had captured you, but since his men were searching for you too, no one, including myself, gave much credence to that."

"I like the story about the owls," Richard said. "It reminds me of Wolphard."

"Aye," Hugh said. "I had that story told to me more than once. I decided it was a sign, so I headed to the Soddenwood by way of Lamberton, hoping to find you there, which of course you weren't, and no one knew where you were. That reminds me, Ceonald left something there for you." He left the room and came back carrying a small wooden box with the symbols on her brooch carved into the top.

Claire ran her fingers over the top, then carefully opened it. It was filled with dried rose petals.

"I was told," Hugh said quietly, "by the contents you would know where William was."

"Oakrose Abbey," Richard whispered.

Hugh nodded.

Claire slowly closed the box and held it close. She thought of arching sprays of red roses and the faint stone arches underneath. And of Ceonald's poem, No, not Oakrose Abbey. The rose sings of her cries for the King, Ceonald had said. William was, where Breona would someday be. "Thank you," she said. For now, it was for her alone to know.

She felt Hugh watching her. "It was in desperation I finally went to Ulric," he said finally. "And as I said, I had a hard time convincing him to tell me where you were."

They left her then, but it was to be a day to tell what needed to be told. Claire and Ellen were at their needlework that afternoon, when Hugh came in, bringing Richard with him.

"I must tell you of Cedric's council," Hugh said. Ellen pushed her needle into the garment and stood.

"This is of concern to you, Lady Ellen," he said. "Please stay."

She sat and took up her needlework, but not the needle.

"There was a truce after Nettlerue," Hugh said, "and Cedric announced a council. All men of title were to present themselves, or forfeit all lands and all property, their families outlawed and they themselves to be imprisoned."

Claire shuddered.

"You know the man," Hugh said. "It was a final defeat that we went and Cedric gloried in it. When we were all assembled, the Marsh King was announced. I do not need to tell you few were happy to see him."

Ellen looked down, her face flushed.

"I will tell you as I witnessed it," Hugh said, "and say the words as well as I remember, but only so you may know I speak the truth. I have no design to cause pain."

Ellen sat immobile. Hugh's voice was gentler than Claire would have thought it could be, knowing of his hatred for the Marsh King. She nodded.

"The Marsh King did not strut or act in any manner other than the rest of us, but took his place with us. Cedric addressed him first."

"Swear you, as my liege lord, Leveric of Morimond?" Cedric asked him.

Hugh glanced at Ellen.

"You wish my oath, My Lord?' the Marsh King said. "I must have my speech before I swear, or there will be no oath."

The room was still then, none of us wanting to breathe. Cedric shrugged.

The Marsh King seemed to straighten and looked Cedric full in the face, more, I think than any of the rest of us would've dared. "A decade and more ago," he said, "I swore to William, as to his sire before him, and as my father before me swore to the High King. But the bond that bound us proved irksome, and while William did not fail me in his duty, I failed him in mine. I did not ride to him when summoned, but sent only my men, with no thought or care to their provision. I would like to say that I meant to attend the High King before he engaged in battle, but I cannot swear I did not hope it would end before the inconvenience. It seemed a trifling thing. How was I to know that you, Cedric, were more false in your word than I was in mine? And yet, mine is the greater fault, for I was a friend, and you the enemy."

"I can tell you," Hugh said, "not a sound was heard save for the Marsh King's voice, and it had an elegance I had not previously noted in him."

Cedric grew very pale. "You dance on quicksand," he said. "Do not think to stretch my patience, for I swear you'll dance on the wind if you vex me overmuch."

His voice made my blood run cold, but the Marsh King seemed not to hear it.

"If I am to be condemned, I will claim my right to final words and will finish what I have set out to say."

"I have not condemned you, but take care, you may condemn yourself."

"Windrush castle stands,' the Marsh King said, "where other homes do not. My fields are fertile and my livestock fattens, but my knights fought and died, while I slept safely. My neighbors, forced to pay where I would not, grow cold and the distance between us lengthens. My wife cries at an empty hearth for a child whose laughter has been stilled. And my child, just blossoming into womanhood, will never know the joy of a child at her breast. And I? I have lost my honor, lost my good name, lost all that has meaning and to my greatest shame, have lost all this not because of something I did, for as you know full well, Cedric, I am no traitor, but because I did not do what I ought. What can you do to me Cedric, that is worse than what I have done to myself?"

"Enough!" Cedric shouted.

"We were all pale then, I can tell you", Hugh said. He is no man to anger, especially when he is the only one armed.

"We're agreed," the Marsh King said. "It is enough.

Would I could change the past but I cannot. So, I will swear my oath. I swear by all the saints that my allegiance is to the house of Aethelstwin, to Richard if he lives, or to Edward or James if he does not, and I swear I will honor my pledge."

"You will honor it with your life," Cedric said.

"We are all at your whim, Cedric," the Marsh King said, "and we know you are both capricious and evil. I say now to all my subjects, all good men of Morimond, that I believe Richard lives, and I transfer any allegiance they have, from me to him, since my own line is dead. Swear false oath to the false King, if you will, and pray the priest absolve you, but remember the rightful King."

"Cedric's guards had him by then," Hugh said. "There was a brief struggle. No man dared help him, but all met his eye, where before we had not."

Ellen cried quietly, her face in her hands.

"Darek of Norvik and Reginald of Norwood fled that night, with most of their men," Hugh said, "and sent word that if Richard lived, they would not swear to Cedric and enjoined their men to swear false oaths, if they must swear. They are, by all reports, safe in their castles. The Bishop declared he would not release any man from his allegiance to his own lord, nor allow them to swear falsely. Even Cedric was not prepared for such a defiance and so large a massacre as must ensure, so he disbanded the council."

"The Marsh King has done a great service to stop this oath," Claire said, "and this seems to me, to balance out what took place earlier."

"The Marsh King has regained his good name," Richard said, "at least as far as I am concerned."

Ellen wiped her eyes.

"He was executed," Hugh said, his voice strained. "Drawn and quartered like a common criminal. I disguised myself and bribed the priest, so I could stand near to where he passed on his way to his execution. I told him, Lady Ellen, that you lived and are safe with the King. He smiled when it was whispered. He died bravely."

CHAPTER THIRTY-SEVEN

The winter snow came early that year, flirting briefly with the mountaintops before covering them in earnest. In the valley and the environs of Mowcop, there had been only a dusting, but the ground had frozen and remained hard.

"He's a shrewd man," Claire said, looking out over the frozen arbors.

"Who, Your Grace?" Hugh lounged near the fire. He'd been drilling Richard on the history of Bridland and had reached the list of successions, the king's names punctuated only by dates, driving everyone but Richard and Claire from the room. Richard sat at a table, laboriously copying the names from his lesson.

"Ulric," Claire said. "He installed Aldwin's wife and baby in the same castle where we once stayed. In a few years, perhaps even less, who will remember there were two babies, not just the one? If anyone inquires, it will be Ulric's little granddaughter they remember, not the youngest son . . ."

"Does he say when he'll return to Mowcop?" Hugh said.

"No time soon, I think," she said. "Did I tell you, he sent a message last spring, proposing we join our households? It was when his Bishop, Wido, came," she said nodding toward Richard. "Ulric has his granddaughter now, but no heir, and he proposed I pledge one of the boys to his granddaughter. When they wed, Ulric will name him as heir. Wido said Ulric did not press for a formal declaration now, but rather asked that I consider it, and give some thought to which of my sons would be most suitable."

"I am already pledged," Richard said.

Claire started and turned away from the window to look at her son. What in heaven's name—

"You cannot treat on your own in this matter, until you are of age," Hugh said. "Even then you need meet with your council."

Claire started to speak but Richard cut her off. "I assure you, I didn't," he said, "but I'm going to marry Faythe all the same."

"Faythe, Breona's daughter?" Claire tried not to smile. "She's much older than you."

"She's two years older and it was Faythe who told me we were going to marry. I suppose she knows."

Claire felt the whisper of a breeze and touched her neck. And remembered, it was Garwyn's sign for Faythe.

"Warin, perhaps," she found herself saying. "He was born in Amadee and will have no memory of anything else to claim his allegiance. He may be too close in age to Ulric's granddaughter though, and thus make any connection too far into the future for Ulric's needs."

Richard nodded, but to which part of what she just said, Claire didn't know.

"Ulric proposed a union in your households when I met with him," Hugh said. "He said to wait to speak of it, until you'd had time to absorb all my news. It was not his granddaughter, though, it was himself. He wants to marry you, Your Grace."

Hugh did not look at her, while Richard stared. She felt her face redden. Ulric! She bit back her first words. Finally, she said, "Ulric is a good man and I believe he is a good King to his people. We are indebted to him for our lives, and we are here on his mercy." Hugh still did not look at her. "I have no wish to marry, Ulric," she said slowly, "or indeed any man. If I did, it would not be until all of my children have their futures secured. I will send him thanks and tell him I must tend to all of them before I think of anything else." Both Richard and Hugh nodded and the tension that had suddenly come into the room left just as quickly. She knew though, she would marry Ulric if she needed to protect her children, and she suspected Hugh knew as much. As would Ulric.

She picked up her needlework and Richard and Hugh resumed the lessons.

"We've talked much of the past since you've been here, Hugh," she said. "And now we've touched on the future. It seems to me it is time we make some plans."

Richard looked up from his lesson.

"Your Grace?" Hugh said.

She stretched her hands out to the fire. "We must raise an army, Hugh."

He sat up. "Your Grace, you and King Richard have my sword while I have the strength to raise it, and there's not one of William's knights, indeed in the four kingdoms, who, if he lives, will not ride for Richard. But it will be an army without arms; old men and boys must fill its ranks. Forgive me, Your Grace, but it will be a slaughter."

"You miss my meaning, Hugh."

"Your Grace?"

Richard put down the quill.

"The badger is both vicious and cunning, it is not?" she said.

"Yes." They both nodded.

"What always conquers the badger, Hugh?"

"Always? Nothing that I know of, but then I'm no woodsman."

"I will solve my riddle, then," she said. "The answer is time, Hugh, time. Even the badger grows old. Time will alter those boys you would have in your army, Hugh, and like my own, they will grow, and they will grow into fine, strong men. In the time it takes to raise my army, cannot bows be fashioned and swords hammered?"

Hugh looked from her to Richard's bright face.

"Six years," she said. "Old enough to begin, I think, with good men beside him. You may think year or two one way or the other. Still, the time will come."

"Those boys will not wake up knights, Your Grace," Hugh said. "They must have years of training."

"Look around Mowcop, Hugh," she said. An army could camp here and none would be the wiser."

"None save Ulric," Hugh said. "It's dangerous for us and more for him. He would never allow it."

Claire picked up her needlework and bent over it. "When a wolf moves into the neighborhood, a man does well to raise wolfhounds."

Hugh stroked his chin. "It wouldn't have to be this valley," he said.

The needle stopped.

"There are many valleys in many places."

Claire, Queen of Bridland, High Queen of Threbant nodded to her son and smiled.

CHAPTER THIRTY-EIGHT

"Ride with me on the morrow," Richard said one afternoon, when his studies were finished.

Hugh started. William's very words, not so very long ago.

They met just as it began to get light, their horses seemingly glad to be on the move, shaking their heads and snorting soft clouds in the frozen air. They rode slowly, letting the horses pick their way through the fresh unspoiled snow. As they reached the top of a nearby hill, the sun rose over the distance mountains, turning them shades of purple and rose. Richard reined in his horse and watched as the rose changed to a golden glow on the mountain peaks. "I will be the High King," he said.

The boy had no sense of bluster or self-aggrandizement, and spoke as if it was a simple statement of fact. As if, somehow, he knew. A hawk soared overhead, circling until it found prey and then dove down, disappearing into the stillness.

"It is your birthright," Hugh said.

"It is more than that," Richard said. "It is my duty. And perhaps, simply my destiny."

"Do you think it's your duty to avenge your father?"

Richard shook his head and gave Hugh a look as if he pitied

him. "Vengeance is the province of the Almighty," he said. "Cedric is evil. I would answer that evil with justice. I would free the people from his bondage."

"It will not be without cost," Hugh said.

"It will cost some their lives," Richard said slowly. "Perhaps many. Probably many. Perhaps, even mine, although I don't think so. If that happens, at least I have brothers to take my place. Whatever the cost, Hugh, it will be less than the cost of doing nothing."

"I wish there was an easier way," Hugh said.

Richard shrugged. "I have been thinking about other things," he said. "More immediate things. I believe my Mother means to marry you off to Ellen."

Hugh started and his horse shied nervously. He hadn't seen that coming. "I can't imagine where you got that idea, son," he said. "Perhaps all the talk of Ulric's proposals."

Richard shook his head and grinned. "I heard her tell Phoebe that Ellen needed to wed, and I've heard her say all kinds of nice things about you to Ellen. So nice, sometimes I can't tell she's talking about you."

Hugh leaned over and lightly cuffed him. "You, young rapscallion."

"Maybe you'd like that, though?"

Ellen was competence and capable, and she would make a good wife - to someone. "My duty is to you, Richard, I do not think to marry until your future is secure. If ever."

Richard laughed. "You sound like my mother. You'd better bring in a replacement then, or you won't know what's happened."

"That's a thought."

"My mother is a comely woman, is she not, Sir Hugh?"

Hugh studied the distant hilltops. "Indeed," he said.

"I've thought about this a lot," Richard said. "I don't want her to marry Ulric, but I think someday she should marry. I think she's afraid."

"I can't imagine that," Hugh said. "She is a brave woman."

"You didn't see her after Warin was born," Richard said. "I

331

think that may be what she is afraid of."

"She was very ill, I know that," Hugh said. "Still—"

"I'll race you to the tree over there," Richard said pointing. He kicked his horse.

Hugh barely beat him, and with a better horse, it may well have been a different outcome. "You need a better horse now that you're older," Hugh said.

Richard grinned. "And will you get me one, Hugh?"

"I'll come up with something."

"Good." Richard smiled again, but quickly sobered. "I have one wish for my mother."

"What's that?"

"I would like to see her laugh. I don't ever remember her ever doing so, but maybe she did when I was little."

"The war has exacted a steep price, lad."

Richard nodded.

Hugh suddenly remembered Fern and Buttercup and oak groves. She had laughed on the Elstow. "I'll race you back up the hillside," he said. This time the race was even and no victor declared.

"Do I still get a new horse?" Richard asked.

"Indeed, you do," Hugh said. "I believe it would be prudent to send a message to Percival, and he can bring a string of good horses. Your brothers will need better mounts soon."

Richard laughed. "Best he stay to help with them."

Hugh smiled. The snow began to fall gently, as they turned toward home. When darkness settled, a great owl glided silently over the compound, and returned to its new nest in the valley below.

ABOUT THE AUTHOR

Trish Howell has always lived in the Pacific Northwest. The beauty and diversity of geography of the Northwest served as inspiration for the geography in 'From Mountain to Marshland'. She has always loved to read and began writing at a young age. This is her first published work. She enjoys many hobbies, including genealogy, quilting and watercolor.

Made in United States
Orlando, FL
24 November 2021

10693934R00196